NAN

Robert Ludlum's
THE HADES
FACTOR

Also by Robert Ludlum

The Scarlatti Inheritance
The Osterman Weekend
The Matlock Paper
The Rhinemann Exchange
The Gemini Contenders
The Chancellor Manuscript
The Holcroft Covenant
The Bourne Identity
The Matarese Circle
The Road to Gandolfo
The Parsifal Mosaic
The Aquitaine Progression
The Bourne Supremacy
The Icarus Agenda
Trevayne
The Bourne Ultimatum
The Road to Omaha
The Scorpio Illusion
The Apocalypse Watch
The Cry of the Halidon
The Matarese Countdown

Also by Gayle Lynds

Mosaic
Masquerade

Robert Ludlum's
THE HADES
FACTOR

Robert Ludlum and
Gayle Lynds

HarperCollins*Publishers*

HarperCollinsPublishers
77–85 Fulham Palace Road,
Hammersmith, London W6 8JB

www.**fire**and**water**.com

Published by HarperCollinsPublishers 2000
1 3 5 7 9 8 6 4 2

First published in the USA by
St Martin's Griffin 2000

A catalogue record for this book
is available from the British Library

ISBN 0 00 710165 1

Set in Electra

Printed and bound in Great Britain by
Clays Ltd, St Ives plc

Acknowledgment

From cells to viruses, antigens to antibodies, Stuart C. Feinstein, Ph.D., has been enormously generous in sharing his cutting-edge expertise in the creation of *The Hades Factor*. Dr. Feinstein is professor and chair of the Department of Molecular, Cellular, and Developmental Biology at the University of California, Santa Barbara. In addition, he is also associate director of the Neuroscience Research Institute.

Prologue

7:14 P.M., Friday, October 10
Boston, Massachusetts

Mario Dublin stumbled along the busy downtown street, a dollar bill clutched in his shaking hand. With the intense purpose of a man who knew exactly where he was going, the homeless derelict swayed as he walked and slapped at his head with the hand that was not clutching the dollar. He reeled inside a cut-rate drugstore with discount signs plastered across both front windows.

Trembling, he shoved the dollar across the counter to the clerk. "Advil. Aspirin kills my stomach. I need Advil."

The clerk curled his lip at the unshaved man in the ragged remnants of an army uniform. Still, business was business. He reached back to a shelf of analgesics and held out the smallest box of Advil. "You'd better have three more dollars to go with that one."

Dublin dropped the single bill onto the counter and reached for the box.

The clerk pulled it back. "You heard me, buddy. Three more bucks. No ticky, no shirty."

"On'y got a dollar . . . my head's breakin' open." With amazing speed, Dublin lurched across the counter and grabbed the small box.

The clerk tried to pull it back, but Dublin hung on. They struggled, knocking over a jar of candy bars and crashing a display of vitamins to the floor.

"Let it go, Eddie!" the pharmacist shouted from the rear. He reached for the telephone. "Let him have it!"

As the pharmacist dialed, the clerk let go.

Frantic, Dublin tore at the sealed cardboard, fumbled with the safety cap, and dumped the tablets into his hand. Some flew across the floor. He shoved the tablets into his mouth, choked as he tried to swallow all at once, and slumped to the floor, weak from pain. He pressed the heels of his hands to his temples and sobbed.

Moments later a patrol car pulled up outside the shop. The pharmacist waved the policemen to come inside. He pointed to Mario Dublin curled up on the floor and shouted, "Get that stinking bum out of here! Look what he did to my place. I intend to press charges of assault and robbery!"

The policemen pulled out their nightsticks. They noted the minor damage and the strewn pills, but they smelled alcohol, too.

The younger one heaved Dublin up to his feet. "Okay, Mario, let's take a ride."

The second patrolman took Dublin's other arm. They walked the unresisting drunk out to their patrol car. But as the second officer opened the door, the younger one pushed down on Dublin's head to guide him inside.

Dublin screamed and lashed out, twisting away from the hand on his throbbing head.

"Grab him, Manny!" the younger cop yelled.

Manny tried to grip Dublin, but the drunk wrenched free. The younger cop tackled him. The older one swung his nightstick and knocked Dublin down. Dublin screamed. His body shook, and he rolled on the pavement.

The two policemen blanched and stared at each other.

Manny protested, "I didn't hit him that hard."

The younger bent to help Dublin up. "Jesus. He's burning up!"

"Get him in the car!"

They picked up the gasping Dublin and dumped him onto the car's rear seat. Manny raced the squad car, its siren wailing, through the night streets. As soon as he screeched to a stop at the emergency room, Manny flung open his door and tore inside the hospital, shouting for help.

The other officer sprinted around the car to open Dublin's door.

When the doctors and nurses arrived with a gurney, the younger cop seemed paralyzed, staring into the car's rear, where Mario Dublin lay unconscious in blood that had pooled on the seat and spilled onto the floor.

The doctor inhaled sharply. Then he climbed inside, felt for a pulse, listened to the man's chest, and backed outside, shaking his head.

"He's dead."

"No way!" The older cop's voice rose. "We barely touched the son of a bitch! They ain't gonna lay this one on us."

■

Because the police were involved, only four hours later the medical examiner prepared for the autopsy of the late Mario Dublin, address unknown, in the morgue on the basement level of the hospital.

The double doors of the suite flung wide. "Walter! Don't open him!"

Dr. Walter Pecjic looked up. "What's wrong, Andy?"

"Maybe nothing," Dr. Andrew Wilks said nervously, "but all that blood in the patrol car scares the hell out of me. Acute respiratory distress syndrome shouldn't lead to blood from the mouth. I've only seen that kind of blood from a hemorrhagic fever I helped treat when I was in the Peace Corps in Africa. This guy was carrying a Disabled American Vets card. Maybe he was stationed in Somalia or somewhere else in Africa."

Dr. Pecjic stared down at the dead man he was about to cut open.

Then he returned the scalpel to the tray. "Maybe we'd better call the director."

"And call Infectious Diseases, too," Dr. Wilks said.

Dr. Pecjic nodded, the fear naked in his eyes.

7:55 P.M.
Atlanta, Georgia

Packed inside the high-school auditorium, the audience of parents and friends was hushed. Up on the bright stage, a beautiful teenage girl stood in front of scenery intended to depict the restaurant in William Inge's *Bus Stop*. Her movements were awkward, and her words, ordinarily free and open, were stiff.

None of that bothered the stout, motherly woman in the first row. She wore a silver-gray dress of the kind the bride's mother at a formal wedding would choose, topped by a celebratory corsage of roses. She beamed up at the girl, and when the scene ended to polite applause, her clapping rang resoundingly.

At the final curtain, she leaped to her feet to applaud. She went around to the stage door to wait as the cast emerged in twos and threes to meet parents, boyfriends, and girlfriends. This was the last performance of the annual school play, and they were flushed with triumph, eager for the cast party that would last long into the night.

"I wish your father could've been here to see you tonight, Billie Jo," the proud mother said as the high-school beauty climbed into the car.

"So do I, Mom. Let's go home."

"Home?" The motherly woman was confused.

"I just need to lie down for a while. Then I'll change for the party, okay?"

"You sound bad." Her mother studied her, then turned the car into traffic. Billie Jo had been snuffling and coughing for more than a week but had insisted on performing anyway.

"It's just a cold, Mother," the girl said irritably.

By the time they reached the house, she was rubbing her eyes and groaning. Two red fever spots showed on her cheeks. Frantic, her terrified mother unlocked the front door and raced inside to dial 911. The police told her to leave the girl in the car and keep her warm and quiet. The paramedics arrived in three minutes.

In the ambulance, as the siren screamed through the Atlanta streets, the girl moaned and writhed on the gurney, struggling for breath. The mother wiped her daughter's fevered face and broke into despairing tears.

At the hospital emergency room, a nurse held the mother's hand. "We'll do everything necessary, Mrs. Pickett. I'm sure she'll be better soon."

Two hours later, blood gushed from Billie Jo Pickett's mouth, and she died.

5:12 P.M.
Fort Irwin, Barstow, California

The California high desert in early October was as uncertain and changeable as the orders of a new second lieutenant with his first platoon. This particular day had been clear and sunny, and by the time Phyllis Anderson began preparing dinner in the kitchen of her pleasant two-story house in the best section of the National Training Center's family housing, she was feeling optimistic. It had been a hot day and her husband, Keith, had taken a good nap. He had been fighting a heavy cold for two weeks, and she hoped the sun and warmth would clear it up once and for all.

Outside the kitchen windows, the lawn sprinklers were at work in the afternoon's long shadows. Her flower beds bloomed with late-summer flowers that defied the harsh wilderness of thorny gray-green mesquite, yucca, creosote, and cacti growing among the black rocks of the beige desert.

Phyllis hummed to herself as she put macaroni into the microwave. She listened for the footsteps of her husband coming down the stairs. The major had night operations tonight. But the stumbling clatter sounded more like Keith Jr., sliding and bumping his way down, excited about the movie she planned to take both children to while their father was working. After all, it was Friday night.

She shouted, "Jay-Jay, stop that!"

But it was not Keith Jr. Her husband, partially dressed in desert camouflage, staggered into the warm kitchen. He was dripping with sweat, and his hands squeezed his head as if to keep it from exploding.

He gasped, ". . . hospital . . . help . . ."

In front of her horrified eyes, the major collapsed on the kitchen floor, his chest heaving as he strained to breathe.

Shocked, Phyllis stared, then she moved with the speed and purpose of a soldier's wife. She tore out of the kitchen. Without knocking, she yanked open the side door of the house next to theirs and burst into the kitchen.

Capt. Paul Novak and his wife, Judy, gaped.

"Phyllis?" Novak stood up. "What's wrong, Phyllis?"

The major's wife did not waste a word. "Paul, I need you. Judy, come watch the kids. Hurry!"

She whirled and ran. Captain Novak and his wife were right behind. When called to action, a soldier learns to ask no questions. In the kitchen of the Anderson house, the Novaks took in the scene instantly.

"Nine-one-one?" Judy Novak reached for the telephone.

"No time!" Novak cried.

"Our car!" Phyllis shouted.

Judy Novak ran up the stairs to where the two children were in their bedrooms getting ready to enjoy an evening out. Phyllis Anderson and Novak picked up the gasping major. Blood trickled from his nose. He was semiconscious, moaning, unable to speak. Carrying him, they rushed across the lawn to the parked car.

Novak took the wheel, and Phyllis climbed into the rear beside her husband. Fighting back sobs, she cradled the major's head on her shoulder and held him close. His eyes stared up at her in agony as he fought for air. Novak sped through the base, blasting the car's horn. Traffic parted like an infantry company with the tanks coming through. But by the time they reached the Weed Army Community Hospital, Maj. Keith Anderson was unconscious.

Three hours later he was dead.

In the case of sudden, unexplained death in the State of California, an autopsy was mandated. Because of the unusual circumstances of the death, the major was rushed to the morgue. But as soon as the army pathologist opened the chest cavity, massive quantities of blood erupted, spraying him.

His face turned chalk white. He jumped to his feet, snapped off his rubber gloves, and ran out of the autopsy chamber to his office.

He grabbed the phone. "Get me the Pentagon and USAMRIID. Now! Priority!"

Part One

Part One

Chapter One

A cold October rain slanted down on Knightsbridge where Brompton Road intersected Sloan Street. The steady stream of honking cars, taxis, and red double-decker buses turned south and made their halting way toward Sloan Square and Chelsea. Neither the rain nor the fact that business and government offices were closed for the weekend lessened the crush. The world economy was good, the shops were full, and New Labor was rocking no one's boat. Now the tourists came to London at all times of the year, and the traffic this Sunday afternoon continued to move at a snail's pace.

Impatient, U.S. Army Lt. Col. Jonathan ("Jon") Smith, M.D., stepped lightly from the slow-moving, old-style No. 19 bus two streets before his destination. The rain was letting up at last. He trotted a few quick steps beside the bus on the wet pavement and then hurried onward, leaving the bus behind.

A tall, trim, athletic man in his early forties, Smith had dark hair worn smoothly back and a high-planed face. His navy blue eyes automatically surveyed vehicles and pedestrians. There was nothing unusual about him as he strode along in his tweed jacket, cotton trousers, and trench coat. Still, women turned to look, and he occasionally noticed and smiled, but continued on his way.

He left the drizzle at Wilbraham Place and entered the foyer of the genteel Wilbraham Hotel, where he took a room every time USAMRIID sent him to a medical conference in London. Inside the old hostelry, he climbed the stairs two at a time to his second-floor room. There he rummaged through his suitcases, searching for the field reports of an outbreak of high fever among U.S. troops stationed in Manila. He had promised to show them to Dr. Chandra Uttam of the viral diseases branch of the World Health Organization.

Finally he found the reports under a pile of dirty clothes tossed into the larger suitcase. He sighed and grinned at himself—he had never lost the messy habits acquired from his years in the field living in tents, focusing on one crisis or another.

As he rushed downstairs to return to the WHO epidemiology conference, the desk clerk called out to him.

"Colonel? There's a letter for you. It's marked 'Urgent.' "

"A letter?" Who would mail him here? He looked at his wristwatch, which told him not only the hour but reminded him of the day. "On a Sunday?"

"It came by hand."

Suddenly worried, Smith took the envelope and ripped it open. It was a single sheet of white printer paper, no letterhead or return address.

Smithy,

> *Meet me Rock Creek park, Pierce Mill picnic grounds, midnight Monday. Urgent. Tell no one.*

> *B*

Smith's chest contracted. There was only one person who called him Smithy—Bill Griffin. He had met Bill in third grade at Hoover elementary school in Council Bluffs, Iowa. Fast friends from then on, they had gone to high school together, college at the University of Iowa, and on to grad school at UCLA. Only after Smith had gotten his M.D. and Bill his Ph.D. in psychology had they taken different paths. Both had fulfilled boyhood dreams by joining the military, with Bill going into military intelligence work. They had not actually seen each other in more than a decade, but through all their distant assignments and postings, they had kept in touch.

Frowning, Smith stood motionless in the stately lobby and stared down at the cryptic words.

"Anything wrong, sir?" the desk clerk inquired politely.

Smith looked around. "Nothing. Nothing at all. Well, better be on my way if I want to catch the next seminar."

He stuffed the note into his trench-coat pocket and strode out into the soggy afternoon. How had Bill known he was in London? At this particular secluded hotel? And why all the cloak-and-dagger, even to the extent of using Bill's private boyhood name for him?

No return address or phone number.

Only an initial to identify the sender.

Why midnight?

Smith liked to think of himself as a simple man, but he knew the truth was far from that. His career showed the reality. He had been a military doctor in MASH units and was now a research scientist. For a short time he had also worked for military intelligence. And then there was the stint commanding troops. He wore his restlessness like another man wore his skin—so much a part of him he hardly noticed.

Yet in the past year he had discovered a happiness that had given him focus, a concentration he had never before achieved. Not only did he find his work at USAMRIID challenging and exciting, the confirmed bachelor was in love. Really in love. No more of that high-school stuff of women coming and going through his life in a revolving door of drama. Sophia Russell was everything to him—fellow scientist, research partner, and blond beauty.

There were moments when he would take his eyes from his electron microscope just to stare at her. How all that fragile loveliness could conceal so much intelligence and steely will constantly intrigued him. Just thinking about her made him miss her all over again. He was scheduled to fly out of Heathrow tomorrow morning, which would give him just enough time to drive home to Maryland and meet Sophia for breakfast before they had to go into the lab.

But now he had this disturbing message from Bill Griffin.

All his internal alarms were ringing. At the same time, it was an opportunity. He smiled wryly at himself. Apparently his restlessness still was not tamed.

As he hailed a taxi, he made plans.

He would change his flight tickets to Monday night and meet Bill Griffin at midnight. He and Bill went too far back for him to do otherwise. This meant he would not get into work until Tuesday, a day late. Which would make Kielburger, the general who directed USAMRIID, see red. To put it mildly, the general found Smith and his freewheeling, field-operations way of doing things aggravating.

Not a problem. Smith would do an end run.

Early yesterday morning he had phoned Sophia just to hear her voice. But in the middle of their conversation, a call had cut in. She had been ordered to go to the lab immediately to identify some virus from California. Sophia could easily work the next sixteen or twenty-four hours nonstop and, in fact, she might be at the lab so late tonight, she would not even be up tomorrow morning, when he had been planning to share breakfast. Smith sighed, disappointed. The only good thing was she would be too busy to worry about him.

He might as well just leave a message on their answering machine at home that he would arrive a day late and she should not be concerned. She could tell General Kielburger or not, her call.

That was where the payoff came in. Instead of leaving London tomorrow morning, he would take a night flight. A few hours' difference, but a world to him: Tom Sheringham was leading the U.K. Microbiological Research Establishment team that was working on a potential vaccine against all hantaviruses. Tonight he would not only be able to attend Tom's presentation, he would twist Tom's arm to join him for a late dinner and drinks. Then he would pry out all the inside, cutting-edge details Tom was not ready to make public and wangle an invitation to visit Porton Down tomorrow before he had to catch his night flight.

Nodding to himself and almost smiling, Smith leaped over a puddle and yanked open the back door of the black-beetle taxi that had stopped in the street. He told the cabbie the address of the WHO conference.

But as he sank into the seat, his smile disappeared. He pulled out the letter from Bill Griffin and reread it, hoping to find some clue he had missed. What was most noteworthy was what was not said. The furrow between his brows deepened. He thought back over the years, trying to figure out what could have happened to make Bill suddenly contact him this way.

If Bill wanted scientific help or some kind of assistance from USAM-RIID, he would go through official government channels. Bill was an FBI special agent now, and proud of it. Like any agent, he would request Smith's services from the director of USAMRIID.

On the other hand, if it were simply personal, there would have been no cloak-and-dagger. Instead, a phone message would have been waiting at the hotel with Bill's number so Smith could call back.

In the chilly cab, Smith shrugged uneasily under his trench coat. This meeting was not only unofficial, it was secret. Very secret. Which meant Bill was going behind the FBI. Behind USAMRIID. Behind all government entities . . . all apparently in the hopes of involving him, too, in something clandestine.

Chapter Two

9:57 A.M., Sunday, October 12
Fort Detrick, Maryland

Located in Frederick, a small city surrounded by western Maryland's green, rolling landscape, Fort Detrick was the home of the United States Army Medical Research Institute for Infectious Diseases. Known by its initials, USAMRIID, or simply as the Institute, it had been a magnet for violent protest in the 1960s when it was an infamous government factory for developing and testing chemical and biological weapons. When President Nixon ordered an end to those programs in 1969, USAMRIID disappeared from the spotlight to become a center for science and healing.

Then came 1989. The highly communicable Ebola virus appeared to have infected monkeys dying at a primate quarantine unit in Reston, Virginia. USAMRIID's doctors and veterinarians, both military and civilian, were rushed to contain what could erupt into a tragic human epidemic.

But better than containment, they proved the Reston virus to be a genetic millimeter different from the extremely lethal strains of Ebola

Zaire and Ebola Sudan. Most important was that the virus was harmless to people. That exciting discovery skyrocketed USAMRIID scientists into headlines across the nation. Suddenly, Fort Detrick was again on people's minds, but this time as America's foremost military medical research facility.

In her USAMRIID office, Dr. Sophia Russell was thinking about these claims to fame, hoping for inspiration as she waited impatiently for her telephone call to reach a man who might have some answers to help resolve a crisis she feared could erupt into a serious epidemic.

Sophia was a Ph.D. scientist in cell and molecular biology. She was a leading cog in the worldwide wheels set in motion by the death of Maj. Keith Anderson. She had been at USAMRIID for four years, and like the scientists in 1989, she was fighting a medical emergency involving an unknown virus. Already she and her contemporaries were in a far more precarious position: This virus *was* fatal to humans. There were three victims—the army major and two civilians—all of whom had apparently died abruptly of acute respiratory distress syndrome (ARDS) within hours of one another.

It was not the timing of the deaths or the ARDS itself that had riveted USAMRIID; millions died of ARDS each year around the planet. But not young people. Not healthy people. Not without a history of respiratory problems or other contributing factors, and not with violent headaches and blood-filled chest cavities.

Now three cases in a single day had died with identical symptoms, each in a different part of the country—the major in California, a teenage girl in Georgia, and a homeless man in Massachusetts.

The director of USAMRIID—Brig. Gen. Calvin Kielburger—was reluctant to declare a worldwide alert on the basis of three cases they had been handed only yesterday. He hated rocking the boat or sounding like a weak alarmist. Even more, he hated sharing credit with other Level Four labs, especially USAMRIID's biggest rival, Atlanta's Centers for Disease Control.

Meanwhile, tension at USAMRIID was palpable, and Sophia, leading a team of scientists, kept working.

She had received the first of the blood samples by 3:00 A.M. Saturday and had immediately headed to her Level Four lab to begin testing. In the small locker room, she had removed her clothes, watch, and the ring Jon Smith gave her when she agreed to marry him. She paused just a moment to smile down at the ring and think about Jon. His handsome face flashed into her mind—the almost American Indian features with the high cheekbones but very dark blue eyes. Those eyes had intrigued her from the beginning, and sometimes she had imagined how much fun it would be to fall into their depths. She loved the liquid way he moved, like a jungle animal who was domesticated only by choice. She loved the way he made love—the fire and excitement. But most of all, she just simply, irrevocably, passionately loved *him*.

She had had to interrupt their phone conversation to rush here. *"Darling, I have to go. It was the lab on the other line. An emergency."*

"At this hour? Can't it wait until morning? You need your rest."

She chuckled. "You called me. I was resting, in fact sleeping, until the phone rang."

"I knew you'd want to talk to me. You can't resist me."

She laughed. "Absolutely. I want to talk to you at all hours of the day and night. I miss you every moment you're in London. I'm glad you woke me up out of sound sleep so I could tell you that."

It was his turn to laugh. "I love you, too, darling."

In the USAMRIID locker room, she sighed. Closed her eyes. Then she put Jon from her mind. She had work to do. An emergency.

She quickly dressed in sterile green surgical scrubs. Barefoot, she labored to open the door to Bio-Safety Level Two against the negative pressure that kept contaminants inside Levels Two, Three, and Four. Finally inside, she trotted past a dry shower stall and into a bathroom where clean white socks were kept.

Socks on, she hurried into the Level Three staging area. She snapped on latex rubber surgical gloves and then taped the gloves to the sleeves to create a seal. She repeated the procedure with her socks and the legs of the scrubs. That done, she dressed in her personal bright-blue plastic biological space suit, which smelled faintly like the inside of a plastic bucket. She carefully checked it for pinholes. She lowered the flexible plastic helmet over her head, closed the plastic zipper that ensured her suit and helmet were sealed, and pulled a yellow air hose from the wall.

She plugged the hose into her suit. With a quiet hiss, the air adjusted in the massive space suit. Almost finished, she unplugged the air hose and lumbered through a stainless steel door into the air lock of Level Four, which was lined with nozzles for water and chemicals for the decontamination shower.

At last she pulled open the door into Level Four. The Hot Zone.

There was no way she could rush anything now. As she advanced each step in the cautious chain of protective layers, she had to take more care. Her one weapon was efficient motion. The more efficient she was, the more speed she could eke out. So instead of struggling into the pair of heavy yellow rubber boots, she expertly bent one foot, angled it just right, and slid it in. Then she did the same with the other.

She waddled as fast as she could along narrow cinder-block corridors into her lab. There she slipped on a third pair of latex gloves, carefully removed the samples of blood and tissue from the refrigerated container, and went to work isolating the virus.

Over the next twenty-six hours, she forgot to eat or sleep. She lived in the lab, studying the virus with the electron microscope. To her amazement, she and her team ruled out Ebola, Marburg, and any other filovirus. It had the usual furry-ball shape of most viruses. Once she had seen it, given the ARDS cause of death, her first thought was a hantavirus like the one that had killed the young athletes on the Navajo reservation in 1993. USAMRIID was expert on hantaviruses. One of its legends, Karl Johnson, had been a discoverer of the first hantavirus to be isolated and identified back in the 1970s.

With that in mind, she had used immunoblotting to test the unknown pathogen against USAMRIID's frozen bank of blood samples of previous victims of various hantaviruses from around the world. It reacted to none. Puzzled, she ran a polymerase chain reaction to get a bit of DNA sequence from the virus. It resembled no known hantavirus, but for future reference she assembled a preliminary restriction map anyway. That was when she wished most fervently that Jon was with her, not far away at the WHO conference in London.

Frustrated because she still had no definitive answer, she had forced herself to leave the lab. She had already sent the team off to sleep, and now she went through the exiting procedure, too, peeling away her space suit, going through decontamination procedures, and dressing again in her civilian clothes.

After a four-hour on-site nap—that was all she needed, she told herself firmly—she had hurried to her office to study the tests' notes. As the other team members awakened, she sent them back to their labs.

Her head ached, and her throat was dry. She took a bottle of water from her office mini-refrigerator and returned to her desk. On the wall hung three framed photos. She drank and leaned forward to contemplate them, drawn like a moth to comforting light. One showed Jon and herself in bathing suits last summer in Barbados. What fun they had had on their one and only vacation. The second was of Jon in his dress uniform the day he'd made lieutenant colonel. The last pictured a younger captain with wild black hair, a dirty face, and piercing blue eyes in a dusty field uniform outside a Fifth MASH tent somewhere in the Iraqi desert.

Missing him, needing him in the lab with her, she had reached for the phone to call him in London—and stopped. The general had sent him to London. For the general, everything was by the book, and every assignment had to be finished. Not a day late, not a day early. Jon was not due for several hours. Then she realized he was probably aloft now anyway, but she wouldn't be at his house, waiting for him. She dismissed her disappointment.

She had devoted herself to science, and somewhere along the way she had gotten extremely lucky. She had never expected to marry. Fall in love, perhaps. But marry? No. Few men wanted a wife obsessed with her work. But Jon understood. In fact, it excited him that she could look at a cell and discuss it in graphic, colorful detail with him. In turn, she had found his endless curiosity invigorating. Like two children at a kindergarten party, they had found their favorite playmates in each other—well suited not only professionally but temperamentally. Both were dedicated, compassionate, and as in love with life as with each other.

She had never known such happiness, and she had Jon to thank for it.

With an impatient shake of her head, she turned on her computer to examine the lab notes for anything she might have missed. She found nothing of any significance.

Then, as more DNA sequence data was arriving, and she continued to review in her mind all the clinical data so far on the virus, she had a strange feeling.

She had seen this virus—or one that was incredibly similar—somewhere.

She wracked her brain. Dug through her memory. Rooted through her past.

Nothing came to mind. Finally she read one of her team members' reports that suggested the new virus might be related to Machupo, one of the first discovered hemorrhagic fevers, again by Karl Johnson.

Africa pushed none of her buttons. But Bolivia . . . ?

Peru!

Her student anthropology field trip, and—

Victor Tremont.

Yes, that had been his name. A biologist on a field trip to Peru to collect plants and dirts for potential medicinals for . . . what company? A pharmaceutical firm . . . Blanchard Pharmaceuticals!

She turned back to her computer, quickly entered the Internet, and searched for Blanchard. She found it almost at once—in Long Lake,

New York. And Victor Tremont was president and Chief Operating Officer now. She reached for her phone and dialed the number.

It was Sunday morning, but giant corporations sometimes kept their telephones open all weekend for important calls. Blanchard did. A human voice answered, and when Sophia asked for Victor Tremont, the voice told her to wait. She drummed her fingers on the desk, trying to control her worried impatience.

At last a series of clicks and silences on the far end of the line were interrupted by another human voice. This time it was neutral, toneless: "May I ask your name and business with Dr. Tremont?"

"Sophia Russell. Tell him it's about a trip to Peru where we met."

"Please hold." More silence. Then: "Mr. Tremont will speak with you now."

"Ms. . . . Russell?" Obviously he was consulting the name handed to him on a pad. "What can I do for you?" His voice was low and pleasant but commanding. A man clearly accustomed to being in charge.

She said mildly, "Actually, it's *Dr.* Russell now. You don't remember my name, Dr. Tremont?"

"Can't say I do. But you mentioned Peru, and I do remember Peru. Twelve or thirteen years ago, wasn't it?" He was acknowledging why he was talking to her, but giving nothing away in case she was a job seeker or it was all some hoax.

"Thirteen, and I certainly remember you." She was trying to keep it light. "What I'm interested in is that time on the Caraibo River. I was with a group of anthropology undergrads on a field trip from Syracuse while you were collecting potential medicinal materials. I'm calling to ask about the virus you found in those remote tribesmen, the natives the others called the Monkey Blood People."

In his large corner office at the other end of the line, Victor Tremont felt a jolt of fear. Just as quickly, he repressed it. He swiveled in his desk chair to stare out at the lake, which was shimmering like mercury in the early-morning light. On the far side, a thick pine forest stretched and climbed to the high mountains in the distance.

Annoyed that she had surprised him with such a potentially devastating memory, Tremont continued to swivel. He kept his voice friendly. "Now I remember you. The eager blond young lady dazzled by science. I wondered whether you'd go on to become an anthropologist. Did you?"

"No, I ended up with a doctorate in cell and molecular biology. That's why I need your help. I'm working at the army's infectious diseases research center at Fort Detrick. We've come across a virus that sounds a lot like the one in Peru—an unknown type causing headaches, fever, and acute respiratory distress syndrome that can kill otherwise healthy people within hours and produce a violent hemorrhage in the lungs. Does that ring a bell, Dr. Tremont?"

"Call me Victor, and I seem to recall your first name is Susan . . . Sally . . . something like . . . ?"

"Sophia."

"Of course. Sophia Russell. Fort Detrick," he said, as if writing it down. "I'm glad to hear you remained in science. Sometimes I wish I'd stayed in the lab instead of jumping to the front office. But that's water over a long-ago dam, eh?" He laughed.

She asked, "Do you recall the virus?"

"No. Can't say I do. I went into sales and management soon after Peru, and probably that's why the incident escapes me. As I said, it was a long time ago. But from what I recall of my molecular biology, the scenario you suggest is unlikely. You must be thinking of a series of different viruses we heard about on that trip. There was no shortage. I remember that much."

She dug the phone into her ear, frustrated. "No, I'm certain there was this one single agent that came from working with the Monkey Blood People. I didn't pay a lot of attention at the time. But then, I never expected to end up in biology, much less cell and molecular. Still, the oddness of it stuck with me."

" 'The Monkey Blood People'? How bizarre. I'm sure I'd recall a tribe with such a colorful name as that."

Urgency filled her voice. "Dr. Tremont, listen. Please. This is vital. Critical. We've just received three cases of a virus that reminds me of the one in Peru. Those natives had a cure that worked almost eighty percent of the time—drinking the blood of a certain monkey. As I recall, that's what astonished you."

"And still would," Tremont agreed. The accuracy of her memory was unnerving. "Primitive Indians with a cure for a fatal virus? But I know nothing about it," he lied smoothly. "The way you describe what happened, I'm certain I'd remember. What do your colleagues say? Surely some worked in Peru, too."

She sighed. "I wanted to check with you first. We have enough false alarms, and it's been a long time since Peru for me, too. But if you don't remember . . ." Her voice trailed off. She was terribly disappointed. "I'm certain there was a virus. Perhaps I'll contact Peru. They must have a record of unusual cures among the Indians."

Victor Tremont's voice rose slightly. "That may not be necessary. I kept a journal of my trips back then. Notes on the plants and potential pharmaceuticals. Perhaps I jotted down something about your virus as well."

Sophia leaped at the suggestion. "I'd appreciate your looking. Right away."

"Whoa." Tremont gave a warm chuckle. He had her. "The notebooks are stored somewhere in my house. Probably the attic. Maybe the basement. I'll have to get back to you tomorrow."

"I owe you, Victor. Maybe the world will. First thing tomorrow, please. You have no idea how important this could be." She gave him her phone number.

"Oh, I think I know," Tremont assured her. "Tomorrow morning at the latest."

He hung up and rotated once more to gaze out at the brightening lake and the high mountains that suddenly seemed to loom close and ominous. He stood up and walked to the window. He was a tall man of medium build, with a distinctive face on which nature had played one of her more kindly tricks: From a youth's oversized nose, gawky ears, and thin cheeks, he had grown into a good-looking man. He was now in his fifties, and his features had filled out. His face was aquiline, smooth, and aristocratic. The nose was the perfect size—straight and strong, a fitting centerpiece for his very English face. With his tan skin and thick, iron-gray hair, he drew attention wherever he went. But he knew it was not his dignity and attractiveness that people found so appealing. It was his self-confidence. He radiated power, and less-assured people found that compelling.

Despite what he had told Sophia Russell, Victor Tremont made no move to go home to his secluded estate. Instead, he stared unseeing at the mountains and fought off tension. He was angry . . . and annoyed.

Sophia Russell. My God, Sophia Russell!

Who would have thought? He had not even recognized her name initially. In fact, still did not remember any of the names of that insignificant little student group. And he doubted any would recall his. But Russell had. What kind of brain retained such detail? Obviously the trivial was too important to her. He shook his head, disgusted. In truth, she was not a problem. Just a nuisance. Still, she must be dealt with. He unlocked the secret drawer in his carved desk, took out a cell phone, and dialed.

An emotionless voice with a faint accent answered. "Yes?"

"I need to talk to you," Victor Tremont ordered. "My office. Ten minutes." He hung up, returned the cell phone to the locked drawer, and picked up his regular office phone. "Muriel? Get me General Caspar in Washington."

Chapter Three

9:14 A.M., Monday, October 13
Fort Detrick, Maryland

As employees arrived at USAMRIID that Monday morning, word quickly spread through the campus's buildings of the weekend's fruitless search to identify and find a way to contain some new killer virus. The press still had not discovered the story, and the director's office ordered everyone to maintain media silence. No one was to talk to a reporter, and only those working in the labs were kept in the loop about the agonizing quest.

Meanwhile, regular work still had to be done. There were forms to be filed, equipment to be maintained, phone calls to be answered. In the sergeant major's office, Specialist Four Hideo Takeda was in his cubicle sorting mail when he opened an official-looking envelope emblazoned with the U.S. Department of Defense logo.

After he read and reread the letter, he leaned over the divider between his cubicle and that of Specialist Five Sandra Quinn, his fellow clerk. He confided in an excited whisper, "It's my transfer to Okinawa."

"You're kidding."

"We'd given up." He grinned. His girlfriend, Miko, was stationed on Okinawa.

"Better tell the boss right away," Sandra warned. "It means teaching a new clerk to deal with the goddamned absentminded professors we got here. She'll be pissed. Man, they're all out of their minds today anyway with this new crisis, aren't they?"

"Screw her," Specialist Takeda swore cheerfully.

"Not in my worst nightmare." Sgt. Maj. Helen Daugherty stood in her office doorway. "Would you care to step in here, Specialist Takeda?" she said with exaggerated politeness. "Or would you prefer I beat you senseless first?"

An imposing six-foot blonde with the shoulders to offset all her whistle-producing curves, the sergeant major looked down with her best piranha smile at the five-foot-six Takeda. The clerk hurried out of his cubicle with a nervous show of fear not entirely faked. With Daugherty, as befitted any good sergeant major, you were never fully sure you were safe.

"Close the door, Takeda. And take a seat."

The specialist did as instructed.

Daugherty fixed him with a gimlet eye. "How long have you known about the possibility of this transfer, Hideo?"

"It came out of the blue this morning. I mean, I just opened the letter."

"And we put it in for you . . . what, almost two years ago?"

"Year and a half, at least. Right after I came back from leave over there. Look, Sergeant, if you need me to stick around awhile, I'll be—"

Daugherty shook her head. "Doesn't look like I could do that if I wanted to." With her finger she stabbed a memo on her desk. "I got this E-mail from the Department of the Army about the same time you must've opened your letter. Looks like your replacement's already on her way. Coming from Intelligence Command over in Kosovo, no less. She must've been on a plane before the letter even got to the office." Daugherty's expression was thoughtful.

"You mean she'll be here today?"

Daugherty glanced at the clock on her desk. "A couple of hours, to be exact."

"Wow, that's fast."

"Yes," Daugherty agreed, "it sure is. They've even cut travel orders for you. You've got a day to clear out your desk and quarters. You're to be on a plane tomorrow morning."

"A day?"

"Better get at it. And best of luck, Hideo. I've enjoyed working with you. I'll put a good report in your file."

"Yessir, er, Sergeant. And thanks."

Still a little stunned, Takeda left Sergeant Major Daugherty contemplating the memo. She was rolling a pencil between her hands and staring off into space as he enthusiastically dumped out his desk. He repressed a war whoop of victory. He was not only tired of being away from Miko, he was especially tired of living in the USAMRIID pressure cooker. He had been through plenty of emergencies here, but this new one had everyone worried. Even scared. He was glad to get the hell out.

.

Three hours later, Specialist Four Adele Schweik stood at attention in the same office in front of Sergeant Major Daugherty. She was a small brunette with almost black hair, a rigid carriage, and alert gray eyes. Her uniform was impeccable, with two rows of medal ribbons showing service overseas in many countries and campaigns. There was even a Bosnian ribbon.

"At ease, Specialist."

Schweik stood at ease. "Thank you, Sergeant Major."

Daugherty read her transfer papers and spoke without looking up. "Kind of fast, wasn't it?"

"I asked to be transferred to the D.C. area a few months ago. Personal reasons. My colonel told me an opening had suddenly come up at Detrick, and I jumped at it."

Daugherty looked up at her. "A little overqualified, aren't you? This is a backwater post. A small command not doing much and never going overseas."

"I only know it's Detrick. I don't know what your unit is."

"Oh?" Daugherty raised a blond eyebrow. There was something too cool and composed about this Schweik. "Well, we're USAMRIID: U.S. Army Medical Research Institute for Infectious Diseases. Scientific research. All our officers are doctors, vets, or medical specialists. We even have civilians. No weapons, no training, no glory."

Schweik smiled. "That sounds peaceful, Sergeant Major. A nice change after Kosovo. Besides, haven't I heard USAMRIID is on the cutting edge, working with pretty deadly Hot Zone diseases? Sounds like it could be exciting."

The sergeant major cocked her head. "It is for the docs. But for us it's just office routine. We keep the place running. Over the weekend there was some kind of emergency. Don't ask any questions. It's none of your business. And if any journalist contacts you, refer them to public affairs. That's an order. Okay, there's your cubicle next to Quinn's. Introduce yourself. Get settled, and Quinn will bring you up to speed."

Schweik came to attention. "Thank you, Sergeant Major."

Daugherty rotated her pencil again, studying the door that had just closed behind the new woman. Then Daugherty sighed. She had not been completely truthful. Although there was plenty of routine, there were moments like this when all of a sudden the army didn't make a damn bit of sense. She shrugged. Well, she had seen stranger things than an abrupt shift in personnel that made both transferring parties happy. She buzzed Quinn, asked for a cup of coffee, and put out of her mind the latest lab crisis and the strange personnel transfer. She had work to do.

■

At 1732 hours, Sergeant Major Daugherty locked her cubicle door, preparing to leave the empty office. But the office was not empty.

The new woman, Schweik, said, "I'd like to stay and learn as much as I can, if that's all right, Sergeant Major."

"Fine. I'll tell security. You have an office key? Good. Lock up when you're finished. You won't be alone. That new virus is driving the docs crazy. I expect some of them will be on campus all night. If this goes on much longer, they're going to start getting cantankerous. They don't like mysteries that kill people."

"So I've heard." The small brunette nodded and smiled. "See, plenty of action and excitement at Fort Detrick."

Daugherty laughed. "I stand corrected," she said, and went out.

At her desk in the silent office, Specialist Schweik read memos and made notes for another half hour until she was sure neither the sergeant major nor security was coming back to check on her. Then she opened the attaché case she had brought inside during her first coffee break. When she had arrived at Andrews Air Force Base this morning, it had been waiting in the car assigned to her.

From the case she withdrew a schematic diagram of the phone installations in the USAMRIID building. The main box was in the basement, and it contained connections for all the internal extensions and private outside lines. She studied it long enough to memorize its position. Then she returned the diagram, closed the case, and stepped into the corridor, carrying it.

With innocent curiosity on her face, she looked carefully around.

The guard inside the front entrance was reading. Schweik needed to get past him. She inhaled, keeping herself calm, and glided silently along the rear corridor to the basement entrance.

She waited. No movement or noise from the guard. Although the building was considered high security, the protection was less to keep people out than to shield the public from the lethal toxins, viruses, bacteria, and other dangerous scientific materials that were studied at USAMRIID. Although the guard was well trained, he lacked the aggressive edge of a sentry defending a lab where top-secret war weapons were created.

Relieved that he remained engrossed in his book, she tried the heavy metal door. It was locked. She took a set of keys from the case. The third one opened the basement door. She padded soundlessly downstairs, where she wound in and out among giant machines that heated and cooled the building, supplied sterile air and negative pressure for the labs, operated the powerful exhaust system, supplied water and chemical solutions for the chemical showers, and handled all the other maintenance needs of the medical complex.

She was sweating by the time she located the main box. She set the attaché case on the floor and withdrew from it a smaller case of tools, wires, color-coded connections, meters, switching units, listening devices, and miniature recorders.

It was evening, and the basement was quiet but for the occasional snap, gurgle, and hum of the pipes and shafts. Still, she listened to make sure no one else was around. Nervous energy sent chills across her skin. Warily she studied the gray walls. At last she opened the main box and went to work on the multitude of connections.

■

Two hours later, back in her office, she checked her telephone, attached a miniature speaker-earphone set, flipped a switch on the hidden control box in her desk drawer, and listened. ". . . Yeah, I'll be here at least two more hours, I'm afraid. Sorry, honey, can't be helped. This virus is a bear. The whole staff's on it. Okay, I'll try to get there before the kids go to bed."

Satisfied her listening and rerouting equipment was working, she clicked off and dialed an outside line. The male voice that had contacted her last night and given her instructions answered. "Yes?"

She reported: "Installation is complete. I'm connected to the recorder for all phone calls, and I've got a line on my set to alert me to any from the offices you're interested in. It'll connect me with the shunt to intercept calls."

"You were unobserved? You are unsuspected?"

She prided herself on her ear for voices, and she knew all the major languages and many minor. This voice was educated, and his English was good but not perfect. A non-English speech pattern, and the smallest trace of a Middle-Eastern accent. Not Israel, Iran, or Turkey. Possibly Syria or Lebanon, but more likely Jordan or Iraq.

She filed the information for future reference.

She said, "Of course."

"That is well. Be alert to any developments that concern the unknown virus they are working on. Monitor all calls in and out of the offices of Dr. Russell, Lieutenant Colonel Smith, and General Kielburger."

This job could not last too long, or it would become too risky. They would probably never find the body of the real Specialist Four Adele Schweik. Schweik had no known relatives and few friends outside the army. She had been selected for those reasons.

But Schweik sensed Sergeant Major Daugherty was suspicious, vaguely disturbed by her arrival. Too much scrutiny could expose her.

"How long will I remain here?"

"Until we do not need you. Do nothing to call attention to yourself."

The dial tone hummed in her ear. She hung up and leaned forward to continue familiarizing herself with the routines and requirements of the sergeant major's office. She also listened to live conversations in and out of the building and monitored the light on the desk phone that would alert her to calls from the Russell woman's laboratory. For a moment she was curious about what was so important about Dr. Russell. Then she banished the thought. There were some things it was dangerous to know.

Chapter Four

Midnight
Washington, D.C.

Washington's magnificent Rock Creek park was a wedge of wilderness in the heart of the city. From the Potomac River near the Kennedy Center it wound narrowly north to where it expanded into a wide stretch of woods in the city's upper Northwest. A natural woodland, it abounded in hiking, biking, horse trails, picnic grounds, and historical sites. Pierce Mill, where Tilden Street intersected Beach Drive, was one of those historical landmarks. An old gristmill, it dated from pre–Civil War days when a line of such mills bordered the creek. It was now a museum run by the National Park Service and, in the moonlight, a ghostly artifact from a faraway time.

Northwest of the mill, where the brush was thick in the shadows of tall trees, Bill Griffin waited, holding a highly alert Doberman on a tight leash. Although the night was cold, Griffin sweated. His wary gaze scanned the mill and picnic grounds. The sleek dog sniffed the air, and its erect ears rotated, listening for the source of its unease.

From the right, in the general direction of the mill, someone approached. The dog had caught the faint sounds of autumn leaves being crunched underfoot long before they were audible to Griffin. But once Griffin heard the footfalls, he released the animal. The dog remained obediently seated, every taut muscle quivering, eager.

Griffin gave a silent hand signal.

Like a black phantom, the Doberman sprang off into the night and made a wide circle around the picnic grounds, invisible among the ominous shadows of the trees.

Griffin desperately wanted a cigarette. Every nerve was on edge. Behind him something small and wild rustled through the underbrush. Somewhere in the park a night owl hooted. He acknowledged neither the sounds nor his nerves. He was highly trained, a complete professional, and so he maintained watch, vigilant and unmoving. He breathed shallowly so as to not reveal his presence by clouds of white breath in the cold night air. And although he kept his temper under control, he was an angry, worried man.

When at last Lt. Col. Jonathan Smith came into view, striding across the open area in the silver-blue moonlight, Griffin still did not move. On the far side of the picnic grounds, the Doberman went to ground, invisible. But Griffin knew he was there.

Jon Smith hesitated on the path. He asked in a hoarse whisper, "Bill?"

In the umbra of the trees, Griffin continued to concentrate on the night. He listened to the traffic on the nearby parkway and to the city noises beyond. Nothing was unusual. No one else was in this part of the massive preserve. He waited for the dog to tell him otherwise, but he had resumed his rounds, apparently satisfied, too.

Griffin sighed. He stepped out to the edge of the picnic grounds where the moonlight met the shadows. His voice was low and urgent. "Smithy. Over here."

Jon Smith turned. He was jumpy. All he could see was a vague shape wavering in the moonlight. He walked toward it, feeling exposed and vulnerable, although he did not know to what.

"Bill?" he growled. "Is that you?"

"The bad penny," Griffin said lightly and returned deep into the shadows.

Smith joined him. He blinked, willing his eyes to adjust quickly. At last he saw his old friend, who was smiling at him. Bill Griffin had the same round face and bland features Smith remembered, although he looked as if he had lost ten pounds. His cheeks were flatter, and his shoulders appeared heavier than usual since his torso and waist were slimmer. His brown hair hung mid-length, limp and unruly. He was two inches shorter than Smith's six feet—a good-sized, strong-looking, stocky man.

But Smith had also witnessed Bill Griffin make himself appear neutral, ordinary really, as if he had just gotten off work from a factory job assembling computer parts or was on his way to the local café where he was the head hamburger flipper. It was a face and body that had stood him in good stead in army intelligence and in the FBI monitoring covert operations, because under that bland exterior was a sharp mind and iron will.

To Smith, his old friend had always been something of a chameleon, but not tonight. Tonight, Smith looked at him and saw the star Iowa football player and man of opinions. He had grown up to be honest, decent, and daring. The real Bill Griffin.

Griffin held out his hand. "Hello, Smithy. Glad to see you after so long. It's about time we caught up. When was it last? The Drake Hotel, Des Moines?"

"It was. Porterhouses and Potosi beer." But Jon Smith did not smile at the good memory as he shook Griffin's hand. "This is a hell of a way to meet. What have you got yourself into? Is it trouble?"

"You might say." Griffin nodded, his voice still light. "But never mind that right now. How the hell are you, Smithy?"

"I'm fine," Smith snapped, impatient. "It's you we're talking about. How'd you know I was in London?" Then he chuckled. "No, never mind. Stupid question, right? You always know. Now, what's the—"

"I hear you're getting married. Finally found someone to tame the cowboy? Settle down in the suburbs, raise kids, and mow the lawn?"

"It'll never happen." Smith grinned. "Sophia's a cowboy herself. Another virus hunter."

"Yeah. That makes sense. Might actually work." Griffin nodded and gazed off, his eyes as restless and uneasy as the now-invisible Doberman. As if the night might explode into flames around them. "How're your people doing on the virus anyway?"

"Which virus? We work on so damn many at Detrick."

Bill Griffin's gaze still traversed the moonlight and shadows of the park like a tank gunner searching for a target. He ignored the sweat collecting under his clothes. "The one you were assigned to investigate early Saturday."

Smith was puzzled. "I'd been in London since last Tuesday. You must know that." He swore aloud. "Damn! That must be the 'emergency' Sophia was called in about while we were talking. I've got to get back—" He stopped and frowned. "How do you know Detrick's got a new virus? Is that what this is all about? You figure they told me all about it while I was away, and now you want to tap me for information?"

Griffin's face revealed nothing. He scrutinized the night. "Calm down, Jon."

"Calm down?" Smith was incredulous. "Is the FBI so interested in this particular virus that they sent you to pump me in secret? That's damn stupid. Your director can call my director. That's the way these things are done."

Griffin finally looked at Smith. "I don't work for the FBI anymore."

"You don't . . . ?" Smith stared into the steady eyes, but now there was nothing there. Bill Griffin's eyes, like the rest of his featureless face, had gone empty. The old Bill Griffin was gone, and for a moment Smith felt an ache in the pit of his stomach. Then his anger rose, every sensor of his military and virus-hunter experience sounding loudly. "What's so special about this new virus? And what do you want information for? Some sleazy tabloid?"

"I'm not working for any newspapers or magazines."

"A congressional committee, then? Sure, what better for a committee looking to cut science funding than using an ex–FBI man!" Smith took a deep breath. He did not recognize this man whom he had once thought of as his best friend. Something had changed Bill Griffin, and Griffin was showing no signs of revealing any of it. Now Griffin seemed to want to use their friendship for his own ends. Smith shook his head. "No, Bill, don't tell me who or what you're working for. It doesn't matter. If you want to know about any viruses, go through army channels. And don't call me again unless you're my friend and nothing more." Disgusted, he stalked away.

"Stay, Smithy. We need to talk."

"Screw you, Bill." Jon Smith continued toward the moonlight.

Griffin gave a low whistle.

Suddenly a large Doberman bounded in front of Jon Smith. Snarling, it spun to face him. Smith froze. The dog planted all four paws, lifted his muzzle, and growled long and deep. His sharp teeth glistened white and moist, so pointed that with one slash they could tear out a man's throat.

Smith's heart thundered. He stared unmoving at the dog.

"Sorry." Griffin's voice behind him was almost sad. "But you asked if there was bad trouble. Well, there is—but not for me."

As the dog continued to make low growls of warning in his throat, Smith remained immobile, except for his face. He sneered in contempt. "You're saying I'm in some kind of trouble? Give me a break."

"Yes." Griffin nodded. "That's exactly what I'm saying, Smithy. That's why I wanted to meet. But it's all I can tell you. You're in danger. Real danger. Get the hell out of town, fast. Don't go back to your lab. Get on a plane and—"

"What are you talking about? You know damn well I'd never do that. Run away from my work? Damn. What's happened to you, Bill?"

Griffin ignored him. "Listen to what I'm saying! Call Detrick. Tell the general you need a vacation. A long vacation. Out of the country. Do it now, and get as far away as possible. Tonight!"

"That won't cut it. Tell me what's so special about this virus. What danger am I in? If you want me to act, I've got to know why."

"For Christ's sake!" Griffin exclaimed, losing his temper. "I'm trying to help. Go away. Go fast! Take your Sophia."

Before he had finished speaking, the growling Doberman abruptly lifted his front paws off the path and whirled, landing ninety degrees south. His gaze indicated the far side of the park.

Griffin said softly, "Visitors, boy?" He gave a hand signal, and the dog raced into the trees. Griffin turned on Smith and exploded, *"Get out of here, Jon! Go. Now!"* He dashed after the Doberman, a stocky shadow moving with incredible speed.

Man and dog vanished among the thick trees of the dark park.

For a moment Smith was stunned. Was it for him Bill was afraid or for himself? Or for both of them? It appeared his old friend had taken a great risk to warn him and to ask him to do what neither would have once considered—abandon job and accountability.

To go this far, Bill's back had to be slammed up against a very unyielding wall.

What in God's name was Bill Griffin mixed up in?

A shiver shot up Smith's spine. A pulse at his temple began to throb. Bill was right. He was in danger, at least here in this dark park. Old habits resettled themselves on him like a long-forgotten cloak. His senses grew acute, and he expertly surveyed the trees and lawns.

He sprinted away along the edge of the dark trees while his mind continued to work. He had assumed the way Bill had found him was through FBI channels, but Bill was no longer in the FBI.

Smith's stay at the Wilbraham Hotel had been known only to his fiancée, to his boss, and to the clerk who had made his travel arrangements at Fort Detrick. No way would any of them have revealed his whereabouts to a stranger, no matter how convincing the stranger was.

So how had Bill—a man who claimed to be out of government—managed to learn where he had been staying in London?

∎

An unlighted black limousine lurked in the shadow of the old mill near the Tilden Street entrance to Rock Creek park. Alone in the backseat sat Nadal al-Hassan, a tall man with a dark face as narrow and sharp as a hatchet. He was listening to his subordinate, Steve Maddux, who leaned inside the window, reporting.

Maddux had been running, and his face was red and sweaty. "If Bill Griffin's in that park, Mr. al-Hassan, he's a goddamn ghost. All I saw was the army doc taking a walk." He breathed hard, trying to catch his breath.

Inside the luxury car, the bones and hollows of the tall man's face were deeply pocked, the mark of a rare survivor of the once-dreaded smallpox. His black eyes were hooded, cold, and expressionless. "I have told you before, Maddux, you will not blaspheme while you work for me."

"Hey, sorry. Okay? *Jesus Chr*—"

Like a cobra striking, the tall man's arm snaked out, and his long fingers clamped on Maddux's throat.

Maddux went pasty with fear, and he made strangling sounds as he bit off the curse. Still, the unsaid syllables hung in the darkness through an ominous silence. Finally, the hand on his throat relaxed a fraction. Sweat dripped off Maddux's forehead.

The eyes inside the car were like mirrors, glistening surfaces no one could see behind. The voice was deceptively quiet. "You wish to die so soon?"

"Hey," the scared man said hoarsely, "you're a Muslim. What's wrong with—"

"All the prophets are sacred. Abraham, Moses, Jesus. All!"

"Okay, okay! I mean, Jes—" Maddux quaked as the claw tightened on his throat. "How'm I s'posed to know that?"

For another instant, the fingers squeezed. Then the tall man let go. His arm withdrew. "Perhaps you are right. I expect too much from stupid Americans. But you know now, yes, and you will not forget again." It wasn't a question.

Wheezing, Maddux gasped, "Sure, sure, Mr. al-Hassan. Okay."

The sharp-faced man, al-Hassan, examined Maddux with his cold, mirrored eyes. "But Jon Smith *was* there." He sat back in the gloom of the car, talking softly as if to himself. "Our man in London finds Smith changed his flight and was missing from London all day. Your men pick him up at Dulles, but instead of driving home to Maryland, he comes here. At the same time, our esteemed colleague slips away from our hotel and I follow him to this vicinity before he eludes me. You fail to find him in the park, but it is a strange coincidence, wouldn't you say? Why is the associate of Dr. Russell here if not to meet our Mr. Griffin?"

Maddux said nothing. He had learned most of his boss's questions were spoken aloud to some unseen part of himself. Nervously he let the silence stretch. Around the limo and the two men, the wild park seemed to breathe with a life of its own.

Eventually al-Hassan shrugged. "Perhaps I am wrong. Perhaps it is a mere coincidence, and Griffin has nothing to do with why Colonel Smith is here. It does not really matter, I suppose. The others will take care of Colonel Smith, yes?"

"You got it." Maddux nodded emphatically. "No way he gets out of D.C."

Chapter Five

1:34 A.M., Tuesday, October 14
Fort Detrick, Maryland

In her office, Sophia Russell flicked on her desk lamp and collapsed into her chair, weary and frustrated. Victor Tremont had called this morning to report that nothing in his Peru journals mentioned the strange virus she had described or the Indian tribe called the Monkey Blood People. Tremont was her best outside lead, and she was devastated he had been unable to help.

Although she and the rest of the Detrick microbiology staff had continued to work around the clock, they were no closer to resolving the threat posed by the virus. Under the electron microscope the new virus showed the same globular shape with hairlike protrusions of some of its proteins, much like a flu virus. But this virus was far simpler than any influenza mutation and far more deadly.

After they had failed to find a match among the hantaviruses, they had rechecked Marburg, Lassa, and Ebola, even though those related killers had no microscopic similarities to the unknown virus. They tried every other identified hemorrhagic fever. They tried typhoid, bubonic plague, pneumonic plague, meningitis, and tularemia.

Nothing matched, and this afternoon she had finally insisted General Kielburger reveal the virus and enlist the aid of the CDC and the other Level Four installations worldwide. He had still been reluctant; there were still only the three cases. But at the same time, the virus appeared to be totally unknown and highly lethal, and if he did not take the proper steps and a pandemic resulted, he would be responsible. So, grumbling, he had finally acquiesced and sent off full explanatory memos and blood samples to the CDC, the Special Pathogens Branch of WHO, Porton Down in the U.K., the University of Anvers in Belgium, Germany's Bernard Nocht Institute, the special pathogens branch of the Pasteur Institute in France, and all the other Level Four labs around the globe.

Now the first of the reports were coming in from the other Hot Zone labs. Everyone agreed the virus seemed like a hantavirus, but matched nothing in any of their data banks. All the reports from the CDC and the foreign laboratories showed no progress. All contained desperate, if informed, guesses.

In her office, tired to the marrow, Sophia leaned back in her desk chair and massaged her temples, trying to ward off a headache. She glanced at her watch and was shocked to see the time. Good God, it was nearly 2:00 A.M.

Worry lines furrowed her brow. Where was Jon? If he had arrived home last night as scheduled, he would have been in the lab today. Because of her frantic work schedule, she had not thought too much about his absence. Now, despite her tiredness and headache and her initial worries about Jon, she could not help smiling. She had a forty-one-year-old fiancé who still had all the curiosity and impulsiveness of a twenty-year-old. Wave a medical mystery in front of Jon, and he was off like a racehorse. He must have found something fascinating that had delayed him.

Still, he should have called by now. Soon he would be a full day late.

Maybe Kielburger had ordered him somewhere in secret, and Jon could not call. That'd be just like the general. Never mind she was Jon's fiancée. If the general had sent Jon off, she would learn about it with the rest of the staff, when the general was good and ready to announce it.

She sat up in her chair, thinking. The scientific staff was working through the night, even the general, who never passed up an opportunity to be noticed in the right way. Abruptly furious and anxious about Jon, she marched out, heading for his office.

■

Brig. Gen. Calvin Kielburger, Ph.D., was one of those big, beefy men with loud voices and not too many brains the army loved to raise to the rank of colonel and then freeze there. These men were sometimes tough and always mean but had few people skills and less diplomacy. They tended to be called Bull or Buck. Sometimes officers with those nicknames made higher rank, but they were small, feisty men with big jaws.

Having achieved one star beyond what he could reasonably have expected, Brigadier General Kielburger abandoned actual medical research in the heady illusion of rising to full general with troop command. But to lead armies, the service wanted smart officers who could work well with the necessary civilian officials. Kielburger was so busy promoting himself he did not see his smartest move was to be intelligent and tactful. As a result, he was now stuck administering an irreverent gang of military and civilian scientists, most of whom did not take well to authority in the first place, particularly not to narrow-minded bombast like Kielburger's.

Of the unruly lot, Lt. Col. Jon Smith had turned out to be the most irreverent, the most uncontrollable, the most irritating. So in answer to Sophia's question, Kielburger bellowed, "I sure as hell didn't send Colonel Smith on any assignment! If we had a sensitive task, he'd be the last one I'd send, exactly because of stunts like this!"

Sophia was as frosty as Kielburger was choleric. "Jon doesn't pull 'stunts.' "

"He's a full day late when we need him here!"

"Unless you phoned him, how would he know we needed him?" Sophia snapped. "Even I didn't know how bad the situation was until I started examining the virus. Then I was busy in the lab. Working. I'm sure you remember what that's like." The truth was, she doubted he had any memories of the pressures and excitement of lab work, because she had heard that even in those days he had preferred to shuffle papers and critique other scientists' notes. She insisted, "Jon must have a reason for being late. Or something he can't control is detaining him."

"Such as what, Doctor?"

"If I knew, I wouldn't be wasting your valuable time. Or mine. But it's not like him to be late without calling me."

Kielburger's florid face sneered. "I'd say it's very much like him. He's a goddamn pirate looking for the next chest of gold, and he always will be. Take my word for it, he's run into an 'interesting' medical problem or treatment or both and missed his flight. Face it, Russell, he's a goddamn loose cannon, and after you're married you're going to have to deal with that. I don't envy you."

Sophia compressed her lips, fighting a strong desire to tell the general exactly what she thought of him.

He stared back, idly undressing her in his mind. He had always liked blondes. It was sexy the way she pulled back her pale hair in a ponytail. He wondered whether she was blond everywhere.

When she made no answer, he went on in a more conciliatory voice. "Don't sweat it, Dr. Russell. He'll turn up soon. I hope so, anyway, because we need everyone we can get on this virus. I suppose you have nothing to report?"

Sophia shook her head. "To be frank, I'm about out of ideas, and so is the rest of the staff. The other labs are struggling, too. It's early, but all we're getting so far from everyone is negatives and guesses."

Kielburger tapped his desk in frustration. He was a general, so he felt obligated to do something. "You say this is a totally unique virus of a type never seen before?"

"There's always a first one to be discovered."

Kielburger groaned. This could ruin any chance he had to break out of the medical ghetto and move into line command.

Sophia was studying him. "May I make a suggestion, General?"

"Why not?" Kielburger said bitterly.

"The three victims we have are widely separated geographically. Plus two are about the same age, while one is much younger. Two are male; one is female. One in active service, one a veteran, and one civilian. How did they get the virus? What was the source? It has to have been centered somewhere. The odds are astronomical against three outbreaks within twenty-four hours of the same unknown virus thousands of miles apart."

As usual, the general did not get it. "What's your point?"

"Unless we begin to see other victims centered in one of the three locations, we have to find the connection among the three we do have. We need to start investigating their lives. For instance, maybe they were all in the same hotel room in Milwaukee six months ago. Maybe that's when all three contracted it." She paused. "At the same time, we should comb the medical records in the three areas for signs of previous infections that could have produced antibodies."

At least it was a positive step, and it would make Kielburger look as if he was acting decisively. "I'll instruct the staff to begin at once. I want you and Colonel Smith to fly out to California first thing in the morning to talk to the people who knew Major Anderson. Is that clear?"

"Perfectly, General."

"Good. Let me know when Smith decides to return to work. I'm going to chew his ass!"

So mad she could not even enjoy the spectacle of Kielburger acting out his Hollywood conception of a tough, no-nonsense American hero, Sophia stalked out of his office.

In the corridor, she looked up at the wall clock: 1:56 A.M. Fresh worry overwhelmed her. Had something happened to Jon? Where was he?

2:05 A.M.
Washington, D.C.

As he drove his small Triumph through the night city, Jon Smith mulled what Bill Griffin had told him, trying to comprehend even the unspoken hints.

Bill said he had left the FBI. Voluntarily or by request?

Either way, Bill was connected somehow to a new virus sent from some armed forces unit for USAMRIID to study. Probably for the lab to identify and suggest the best method of treatment. To Smith, it sounded routine—one of the vital tasks Fort Detrick had been established to handle.

Still, Bill Griffin claimed Smith was in danger.

His trained Doberman said more about Griffin's state of mind than any words he had uttered. Obviously, Griffin believed there was peril, and not just for Jon but for himself.

After their meeting, Jon had made his way carefully along the park's dark paths, stopping often to melt into the trees to make certain he was not being followed. When at last he had reached his restored 1968 Triumph, he had looked carefully around before getting in the car, then had driven south out of the park, heading away from Maryland and home, the opposite of what a pursuer would expect. Despite the late hour, traffic had been moderate. Not until the depths of night, sometime around 4:00 A.M., would the bustling metropolis finally grow weary and its main arteries empty.

At first he had thought a car was pacing him. So he had turned corners, sped up and slowed down, and wound his way to Dupont Circle and Foggy Bottom and then north again. It had taken him more than an hour of driving, but now he felt certain no one was following him.

Still warily watching, he turned south again, this time on Wisconsin Avenue. Traffic was very light here, and street lamps cast wide yellow pools of illumination against the dark night. He sighed wearily. God, he wanted to see Sophia. Maybe it was safe at last to go to her. He would cross the Potomac and take the George Washington Parkway to 495 north—heading to Maryland. To Sophia. Just thinking about her made him smile. The longer he was gone, the more he missed her. He could not wait to hold her in his arms. He was nearing the river and driving tiredly between Georgetown's long rows of trendy boutiques, elegant bookstores, fashionable restaurants, bars, and clubs when a mammoth truck, its engine rumbling, pulled up in the left lane next to his small car.

It was a six-wheel delivery truck, the kind that dotted every beltway and interstate around every city from the Atlantic seaboard to the Pacific coast. At first Smith wondered what a truck was doing here since businesses and restaurants would not open for deliveries for another three or four hours. Interestingly, neither the cab nor the white cargo section displayed a company name, address, logo, slogan, phone number, or anything to mark what it was delivering or for whom.

Thinking longingly of Sophia, Smith did not dwell on the truck's unusual anonymity. Still, the events of the evening had activated the finely honed sense of danger he had developed over the years of practicing medicine and commanding at the front lines where violence could erupt minute to minute, where death was close and real, where disease waited to strike from every hut and bush. Or maybe some movement, action, or sound inside the truck had caught his attention.

Whatever it was, a split second before the behemoth vehicle suddenly pulled ahead and moved to cut off Smith's sports car, Smith knew it was going to do it.

Adrenaline jolted him. His throat tightened. Instantly he assessed the situation. As the truck turned into him, he yanked his steering wheel to the right. His car skidded and bounced up over the curb and onto the deserted sidewalk. He had not been going all that fast—just thirty miles an hour—but driving on a sidewalk, not even a wide one like this, at thirty miles an hour was insanity.

As the truck roared alongside, he fought to control his car. With explosive crashes, he sideswiped a mailbox and litter bin and smashed a table off its pedestal. He careened past the closed, silent doors of shops, bars, and clubs. Darkened windows flashed past like blind eyes winking at him. Sweating, he glanced left. The huge truck continued to parallel him out on the street, waiting for a chance to bore in again and squash him against the facade of a building. He said a silent prayer of thanks that the sidewalk was empty of people.

Dodging trash cans, he saw the truck's passenger-side window suddenly lower. A gun barrel thrust out, aimed directly at him. For an instant he was terrified. Trapped on the sidewalk, the truck blocking the avenue from him, he could neither hide nor evade. And he was unarmed. Whatever their plans had been earlier, now they were counting on shooting him dead.

Smith tapped his brake and swerved so the thug in the truck cab would have to contend with a shifting target as he tried to find his aim.

Sweat beaded on Smith's brow. Then for an instant he felt a sense of hope. Ahead lay an intersection. His hands were white on the steering wheel as he pushed the Triumph toward it.

Just as he accelerated, the gun in the truck fired. The noise was explosive, but the bullet was too late. It blasted across the Triumph's tail and shattered a store window. As glass burst into the air, Smith inhaled sharply. That had been too damn close.

He glanced warily again at the gun barrel as it bounced in the truck's open window. Fortunately, he was closing in on the intersection. A bank stood on one corner, while retail businesses occupied the other three.

And then he had no more time. The intersection was immediately ahead, and this might be his only chance. He took a deep breath. Gauging distance carefully, he slammed his brakes. As the Triumph shuddered, he swung the steering wheel sharply right. He had only seconds to check the truck as his fleet sports car swerved away off onto the cross street. But in those few moments he saw what he had hoped for: The victim of its own speed, the truck hurtled ahead down the avenue and out of sight.

Exulting inside, he gunned to full speed, hit the brakes again, and turned another corner, this time onto a leafy street of Federalist row houses. He drove on, turning more corners and watching his rearview mirror the whole time even though he knew the long truck could not possibly have made a U-turn despite the light traffic of the late night.

Breathing hard, he stopped the car at last in the lacy shadows of a branching magnolia on a dark residential street where BMWs, Mercedeses, and other artifacts of the rich indicated that this was one of Georgetown's most elite neighborhoods. He forced his hands from the steering wheel and looked down. The hands were trembling, but not from fear. It had been a long time since he had been in trouble like this—violent trouble he had not anticipated and did not want. He threw back his head and closed his eyes. He inhaled deeply, amazed as always at how quickly everything could change. He did not like the trouble. . . . Yet there was an older part of him that understood it. That wanted to be involved. He thought his commitment to Sophia had ended all that. With her, he had not seemed to need the outside peril that in the past had affirmed he was fully, actively alive.

On the other hand, at this point he had no choice.

The killers in the truck who had attacked him had to be part of what Bill Griffin had tried to warn him about. All the questions he had been mulling ever since leaving their midnight meeting returned:

What was so special about this virus?

What was Bill hiding?

Warily, he shoved the car into gear and drove onto the street. He had no answers, but maybe Sophia did. As he thought that, his chest contracted. His mouth went dry. A terrible fear shot ice into his veins.

If they were trying to kill him, they could be trying to kill her, too.

He glanced at his watch: 2:32 A.M.

He had to call her, warn her, but his cell phone was still at his house.

He had seen no compelling reason to take it to London. So now he needed a pay phone quickly. His best chance would be on Wisconsin Avenue, but he did not want to risk another attack from the truck.

He needed to get to Fort Detrick. *Now*.

He hit his gas pedal, rushing the Triumph toward O Street. Tall trees passed in a blur. Old Victorians with their ornate scrollwork and sharply pointed roofs loomed over the sidewalks like ghost houses. Ahead was an intersection with lamplight spilling across it in silver-gray splashes. Suddenly car headlights appeared ahead, bright spotlights in the dark night. The car was approaching the same intersection as Smith's Triumph, but from the opposite direction and at twice the speed.

Smith swore and checked the crosswalk. Bundled against the cool night air, a solitary pedestrian had stepped off the sidewalk. As the man swayed and sang off-key from too much whiskey, he staggered toward the other curb, swinging his arms like a toy soldier. Smith's chest tightened. The man was heading heedlessly into the path of the accelerating car.

The drunk pedestrian never looked up. There was a sudden scream of brakes. Helplessly Smith watched as the speeding car's fender struck him, and he flew back, arms wide. Without realizing it, Smith had been holding his breath. Before the drunk could land in the gutter, Smith slammed his brakes. At the same time, the hit-and-run driver slowed for a moment as if puzzled and then rushed off again, vanishing around the corner.

The instant his Triumph stopped, Smith was out of the car and running to the fallen man. All the night sounds had disappeared from the street. The shadows were long and thick around the artificial illumination of the intersection. He dropped to his haunches to examine the man's injuries just as another car approached. Behind him, he heard a screech of brakes, and the car stopped beside him.

Relieved, he lifted his head and waved for help. Two men jumped out and ran toward him. At the same time, Smith sensed movement from the injured man.

He looked down: "How do you feel?—" And froze. Stared.

The "victim" was not only appraising him with alert, sober eyes, he was pointing a Glock semiautomatic pistol with a silencer up at him. "Christ, you're a hard man to kill. What the hell kind of doctor are you anyway?"

Chapter Six

2:37 A.M.
Washington, D.C.

A part of Jon Smith was already in the past, back in Bosnia and his undercover stint in East Germany before the wall came down. Shadows, memories, broken dreams, small victories, and always the restlessness. Everything he had thought he had put behind him.

As the two strangers pulled out weapons and sped toward him through the intersection's light, Smith grabbed the wrist and upper arm of the thug at his feet. Before the man could react, Smith expertly pushed and pulled, feeling the tendons and joint do exactly what he wanted.

The man's elbow snapped. He screamed and jerked, and his face turned white and twisted in pain. As he passed out, the Glock fell to the pavement. All this happened in seconds. Smith gave a grim smile. At least he did not have to kill the man. In a single motion, he scooped up the weapon, rolled onto his shoulder, and came up on one knee with the pistol cocked. He fired. The silenced bullet made a *pop*.

One of the two men running at him pitched forward, twisting in agony on the cold pavement. As the man grabbed his thigh where Smith's bullet had entered, the second man dropped beside him. Lying on his belly, he lifted his head as if he were on a firing range and Smith were a stationary target. Big mistake. Smith knew exactly what the man was going to do. Smith dodged, and his attacker's silenced gunshot burned past his temple.

Now Smith had no choice. Before the man could shoot again or lower his head, Smith fired a second time. The bullet exploded through the attacker's right eye, leaving a black crater. Blood poured out, and the man pitched facedown, motionless. Smith knew he had to be dead.

His pulse throbbing at his temples, Smith jumped up and walked cautiously toward them. He had not wanted to kill the man, and he was angry to have been put in the position where he had to. Around him, the air seemed to still vibrate from the attack. He gazed quickly up and down the street. No porch lights turned on. The late hour and the silenced bullets had kept secret the ambush.

He pulled an army-issue Beretta from the limp hand of the man he had shot in the eye and, with little hope, checked his vital signs. Yes, he was dead. He shook his head, disgusted and regretful, as he removed weapons from the reach of the two injured men. The man with the broken elbow was still unconscious, while the one with the bullet through his thigh swore a string of curses and glared at Smith.

Smith ignored him. He hurried back toward his Triumph. Just then the night rocked with the sound of a large truck's approach. Smith whirled. The broad white expanse of the unmarked, six-wheel delivery truck sped into the intersection. Somehow these killers had found him again.

How?

In combat, there is a time to stand and fight, and a time to run like hell. Smith thought about Sophia and sprinted down a row of looming Victorian houses close to the sidewalk. In some backyard a lonely dog barked, followed instantly by an answering bark. Soon the animals' calls echoed across the old neighborhood. As they died away, Smith slid into the black shadows of a three-story Victorian with turrets, cupolas, and a wide porch. He was at least a hundred yards from the intersection. Crouched low, he looked back and studied the scene. He memorized the parked cars and then focused on the truck, which had stopped. A short, heavy man had jumped from the cab to bend over the three wounded men. Smith did not recognize him, but he knew that truck.

The man waved urgently. Another two men exited the cab and ran to carry away the injured attackers while the first man raised the truck's rear accordion door. A half-dozen men piled out over the tailgate and waited, their heads swiveling as they examined the night. Even in the capricious moonlight, Smith could see the heavy man's face glisten with sweat as he issued orders.

The two wounded men and the corpse were put into the car that had pulled up alongside Smith, and one of the men drove it quickly away, heading north. Then the big delivery truck left, too, going south toward the river, while the leader sent his men off in pairs, no doubt to search for Jon Smith. With luck, each would assume he was more than a match for a forty-year-old, sedentary research scientist, despite the reports of their two surviving comrades. An ivory-tower freak who wore a military uniform as a courtesy and had gotten lucky—people had made that mistake about Smith before.

He listened from his hiding place until two of them drew close. This pair he would have to neutralize somehow. He turned and loped off into the shadows, making sure they heard him. They took the bait, and a wide gap opened between the pair and the others as they pursued him. All his nerves were afire as he trotted across dark yards, watching everywhere. Four blocks beyond the intersection, he found a combination that would work: A white, Colonial-style mansion stood lightless up at the end of a short drive, while off to the side was a gazebo, nearly invisible in the camouflage of night and the thick trees and bushes that marked the property.

He coughed and scuffed his shoes against the driveway to make sure they would hear and think he was heading off to hide at the mansion.

Then he slipped into the secluded gazebo. He had been right—through its latticed walls he had a clear view of the property. He set the Glock and Beretta on a bench; he did not plan to use them for anything more than intimidation. No, this work had to be done in silence and with speed.

One long minute passed.

Could they have somehow guessed what he was doing and called in the rest of the team? At this moment, were they circling to come up from behind? He wiped a hand across his forehead, removing sweat. His heart seemed to thunder.

Two minutes . . . three minutes . . .

A shadow emerged from the trees and ran toward the left side of the big house.

Then a second ran toward the right side.

Smith inhaled. Thugs, civilian or military, were predictable. Without much imagination, their tactical ideas were rudimentary—the direct charge of the bull, or the simple ruse of a schoolboy quarterback who always looked the opposite way from where he intended to throw the football.

The two closing in like pincers in the night were better than most, but like Custer at Little Big Horn or Lord Chelmsford at Isandhlwana against the Zulu, they had done him the favor of splitting their forces so he could take them on one at a time. He had hoped they would.

The bolder padded around the mansion's right side, between it and the gazebo. That was a break for Smith. As the man continued on, Smith crept toward him from behind. He stepped on a twig. It was a soft snap, but loud enough to alert the attacker. Smith's heart seemed to stop. The man whirled around, pistol rising to fire.

Smith acted instantly. A single powerful right fist to the throat paralyzed the vocal cords, a sweeping arc of right leg smashed a size-twelve shoe to the side of the man's head, and he dropped quietly.

Smith slid back into the gazebo.

One . . . two minutes.

The more cautious of the pair materialized in a patch of moonlight between the gazebo and the fallen man. He had had the sense to circle his partner out of sight. But that was where his imagination ended, and he hurried to kneel over the fallen man.

"Jerry? Jesus, what—" Smith's appropriated Beretta smashed across the back of the bent head.

Smith dragged both unconscious men into the gazebo. Crouched over them, he panted as he listened to the night. The only distinctive sound was of a distant car heading south. With relief, he left the gazebo and loped through the shadows of houses and trees back the way he had come. As he neared the intersection where he had been attacked, he slowed and listened again. The only noise was what sounded like the same car driving in the opposite direction, this time north.

On elbows and knees, a pistol in each hand, he crawled to within a front yard of the intersection. The sprinkling of parked cars on either side had not changed, and his Triumph still waited at the curb where he had left it to go to the aid of the fake victim. No one was in sight.

There was no way the six-wheeler truck could have found him first on Wisconsin Avenue and then here. No one had that kind of luck. Yet the truck, the car, and the "drunk" had created a diversion, intending his death.

They had to have known exactly where he was.

He waited as the moon went down. The night grew darker, a large owl hunted through the trees, and the distant car continued to drive south, then north, then south again, slowly making its way closer to the intersection.

Satisfied that no one was lurking there, Smith jumped up and ran to his Triumph. He took a small flashlight from the glove compartment and slid under the car's rear. And there it was. No imagination, no originality. The bright funnel of his flashlight revealed a transmitter no larger than his thumbnail attached to the car's undercarriage by a powerful mini-magnet. The tracking device's reader was probably in the truck or with the short, heavy leader.

He flicked off the flashlight, slipped it into his pocket, and removed the tracking device. He admired the creativity that had manufactured such delicate engineering. As he crawled out from under the Triumph, he noticed the car he had been monitoring was almost at the intersection. He knelt beside the Triumph, watching. The car was moving slowly as the driver pitched newspapers from his rolled-down window onto the lawns and driveways of the neighborhood.

The driver made a U-turn.

Smith stood up and whistled. As the car slowed in the intersection, he ran toward the open window. "Can I buy a paper from you?"

"Yeah, sure. I've got some extras."

Smith reached into his pocket for change. He dropped a coin, bent to pick it up, and with a cool smile he stuck the microtransmitter to the car's undercarriage.

Straightening, he took the newspaper and nodded. "Thanks. I appreciate it."

The car drove on, and Smith jumped into the Triumph. He peeled away, hoping his trick would occupy his assailants long enough for him to reach Sophia. But if these attacks where part of what Bill Griffin had warned him would happen, they knew who he was and where to find him. And where to find Sophia.

4:07 A.M.
Fort Detrick, Maryland

The report from the Prince Leopold Institute of Tropical Medicine in Belgium was the third Sophia read after plunging back into work, the last scientist still there. She was too worried to sleep. If the damned general was right that Jon was off on one of his enthusiasms over some medical development, she would be furious. Still, she hoped Kielburger *was* right, as that would mean she had no reason to be concerned.

She continued studying the latest reports, but not until she reached the one from the Prince Leopold lab did something finally offer hope: Dr. René Giscours recalled a field report he had read years ago while doing a stint at a jungle hospital far upriver in Bolivian Amazonia. He had been preoccupied at the time battling what appeared to be a new outbreak of Machupo fever, not far from the river town of San Joaquin where Karl Johnson, Kuns, and MacKenzie had first found the deadly virus many years before. He had had no time for even thinking about an unconfirmed rumor from far-off Peru, so he had made a note and forgotten about it.

But the new virus had jogged his memory. He had checked through his papers and found his original note—but not the actual report. Still, the note to himself back then had emphasized an apparent combination of hantavirus and hemorrhagic fever symptoms, as well as some connection to monkeys.

A surge of angry justification rushed through Sophia. Yes! After Victor Tremont had been unable to help her, she had doubted herself. Now Giscours's report confirmed her recollection. What contact did USAMRIID have down there? If she was right, there had been no major or even minor outbreaks of that virus since. Which meant it must still be confined to the narrow, deep jungle in a remote part of Peru.

In her daily logbook, she described her reaction to the Prince Leopold report, and she summarized what she recalled of the strange virus and her two conversations with Victor Tremont, since they might be relevant now. She also wrote some speculations about how a Peruvian virus could have been transmitted beyond the jungle.

As she was writing, she heard the door to her office open. Who—? Hope filled her.

Excited, she spun her chair around. "Jon? Darling. Where the hell—"

In the instant before her head exploded in violent pain and color, she had a glimpse of four men surrounding her. None was Jon. Then darkness.

■

Nadal al-Hassan, disguised from head to foot in lab scrubs, methodically searched the female scientist's office desk. He read each document, report, notebook, and memo. He studied every file. The task was offensive, even though he was protected by surgical gloves. He knew such modern blasphemies occurred in his own country as well as many other Islamic, even Arab, nations, but he made no secret of his distaste. Allowing females to study and work beside men was not only heresy, it defiled both the dignity of the men and the chastity of the women. Touching what the woman had touched defiled him.

But the search was necessary, so he performed it meticulously, leaving nothing unexamined. He found the two damaging documents almost at once. One was the only report open on her desk—from the Prince Leopold Institute, by a Dr. René Giscours. The other was her handwritten phone record of outgoing calls that the USAMRIID director apparently required all personnel to complete each month.

Then he found her logbook musings about the Belgian report. Fortunately, it filled an entire page, beginning at the top and ending at the bottom. From a small leather case, he took out a pen-shaped, razor-sharp draftsman's blade. With care and delicacy, he excised the page. He examined the cut to be certain it was invisible, then hid the page in his scrubs. After that he found nothing more of importance.

His three men, dressed in identical scrubs, were completing their search of the rows of file cabinets.

One said, "Got a new memo in a file 'bout Peru."

Another said, "Couple of old files talked about stuff down in South America."

The third just shook his head.

"You read every document?" al-Hassan snapped. "Every file? Looked in every drawer?"

"Like you told us."

"Under everything? Behind anything that moved?"

"Hey, we ain't stupid."

Al-Hassan had strong doubts about that. He found most Westerners lazy and incompetent. But from the mess in the office, he decided they had been thorough this time.

"Very well. You will now erase any indications of a search. Everything is to be as it was."

While they grumbled and returned to work, al-Hassan slipped on a second, thicker pair of white rubber gloves. He took a small refrigerated metal container from a leather case, released a pressure seal, and extracted a glass vial. He carefully removed a hypodermic syringe from the case, filled it from the sealed vial, and injected Sophia in the vein of her left ankle.

At the prick of the needle, she stirred and moaned.

The three men heard. They turned to look, and their faces went ashen.

"Complete your tasks," al-Hassan said harshly.

The men dropped their gazes. As they finished straightening the office, al-Hassan put the used syringe inside a plastic container, sealed it, and returned it to the leather case. His men indicated they were finished. Al-Hassan inspected the office once more. Satisfied, he ordered them to leave. He gave one final glance at the now-motionless Sophia and saw the sweat that had beaded up on her face. When she groaned, he smiled and followed them out.

Chapter Seven

4:14 A.M.
Thurmont, Maryland

A light wind rustled through bushes and trees, carrying the stink of apples rotting on the ground. Jon Smith's three-story, saltbox-style house was set back into the looming shoulder of Catoctin Mountain. The place was dark, not even a porch light to welcome him home, which made him think Sophia must still be at the lab. But he had to be sure.

He was a block away, crouched behind an SUV, as he studied his house, yard, and street. He saw telltale signs: The trunk of the old apple tree was too thick where someone stood behind it, watching. Farther up the block, almost hidden by two tall oak trees, the hood of a black Mercedes protruded from a driveway of neighbors Smith knew owned only a 2000 Buick Le Sabre, which they always parked in the garage.

Considering how quickly he had driven home from Georgetown on the almost-deserted highway and roads, there was no way the pair waiting here could have arrived first. Which meant this was a second surveillance team, and that alarmed him.

The sentry in front could see the driveway and garage doors. There was probably a man in back, too, to cover the rear of the house and garage. But Smith could see no reason to waste a man on the side of the garage away from the house.

He felt the familiar hollow of fear in his stomach every soldier knows, but also the hot rush of adrenaline. He slipped down an alley and sprinted behind the houses until past his street. Then he recrossed out of sight of the hunters. Beginning to sweat again, he worked through a stand of sycamores to the near side of his garage and slithered the last five yards on his elbows and belly.

He listened. There was no sound behind the house. He raised up to peer inside the garage.

And sighed with relief. It was empty. Sophia's old green Dodge was gone. She must have been at Fort Detrick all this time. If so, she had never received his message, and that explained the lack of a porch light. He breathed deeply, instantly feeling better.

Retracing his path, he hurried back to his Triumph and drove to a phone booth a quarter mile away. He could not wait to hear her voice. He dialed her work number. After four rings, the machine picked up. "I'm out of my office or in the lab. Please leave a message. I'll return your call as soon as possible. Thank you."

The bright sound of her strong voice gave him a sharp pang and another feeling he could not explain. Loneliness?

He dialed again. The voice that answered was all business, which was reassuring, particularly considering the circumstances: "United States Army, Fort Detrick. Security."

"This is Lt. Col. Jonathan Smith, USAMRIID."

"Base ID, Colonel?"

He gave his number.

There was a pause. "Thank you, Colonel. How can we help you?"

"Connect me to the desk guard at USAMRIID."

Clicks, beeps, and a new voice. "USAMRIID. Security. Grasso."

"Grasso, Jon Smith. Listen—"

"Hey, Colonel, you're back. Everything okay? Doc Russell's been askin'—"

"I'm fine, Grasso. It's Dr. Russell I'm calling about. She's not answering her phone. You know where she is?"

"She's on the night list I got when I came on, and I ain't seen her leave."

"What time did you come on?"

"Midnight. She's probably in the lab and not hearing nothing."

Smith glanced at his watch: 4:42 A.M.

"Could you go up and check?"

"Sure, Colonel. Call you back."

Smith recited the phone number. Every second seemed like a minute, and every minute it was harder to breathe. The cool night seemed stifling. The phone booth suffocated him.

When the phone rang at last, he almost jumped. "Yes?"

"Not there, Colonel. Office and lab are both closed up."

"Any sign of trouble?"

"Nope. Everything's packed away and covered up." Grasso sounded a little defensive. "Damned if I know how I missed her. I guess she could've gone out one of the other exits. You could check with the gate guard."

"Thanks, Grasso. You want to transfer me?"

"Hold on, Doc."

A different and very sleepy voice spoke: "Fort Detrick. Gate. Schroeder."

"This is Lt. Col. Jonathan Smith, USAMRIID. Did Dr. Sophia Russell leave the base tonight, Schroeder?"

"Don't know, Colonel. Don't know Dr. Russell. Try the guy at USAMRIID."

Smith swore under his breath. The civilian security guards were always changing, and they worked longer shifts than MPs. It was not unknown for them to doze in the gate kiosk. The barrier would stop any cars trying to enter, and if it did not, the noise would certainly wake them up. But no barrier stopped cars leaving.

He hung up. It sounded as if she could have been too tired to drive all the way to Thurmont. Which meant she was likely at her old condo in Frederick, which she had just sold but had not yet fully moved out of. He could call the condo, but that would tell him nothing. When they worked around the clock, they always turned off their phone's ringer to get a few hours sleep.

As he sped the car away, his mind raced. *She had been so tired she left the lab through one of the side doors, not wanting to run into anyone. That was logical. Just what she would have done. The gate guard had missed her, probably asleep. She would go to her condo. He would slip into bed beside her. She would sense his presence without waking up. She would smile in her sleep, murmur, and move close to touch him. Her hip would press warm against him. He would smile, kiss her shoulder lightly, watch her sleep before he fell asleep himself. He would . . .*

•

Few guidebooks listed Fort Detrick as one of the attractions to the historic City of Frederick. With its chain-link fence and guard post at the entrance, Detrick was a medium-secure army base set in the middle of a residential area. Sophia's condo was five blocks away. Parked up the street again, Smith saw no signs of anyone watching here. He stepped from the Triumph, closed the door softly, and listened. He heard the distant coughs of sleepers. The occasional laughter or a voice raised in drunken anger. A solitary car squealing around a turn. The constant low hum that was the city itself.

But no clandestine sounds or movements he could identify as threatening.

He used his key to the lobby of the three-story condo building and strode across the exposed expanse of the tile and carpet to the elevators. All were empty at this hour.

On the third floor, the Glock in his hand, he stepped off warily. The corridor echoed to his footfalls like the empty rooms of an ancient tomb. When he reached her door, he listened again. He heard nothing from inside. He turned the key, the quiet tumblers clicking in his mind loud as explosions.

Silently he pulled open the door and dropped flat to the carpeting inside.

The apartment was dark. Nothing stirred. His hand felt a film of dust covering the side table near the door.

He stood and glided through the shadowy living room to the short corridor that led to the two bedrooms. Both were empty, the beds made and unused. The kitchen showed no sign that anyone had eaten a meal or prepared even a cup of coffee. The sink was dry. The refrigerator was silent, turned off weeks ago.

She had not been here.

Feeling numb, Smith walked like a robot back into the living room. He turned on lights. He inspected for signs of an attack, an injury, even a search.

Nothing. The condo was as clean and undisturbed as an exhibit in a museum.

If they had killed or kidnapped her, it had not been here.

She was not at the lab. She was not at the house in Thurmont. She was not here. And he had no indications that anything had happened to her at any of those places.

He needed help, and he knew it.

The first step was to call the base and alert them to her disappearance. Then the police. FBI. He grabbed the portable telephone to dial Detrick.

His hand froze midair. Outside in the corridor, footsteps echoed along the walls.

He switched off the lights and set the phone on the table. He dropped to one knee behind the couch, the Glock in his hand trained on the door.

Someone advanced haltingly toward Sophia's condo, bumping into walls, progressing in fits and starts. A drunk staggering home?

The steps stopped with a hard thump against Sophia's door. There was ragged breathing. A key probed for the lock.

He tensed. The door swung open as if flung.

In the shaft of light, Sophia swayed. Her clothes were torn and stained as if she had been crawling in a gutter.

Smith leaped forward. "Sophia!"

She staggered in, and he caught her before she collapsed. She gasped, battled for breath. Her face burned with fever.

Her black eyes stared up at him, tried to smile. "You're . . . back, darling. Where . . . where were you?"

"I'm so sorry, Soph. I had an extra day, I wanted . . ."

Her hand reached up to interrupt him. Her voice sounded delirious. ". . . lab . . . at the lab . . . someone . . . hit . . ."

She fell back in his arms, unconscious. Her skin was pasty. Two bright fevered spots glowed on her cheeks. Her beautiful face was pinched with pain. She was terribly ill. What had happened to her? This was not just simple exhaustion.

"Soph? Soph! Oh my God, Soph?"

There was no response. She was limp, unconscious.

Shaken and terrified, he fell back on his medical training. He was a doctor. He knew what to do. He laid her on the couch, grabbed the portable phone, and dialed 911 as he checked her pulse and breathing. The pulse was weak and rapid. She breathed in labored gasps. She burned. The symptoms of acute respiratory distress plus fever.

He yelled into the phone, "Acute respiratory distress. Dr. Jonathan Smith, dammit. *Get here. Now!*"

•

The unmarked van was almost invisible beneath the tree on the street outside Sophia Russell's apartment. Above, a weak streetlight hardly pierced the night, giving the van's inhabitants exactly what they wanted—darkness and camouflage. From the interior gloom, Bill Griffin watched the paramedic van, its beacons flashing blue and red, in front of the three-story condo building that blazed with light across the street.

Nadal al-Hassan's hatchet face spoke from the driver's seat, "Dr. Russell should not have been able to leave her laboratory alone. She should never have reached this far."

"But she did both." Griffin's round face was neutral. In the darkness, his brown, mid-length hair was ebony. His big shoulders and muscular body appeared relaxed. This was a different, harder, colder man than the one who had met his friend Jon Smith just hours ago in Washington's Rock Creek park.

Al-Hassan said, "I did what was ordered for the woman. It was the only way she could be handled without suspicion."

Griffin's silence covered the turmoil inside him. The sudden and unforeseen involvement of Jon was something he had never imagined. He had tried to warn Jon off, but al-Hassan had sent Maddux after Jon in Washington before Jon even had a chance to think about running. That would have told Jon the warning was true, but with the woman attacked, too, Jon would not back away. How in hell was he going to save his oldest friend now?

He and al-Hassan had been waiting for the others to locate Smith again when the call from their spy inside USAMRIID, fake Specialist Four Adele Schweik, came in on al-Hassan's cell phone. The motion sensor she had planted in Sophia Russell's office and lab had gone off, and when she had activated the hidden video camera, she had seen Sophia staggering from her office. She had rushed to Fort Detrick, but by the time she had gotten there, Russell had vanished.

"She couldn't drive in her condition," Schweik had told al-Hassan, "so I checked her file. She owns a condo close to the fort."

They had driven straight to the building only to find the paramedics already there, and the whole building awakened by the commotion. There was no way they could get inside without attracting attention.

Bill Griffin said, "Only way or not, if she can talk and tells Smith too much, the boss isn't going to be happy. And look at this."

Four paramedics pushed a gurney out through the lobby doors. Jon Smith strode alongside the gurney holding the hand of the woman on the stretcher as he bent close to talk to her. He appeared oblivious to anything else. He went on talking and talking.

Al-Hassan cursed in Arabic. "We should have known of the condo."

Griffin had to take the chance of making al-Hassan hate him more than he already did in hopes of goading the Arab into making a mistake. "But we didn't, and now they're talking. She's alive. You blew it, al-Hassan. Your hide's going to be stretched for this. Now what do we do?"

Nadal al-Hassan's words were soft. "We follow them to the hospital. Then we make her dead for certain. And him, too." He turned to stare at Griffin.

Griffin knew al-Hassan was watching his reaction for even the slightest hint of discomfort with the idea of killing Jon. A faint stiffening, a flinch, a microscopic shudder.

Instead, Griffin nodded at the paramedic van. His expression was arctic. "If necessary, we may have to kill them, too. Maybe they heard her say something. I hope you're prepared for that. You're not going to wimp out on me, are you? Turn soft?"

Al-Hassan bristled. "I had not thought of the paramedics. Of course, if it is necessary, we will kill them." His eyes narrowed. He paused. "It is possible Jon Smith is conversing with a corpse. Love makes fools of even the most intelligent. We will see whether she dies on her own. If so, then we have only Jon Smith to eliminate. That makes our jobs easier, yes?"

Chapter Eight

5:52 A.M.
Frederick, Maryland

Sophia lay in the curtained ICU bed gasping for breath, even under oxygen. Hooked to all the machines of a modern hospital, she was held captive by apparatus untouched by who she was or what was wrong with her. Smith held her fevered hand and wanted to yell at the machines: *"She's Sophia Russell. We talk. We laugh. We work together. We make love. We live! We're going to be married this spring. She's going to get well, and we'll marry in just a few months. We're going to live together until we're old and gray and still in love."*

He leaned close and said in a strong voice, "You'll be fine, Soph, my darling." As he had told countless young soldiers lying shattered in a MASH unit at some front line, he reassured, "You're going to be well soon. You'll be up and about and feeling a lot better." He kept the fear and worry from his tones. He had to bolster their morale; there was always hope. But this was Sophia, and he had to fight harder than he had ever fought in his life to hide his despair. "Just hang on, darling. *Please*, darling," he whispered. "Hang on."

When she was conscious, she tried to smile up at him between shuddering gasps for breath. She squeezed his hand weakly. The fever and struggle to breathe were draining her.

She tried to smile. ". . . where . . . were . . . you . . ."

Tenderly he laid a finger on her lips. "Don't try to talk. You need to concentrate on getting well. Sleep, darling. Rest, my beautiful darling."

Her eyes fell closed as if they were curtains dropping at the end of a play. She seemed to be concentrating, directing all her faculties inward to battle whatever was attacking her. He studied the translucent skin, the fine bones, the graceful arches of her brows. Her face had always had a kind of refined beauty that was somehow made more appealing by the intelligence that lay beneath. But now that fever wracked her, she looked thin and frail against the white hospital sheets. Her skin was almost transparent. Her fevered face had a touch of brilliance to it that frightened him.

A trickle of blood appeared at her left nostril.

Surprised, Smith dabbed at it with a tissue and motioned to the nurse. "Stop that bleeding."

The nurse took the box of gauze pads. "She must've broken a capillary in her nose, poor dear."

Smith didn't answer. He strode across the room of machines and blinking lights to where Dr. Josiah Withers, the hospital's pulmonary specialist, Dr. Eric Mukogawa, the internist from Fort Detrick, and Capt. Donald Gherini, USAMRIID's best virologist, were consulting in low voices. They looked up as Smith reached them, concern on their faces.

"Well?"

"We've tried every antibiotic we can think of that might help," Dr. Withers told him. "But it appears to be a virus, Dr. Smith. All our efforts to alleviate the symptoms have been useless. She's responded to nothing."

Smith swore. "Come up with *something*. At least stabilize her!"

"Jon"—Captain Gherini put a hand on Smith's shoulder—"it looks like the virus we got in the lab last weekend. We have every Level Four lab in the world working on it, and so far we haven't a clue what it is or how to treat it. It looks like a hantavirus, but it isn't. At least not like any hanta we know." He grimaced and shook his head sadly. "She must've somehow been contaminated—"

Smith stared at Gherini. "You're saying she made a mistake in the lab, Don? In the Hot Zone? No way! She's a hell of a lot more careful and skilled than that!"

The base internist said quietly, "We're doing everything we can, Colonel."

"Then do more! Do better! Find *something*, for God's sake!"

"*Doctors! Colonel!*"

The nurse stood over the ICU bed where Sophia's whole body had jerked up into a bow of agony, as if trying to draw one single long breath.

Smith slammed the others aside and ran. "Sophia!"

As he reached her side, she tried to smile.

He took her hand. "Darling?"

Her eyes fell closed, and her hand went limp.

"No!" he roared.

She settled into the bed as if she were weary from a long journey. Her chest stopped moving. After her long battle of gasps and pants, there was sudden, irrevocable silence. And before that could really register, blood gushed from her nose and mouth.

Horrified, unbelieving, Smith jerked his head up to check the monitor. A green line plodded steadily across the screen. Flat. A flatline. Death.

"Paddles!" he bellowed.

The nurse bit back a sob and produced the shock resuscitation electrodes.

He fought panic. He reminded himself that he had treated injured bodies in bloody skirmishes in hot spots around the world. He was a trained physician. *He saved lives.* That was his job. What he did best. *He was going to save Sophia's life.* He could do it.

His gaze on the monitor, he initiated the shock. Sophia's body curved silently in an arc and fell back.

"Again!"

Five times he tried, increasing the shock each time. He thought he had brought her back a couple of times. He was almost sure she had responded at least once. She could not be dead. It was impossible.

Captain Gherini touched his wrist. "Jon?"

"No!"

He shocked her again. The monitors remained flat, unresponsive. It had to be a mistake. Certainly a nightmare. He must be asleep and having a nightmare. Sophia was alive. Full of vitality. Beautiful as a summer day. And a smart-aleck. He loved the way she teased him—

He snapped, "Again!"

The pulmonary specialist, Dr. Withers, put his arm around Smith's shoulders. "Jon, let go of the paddles."

Smith looked at him. "What?"

But he released the paddles, and Withers took them.

The internist, Dr. Mukogawa, said, "I'm very sorry, Jon. We all are. This is horrible. Unbelievable." He motioned to the others. "We'll leave you alone. You'll need some time."

They filed out. The curtains closed around Sophia's bed, and a wasteland of pain took over Smith's heart. He shook. He dropped down on his knees and pressed his forehead against Sophia's limp arm. It was warm. He wanted to keep telling himself she was alive. He wanted her to move, to sit up and laugh, to tell him it was all just a bad joke.

A tear slid down his cheek. Angrily he wiped it away. He removed the oxygen tent so he could really see her. She looked so alive still, her skin pink and moist. He sat beside her on the bed. He picked up both her hands and held them in his. He kissed her fingers.

I remember when I first saw you. Oh, you were lovely. And giving that poor researcher hell because he had misread the slide. You're a great scientist, Sophia. The best friend I've ever had. And the only woman I ever loved—

He sat and talked to her in his thoughts. He poured out his love. Sometimes he squeezed her hands just as he did when they went to the movies together. Once he looked down and saw his tears had puddled on the sheet. It was a long time before he finally said, "Good-bye, darling."

■

In the hospital waiting room, the long, slow night was over but the morning bustle had yet to begin. Miserable and numb, Smith sat slumped alone in an armchair.

The first day Sophia had walked into the lab at USAMRIID she had started talking before he had even taken his gaze from his microscope. "Randi hates your guts," she had told him. "I don't know why. I kind of like the way you took the blame for whatever you did to her and that you were sorry. It was clear you meant it, and you were suffering for it."

He had turned then, took one look, and knew again why he had badgered the army into bringing her to Fort Detrick. He had seen her first in the NIH lab where she had castigated a careless researcher, and he had been shocked to meet her again at her sister's place, but those two encounters had been enough to know he wanted to spend time with her. He had sat there under Randi's angry gaze admiring Sophia. She had long cornsilk hair pulled back in a ponytail and a slim figure full of curves.

She had not missed his interest. That first day in the USAMRIID lab, she had told him, "I'll take the empty bench over there. You can stop staring at me, and I'll get to work. Everyone tells me you're a hotshot combat doctor. I respect that. But I'm a better researcher than you'll ever be, and you'd better get used to it."

"I'll remember that."

She had stared him straight in the eye. "And keep your dick in your pants until I say take it out."

He nodded, smiled, and told her, "I can wait."

The hospital's waiting room was an island out of time. In his mind the world was somewhere else. Crazy memories rampaged through his brain. He seemed to be out of control. He would have to call the wedding off. Cancel everything. The caterers, the limousine, the . . .

My God, what was he doing?

He shook his head violently. Tried to focus his mind. He was in the hospital.

Dawn's light reflected pink and yellow on the buildings across the street. He would have to put his dress uniform back into mothballs.

Where had she been in recent weeks? He should have been with her. He should never have gotten her the job at USAMRIID.

How many people had they invited to the wedding? He had to write each one. Personally. Tell them she was gone . . . gone . . .

He had killed her. Sophia. He had made USAMRIID make an offer so good she had taken the job at Detrick, and he had killed her. He had known he wanted her the moment he saw her at Randi's. When he had tried to tell Randi how sorry he was her fiancé had died, Randi had been too angry to listen. But Sophia had understood. He had seen it in her eyes—those black eyes, so intense, so lively, so alive . . .

He had to tell her family. But she had no family. Only Randi. He had to tell Randi.

He lurched to his feet to find a pay telephone, and Somalia came back to him in a rush. He had been posted to a hospital ship in the minor invasion to bring order and protect our citizens in a country torn apart by the war raging between two warlords who had divided Mogadishu and the country. They summoned him into the remote bush to treat a major with fever. Exhausted from a twelve-hour shift, he had diagnosed malaria, but then it had turned out to be the far-less-known and far-more-deadly Lassa fever. The major had died before the diagnosis could be corrected and better treatment begun.

The army exonerated him of wrongdoing. It was a mistake many more experienced doctors—unfamiliar with virology—had made before and would make again, and Lassa usually killed even with the best treatment. There was no cure. But he knew he had been arrogant, so full of himself that he had not called for help until too late. He blamed himself. So much so that he had pressured the army to assign him to Fort Detrick to become an expert in virology and microbiology.

There, after he really understood the rarity of Lassa compared to malaria, he finally accepted his error as a risk of field medicine in distant and unfamiliar places. But the major had been Randi Russell's fiancé, and Randi had never forgiven Smith, never stopped blaming him for his death. Now he had to tell her he had killed another person she loved.

He slumped back onto the couch.

Sophia. Soph. He had killed her. Darling Sophia. They would marry in the spring, but she was dead. He should never have brought her to Detrick. Never!

■

"Colonel Smith?"

Smith heard the voice as if from under miles of water at the bottom of a murky lagoon. He saw a shape. Then a face. And burst through the surface to blink in the hard light.

"Smith? Are you all right?" Brigadier General Kielburger stood over him.

Then it struck him and left him chilled to the marrow. *Sophia was dead.*

He sat up. "I have to be there at the autopsy! If—"

"Relax. They haven't started yet."

Smith glared. "Why the hell wasn't I told about this new virus? You knew damn well where I was."

"Don't use that tone with me, Colonel! You weren't contacted at first because the matter didn't seem urgent—a single soldier in California. By the time the two other cases were reported, you were due home in a little over a day anyway. If you'd returned when your orders instructed, you would have known. And perhaps—"

Smith's stomach clenched into an enormous fist, and his hands followed suit. Was Kielburger suggesting he might have saved Sophia had he been here? Then he slumped back. He did not need the general to do what he was already doing himself. Over and over as he sat in the dawn waiting room he blamed himself.

He stood up abruptly. "I have to make a call."

He walked to the telephone near the elevators and dialed Randi Russell's home. After two rings the machine picked up, and he heard her precise, get-to-the-point voice: "Randi Russell. Can't talk now. After the beep, leave a message. . . . Thanks."

That "thanks" came grudgingly, as if an inner voice had told her to not be all business all the time. That was Randi.

He dialed her office at the Foreign Affairs Inquiries Institute, an international think tank. This message was even crisper: "Russell. Leave a message." No thanks this time, not even as an afterthought.

Bitterly, he considered leaving the same kind of message: "Smith here. Bad news. Sophia's dead. Sorry."

But he simply hung up. There was no way he could leave a death message. He would have to keep trying to reach her, no matter how much it hurt. If he could not get her by tomorrow, he would tell her boss what had happened and ask him or her to have Randi call him. What else could he do?

Randi had always been a sometime thing, frequently away on long business trips. She saw Sophia rarely. After he and Sophia grew close, Randi seldom called and never came around.

Back in the waiting room, he found Kielburger impatiently swinging a knife-creased uniform leg and polished boot.

Smith dropped into a chair beside the general. "Tell me about this virus. Where did it break out? What kind is it? Another hemorrhagic like Machupo?"

"Yes to all of that, and no to all of that," Kielburger told him. "Major Keith Anderson died Friday evening out in Fort Irwin of acute respiratory distress syndrome, but it was not like any ARDS we'd ever seen. There was massive hemorrhaging from the lungs, and blood in the chest cavity. The Pentagon alerted us, and we got blood and tissue samples early Saturday morning. By then two other deaths had occurred in Atlanta and Boston. You weren't here, so I put Dr. Russell in charge, and the team worked around the clock. When we did the DNA restriction map, it turned out to be unlike any known virus. It failed to react to any of the antibody samples we had for any virus. I decided to bring in CDC and the other Level Four facilities worldwide, but everything is still negative. It's new, and it's deadly."

In the corridor, Dr. Lutfallah, the hospital pathologist, passed with two orderlies pushing a sheet-draped gurney. He nodded to Smith.

The general continued talking. "What I want you to do is—"

Smith ignored him. What he had to do was more important than anything Kielburger wanted. He jumped up and followed the procession to the autopsy rooms.

∎

Hospital orderly Emiliano Coronado slipped out into the service alley behind the hospital to have a cigarette. Proud of his distant ancestor's daring and fame, he stood erect, his shoulders squared, and in his imagination he stared off into the vast distances of Colorado four centuries ago, looking for the Cities of Gold.

A sudden pain sliced across his throat. His cigarette dropped from his mouth, and his vision of glory sank into the refuse littering the dark alley. A knife blade had cut a thin trickle of blood from his neck. The blade pressed against the wound.

"Not a sound," the voice said from behind.

Terrified, Emiliano could only grunt.

"Tell me about Dr. Russell." Nadal al-Hassan dug the razor-sharp knife deeper as encouragement. "Is she alive?"

Coronado tried to swallow. "She die."

"What did she say before she died?"

"Nothin' . . . she don' say nothin' to no one."

The knife dug in. "You are sure? Not to Colonel Smith, her fiancé? That does not sound possible."

Emiliano was desperate. "She unconscious, you know? How she gonna talk?"

"That is good."

The knife did its work, and Emiliano Coronado lay unconscious and dying as his blood soaked the refuse of the shadowed alley.

Al-Hassan looked carefully around. He left the alley and circled the block to where the van waited.

"Well?" Bill Griffin asked as al-Hassan climbed in.

"According to the orderly, she said nothing."

"Then maybe Smith knows nothing. Maybe it's good Maddux missed him in D.C. Two murders at USAMRIID increases the risk of someone figuring it out."

"I would prefer Maddux had killed him. Then we would not be having this discussion."

"But Maddux didn't kill him, and we can rethink the necessity."

"We cannot be certain she did not speak in her condominium."

"We can if she was unconscious the whole time."

"She was not unconscious when she went into her building," al-Hassan replied. "Our leader will not like the possibility she told him of Peru."

Griffin shot back: "I've got to say it again, al-Hassan, too many unexplained deaths and killings can draw a lot of attention. Especially if Smith's told anyone about the attacks on him. The boss could like that even less."

Al-Hassan hesitated. He distrusted Griffin, but the ex–FBI man could be right. "Then we must let him decide which course of action he likes least."

Bill Griffin felt a weight lift from him. Not all the way off, because he knew Smithy. If Jon even suspected that Sophia's death was not an accident, he would never back off. Still, Bill hoped the hardhead would believe she had made a mistake in the lab, and the attacks on him had no relation to her death. When there were no more attacks, he would give it up. Then Smithy would be out of danger, and Griffin could stop worrying.

•

In the tile and stainless-steel autopsy room in the basement of the Frederick hospital, Smith looked up as pathologist Lutfallah stepped from the dissecting table. The air was cold and singed with the stink of formaldehyde. Both men were dressed completely in green scrubs.

Lutfallah sighed. "Well, that's it, Jon. No doubt at all. She died of a massive viral infection that destroyed her lungs."

"What virus?" Smith's masked voice demanded, although he was pretty sure he knew the answer.

Lutfallah shook his head. "I'll leave that part to you Einsteins at Detrick. The lungs and almost nothing else . . . but it's not pneumonia, tuberculosis, or anything else I've ever seen. Swift and devastating."

Smith nodded. With a giant effort of will, he blanked his mind against who was lying cut open on the stainless-steel table with its channels and slopes to catch blood. He and Lutfallah began the grim business of collecting tissue and blood samples.

•

Only later after the autopsy was finished and Smith had taken off his green cap and mask and gloves and scrubs and sat outside the autopsy room alone on a long bench did he let himself grieve for Sophia again.

He had waited too long. He had let his excited chase of science and medicine around the globe keep him away too much. He had been lying to himself that with Sophia he was no longer a cowboy. It was not true. Even after he had asked her to marry him, he had still left her for his pursuits. And now he could not get that lost time back.

The pain of missing her was sharper than anything physical he had ever felt. With a rush of aching comprehension, he tried to come to terms with the fact that they would never be together again. He leaned forward, and his face fell into his hands. He yearned for her. Thick tears poured through his fingers. Regret. Guilt. Mourning. He shook with silent sobs. She was gone, and all he could think about was that his arms ached to hold her one more time.

Chapter Nine

9:18 A.M.
Bethesda, Maryland

Most people think of the behemoth National Institutes of Health as a single entity, which is far from the truth. Set on more than three hundred lush acres in Bethesda, just ten miles from the Capitol's dome, the NIH consists of twenty-four separate institutes, centers, and divisions that employ sixteen thousand people. Of those, an astounding six thousand are Ph.D.s. It is a collection of more advanced degrees in one location than most colleges and some entire states are able to boast.

Lily Lowenstein, RRL, was thinking about all that as she stared out her office suite's windows on the top floor of one of the seventy-five campus buildings. Her gaze swept over the flower beds, the rolling lawns, the tree-rimmed parking lots, and the office structures where so many highly educated and intelligent people labored.

She was looking for an answer where there was none.

As director of the Federal Resource Medical Clearing house (FRMC), Lily was herself highly educated, well-trained, and at the top of her profession. Alone in her office, she stared out at the prestigious

NIH, but she did not see the people or buildings or anything else. What she was actually seeing and thinking about was her problem. A problem that had grown almost imperceptibly over many years until it weighed her down like the proverbial thousand-pound gorilla.

Lily was a compulsive gambler. It made no difference what kind; she was addicted to them all. At first she spent her vacations in Las Vegas. Later, after she took her first job in Washington, she went to Atlantic City because she could get to the tables faster. She could play Atlantic City on weekends, or on a single day off, or even a one-night stand in recent years as the compulsion grew with the size of her debts.

If it had stopped there—casino gambling and an occasional trip to the track at Pimlico and Arlington—perhaps it would have remained a minor monkey. It would have been annoying, draining away her good salary, causing rifts in her family when she canceled visits and failed to send Christmas or birthday presents to her nieces and nephews. It would have left her with few friends, but it would never have grown into the terrifying beast she now faced.

She placed bets by telephone with bookmakers, placed bets in bars with other bookmakers, and, finally, borrowed money from those who lent money to faceless, frantic souls like herself. Now she owed more than fifty thousand dollars, and a man who would not give his name had called to tell her he had bought up all her debts and would like to discuss payment. It shot chills up her spine. Her hand shook as if from palsy. He was polite, but there was an implied threat in his words. At exactly nine-thirty she was to meet him at a downtown Bethesda sports bar she knew only too well.

Terrified, she had tried to figure out what to do. She had no illusions. She could, of course, go to the police, but then everything would come out. She would lose her job and probably go to prison because, inevitably, she had cut a few corners in buying office supplies, and she had pocketed the difference. She had even dipped into petty cash. That was what compulsive gamblers did.

There were no more friends or family who would lend her money, even if she were willing to let them know she had a problem. One of her two cars, the Beemer, had been repossessed, and her house was mortgaged to the maximum. She had no husband, not anymore. Her share of her son's private school tuition was in arrears. She had no bonds, no stocks, no real estate. No one was going to help her, not even a loan shark. Not anymore.

She could not even run away. Her only means of support was her job. Without her job she had nothing. She was nothing.

■

From a rear booth in the sports bar, Bill Griffin watched the woman enter. She was about what he had expected. Middle-aged, middle-class, almost prim, nondescript. A few inches taller, maybe five-foot-nine. A few pounds heavier. Brown hair, brown eyes, heart-shaped face, small chin. There was a certain telltale carelessness about her clothes: Her suit bordered on shabby and did not fit as well as it should on the director of a big government facility. Her hair was ragged, and her gray roots were showing. The gambler.

But she was also a shade haughty as she stood inside the door looking for someone to come forward and claim her, the sign of the middle-rank bureaucrat.

Griffin let her stew.

Finally he stepped out of the booth, caught her eye, and nodded. She walked stiffly past tables and booths toward him.

"Ms. Lowenstein," he said.

Lily nodded to control her apprehension. "And you are?"

"That doesn't matter. Sit down."

She sat, nervous and uneasy, so she went on the attack. "How did you find out about my debts?"

Bill Griffin smiled thinly. "You don't really care about all that, Ms. Lowenstein, do you? Who I am, where I got the debts, why I bought them up. None of it matters a damn, right?" He gazed at her trembling cheeks and lips. She caught his look and stiffened her face. Inwardly he nodded. She was terrified, which made her vulnerable to alternatives. "I have your markers." He watched her brown eyes as they shifted uneasily. "I'm here to offer you a way to get out from under."

She snorted derisively. "Out from under?"

No gambler cared much about simply erasing debt. Gambling was a compulsion, an illness. Debt was an embarrassment and danger, but it had little impact until it meant the tracks, the bookmakers, anyone who ran a game would refuse to let you play without cash on the table. Griffin knew Lily was in a daily scramble to come up with enough to place more than a five-dollar track bet.

So he offered her the bone that wagged this dog's tail: "You can start fresh. I wipe away your debts. No one ever knows, and I give you enough to start over. Sound good?"

"A fresh start?" An excited flush appeared above Lowenstein's collar. For a moment, her eyes were bright with excitement. But just as quickly, she frowned. She was in trouble, but she was not an idiot. "That depends on what I have to do for it, doesn't it?"

In his military intelligence days, Griffin had been one of the army's best recruiters of assets behind the Iron Curtain. Lure them with the personal advantages, the moral principles, the rightness of the cause until they were compromised. Then when they balked at what you asked them to do, and they always did sooner or later, drop the carrot, tighten the screws, and lean. It was not the aspect of his job he had liked most, but he had been good at it, and it was time to lean on this woman.

"No, not really." His voice dropped thirty degrees. "It depends on nothing. You can't pay me off, and you can't be exposed. If you think you can do either, get up and walk out now. Don't waste my time."

Lily turned red. She bristled. "Now you listen to me, you arrogant—"

"I know," Griffin cut her off. "It's hard. You're the boss, right? Wrong. *I'm* the boss now. Or tomorrow you'll be out of a job, with no chance of getting another. Not in the government, not in D.C., probably not anywhere."

Lily's stomach turned to stone. Then to mush. She started to cry. No! She would not cry! She never cried. She was the boss. She . . .

"It's okay," Griffin said. "Cry. Get it out. It's hard, and it's going to get harder. Take your time."

The more he spoke compassionately, the harder Lily wept. Through her tears, she watched him lean back, relaxed. He waved to the waitress and pointed at his glass. He did not point at her or ask what she wanted. This was not social; this was business. Whoever he was, she realized suddenly, it was not he who was blackmailing her. He was only the messenger. Doing a job. Indifferent. Nothing personal.

When the waitress brought his beer, Lily turned her head away, ashamed to be seen red-eyed and crying. She had never had to deal with anything like this, anyone like this, and she felt terribly alone.

Griffin sipped his beer. It was time to produce the carrot again. "Okay, feel better? Maybe this'll help. Think about it this way—the ax was going to fall someday. This way, you get it over with, wipe the slate clean, and I give you a little extra, say fifty thousand, to get you started again. All for a couple of hours' work. Probably less time, if you're as good at your job as I think you are. Now, that's not so bad, is it?"

Wipe the slate clean . . . fifty thousand . . . The words burst into her brain like a blaze of sunshine. Start again. The nightmare over. And money. She could really start over. Get help. Therapy. Oh, this was never going to happen again. Never!

She dabbed her eyes. She suddenly wanted to kiss this man, hug him. "What . . . what do you want me to do?"

"There, right to the point," Griffin said approvingly. "I knew you were smart. I like that. I need a smart person for this."

"Don't try to flatter me. Not now."

Griffin laughed. "Feisty too. Got the spirit back, right? Hell, no one's even going to get hurt. Just a few records erased. Then you're home free."

Records? Erased? Her records! Never. She shuddered, and then she took hold of herself. What had she expected? Why else would they need her? She was a record librarian. Chief of Federal Resource Medical Clearing House. Of course, it was medical records.

Griffin watched her. This was the critical moment. That first shock of a new asset knowing what he or she was actually going to have to do. Betray their country. Betray their employer. Betray their family. Betray a trust. Whatever it was. And as he watched, he saw the moment pass. The internal battle. She had gotten a grip on herself.

He nodded. "Okay, that's the bad part. The rest is all downhill. Here's what we want. There's a report to Fort Detrick and CDC and probably to a lot of other places overseas, too, that we need deleted from all the records. Wiped out, erased clean. All copies. It never existed. The same with any World Health Organization reports of virus outbreaks and/or cures in Iraq in the last two years. Those, plus all records of a couple of telephone calls. Can you do that?"

She was still too shocked to speak. But she nodded.

"Now, there's one other condition. It must be done by noon."

"By noon? *Now?* During office hours? But how—?"

"That's your problem."

All she could do was nod again.

"Good." Griffin smiled. "Now, how about that drink?"

Chapter Ten

1:33 P.M.
Fort Detrick, Maryland

Smith worked feverishly in the Level Four lab, pushing against a wall of fatigue. How had Sophia died? With Bill Griffin's warning ringing in his head, and considering the lethal attacks on him in Washington, he could not believe her death had been an accident. Yet there was no doubt how she had died—acute respiratory distress syndrome from a deadly virus.

At the hospital, the doctors had told him to go home, to get some sleep. The general had ordered him to follow the doctors' advice. Instead, he had said nothing and driven straight to Fort Detrick's main gate. The guard saluted sadly as he passed. He had parked in his usual spot near USAMRIID's monolithic, yellow brick-and-concrete building. Exhaust ventilators on the roof blew an endless stream of heavily filtered air from the Level Three and Four labs.

Walking in a semi-trance of grief and exhaustion, carrying the refrigerated containers of blood and tissue from the autopsy, he had showed his security ID badge to the guard at the desk, who nodded to him sympathetically. On automatic pilot, he had continued walking. The corridors were like something in a hazy dream, a floating maze of twists and turns, doors and thick glass windows on the containment labs. He paused at Sophia's office and looked in.

A lump formed in his throat. He swallowed and hurried on to the Level Four suite where he suited up in his containment suit.

Using Sophia's tissue and blood, he worked alone in the Hot Zone lab against advice, orders, and the directives of safe procedure. He repeated all the lab work she had done with the samples from the three other victims—isolating the virus, studying it under the electron microscope, and testing it against USAMRIID's frozen bank of specimens from previous victims of various viruses from around the world. The virus that had killed Sophia reacted to none. He ran yet another polymerase-chain-reaction-driven DNA sequencing analysis to identify the new virus, and he made a preliminary restriction map. Then he transmitted his data to his office computer and, after seven minutes of decon showering in the air lock, removed his space suit and scrubs.

Dressed again, he hurried to his office, where he checked his data against Sophia's. At last he sat back and stared into space. The virus that had killed Sophia matched none he had ever heard of or seen. It had been close here and there, yes, but always to a different known virus.

What it did match was the unknown virus she had been working on.

Obsessed as he was with Sophia's death, he still felt horror at the potential threat to the world from this new, deadly virus. Four victims might be only the beginning.

How had Sophia contracted it?

If she had had an accident in which she had any possible contact with the new virus, she would have reported it instantly. Not only was that a standing order, it was insanity not to. The pathogens in a Hot Zone were lethal. There was no vaccine and no cure, but prompt treatment to bolster the body's resistance and maintain the best possible health; plus normal medical steps for any virus, had saved many who all but certainly would have died untreated.

Detrick had a biocontainment hospital where the doctors knew everything there was to know about treating victims. If anyone could have saved her, it would have been them, and she knew it.

On top of everything, she was a scientist. If she had thought there was the remotest possibility she could have contracted the virus, she would have wanted everything that had happened to her recorded and analyzed to add to the body of knowledge about the virus and perhaps save others.

She would have reported anything. Anything at all.

Add to that the violent attacks on him in Georgetown, and Smith could draw only one conclusion: Her death had been no accident.

In his mind, he heard her gasping voice *"... lab ... someone ... hit ..."*

The tortured words had meant nothing to him in the horror of the moment, but now they reverberated in his mind. Had someone entered her lab and attacked her the way they had attacked him?

Galvanized, he read again through her notes, memos, and reports for any clue, any hint of what had really happened.

And saw the number in her careful printing at the top of the next-to-last page of her logbook. Her logbook detailed each day's work on the unknown virus. The entry number was *PRL-53-99.*

He understood the notation. "PRL" referred to the Prince Leopold Institute in Belgium. There was nothing special about that, simply her way to identify a report from some other researcher she had used in her work. The number referred to a specific experiment or line of reasoning or a chronology. What was important about this reference and number was that she always—always—wrote them at the end of her report.

At the *end.*

This notation was at the top of a page—at the beginning of a commentary concerning the problem of three victims separated widely by geography, circumstances, age, gender, and experience dying from the same virus at the same time, and no one else in the surrounding areas even contracting it.

The commentary mentioned no other reports, so the log number was in the wrong place.

He examined the two last pages carefully, pushing apart the sheets so he could study the gutter where the paper was sealed into the book's spine. His magnifying glass revealed nothing.

He thought a moment and then carried the open logbook to his large dissecting microscope. He positioned the book's exposed gutter under the viewing lens and peered into the binocular eyepiece. He slid the spine under the viewer.

He inhaled sharply when he saw it—a cut almost as straight and delicate as a laser scalpel. But although very good, it was not good enough to hide the truth from the powerful microscope. A knife-edge showed, faintly jagged.

A page had been cut out.

■

Brig. Gen. Calvin Kielburger stood in the open doorway to Jon Smith's office. His hands clasped behind his back, legs spread apart, beefy face set firmly in a severe expression, he looked like Patton on a tank in the Ardennes inspiring the Fourth Armored.

"I ordered you to go home, Colonel Smith. You're no good to anyone out on your feet. We need a full, clear-thinking staff on this effort. Especially without Dr. Russell."

Smith did not look up. "Someone cut a page from her logbook."

"Go home, Colonel."

Now Smith raised his head. "Didn't you hear me? There's a page missing from the last work she did. Why?"

"She probably removed it because she didn't want it."

"Have you forgotten everything you know about science since you got that star? *No one* destroys a research note. I can tell you what was cut out was connected to some report she had read from the Prince Leopold Institute in Belgium. I've found no copy of such a report in her papers."

"It's probably in the computer data bank."

"That's where I'm going to look next."

"You'll have to do it later. First I want you to get some rest, and then I need you to go to California in Dr. Russell's place. You've got to talk to Major Anderson's family, friends, anyone and everyone who knew him."

"No, dammit! Send someone else." He wanted to tell Kielburger about the attacks on him in Washington. That might go a long way to making the general believe that he had to keep trying to find out how Sophia had contracted the virus. But Kielburger would want to know what he had been doing in Washington in the first place when he was supposed to be back at Detrick, which would force him to reveal his clandestine meeting with Bill Griffin. He could not expose an old friend until he knew more, which meant he had to convince the general to let him go on. "Something's *wrong* about Sophia's death, I know it. I'm going to find out what."

The general bristled. "Not on the army's time, you're not. We've got a far bigger problem than the death of one staff member, Colonel, no matter who she was."

Smith reared up from his seat like a stallion attacked by a rattlesnake. "Then I'm out of the army!"

For a moment Kielburger glared, his thick fists clenched at his sides. His face was beet red, and he was ready to tell Smith to go ahead and quit. He had had enough of his insubordination.

Then he reconsidered. It would look bad on his record—an officer unable to command loyalty in his troops. This was not the time to deal with Smith's arrogance and insubordination.

He forced his face to relax. "All right, I suppose I don't blame you. Continue working on Dr. Russell's case. I'll send someone else to California."

2:02 P.M.
Bethesda, Maryland

Even though she had rushed, it took Lily Lowenstein the entire morning to do what the nameless man had ordered. Now she was finishing a celebratory lunch at her favorite restaurant in downtown Bethesda. On the other side of the window, the city's tall buildings, reminding her again of a mini-Dallas, reflected the bright October sunlight as she sipped her second daiquiri.

Surprisingly, tapping into WHO's worldwide computerized medical network had turned out to be the simplest of her tasks. Nobody had thought it necessary to put stringent security on a scientific and humanitarian information network. So it had been child's play to erase all trace of a series of reports from WHO records concerning the victims and survivors of two minor viral outbreaks in the cities of Baghdad and Basra.

The Iraqi computer system was five years out of date, so going in to remove the originals of the same reports at the source was almost as easy. Oddly, Lily had found most of the original information from Iraq had already been erased by the Saddam Hussein regime. Not wanting to reveal any weakness or need, no doubt.

Clearing the single Belgian report from all electronic records of her own FRMC master computer, from USAMRIID and CDC's databases, and from all the other databases worldwide had been more time consuming. But the hardest task proved to be erasing the item from the telephone log at Fort Detrick. She had been forced to call in favors from high-level phone company contacts who owed her.

Curious, she had attempted to comprehend the reason behind the blackmailer's demands, but there seemed to be no common ground among the items she deleted except that most dealt with a virus. There had been hundreds of other research reports flying back and forth over the electronic circuits among a dozen Level Four research institutions worldwide, and her blackmailer had shown no interest in those.

Whatever he had wanted, her part was successfully completed. She had not been discovered, had left no trace, and would soon be free of her financial problems for good. She would never get in so deep again, she promised herself. With fifty thousand dollars in cash, she could go to Vegas or Atlantic City with enough to recoup everything she had lost. With a carefree smile, she quickly decided she would begin with a thousand on the Capitals to win tonight.

She almost laughed aloud as she left the restaurant and turned the corner toward the bar where her favorite bookmaker had his private booth. She felt a fiery surge that told her she could not lose. Not now. Not anymore.

Even when she heard the screams behind her, the screech and rumble of rubber and metal, and turned to see the big black SUV careening along the sidewalk directly at her, she had a wide smile on her face. The smile was still there when the SUV struck her and swerved back onto the street, leaving her dead on the sidewalk.

3:16 P.M.
Fort Detrick, Maryland

Smith pushed away from the computer screen. There were five reports from the Prince Leopold Institute, but none had arrived yesterday or early today, and none reported anything but more failure to classify the unknown virus.

There had to be a report with new information in it—at least one fact important enough for Sophia to be inspired in some new line of investigation she had chronicled as a full-page note last night. But he had searched Detrick's database, CDC's database, and tied into the army's supercomputer to search every other Level Four lab in the world, including the Prince Leopold itself.

There was nothing.

Frustrated, he stared at the uncooperative screen. Either Sophia had made a mistake, put the wrong code on her designation, and the report had never existed, or—

Or it had been erased from every database in the world, including its source.

That was difficult to believe. Not impossible to do, but hard to believe someone would go to such trouble over a virus when it was in everyone's best interests to investigate. Smith shook his head, trying to dismiss the idea that there had been anything critical on that missing page, but he could not. The page *had* been cut out.

And by someone who had gotten on and off the base unseen. Or had they?

He reached again for the phone to find out who else had been in the lab last night, but after speaking to the whole staff and Sergeant Major Daugherty, he was no closer to an answer. All of Daugherty's people had gone home by 6:00 P.M. while the scientific staff had stayed until 2:00 A.M., even Kielburger. After that, Sophia had been here alone.

On the night desk, Grasso had seen nothing, not even Sophia's leaving, as Smith already knew. At the gate, the guards swore they had seen no one after 2:00 A.M., but they had obviously missed Sophia staggering out on foot, so their report meant little. Besides, he doubted anyone skilled enough to cut out the page without leaving a trace to the naked eye would have drawn attention to himself as he entered or left.

Smith was at a dead end.

Then, in his mind, he heard Sophia gasp. He closed his eyes and saw once again her beautiful face, contorted in excruciating pain. Falling into his arms, struggling to breathe, yet managing to blurt out, "*. . . lab . . . someone . . . hit . . .*"

5:27 P.M.
The Morgue, Frederick, Maryland

Dr. Lutfallah was annoyed. "I don't know what more we can find out, Colonel Smith. The autopsy was clear. Definite. Shouldn't you take a break? I'm surprised you can function at all. You need some sleep . . ."

"I'll sleep when I know what happened to her," Smith snapped. "And I'm not questioning *what* killed her, only *how* it killed her."

The pathologist had reluctantly agreed to remeet Smith in the hospital's autopsy room. He was not happy to have been pulled away from a perfectly good Tanqueray martini.

"*How?*" Lutfallah's eyebrows shot up. This was too much. He made no effort to keep the scathing sarcasm from his voice. "I'd say that'd be the usual way any lethal virus kills, Colonel."

Smith ignored him. He was bent close to the table, fighting to keep from breaking down again at the sight of his vibrant Sophia so pale and lifeless. "Every inch, Doctor. Examine her inch by inch. Look for anything we missed, anything unusual. Anything."

Still bristling, Lutfallah began to search. The two medical men worked in silence for an hour. Lutfallah was starting to make annoyed sounds again when he gave a muffled exclamation through his surgical mask. "What's this?"

Smith jerked alert. "What? What do you have? Show me!"

But it was Lutfallah who did not answer this time. He was examining Sophia's left ankle. When he spoke, it was a question. "Was Dr. Russell diabetic?"

"No. What have you found?"

"Any other intravenous medications?"

"No."

Lutfallah nodded to himself. He looked up. "Did she do drugs, Colonel?"

"You mean narcotics? Hell, no."

"Then take a look."

Smith joined the pathologist, who was standing on Sophia's left side. Together they bent close to the ankle. The mark was all but invisible—a reddening and swelling so small no one had noticed, or perhaps it had not been there before, a late manifestation of the virus.

In the center of the reddening was a single, tiny needle mark for an injection, as expertly administered as the page had been cut from her notebook.

Smith stood up abruptly. Fury enveloped him. He gripped his hands in white-hard fists as his head pounded. He had guessed it. Now he knew it.

Sophia had been murdered.

8:16 P.M.
Fort Detrick, Maryland

Jon Smith slammed into his office and stalked to his desk. But he did not sit. He could not. He paced the room, back and forth, a wild animal in a corral. Despite the turmoil in his body, his mind was diamond sharp. Concentrating. For him right now, despite the needs of the world . . . there was one single goal—to find Sophia's killer.

All right, then. *Think.* She must have learned something so dangerous she had to be killed, and all physical evidence of what she had learned or deduced eliminated. So what else did researchers in a worldwide scientific investigation do? *They talked.*

He grabbed the telephone. "Get me the base security commander."

His fingers tapped a tattoo on the desk like a drummer beating eighteenth- and nineteenth-century regiments into battle.

"Dingman speaking. How can I help you, Colonel?"

"Do you keep a record of incoming and outgoing phone calls from USAMRIID?"

"Not specifically, but we can get one of a call made to or from the base. May I ask what in particular you're interested in?"

"Any and all made by Dr. Sophia Russell since last Saturday. Incoming, too."

"You have authorization, sir?"

"Ask Kielburger."

"I'll get back to you, Colonel."

Fifteen minutes later, Dingman phoned with a list of Sophia's incoming and outgoing calls. There had been few, since Sophia and the rest of the staff had been buried in their labs and offices with the virus. Five outgoing, three overseas, and only four incoming. He called the numbers. All checked out as discussions of what had not been found, of failure.

Disappointed, he sat back—and then shot forward out of his chair. He ran through the corridor into Sophia's office, where he pawed through everything on her desk again. Checked the drawers. He was not wrong—her monthly telephone log, the one Kielburger insisted they keep faithfully, was also missing.

He hurried back to his office and made another call. "Ms. Curtis? Did Sophia turn her October phone log in early? No? You're sure? Thank you."

They had taken her phone log, too. The murderers. Why? Because there *had* been a call that revealed what they were trying to hide. It had been erased along with the Prince Leopold report. They were powerful and clever, and he had hit a seemingly impenetrable wall trying to discover what Sophia had done, or knew, to make someone think he needed to kill her.

He would have to find the answer another way—look into the history of the victims. Something must have connected them before they died, something tragically lethal.

He dialed again. "Jon Smith, Ms. Curtis. The general in his office?"

"He surely is, Colonel. You hold on now." Ms. Melanie Curtis was from Mississippi, and she liked him. But tonight he did not feel like their usual flirtatious banter.

"Thank you."

"General Kielburger here."

"Still want me to go to California tomorrow?"

"What's changed your mind, Colonel?"

"Maybe I've seen the light. The bigger danger should get the priority."

"Sure." Kielburger snorted in disbelief. "Okay, soldier. You'll fly out of Andrews at 0800 tomorrow. Be in my office at 0700, and I'll give you your instructions."

Chapter Eleven

5:04 P.M.
Adirondack Park, New York

Contrary to the assumptions of most of the world, two-thirds of New York was not skyscrapers, jammed subways, and ruthless financial centers. As Victor Tremont, COO of Blanchard Pharmaceuticals, stood on his deck in the vast Adirondack State Park looking west, in his mind's eye he could see the map: stretching from Vermont on the east nearly to Lake Ontario on the west, Canada on the north to just above Albany on the south, some six million acres of lush public and private lands rose from rushing rivers and thousands of lakes to forty-six rugged peaks that towered more than four thousand feet above the Adirondack flatlands.

Tremont knew all this because he had the kind of honed mind that automatically grasped, stored, and used important facts. Adirondack Park was vital to him not only because it was a stunning woodland wilderness, but because it was sparsely settled. One of the stories he liked to tell guests around his fireplace was about a state tax chief who had bought a local summer cabin. When the tax man decided his county bill was too high, he had investigated. In the process, he had—here Tremont would laugh heartily—discovered county tax officials were involved in massive corruption. The official was able to get an indictment against the lowlifes, but no jury could be impaneled. The reason? There were so few permanent residents in the county that all were either involved in the illegal scheme or related to someone who was.

Tremont smiled. This isolation and backwoods corruption made his timbered paradise perfect. Ten years ago he had moved Blanchard Pharmaceuticals into a redbrick complex he had ordered built in the forest near Long Lake village. At the same time, he had made a hidden retreat on nearby Lake Magua his main residence.

Tonight as the sun faded in a fiery orange ball behind pines and hardwoods, Tremont was standing on the roofed veranda of the first floor of his lodge. He studied the play of the brilliant sunset against the rugged outlines of the mountains and drank in the affluence, power, and taste that this view, this lodge, this lifestyle proved.

His lodge had been part of one of the great camps established here by the wealthy toward the end of the nineteenth century. Built with the same log-and-bark siding as the lodge at Great Camp Sagamore on nearby Raquette Lake, his sprawling hideaway was the only surviving structure from the old days. Concealed from above by a thick canopy of trees and from the lake by a dense forest, it was all but invisible to outsiders. Tremont had planned his restoration that way, allowing the vegetation to grow high and wild. There was neither an address post on the road nor a dock in the lake to reveal its presence. No public nor corporate access was provided, or wanted. Only Victor Tremont, a few trusted partners in his Hades Project, and the loyal scientists and technicians who worked in the private high-tech lab on the second floor knew it existed.

As the October sun dropped lower, the chilly Adirondack night bit at Tremont's cheeks and seeped through his jacket and trousers. Still, he was in no hurry to go inside. He savored the thick cigar he smoked and the taste of the fifty-year-old Langavulin he sipped. It warmed his blood and coated his throat with a satisfying burn. The Langavulin was perhaps the globe's finest whiskey, but its heavy peat-smoke flavor and incredibly balanced body were little known outside Scotland. That was because Tremont bought the entire supply each year from the distillery on Islay.

But as he stood in the last golden rays of the sunset on the veranda, it was the wilderness rather than the whiskey that brought a smile to his patrician lips. The pristine lake was only a short canoe portage from overpopulated Raquette. The tall pines swayed gently, and their pungent scent filled the air. In the distance, the naked peak of 5,344-foot Mount Marcy shone like a finger pointing at God.

Tremont had been attracted to the mountains since he had been an unruly teenager in Syracuse. His father, a professor of economics up on the hill at the university, had not been able to control him then any more than the fat-ass chairman of Blanchard could control him now. Both were always insisting upon what could not be done, that no one could do everything he wanted. He had never understood such narrowness. What limitation was there except your imagination? Your abilities? Your daring? The Hades Project itself was an example. If they had known in the beginning what he envisioned, both would have told him it was impossible. No one could do it.

Inwardly he snorted with disgust. They were puny, small men. In a few weeks, the project would be a total success. *He* would be a total success. Then there would be decades of profits.

Maybe it was because this was the final stage of Hades, but he had found himself occasionally drifting off in reverie, thinking about his long-dead father. In a strange way, his father had been the only man he had ever respected. The old man had not understood his only son, but he had stood by him. As a teen, Tremont had been fascinated by the movie *Jeremiah Johnson*. He had seen it a dozen times. Then, in the dead of an icy winter, he had taken off for the mountains, determined to live off the land just as Johnson had. Pick berries and dig roots. Hunt his own meat. Fight Indians. Pit himself against the elements in a heroic venture few had the courage or imagination to attempt.

But there had been little that was noble about the experience. He killed two deer out of season with his father's 30-30 Remington, mistakenly shot at and almost killed some hikers, got violently sick on the wrong berries, and damn near froze to death. Fortunately, because of his missing rifle, parka, and backpack, plus his constant talking about the film, his father had guessed where he had headed. When the forest service wanted to give up the hunt, his father had raged and pushed all the levers of academia and state politics. The result was the forest service grumbled but soldiered on, eventually finding him, miserable and frostbitten, in a cave on the snowy slopes of Marcy.

Despite everything, he counted it as one of the most important experiences of his life. He had learned from the mountain fiasco that nature was hard, indifferent, and no friend to humanity. He had also discovered physical challenge held little allure for him; it was too easy to lose. But his greatest lesson was the critical point of why Johnson had gone to the mountains. At the time, he had thought it was to challenge nature, to fight Indians, to prove manhood. *Wrong.* It was to make money. The mountain men were trappers, and everything they did and suffered was for one goal—to get rich.

He had never forgotten that. The boldness and simplicity of the goal had shaped his life.

As these thoughts flickered through his mind on the rustic veranda, he realized he wished his father were here for the conclusion of Hades. The old man would finally recognize that a man could do anything he wanted as long as he was smart enough and tough enough. Would his father be proud? Probably not. He laughed aloud. Too bad for the old man. His mother would be, but that was meaningless. Women didn't count.

Abruptly he came alert. He cocked his head, listening. The *chop-chop* of helicopter rotors was growing louder. Tremont knocked back his scotch, left his cigar in a large serpentine ashtray to die a natural death, and strode into the enormous high-beamed living room. Peering down from the log walls were the glass eyes of mounted trophy heads. Adirondack wood-and-leather furniture stood on hand-knotted rugs around the walk-in fireplace. Tremont continued past the crackling fire and along a back hall where the aroma of hot baking-powder biscuits scented the air from the kitchen.

Finally he stepped out on the other side of the lodge into the cool dusk. The chopper, a Bell S-92C Helibus, was settling down in a clearing a hundred yards away.

The four men who descended were in their mid-forties or early fifties, like Tremont himself. Unlike Tremont, who was dressed in custom-made chinos, pewter-colored bush shirt, Gore-Tex lined safari jacket, and a broad-brimmed safari hat that hung from its chin strap down his back, they wore expensive, tailored business suits. They were smooth-looking men with the sophisticated manners of the privileged business class.

As the noisy rotors thundered, Tremont greeted each with the broad smile and vigorous handshake of an old friend. The chopper copilot jumped out to unload luggage. Tremont waved toward the lodge and turned to lead his visitors there.

Moments after the Helibus took off into the twilight, a smaller 206B JetRanger III helicopter settled into the clearing. Two men very different from the occupants of the first helicopter stepped from the JetRanger. They wore ordinary, off-the-rack suits no one would look at twice. The tall, swarthy man in the dark blue suit had a pockmarked face with heavy-lidded eyes and a nose as curved and sharp as a scimitar. The round-faced, bland-looking man with the big shoulders and lanky brown hair wore charcoal gray. Neither had luggage. It was not only the ordinary clothes and lack of suitcases that marked them as different. There was something about the way they moved . . . a trained predatory manner that anyone who knew about such things would recognize as dangerous.

The pair ducked under the JetRanger's flashing rotors and followed the others toward the lodge.

Although Victor Tremont never looked back, the four other men noticed the last two. They glanced at each other uneasily, as if they had seen both men before.

Nadal al-Hassan and Bill Griffin showed no reaction to either Tremont's indifference or to the nervousness of the other four. Silently, their gazes swept all around, and they entered the lodge by a different door.

■

At the long Norwegian banquet table, Victor Tremont and his four guests dined on a feast that could have come from Valhalla itself—wild duck confit with shitaki mushrooms, poached local lake trout, and venison shot by Tremont himself, with braised Belgian endive, potatoes dauphin, and a Rhone Hermitage reduction sauce. Flushed and sated, the men chose overstuffed chairs in the vast living room. They indulged in cognac, Rémy Martin Cordon Bleu, and cigars—Cuban Maduros made exclusively for Tremont. After they were settled in around the blazing fire, Tremont finished his status report on the project that had consumed their imaginations, hopes, and lives for the last dozen years.

"... we'd always hypothesized the mutation would take place in the American subjects as much as a year later than it did in the non-American subjects. A matter of general health, nutrition, physical fitness, and genetics. Well ..."

Tremont paused for emphasis and to study their faces. They had all been with him from the start—a year after he had returned from Peru with the odd virus and the monkeys' blood. There was George Hyem far off to the right, like a wing gunner. Tall and ruddy, in those days he had been a young accountant who had seen the financial potential instantly. Now he was chief accountant for Blanchard while actually working for Tremont. Next to him was Xavier Becker, going to fat, a computer genius who had shortened research on improving the virus and the serum by five years. Opposite Tremont sat Adam Cain, post-doc virologist who had seen George's numbers and decided his future was with Blanchard and Tremont, rather than with the CDC. He had found a way to isolate the lethal mutated virus and keep it stable for as much as a week. On Becker's other side was Blanchard's security chief, Jack McGraw, who had covered all their asses from the start.

His four clandestine associates were ready and eager for the payoff.

Tremont held the pause another beat. "The virus has surfaced here in the United States. Soon it's going to appear across the world. Country by country. An epidemic. The press doesn't know about it yet, but they will. No way to stop them or the virus. The only recourse governments will have is to pay our price."

The four men grinned. Their eyes shone with dollar signs. Big dollar signs. But there was something else, too—triumph, pride, anticipation, and eagerness. They were already professional successes. Now they were going to be financial successes, hugely wealthy, achieving the pinnacle of the American dream.

Tremont said, "George?"

George abruptly reset his face. He looked sad, crestfallen. "The profit projection for the stockholders is ready any time." He hesitated. "I'm afraid it's less than we'd hoped. Perhaps only five . . . six at best . . . *billion dollars*." And laughed uproariously at his joke.

Xavier Becker, frowning severely at George's levity, did not wait to be asked. "What about the secret audit I discovered?"

"Jack says that only Haldane has actually seen it," Tremont told them, "and I'll handle him when we meet before the board dinner at the annual meeting. What else, Xavier?" Mercer Haldane was chairman of Blanchard Pharmaceuticals.

"I've manipulated the computer logs to show we've been working on the cocktail of recombinant antibodies that form our serum the whole ten years, improving it since we got the patent, and that we've finished our final tests and submitted it for FDA approval. The logs also now show our astronomical costs." Excitement was in Xavier's voice. "Supply's in the millions of doses and climbing."

Adam laughed. "No one suspects a damn thing."

"Even if they suspect, they'll never find the trail." Jack McGraw, the security chief, rubbed his hands, pleased.

"Just tell us when to move!" George begged.

Tremont smiled and held up his hand. "Don't worry, I've got a complete timetable based on how fast they realize they've got an epidemic on their hands. I'll make my move on Haldane before the board meeting."

The five men drank, their futures growing brighter every second.

Then Tremont put down his brandy. His face grew somber. He again raised a hand to silence them. "Unfortunately, we've run into a situation that could be more of a problem than the audit. How big or small the danger is, or whether there's any danger at all after some, ah, steps we were forced to take, we can't be certain yet. But rest assured it's being watched and thoroughly dealt with."

Jack McGraw scowled. "What kind of problem, Victor? Why wasn't I told?"

Tremont eyed him. "Because I don't want Blanchard even remotely connected." He expected Jack to be jealous of security, but in the end Tremont made all decisions. "As for the problem, it was simply one of those events no one could anticipate. When I was in Peru on that expedition where I found the virus and the potential serum, I ran into a group of young undergraduates on a field trip. Beyond being polite, we paid little attention to each other because we were interested in different studies." He shook his head in wonderment. "But three days ago one called. When she said her name, I vaguely recalled a student who had shown a lot of interest in my work. She went on to become a cell and molecular biologist. The problem was she's now at USAMRIID, which is studying the first deaths. As we expected, they hadn't been able to figure out the virus. But the unique combination of symptoms suddenly brought that trip to Peru back into her mind. She remembered my name. She called me."

"Jesus!" George exclaimed, his ruddy face gone white.

"She tied the virus to you?" Jack McGraw growled.

"To us!" Xavier exploded.

Tremont shrugged. "I denied it. I convinced her she was wrong, that there'd been no such virus. Then I sent Nadal al-Hassan and his people to eliminate her."

There was a collective relaxation in the giant living room. Sighs of relief as the tension eased. They had worked hard and long for more than a decade, had risked their professions and livelihoods on this one visionary gamble, and none had any intention of losing the riches that were now within reach.

"Unfortunately," Tremont went on, "we were unsuccessful in doing the same to her fiancé and research partner. He escaped us, and it's possible she had time to speak to him before she died."

Jack McGraw understood. "That's why al-Hassan is here. I knew something was up."

Tremont shook his head. "Don't make more of this than there is. I sent for al-Hassan to report on how we stood. While I have the most to lose, we're all in it together."

The silence in the room was louder than any noise.

Xavier broke it. "Okay. Let's hear what he's got to say."

The fire had died down to glowing coals and a few flickering flames. Tremont moved to the side of the stone fireplace. He pressed a button in the carved mantlepiece. First Nadal al-Hassan and then Bill Griffin entered the cavernous room. Al-Hassan joined Victor Tremont before the fireplace, while Griffin remained unobtrusive in the background. Al-Hassan related details of Sophia Russell's call to Tremont, her death, and his removal of everything that could connect the virus to the Hades Project. He described Jonathan Smith's reactions. He detailed Griffin's blackmailing of Lily Lowenstein and the subsequent erasure of all electronic evidence.

"Nothing remains to connect us to Russell or the virus," al-Hassan finished, "unless she told Colonel Smith."

Jack McGraw growled, "That's a pretty damn big 'unless.'"

"That is what I think," al-Hassan agreed. "Something has made Smith suspicious that her death was not an accident. He has been investigating vigorously, ignoring his share of the scientific work on the virus itself."

"Can he find us?" the accountant, George, asked nervously.

"Anyone can find anyone if they look long enough and hard enough. That is why I think we must eliminate him."

Victor Tremont nodded to the rear of the room. "But you don't agree, Griffin?"

Everyone rotated to stare at the former FBI man, who was leaning against a wall behind them. Bill Griffin was thinking about Jon Smith. He had done his damnedest to warn his friend off. He had used his old FBI credentials to learn from Jon's office that he was out of town, and then he had gone through a Rolodex of agencies acquiring one bit of information after another until he had finally uncovered which conference Jon was attending and, from there, where in London he had been staying.

So as his canny gaze swept the five who stared at him, he did what he had to do to save himself, while trying to distract the heat from Jon: He shrugged, noncommittal. "Smith's been working so hard to find out what happened to the Russell woman that I think she must've told him nothing about Peru or us. Otherwise, he'd likely be here right now, knocking on the door to talk to you, Mr. Tremont. But our mole inside USAMRIID says Smith's stopped investigating her death and is back concentrating on the virus with the team. He's even flying to California tomorrow to do the routine interviews with the family and friends of Major Anderson."

Tremont nodded thoughtfully. "Nadal?"

"Our contact in Detrick says General Kielburger ordered Smith to California, but he refused," al-Hassan reported. "Later he volunteered to go, and that is a very different matter. I believe he is seeking corroboration in California for what he already suspects."

Griffin said, "He's a doctor, so he was at the autopsy. No big deal. They found nothing. There's nothing to suspect. You've taken care of everything."

"We do not know what Smith found at the autopsy," al-Hassan said.

Griffin grimaced. "Kill him, then. That solves one problem. But every new murder increases the danger of questions and discovery. Especially the murder of Dr. Russell's fiancé and research partner. And especially if he's already told General Kielburger about the attacks on him in D.C."

"To wait could be too late," al-Hassan insisted.

The silence in the room seemed heavy enough to crush the lodge itself. The conspirators glanced at one another and settled their uneasy gazes on their aristocratic leader, Victor Tremont.

He paced slowly in front of the fire, a frown creasing his forehead.

At last he decided, "Griffin could be right. Better we not risk another killing involving the Detrick staff so soon."

Again they looked at one another. This time they nodded. Nadal al-Hassan watched the silent vote, then he moved his hooded eyes to study Bill Griffin where the ex–FBI agent lurked in the room's shadows.

"Well," Tremont said, smiling, "that's settled. We'd better get some sleep. With final plans to make, tomorrow will be a busy day." He shook each man's hand warmly, the gracious host and leader, as they exited the imposing living room.

Al-Hassan and Griffin were last.

Victor Tremont gestured them to him. "Watch Smith carefully. I don't want him to shave without your knowing when, where, and how close." He looked down at the glowing coals of the fire as if they were oracles for the future. Suddenly he lifted his head. Al-Hassan and Griffin were just turning away to leave. He called them back.

When they stood close in front of him, he said in a low, hard voice, "Don't misunderstand me, gentlemen. If Dr. Smith proves to be trouble, of course he has to be purged. Life is a balance of risk and security, victory and loss. What we might lose in a few pointed questions about the coincidences of his and his fiancée's deaths could prove to be more than offset by stopping him from revealing the circumstances of her death."

"If he's really digging around."

Tremont aimed his analytical gaze at Bill Griffin. "Yes, *if*. It's your job to discover that, Mr. Griffin." His voice was abruptly cold, a warning. "Don't disappoint me."

Chapter
Twelve

10:12 A.M., Wednesday, October 15
Fort Irwin, Barstow, California

The C-130 transport from Andrews Air Force Base touched down at the Southern California Logistical Airport near Victorville at 1012 on a warm, windy morning. A military police Humvee met Smith on the runway.

"Welcome to California, sir," the driver greeted Smith as he grabbed his bag and held the vehicle's door open.

"Thanks, Sergeant. Are we driving to Irwin?"

"To the helicopter landing area, sir. There's a chopper from Irwin waiting for you there."

The driver heaved Smith's bag into the rear, climbed behind the wheel, and careened off across the tarmac. Smith hung on as the big combat vehicle bounced across ruts and potholes until it reached a waiting helicopter ambulance marked with the logo of the Eleventh Armored Cavalry Regiment—a rearing black stallion on a diagonal red-and-white field. Its rotors were already pivoting for takeoff.

An older man wearing the gold leaf of a major and a medical caduceus stepped out from beneath the long blades. He held out his hand and shouted, "Dr. Max Behrens, Colonel. Weed Army Hospital."

An enlisted man took Smith's bag, and they climbed into the vibrating ambulance chopper. It lurched into the air and banked at a steep angle, low across the desert. Smith looked down as they passed over two-lane highways and the buildings of small towns. Soon they were following the broad four lanes of Interstate 15.

Dr. Behrens leaned toward him to yell over the wind and noise. "We've kept close watch on all units on the base, and no other cases of the virus have appeared."

Smith said loudly, "Mrs. Anderson and the others ready to talk with me?"

"Yessir. Family, friends, everyone you need. The colonel of OPFOR said you're to have anything you want, and he'd be glad to speak with you himself if that'd help."

"OPFOR?"

Behrens grinned. "Sorry, forgot you've been at Detrick awhile. That's our mission—Opposing Force. What the Eleventh Cav does here is act the role of enemy to all the regiments and brigades that come through for field training. We give them one hell of a hard time. It entertains us and makes them better soldiers."

The helicopter flew across a four-lane highway and plunged deeper into the rock-strewn desert until Smith saw a road below, a WELCOME sign, and at the top of a hill a jumble of piled rocks all painted with the brightly colored logos and patches of units that had been stationed there or passed through Irwin over the years.

They swept on above lines of fast-moving vehicles trailing clouds of dust. It was startling how much the visually modified American vehicles looked like Russian mechanized infantry BMP-2s, BRDM-2s, and armored division T-80 tanks. The chopper swooped over the main post and settled to the desert floor in a cloud of sand. A reception committee was waiting, and Smith was jolted back to why he was here.

∎

Phyllis Anderson was a tall woman and a little heavy, as if she had eaten too many transient meals on too many army bases. Her full face was drawn as they sat on packing boxes in the silent living room of the pleasant house. She had the frightened eyes Smith had seen on so many relatively young army widows. What was she going to do now? She had spent her entire married life living from camp to camp, fort to fort, in on-base or off-base housing that was never her own. She had nowhere to call home.

"The children?" she said in answer to Smith's question. "I sent them to my parents. They're too young to know anything." She glanced at the packed boxes. "I'll join them in a few days. We'll have to find a house. It's a small town. Near Erie, Pennsylvania. I'll have to get some work. Don't know what I can do . . ."

She trailed off, and Smith felt brutal bringing her back to what he needed to ask.

"Was the major ever sick before that day?"

She nodded. "Sometimes he'd run a sudden fever, maybe a few hours, and then it'd go away. Once it went on for twenty-four hours. The doctors were concerned but couldn't find a cause, and he always got better without any problem. But a few weeks ago he came down with a heavy cold. I wanted him to take some sick days, at least stay out of the field, but that wasn't Keith. He said wars and hostile skirmishes didn't stop for a cold. The colonel always says Keith can outlast anyone in the field." She looked down at her lap where her hands twisted a ragged tissue. "Could."

"Anything you can tell me that might be connected to the virus that killed him?"

He saw her flinch at the word, but there was no other way to ask the question.

"No." She raised her eyes. They held the same pain he felt, and he had to fight to keep it from reflecting in his own eyes. She continued, "It was over so fast. His cold seemed better. He took a good afternoon nap. And then he woke up dying." She bit her lower lip to stop a sob.

He felt his eyes moisten. He reached out and put his hand on top of hers. "I'm so sorry. I know how difficult it is for you."

"Do you?" Her voice was forlorn, but there was a question in it, too. They both knew he could not bring back her husband, but might he have a magic remedy to wipe away the endless, bottomless pain that made her ache from every cell?

"I do know," he said softly. "The virus killed my fiancée, too."

She stared, shocked. Two tears slid down her cheeks. "Horrible, isn't it?"

He cleared his throat. His chest burned, and his stomach felt as if it had just been invaded by a cement mixer. "Horrible," he agreed. "Do you think you can go on? I want to find out about this virus and stop it from killing anyone else."

She was still a soldier's wife in her mind, and action was always the best comfort. "What else do you want to know?"

"Was Major Anderson in Atlanta or Boston recently?"

"I don't think he was ever in Boston, and we haven't been in Atlanta since we left Bragg years ago."

"Where else besides Fort Bragg did the major serve?"

"Well . . ." She reeled off a list of bases that covered the country from Kentucky to California. "Germany, too, of course, when Keith was with the Third Armored."

"When was that?" Marburg hemorrhagic fever, a close cousin of Ebola, had first been discovered in Germany.

"Oh, 1989 through '91."

"With the Third Armored? Then he went to Desert Storm?"

"Yes."

"Anywhere else overseas?"

"Somalia."

That was where Smith had his fatal encounter with Lassa fever. It had been a small operation, but had he known everything that happened there? An unknown virus was always possible deep in the jungles and deserts and mountains of that unfortunate continent.

Smith pressed on. "Did he ever talk about Somalia? Was he sick there? Even briefly? One of those sudden fevers that went away? Headaches?"

She shook her head. "Not that I remember."

"Was he ever sick in Desert Storm?"

"No."

"Exposed to any chemical or biological agents?"

"I don't think so. But I remember he did say the medics sent him to a MASH for a minor shrapnel wound and some doctors said the MASH could've been exposed to germ warfare. They inoculated everyone who went through."

Smith's gut did a flip, but he kept the excitement from his voice. "Including the major?"

She almost smiled. "He said it was the worst inoculation he ever got. Really hurt."

"You don't happen to recall the MASH number?"

"No, I'm sorry."

Soon after that he ended the interview. They stood in the shade of her front porch, talking about nothing. There was solace in the normal interactions of everyday life.

But as he stepped off the porch, she said in a tired voice, "Are you the last one, Colonel? I think I've told everything I know."

Smith turned. "Someone else questioned you about the major?"

"Major Behrens over at Weed, the colonel, a pathologist from Los Angeles, and those awful government doctors who called here on Saturday asking terrible things like poor Keith's symptoms, how long he lived, how he looked at the—" She shuddered.

"Last Saturday?" Smith puzzled. What government doctor could have called on *Saturday*? Both Detrick and the CDC had barely started their investigations of the virus. "Did they say who they worked for?"

"No. Just government doctors."

He thanked her again and left. In the glaring sun and hard wind of the high desert, he walked to his next interview thinking about what he had learned. Could the virus have been contracted by Major Anderson in Iraq—or given to him there—and then lain dormant over the next ten years, except for unexplained mild fevers, finally erupting into what seemed like a simple heavy cold . . . and death?

He knew no virus that acted that way. But then no virus they had known had acted like HIV-AIDS until it exploded from the heart of Africa onto the world.

And who were the "government doctors" who had called Phyllis Anderson before anyone outside the CDC and Fort Detrick was even aware that there was a new virus?

8:22 P.M.
Lake Magua, New York

Congressman Benjamin Sloat mopped his balding head and took another gulp of Victor Tremont's single malt. He and Tremont were sitting in the dark sunroom that looked out over the nighttime deck and grassy lawn. While they had been talking, a large-eyed doe had strolled across the deck as if she owned it, and Victor Tremont had merely smiled. Congressman Sloat had decided long ago he would never understand Tremont, but then he did not need to. Tremont meant contacts and campaign contributions and a big chunk of Blanchard Pharmaceuticals stock, an unbeatable combination in this high-priced political age.

The congressman grumbled, "Dammit, Victor, why didn't you clue me in earlier? I could've headed this Smith off. Got him and the woman shipped overseas. We wouldn't have a murder to cover up and a damned snooper nosing in the closet."

From his armchair, Tremont gestured with his cigar. "Her call was such a shock all I could think of was getting rid of her. It's only now that we know how close she and Smith were."

Sloat drank moodily. "Can we just ignore him? Hell, the woman'll be buried and forgotten soon, and it sure looks like Smith doesn't know much yet. Maybe it'll blow over."

"You want to take that chance?" Tremont studied the sweating chairman of the Armed Services Committee. "All hell's going to break loose around the world soon, and we'll be the white knights to the rescue. Unless someone stumbles onto something incriminating and blows the whistle on us."

Half-hidden in the flickering shadows of the farthest corner of the sunroom, Nadal al-Hassan warned, "Dr. Smith is at Fort Irwin at this moment. He may hear of our 'government doctors.'"

Tremont contemplated the thick ash of his cigar. "Smith's come a long way already. Not far enough to hurt us, but enough to get our attention. If he gets too close, Nadal will eliminate him without drawing attention to us or the death of Sophia Russell. Something very different. A tragic accident. Isn't that right, Nadal?"

"Suicide," the Arab offered from the shadows. "He is obviously distraught over Dr. Russell's death."

"That could be good, if you can make it airtight," Tremont agreed. "Meanwhile, Congressman, block his investigation. Keep him in the lab. Get him reassigned. Anything."

"I'll call General Salonen. He'll know the right man," Sloat decided. "We'll need to keep the virus under wraps. Extreme sensitivity. Smith's only a doctor, an amateur, and this is a job for the pros."

"That sounds about right."

Sloat finished his single malt, smacked his lips, nodded in appreciation, and stood. "I'll call Salonen right away. But not from here. Better to use a pay phone in the village."

After the congressman left, Tremont continued to smoke. He spoke without looking at Nadal al-Hassan. "We should've eliminated Smith. You were right. Griffin was wrong."

"Perhaps. Or perhaps, in his view, he was quite right."

Tremont turned. "How so?"

"I have wondered how Dr. Smith appeared to be so alert for our initial attacks. Why was he in that park so late, so far from his home in Thurmont? Why was he so ready to suspect murder?"

Tremont studied the Arab. "You think Griffin warned him. Why? Griffin stands to lose as much as the rest of us if we're exposed." He paused thoughtfully. "Unless he's still working for the FBI?"

"No, I checked that. Griffin is independent, I am sure. But perhaps he and Dr. Smith had some association in the past. My people are investigating."

Victor Tremont had been frowning. Now he suddenly smiled. He told al-Hassan, "There's a solution. An elegant solution. Keep checking the pasts of the two men, but at the same time tell your associate, Mr. Griffin, that I have changed my mind. I want him to personally find Smith . . . and eliminate him. Yes, kill him quickly." He nodded coldly and smiled again. "This way we'll discover where Mr. Griffin's loyalties actually lie."

Chapter Thirteen

9:14 A.M., Thursday, October 16
Fort Detrick, Maryland

The rest of his interviews at Fort Irwin yesterday had added nothing more to what he had learned from Phyllis Anderson. After the last interview, Smith had flown all night from Victorville, sleeping fitfully most of the way. From Andrews, he drove straight to Fort Detrick, seeing no suspicious vehicles either following him or waiting at Detrick. The reports from the other family and associates interviews were in. They told him the homeless victim in Boston and the late father of the dead girl in Atlanta had also been in the army during the Gulf War. He searched the service records of all three soldiers.

Sgt. Harold Pickett had been in 1-502 Infantry Battalion, Second Brigade, 101st Air Assault Division in Desert Storm. He had been wounded and treated at 167th MASH. Specialist Four Mario Dublin had been an orderly at the 167th MASH. There was no record of the then-lieutenant Keith Anderson having been treated at the 167th, but units of the Third Armored had been at the Iraq-Kuwait border near the 167th.

The results made Smith reach once more for the telephone. He dialed Atlanta.

"Mrs. Pickett? Sorry to call you so early. I'm Lt. Col. Jonathan Smith from the U.S. Army Medical Research Institute for Infectious Diseases. May I ask you a few questions?"

The woman at the other end was close to hysterics. "No more. Please, Colonel. Haven't you people—"

Smith pressed on. "I know it's terribly difficult for you, Mrs. Pickett, but we're trying to prevent more girls like your daughter from dying the way she did."

"Please—"

"Two questions."

As the silence stretched, he thought she might have just walked away from the phone. Then her voice sounded again, low and dull. "Go ahead."

"Was your daughter ever injured badly enough to need a blood transfusion, and did your husband donate the blood?"

Now the silence radiated fear. "How . . . how did you know?"

"It had to be something like that. One last question: Did government doctors call you on Saturday to ask questions about her death?"

He could almost hear her nod. "They certainly did. I was shocked. They were like ghouls. I hung up on them."

"No identification beyond just 'government doctors'?"

"No, and I hope you fire them all."

The line went dead, but he had what he needed.

All three soldiers had almost certainly been inoculated against "possible bacteriological warfare agent contamination" at the same MASH unit in Iraq-Kuwait ten years ago.

Smith dialed Brigadier General Kielburger's extension to tell him about the interviews.

"Desert Storm?" Kielburger almost squeaked in alarm. "Are you sure, Smith? Really sure?"

"As sure as I am of anything right now."

"Damn! That'll explode the Pentagon after all the medical headaches and lawsuits about Gulf War syndrome. Don't talk to anyone until I've checked this with the Pentagon. Not a word. You understand?"

Smith hung up in disgust. Politics!

He went to lunch to think and decided the next thing to do was to locate the "government doctors." Someone had ordered them to make those calls, but who?

■

Four long, wasted hours later, it was Smith who was ready to explode as he repeated into the telephone receiver, ". . . Yes, doctors who called Fort Irwin, California, Atlanta, and probably Boston. They asked nasty questions about the virus victims' deaths. The families are steamed, and I'm getting damn mad, too!"

"I'm just doing my job, Dr. Smith." The woman on the other end of the line was testy. "Our director was killed in a hit-and-run accident yesterday, and we're shorthanded. Now tell me your name and your company again."

He took a long breath. "Smith, Lieutenant Colonel Jonathan. From U.S. Army Medical Research Institute for Infectious Diseases at Fort Detrick."

There was silence. She seemed to be writing down his name and "company." She came back on. "Hold, please."

He fumed. He had been running into the same bureaucratic red tape for the past four hours. Only the CDC had confirmed that they had not called the families. The surgeon general's office told him to put his request in writing. The various possible institutes at NIH referred him to general information, and the man there said they had been ordered to not discuss anything to do with those deaths. No matter how much he had explained that *he* was a government researcher already working on those deaths, he had gotten nowhere.

By the time he was turned away by the departments of the navy and air force and Health and Human Services, he knew he was being stonewalled. His last chance was the NIH's Federal Resource Medical Clearing House (FRMC). After that he was out of options.

"This is Acting Director Aronson of FRMC. How can I help you, Colonel?"

He tried to speak calmly. "I appreciate your talking to me. There seems to be a team of government doctors interested in the virus at Fort Irwin, Atlanta, and—"

"Let me save you time, Colonel. All information on the viral incident at Fort Irwin has been classified. You'll have to go through channels."

Smith finally blew up. "I *have* the virus! I'm *working* with it! USAMRIID *is* the information. All I want is—"

The dial tone buzzed angrily in his ear.

What in hell was going on? It looked as if some idiot had clamped a lid on anything to do with the virus. No information without clearance. But from whom? And why?

He rushed out the door, strode furiously along the corridor, and barged past Melanie Curtis and into Kielburger's office. "What the hell's going on, General? I try to find out who had those teams of 'government doctors' call Irwin and Atlanta and everyone yells 'top secret' and won't talk."

Kielburger leaned back in his desk chair. He knitted his thick fingers over his beefy chest. "It's out of our hands, Smith. The whole investigation. *We're* top secret. We do our research and then report to the surgeon general, military intelligence, and NSC. Period. No more detectives."

"In this investigation, we *are* the detectives."

"Tell the Pentagon that."

In a flash of understanding, the past frustrating three hours suddenly made sense. This could not be merely government red tape. There was too much of it, too many agencies were involved. And it was illogical. You did not take an investigation away from those who knew what was going on. Certainly not a scientific investigation. If there were other teams of "government doctors," there was no reason to keep that from him or anyone else at USAMRIID.

Unless they were not government doctors at all.

"Listen, General. I think—"

The general interrupted, disgusted. "Your hearing gone, Colonel? Don't you understand orders anymore? We stand down. The professionals will work on Dr. Russell's death. I suggest you go back to your lab and focus on the virus."

Smith took a deep breath. Now he was not only furious, he was scared. "Something's very wrong here. Either someone very powerful is manipulating the army, or it's the army itself. They want to stop the investigation. They're stonewalling this virus, and they're going to end up killing one hell of a lot of people."

"Are you crazy? *You're* in the army. And those were direct orders!"

Smith glared. He had been fighting grief all day. Every time Sophia's face flashed into his mind, he had tried to banish her. Sometimes he would see something of hers—her favorite pen, the photos on her office wall, the little bottle of perfume she kept on top of her desk—and he would start to fall apart. He wanted to sink to his knees and howl at the unseen forces that had stolen Sophia, and then he wanted to kill them.

Smith snarled, "I resign. You'll have the paperwork this afternoon."

Now Kielburger lost his temper. "You can't quit in the middle of a goddamn crisis! I'll have you court-martialed!"

"Okay. I've got a month's leave coming. I'm taking it!"

"No leave! Be in your lab tomorrow or you're AWOL!"

The two men faced each other across Kielburger's desk. Then Smith sat down. "They murdered her, Kielburger. They killed Sophia."

"Murdered?" Kielburger was incredulous. "That's ridiculous. The autopsy report was clear. She died as a result of the virus."

"The virus killed her, yes, but she didn't contract it by any accident. We missed it at first, maybe because the reddening didn't appear for a few hours. But when we took a second look, we spotted the needle mark in her ankle. They injected the virus."

"A needle mark in her ankle?" Kielburger had a concerned frown. "Are you sure she wasn't—"

Smith eyes were hard blue agates. "There was no reason for an injection except to give her the virus."

"For God's sake, Smith, why? It makes no sense."

"It does if you remember the page cut from her logbook. She knew— or suspected—something they didn't want her to know. So they cut out her notes, stole her phone log, and killed her."

"Who are *they*?"

"I don't know, but I'm going to find out."

"Smith, you're upset. I understand. But there's a new virus loose to run across the world. There could be an epidemic."

"I'm not sure about that. We've got three widely separated cases that haven't infected anyone else in their areas. Did you ever hear of a virus breakout in which only one single person in an area was infected?"

Kielburger considered the question. "No, I can't say I have, but—"

"Neither has anyone else," Smith told him grimly. "We still get new viruses, and nature confounds us all the time. But if the virus is as deadly as it appears, why haven't there been more cases in each of the three areas since? At best it indicates this virus isn't very contagious. The victims' families and neighbors didn't get it. No one in the hospitals got it. Even the pathologist who was sprayed with blood didn't get it. The only person we can be sure of who got it from someone else is the Pickett girl in Atlanta, who had a direct blood transfusion from her father years ago. That indicates two facts: One, the virus, like HIV, appears to exist in a dormant state inside a victim for years, and then it suddenly turns virulent. Two, it seems to take a direct injection into the bloodstream for infection, either in the dormant state or the virulent state. In any event, an epidemic looks remote."

"I wish you were right." Kielburger grimaced. "But you're dead wrong this time. There are already more cases. People are sick and dying. This crazy virus may not be highly contagious in the usual ways, but it's still spreading."

"What about Southern California? Atlanta? Boston?"

"Not in any of those places. It's in other parts of the world—Europe, South America, Asia."

Smith shook his head. "Then it's still all wrong." He paused. "They murdered Sophia. You understand what that means?"

"Well, I'm—"

Smith stood up and leaned across the desk. "It means someone has this virus in a test tube. An unknown, deadly virus no one's been able to match or trace. But someone knows what this virus is, and where it comes from, *because they've got it.*"

The general's heavy face turned purple. "Got it? But—"

Smith hammered his fist on the desk. "We're dealing with people who have given the virus to other people! To *Sophia.* They're willing to use it like a weapon!"

"My God." Kielburger stared at him. "*Why?*"

"Why and who, that's what we've got to find out!"

Kielburger's burly body seemed to quiver in shock. Then he abruptly stood up, his florid face as white as it had ever been. "I'll call the Pentagon. Go and write up what you told me and what you want to do from here on."

"I've got to go to Washington."

"All right. Get whatever you need. I'll cut official orders for you."

"Yessir." Smith stood back, relieved and a little stunned that he had finally gotten through Kielburger's thick brain. Maybe the general was not as rigid and stupid as he had thought. For a moment he almost felt affection for the irritating man.

As he ran out the door, he heard Kielburger pick up his phone. "Get me the surgeon general and the Pentagon. Yes, both of them. No, I don't care which one first!"

·

Specialist Four Adele Schweik flipped the intercept shunt on her telephone inside her cubicle, warily listening for any sound of Sergeant Major Daugherty leaving her office. At last she lied briskly into her phone, "Surgeon General Oxnard's Office. No, General Kielburger, the surgeon general isn't in the office. I'll have him call as soon as he returns."

Schweik glanced around. Fortunately, Sandra Quinn was busy in her cubicle, and the sergeant major was in her office. Kielburger's office was calling out again. Schweik answered in a different voice, "Pentagon. Please hold."

She quickly dialed a number she read from a list in her top drawer. "General Caspar, please? Yes, General Kielburger calling urgently from USAMRIID." She took him off hold, returned to her own line, and dialed again. She spoked softly but rapidly, hung up once more, and went back to her work.

5:50 P.M.
Thurmont, Maryland

Smith finished packing in the empty house under the shoulder of Catoctin Mountain. He felt a little ill, and he figured that was no surprise. Sophia was everywhere, from the bottled water in the kitchen to the scent of her in their bed. It broke his heart. The emptiness of the house echoed through him. The house was a tomb, the sepulchre of his hopes, filled with Sophia's dreams and laughter. He could not stay here. He could never live here again.

Not in the house, and not in her condo. He could think of nowhere in the world he wanted to be. He knew he would have to figure that out eventually, but not now. Not yet. First he had to find her killers. Smash them. Crush them into screaming masses of blood and bones and tissue.

In his office after he had left Kielburger, Smith had written up his reports and notes, printed them out, and driven a circuitous route home, watching behind. He had seen no one follow to the big saltbox house he had shared for so many happy months with Sophia. When he had finished packing for a week of any weather, loaded his service Beretta, and grabbed his passport, address book, and cell phone, he dressed in his uniform and waited for Kielburger's call with the word from the Pentagon.

But Kielburger did not call.

It was growing dark at 1800 as he drove back to Fort Detrick. Ms. Melanie Curtis was not at her secretary's desk, and when he checked the general's office, the general was gone, too, but neither office looked as if it had been tidied up for the night. Very unusual. He looked at his watch: 1827. They must be on coffee breaks. But at the same time?

Neither was in the coffee room.

Kielburger's office was still empty.

The only explanation Smith could think of was the Pentagon had called Kielburger to Washington in person, and he had taken Melanie Curtis with him.

But would not Kielburger have called to tell him?

No. Not if the Pentagon had ordered him not to.

Uneasy, and telling no one, he went back down to his battered Triumph. Pentagon permission or not, he was going to Washington. He could not sleep another night in the Thurmont house. He turned on the ignition and drove out the gate. He saw no one watching from outside, but to be sure, he circled the streets for an hour before driving to I-270 and heading south for the Capital. His mind roamed over the past with Sophia. He was beginning to find comfort in remembering the good times. God knew, that was all he had left.

He had had one good night's sleep in three days and wanted to be sure no one was tailing him, so he pulled off abruptly at Gaithersburg and watched the exit to see whether anyone followed. No one did. Satisfied, he drove to the Holiday Inn and checked in under a false name. He drank two beers in the motel bar, ate dinner in the motel dining

room, and went back to his room to watch CNN for an hour before
dialing Kielburger at the office and at home. There was still no answer.

Suddenly he sat bolt upright, shocked. It was the third item on the
national report: *"The White House has reported the tragic death of Brig.
Gen. Calvin Kielburger, medical commander of the United States Army
Medical Research Institute of Infectious Diseases at Fort Detrick, Maryland. The general and his secretary were found dead in their homes, apparently victims of an unknown virus that has already killed four people
in the United States, including another research scientist at Fort Detrick.
The White House emphasizes these tragic deaths are isolated, and there
is no public danger at this time."*

Stunned, Smith's mind quickly grappled with what he knew: Neither
Kielburger nor Melanie Curtis had worked in the Hot Zone with the
virus. There was no way they could have contracted it. This was no
accident or natural spreading of the virus. This was murder . . . two more
murders! The general had been stopped from going to the Pentagon
and the surgeon general, and Melanie Curtis had been stopped from
telling anyone the general's intentions.

And what had happened to the complete secrecy everyone working
on the virus was supposed to maintain? Now the nation knew. Someone
somewhere had done a complete reversal, but why?

*". . . in connection with the tragic deaths at Fort Detrick, the army is
requesting all local police watch for Lt. Col. Jonathan Smith, who has
been declared absent without leave from Detrick."*

He froze in front of the motel television. For a moment it seemed
as if the walls were closing in on him. He shook his head; he had to
parse this out clearly. They had enormous power, this enemy that had
murdered Sophia, the general, and Melanie Curtis. They were out there
looking for him, and now the police wanted him, too.

He was on his own.

Part Two

Chapter Fourteen

9:30 A.M., Friday, October 17
The White House, Washington, D.C.

President Samuel Adams Castilla had been in office three years and was already campaigning for his second term. It was a cool, gray morning in the District, and he had expected a good turnout at the Mayflower Hotel for a fund-raising breakfast, which he had canceled for this emergency meeting.

Annoyed and worried, he stood up from the heavy pine table he used as his Oval Office desk and stalked to the leather chair by the fireplace, where everyone was gathered. As with every president, the Oval Office reflected President Castilla's tastes. No thin-blooded, Eastern seaboard interior decorator for him. Instead, he had brought his Southwestern ranch furniture from the governor's residence in Santa Fe, and an Albuquerque artist had coordinated the red-and-yellow Navajo drapes with the yellow carpet, woven blue presidential seal, and the vases, baskets, and headdresses that made this the most native Oval Office in history.

"All right," he said, "CNN says we've had six deaths from this virus now. Tell me how bad it *really* is and what we're up against."

Sitting around a simple pine coffee table, the men and women were somber but cautiously optimistic. Surgeon General Jesse Oxnard, seated next to the secretary of Health and Human Services, was the first to answer. "There have now been fifteen deaths from an unknown virus that was diagnosed last weekend. That's here in America, of course. We've just recently learned there were six original cases, with three of them surviving. At least that's a little hopeful."

Chief of Staff Charles Ouray added, "Reports from the WHO indicate ten or twelve thousand people overseas have contracted it. Several thousand have died."

"Nothing to require any special emergency action on our part, I'd say." This was the chairman of the Joint Chiefs, Admiral Stevens Brose. He was leaning against the fireplace mantel under a large Bierstadt Rocky Mountain landscape.

"But a virus can spread like wildfire," Secretary of Health and Human Services Nancy Petrelli pointed out. "I don't see how we can in all good conscience wait for the CDC or Fort Detrick to come up with countermeasures. We need to call on the private sector and contact every medical and pharmaceutical corporation for advice and help." She looked hard at the president. "It's going to get worse, sir. I guarantee it."

When some of the others began to protest, the president cut them off. "Just what kind of details do we know about this virus so far?"

Surgeon General Oxnard grimaced. "It's of a type never seen before, as far as Detrick and the CDC can tell. We don't know how it's transmitted yet. It's apparently highly lethal, since three people who worked with it at Detrick have died, although the mortality rate of the first six cases was only fifty percent."

"Three out of six is lethal enough for me," the president told them grimly. "You say we recently lost three scientists at Fort Detrick, too? Who?"

"One was the medical commander, Brig. Gen. Calvin Kielburger."

"Good Lord." The president shook his head sadly. "I remember him. We talked soon after I took office. That's tragic."

Admiral Brose agreed ominously: "It's blown the lid off. I'd declared the matter top secret after the first four deaths because my exec, General Caspar, reported too many amateurs were bumbling around in what could be a critical situation. I was concerned about public panic." He paused for confirmation of the correctness of his decision. Everyone nodded, even the president. The general inhaled, relieved. "But the police were called to General Kielburger's and his secretary's homes when they were discovered dead. The hospital recognized the same virus that'd killed the first USAMRIID scientist. So now the newspeople have it. I've had to open it up, but the media knows it's got to get its information only from the Pentagon. Period."

"Sounds like a good step," Nancy Petrelli, the HHS secretary, agreed. "There's also a scientist who appears to have gone AWOL from Detrick. That concerns me, too."

"He's missing? You know why?"

"No, sir," Jesse Oxnard admitted. "But the circumstances are suspicious."

"He disappeared soon before Kielburger and his secretary died," the Joint Chiefs chairman explained. "We've got the army, the FBI, and the local police alerted. They'll find him. Right now we're saying it's for questioning."

The president nodded. "That sounds reasonable. And I agree with Nancy. Let's see what the private sector can offer. Meanwhile, everyone keep me informed. A lethal virus no one knows anything about scares the hell out of me. It should scare the hell out of all of us."

Chapter Fifteen

9:22 A.M.
Washington, D.C.

The multiethnic neighborhood of Adams-Morgan is a bustling district of rooftop restaurants with sweeping views of the city. Its main arteries—Columbia Road and Eighteenth Street—offer a lively potpourri of sidewalk cafés, neighborhood bars and clubs, new and secondhand bookstores, record stores, funky used-clothing shops, and trendy boutiques. Newcomers in the exotic dress of Guatemala and El Salvador, Colombia and Ecuador, Jamaica and Haiti, both Congos, and Cambodia, Laos, and Vietnam add color to an already picturesque neighborhood.

At a rear table in a coffee shop just off Eighteenth, where coffee mugs had made circular brands that looked so old they might have been there since the days Indians trod local ridges, Special Agent Lon Forbes, FBI, waited for Lt. Col. Jonathan Smith to come to the point. He knew little personal detail about Smith except he claimed to be a friend of Bill Griffin's. That made Forbes both interested and wary.

Since he had had no time to research Smith's background beyond finding out that he was assigned to Fort Detrick as a research scientist, Agent Forbes had suggested they meet in this grungy coffee shop. He had arrived early and watched from across the street as late breakfast seekers strolled past. Then Smith had arrived.

In his drab-green officer's uniform, the lieutenant colonel had stopped to glance around outside, observed the interior from the door, and finally entered. The FBI man noticed the impressive physique of the man and a sense of repressed power. At least from an initial impression, Smith neither looked nor acted like an egghead research scientist in the arcane field of cell and molecular biology.

Smith sipped coffee, chatted about the weather—unseasonably warm—asked if Forbes wanted a pastry—Forbes declined—and tapped his foot under the minuscule table. Forbes watched and listened. The lieutenant colonel's high-planed face was strong, faintly American Indian, and his black hair was swept neatly back. He had navy blue eyes that seemed full of a darkness that had nothing to do with their inky color. Forbes sensed violence that ached to explode. This officer was not only on edge, he was wound as tight as a steel spring.

"I need to get in touch with Bill," Smith finally announced.

"Why?"

Smith pondered the wisdom of answering. At last he decided he would have to take the chance and reveal something of what he knew. After all, he had come here to get help. "A few days ago Bill contacted me, arranged a clandestine meeting in Rock Creek park, and warned me I might be in danger. Now I am in danger, and I need to know more about how he knew and what he knows now."

"That's plain enough. You care to tell me what the danger is?"

"Someone wants to kill me."

"But you don't know who?"

"In a nutshell, no, I don't."

Forbes looked around at the empty tables. "The circumstances, what we call the environment of the danger, you don't want to get into that?"

"Right now, no. I just need to find Bill."

"It's a big Bureau. Why me?"

"I remembered Bill saying you were about his only friend there. The only one he'd trust, anyway. You'd be on his side if the chips were down."

Which was true, Forbes knew, as far as it went, and another plus for Smith. Bill would have told that only to another person he trusted.

"Okay. Now tell me about you and Bill."

Smith described their childhood together, high school and college, and Forbes listened, comparing it to what Griffin had said and what he knew from the personnel file he had studied after Griffin disappeared. It all appeared to match.

Forbes drank coffee. He leaned forward in the somnolent café and contemplated his hands cupped around the mug. His voice was low and serious. "Bill saved my life. Not once, but twice. We were partners and friends and a lot more. Much, much more." He looked up at Smith. "Okay?"

As Forbes looked up at him, Smith tried to see behind his eyes. There was a world of meaning in that single word with a question mark: *Okay?* Did it mean they were so close there were things between him and Bill the Bureau didn't know? Broken rules together? Covered each other's backs? Bent laws? *We did things, okay? Don't ask. Not the details. Just say, when it comes to Griffin, I can be trusted to help. Can you be trusted, too?*

Smith tried, "You know where he is."

"No."

"Can you get in touch with him?"

"Maybe." Forbes drank the coffee more as a time filler than because he wanted it. "He's not with the Bureau anymore. I guess you didn't know that."

"I knew. He told me when we met. What I don't know is whether I should believe him. He could be working undercover."

"He's not undercover." Forbes hesitated. Finally he continued, "He came from freewheeling army intelligence, and the Bureau has rules.

Rules for everything. Questions about every move you make no matter how good the result. Paperwork that has to be filled out for everything. Bill was too much of a self-starter. Initiative does not go down well with the brass. Not to mention secret initiative. The Bureau likes agents to report every breath they breathe in triplicate. That never sat well with Bill."

Smith smiled. "No, it wouldn't have."

"He got into trouble. Insubordination. Not a team player. I took plenty of that myself. But Bill went farther. He cut rules and corners, and he didn't always account for his actions or expenses. He got accused of misappropriating funds. When he made deals to close cases, the Bureau refused to honor some that involved particularly bad characters. They made it hard for Bill, and he finally got disgusted."

"He quit?"

Forbes reached into his jacket for a handkerchief. Smith saw the big 10mm Browning in his shoulder holster. The Bureau still believed in its agents being the men with the bigger guns. Forbes mopped his face. He was clearly worried. But not for himself. For Bill Griffin.

He said, "Not exactly. He'd met someone on a tax-fraud case, some-one with money and power. I never knew who. Bill started missing meet-ings and staying away from the Hoover Building between assignments. When he was sent to work with a field office, sometimes he didn't show up for days. Then he blew an assignment, and there were signs of high living—too much money, the usual. The director found evidence Bill was secretly moonlighting for the tax-fraud guy and that some of what he was doing skated pretty close to the edge—intimidation, using his badge to lean on people, that sort of thing. In the Bureau, if you work for the Bureau, you represent the Bureau. Period. They fired him. He went to work for someone. I had the feeling it was the tax-fraud guy he'd been moonlighting for." He shook his head regretfully. "I haven't seen him in more than a year."

Smith tried to watch the street outside the front windows, but there were too many signs taped to the dirty glass. "I can see where he'd be frustrated, even disgusted. But to work for someone like that? To intimidate others? That doesn't sound like Bill."

"Call it disgust, disillusion, principles betrayed." Forbes shrugged. "As far as he was concerned, no one at the Bureau really cared about justice. It was all about the rules. The law. And, yeah, I think he wanted money and power, too. No one flips sides like a believer who loses his belief."

"And that's okay with you?"

"It's not okay, and it's not not-okay. It's what Bill wants, and I don't ask questions. He's my man regardless."

Smith considered everything. His position was similar to what Bill's had been. Instead of the Bureau, it was the army that was betraying Smith, and how far from going rogue was he right now? In the Pentagon's eyes, he probably already was rogue. Certainly AWOL. Was he the one to judge Bill? Was this FBI man a better friend of Smith's old friend than was Smith?

Moral actions were not always as absolute as we liked to think.

"You don't know where he is? Or who the man he's working for, or with, is?"

Forbes said, "I don't know where he is, or if he's even working for the same guy. It's only a hunch, and I never knew who the guy was."

"But you can get in touch with Bill?"

Forbes's eyes blinked slowly. "Let's say I can. What would you want me to say?"

Smith had already worked that out. "That I took the warning. That I survived, but they murdered Sophia. That I know they have the virus. But I don't know what they're planning, and I need to talk to him."

Forbes studied the big soldier-scientist. The FBI had been briefed days ago on the worrisome situation with the unknown virus, including the death of Dr. Sophia Russell. Then an army memo had arrived this morning declaring Smith AWOL, a danger to the integrity of the investigation, the facts of which had been declared top secret by the

White House. It asked the Bureau to look for Smith and, if they found him, to return him to Fort Detrick under guard.

But a lifetime of learning to assess people, sometimes in a matter of seconds with his life hanging on the outcome, had made Forbes trust himself. Smith was not the enemy. If anything threatened the integrity of the investigation, it was the paranoid order that took the scientific investigators out of the field. The Pentagon didn't want any more headlines about bacteriological warfare agents and our soldiers' possible exposure during Desert Storm. They were covering their sedentary butts as usual.

"If I can contact him, I'll give him your message, Colonel." Forbes stood up. "A tip. Be careful who you talk to, and watch your back, whatever you plan to do. There's an arrest order out for you—AWOL and a fugitive. Don't try to contact me again."

Smith's chest contracted as he listened to the news. He was not surprised, but the confirmation was still a blow. He felt betrayed and violated, but that was the pattern since he had returned from London. First he had lost Sophia, and now he was losing his profession, his career. It stuck in his throat like broken glass.

As the FBI man walked to the door, Smith glanced around the café with its scattering of patrons bent over their exotic coffees and teas. He looked up just in time to see Forbes push through the doorway and scan the bustling street with a long-accustomed eye. Then he was gone, vanishing like the steam from his coffee. Smith put money on the table and slipped out the back door. He saw no one suspicious outside and no dark sedans parked with people in them. His pulse beating a wary tattoo, he walked away briskly toward the distant Woodley Metro station.

Chapter Sixteen

10:03 A.M.
Washington, D.C.

At Dupont Circle, Smith left the Metro. The morning sun radiated down bright and warm on the thick traffic as it circled the park. He glanced casually around and began to walk, joining the throngs of business and government people taking early coffee breaks. His gaze constantly moved as he headed off through the maze of streets that hosted cafés, cocktail lounges, bookstores, and boutiques. The shops here were more upscale than in Adams-Morgan, and even though it was October, tourists were pulling out their billfolds to make purchases.

Several times as he examined faces, he had bittersweet feelings of déjà vu, and for a few exciting moments it seemed as if he had just caught sight of Sophia . . .

She was not dead.

She was alive and vital. Just a few steps away.

There was one brunette who had the same swinging, sexy gait. He had to fight himself from rushing past so he could turn and stare. Another woman had her long blond hair pulled back in the same kind of loose ponytail that Sophia always wore to keep her hair from her face when she worked. Then there was the woman who breezed past leaving a scent so much like Sophia's that his stomach knotted with anguish.

He had to get over this, he told himself sternly.

He had work to do. Crucial work that would give some meaning to Sophia's tragic death.

He inhaled and kept at it. He made himself watch all around for tails. He walked north up Massachusetts Avenue toward Sheridan Circle and Embassy Row. Halfway to Sheridan, he made one last move to assure himself that he had left behind any surveillance: He stepped quickly into the main entrance of the just-opened Phillips Collection, hurried through empty rooms of remarkable Renoirs and Cézannes, provocative Rothkos and O'Keeffes, and slipped out a side fire door. He paused, leaned back against the building, and studied pedestrians and cars.

At last he was satisfied. No one was watching him. If there had been a tail, he had lost him or her. So he hurried back to Massachusetts Avenue and his Triumph parked on a side street.

After hearing the telecast last night about Kielburger, Melanie Curtis, and the AWOL charge against him, he had intensified these evasive maneuvers. Before dawn he had awakened in Gaithersburg on the inner alarm of all combat surgeons in the field. He had been drenched in a cold, sad sweat following a night of dreaming about Sophia. He forced himself to eat a solid breakfast, and he studied the morning traffic as it increased on the highway and the traffic helicopters that monitored it. Showered, shaved, and determined, he was on the road by seven.

He had called Special Agent Forbes from a pay phone and driven across the Potomac into Washington. He had cruised around for a time before parking the Triumph off Embassy Row and hopping on the Metro to meet Forbes.

After retrieving the Triumph, he drove sedately to a busy residential street between Dupont and Washington Circles where a prominent sign marked the entrance to a narrow driveway bordered by a high, unruly hedge: PRIVATE PROPERTY—KEEP OUT! Beneath it hung smaller signs: NO TRESPASSING. NO SALESMEN. NO SOLICITING. NO COLLECTORS. GO AWAY!

Smith ignored the signs and pulled into the driveway. There was a small white clapboard bungalow with black trim hidden behind the hedge. He parked in front of a brick walk that led from the drive to the front door.

As soon as he stepped out, a mechanical voice announced: "Halt! State your name and purpose of visit. Failure to do so within five seconds will result in defensive measures." The deep voice appeared to emanate from the sky with the authority of the heavens.

Smith grinned. The bungalow owner was an electronic genius, and the driveway surface was booby-trapped with a catalog of nasty discomforts, from a cloud of eye-stinging gas to a mercaptan spray that bathed victims in a foul stench. The owner—Smith's old friend Marty Zellerbach—had been hauled into court a few times many years ago by irate salesmen, meter readers, postal officials, and delivery people.

But Marty had two Ph.D.s, and he always appeared mild and responsible, if a little naive. That he was also extremely wealthy and bought the best defense attorneys did not hurt. Their arguments were passionate and convincing: His victims could not have missed his signs. They had to know they were trespassing. They had been asked to perform a perfectly reasonable act of identification by a disabled man who lived alone. And they had been warned.

His security, while annoying, was neither lethal nor seriously injurious. He had always won his cases, and after a few times the police gave up charging him and advised complainants to settle for compensation and quit trespassing.

"Come on, Marty," Smith said, amused, "it's your old pal, Jonathan Smith."

There was a surprised hesitation. Then: "Approach the front door using the brick path. Do not step off the path. That would activate further defensive measures." The stilted voice disappeared, and suddenly the words were concerned. "Careful, Jon. I wouldn't want you to end up stinking like a skunk."

■

Smith took the route Marty described. Invisible laser beams swept the entire property. A footstep off the path, or intrusion from anywhere else, would activate God-knew-what.

He climbed to the covered porch. "Call off the watchdogs, Marty. I've arrived. Open the door."

From somewhere inside, the voice coaxed, "You have to follow the rules, Jon." Instantly the disembodied voice returned: "Stand in front of the door. Open the box to the right and place your left hand on the glass."

"Oh, please." But Smith smiled.

A pair of ominous metal covers over the door slid up to reveal dark tubes that could contain anything from paint guns to rocket launchers. Marty had always found childlike glee in ideas and games most people left behind at adolescence. But Smith gamely stood in front of the door, opened the metal box, and rested his hand on the glass plate. He knew the routine: A video camera snapped a digital photo of his face, and instantly Marty's supercomputer would convert the facial measurements into a series of numerical values. At the same time, the glass plate recorded Smith's palm print. Then the computer compared the collected data to the bar codes it kept on file for everyone Marty knew.

The wooden voice announced: "You are Lt. Col. Jonathan Jackson Smith. Therefore, you may enter."

"Thanks, Marty," he said dryly. "I've been wondering who in the hell I was."

"Very funny, Jon."

A series of dramatic clicks, clanks, and thuds followed, and the wood-covered steel door swung open on a creaky track. Maintenance was not one of Marty's top priorities, but theatricality was. Smith stepped inside what was a traditional foyer except for one imposing detail—his progress was stopped by a walk-in metal cage. As the front door automatically closed behind, Smith waited, trapped by jail-like bars.

"Hi, Jon." Marty's high, slow, precise voice welcomed him from beyond the foyer. As the cage's gate clicked open, Marty appeared in a doorway to the side. "Come in, please." His eyes twinkled with devilment.

He was a small, rotund man who walked awkwardly, as if he had never really learned how to move his legs. Smith followed him into an enormous computer room in a state of utter disorder and neglect. A formidable Cray mainframe and other computer equipment of every possible description filled all wall space and most of the floor, and what furniture there was looked like Salvation Army discards. Steel cages enclosed the draped windows.

As Marty's right hand flopped aimlessly, he held out his left for Smith to shake, while his brilliant green eyes looked away at the left wall of computer equipment.

Smith said, "It's been a while, Marty. It's good to see you."

"Thanks. Me, too." He smiled shyly, and his green eyes made glittering contact and then skittered away again.

"Are you on your medication, Marty?"

"Oh, yes." He did not sound happy about that. "Sit down, Jon. You want some coffee and a cookie?"

Martin Joseph Zellerbach—Ph.D. D.Litt. (Cantab)—had been a patient of Smith's Uncle Ted, a clinical psychiatrist, since Smith and Marty were in grammar school together. F better adjusted and socially mature, Smith had taken Marty under his wing, protecting him from the cruel teasing of other children and even some teachers. Marty was not stupid. In fact, he had tested at the genius level since the age of five, and Smith had always found him funny, nice, and intellectually stimulating. With the years, Marty had grown even more intelligent— and more isolated. In school, he ran academic circles around everyone, but he had no concept of—or interest in—other people and the relationships so important to preteens and teens.

He obsessed on one arcane curiosity after another and lectured at great length. He knew all the answers in many of his courses, so to relieve his boredom he would disrupt his classes with his wild and dazzling fantasies and manias. No one could believe anyone as smart as Marty was not being intentionally rude and a troublemaker, so teachers frequently sent him to the principal's office. In later years, Smith had to fight a number of enraged boys who thought Marty was "dissing" them or their girlfriends.

All of this unusual behavior was the result of Asperger's syndrome, a rare disorder at the less severe end of the autism spectrum. Diagnosed in childhood with everything from "a dash of autism" to obsessive-compulsive disorder and high-functioning autism, Marty was finally diagnosed accurately by Smith's Uncle Ted. Marty's key symptoms were consuming obsessions, high intelligence, crippling lack of social and communications skills, and outstanding talent in a specific area—electronics.

On the milder end, Asperger sufferers were often described as "active but odd" or "autistic-eccentric." But Marty had a slightly more severe case, and despite specialists' attempts to socialize him, except for the few brief trips to court years ago, he had not left this bungalow—which he had carefully and lovingly created as part electronic paradise and part haven for his eccentricities—in fifteen years.

There was no cure, and the only help for people like Marty was medication, usually central nervous system stimulants like Adderall, Ritalin, Cylert, or the new one Marty took—Mideral. As with schizophrenia, the medicines allowed Marty to function with both feet firmly planted on the earth. They restrained his fantasies, enthusiasms, and obsessions. Although he hated them, he took them when he knew he had to do "normal" activities such as pay bills or when his Asperger's was threatening to spin him completely out of control.

But when medicated, Marty said everything was dull and flat and distant, and much of his genius and creativity was lost. So he had eagerly embraced the new medicine that acted fast to calm him, as most did, but whose effects lasted only six hours at most, which meant a dose could be taken more frequently. Living sealed off from the world in his bungalow, he could be off his meds more than most Asperger's sufferers could.

If you needed a computer genius to do creative, maybe illegal, hacking, you wanted Marty Zellerbach off his meds. It was then up to you to keep him on track and to know when it was time to bring him back to earth if he threatened to fly off into an orbit of his own.

Which was why Smith was here.

"Marty, I need help."

"Of course, Jon." Marty smiled, a stained coffee mug in his hand. "It's almost time for a new dose of meds. I'll stay off."

"I was hoping you'd say that." Smith explained about the report from the Prince Leopold Institute in Belgium that did not appear to exist. About the outside phone calls Sophia could have made or received, yet the records were gone. About his need for any information relating to the unknown virus anywhere in the world. "A couple of other things, too. I want to find Bill Griffin. You remember him from school." And finally he described his tracking the three virus victims to the Gulf War and the MASH unit. "See if you can find anything about the virus in Iraq as far back as ten years ago."

Marty put down his mug and made a beeline for his mainframe. He flashed an enthusiastic smile. "I'll use my new programs."

Smith stood. "I'll be back in an hour or so."

"All right." Marty rubbed his hands together. "This is going to be fun."

Smith left him working his sluggish, awkward fingers on the keyboard. The meds would wear off soon, and then, Smith knew, the fingers and the brain would fly until they came close to spiraling off the earth entirely, and Marty would have to take his Mideral again.

Outside, Smith walked quickly to his Triumph. As traffic drove noisily past, he did not notice a helicopter pause high overhead and then speed on, making a long loop to the left to parallel him as he drove toward Massachusetts Avenue.

∎

The noise of the rotors and wind through the open window of the Bell JetRanger vibrated the chopper. Nadal al-Hassan cupped a microphone close to his mouth. "Maddux? Smith has visited a bungalow near Dupont Circle." He located the bungalow on a city map and described the hidden driveway and high hedge. "Find out who lives there and what Smith wanted."

He clicked off his microphone and stared down at the old, classic Triumph below as it headed toward Georgetown. For the first time, al-Hassan felt uneasy. It was not a feeling he would communicate to Tremont, but as a result he would stay close to this Smith. Bill Griffin, even if he were to be trusted, might not be enough to end the threat.

Chapter Seventeen

10:34 A.M.
Washington, D.C.

Bill Griffin had been briefly married, and Smith had met the woman twice back before the couple was even engaged. Both times they had been happily out on the town, hitting the noisy New York bars Bill frequented in his army days. Bill did a lot of loud bars then, perhaps because his life was spent in remote foreign locations where every step could be his last and every sound was an enemy. Smith knew almost nothing about the woman or the marriage, except that it had lasted less than two years. He had heard she still lived in the same Georgetown apartment she had shared with Bill. If Bill was in danger, he might have holed up there, where few people would know to look.

It was a long shot, but aside from Marty, he had few options.

When he reached her apartment house, he used his cell phone to call her.

She answered promptly and efficiently. "Marjorie Griffin."

"Ms. Griffin, you won't remember me, but this is Jonathan Smith, Bill's—"

"I remember you, Captain Smith. Or is it major or colonel by now?"

"I'm not sure what it is, and it doesn't matter anyway, but it was lieutenant colonel yesterday. I see you kept Bill's name."

"I loved Bill, Colonel Smith. Unfortunately for me, he loved his work more. But you didn't call to inquire about my marriage or divorce. You're looking for Bill, right?"

He was wary. "Well—"

"It's all right. He said you might call."

"You've seen him?"

There was a pause. "Where are you?"

"In front of your building. The Triumph."

"I'll come down."

■

In the large, chaotic room crammed with computer terminals, monitors, and circuit boards, Marty Zellerbach leaned forward, concentrating. Torn printouts were stacked in messy piles near his chair. A radio receiver emitted low static as it eavesdropped on the squeals and beeps of data transmissions. The drapes were closed, and the air was cool and dry, almost claustrophobic, which was good for Marty's equipment and the way he liked it. He was smiling. He had used Jon Smith's codes to connect with the USAMRIID computer system and enter the server. Now the real action began. He felt a deep thrill as he scrolled through the various directories until he found the system administrator's password file. He gave a little laugh of derision. The data was scrambled.

He exited and found the file that revealed that the USAMRIID server used Popcorn—one of the latest encryptors. He nodded, pleased. It was first-rate software, which meant the lab was in good hands.

Except that they had not counted on Marty Zellerbach. Using a program he had invented, he configured his computer to search for the password by scrambling every word from *Webster's Unabridged* plus the dialogue of all four *Star Wars* movies, the *Star Trek* television series and feature movies, Monty Python's *Flying Circus*, and every J. R. R. Tolkien novel—all favorites of cybertechs.

Marty jumped up and paced. He grabbed his hands behind his back, and in his weaving gait he moved around the room as if it were a ship on the high seas and he its pirate captain. His program was incredibly fast. Still, like other mortals, he had to wait. Today the best hackers and crackers could steal most passwords, penetrate even the Pentagon's computers, and ride like Old West outlaws through the worldwide Internet. Even a novice could buy software that enabled him to invade and attack Web sites. For that reason, major corporations and government agencies continually heightened their security. As a result, Marty now wrote his own programs and developed his own scanners to find system weaknesses and to break through the firewalls that would stop others.

Suddenly he heard his computer ring the tones of the doorbell from the old *Leave It to Beaver* television show. *Ding-dong-ding.* With a chuckle, he rushed back to his chair, swiveled to face the monitor, and crowed. The password was his. It was not terribly imaginative—Betazoid, named for the extrasensory natives of the *Star Trek* planet called Beta. He had not had to use his more sophisticated password cracker, which included a number randomizer and avoided all real words. With the system administrator's password file, he acquired the system's internal IP—Internet Protocol—address as well. Now he had the blueprint to USAMRIID's computer network, and soon he was "root," too, which meant he had access to every file and could change and delete and trace all data. He was God.

For him, what Jon Smith had asked was not child's play, but it was not climbing Mount Everest either. Quickly Marty scanned all the E-mail messages from the Prince Leopold Institute, but each reported failure to find a match for the new virus. Those files were not what Jon wanted. To most people's eyes, if there was anything else from the lab, it had been completely erased. Gone forever. They would give up now.

Instead, Marty sent another search program to look in the spaces and cracks between data. As more data was inputted onto a system, the new overwrote the old, and once data was overwritten, it supposedly was not retrievable. When his program could find no evidence of any other E-mail from the Belgium lab, Marty figured that was probably what had happened in this case.

He threw back his head and stretched his arms high to the ceiling. His medication had worn off. A thrill rushed through him as his brain seemed to acquire diamondlike clarity. He looked down, and his fingers flew over the keyboard in a race to keep up with his thoughts. He instructed his program to do a different search, this time focusing on bits of the name, E-mail address, and other identifying qualities. With incredible speed, the program searched . . . and there it was—two tiny pieces of the laboratory's name—*opold Inst.*

With a shout, he followed the E-mail's footprints—traces of data and numbers, almost a scent to Marty—to NIH's Federal Resource Medical Clearing House and a terminal accessed only by the password of the director, Lily Lowenstein. From there, he painstakingly tracked the prints forward to the Prince Leopold Institute itself.

His green eyes flashed as he bellowed: "There you are, you *frumious beast!*" It was a reference to Lewis Carroll and the Jabberwock. In a hidden backup file buried deep within the institute's system language he had located an actual copy of the report.

The report had been E-mailed from the Prince Leopold Institute of Tropical Medicine to Level Four labs across the world. After a quick glance, it was evident Jon might find this useful. That decided, Marty tried to trace the E-mail elsewhere. He frowned as the evidence mounted: Someone had erased it not only from its origination site in the central computer of the Prince Leopold Institute but also at the addresses of the various recipients. Or that was what was supposed to have happened. And that was what the average computer nerd, the ordinary hacker, even most electronic security experts would have found.

But not Marty Zellerbach. They came to him—the other cyberspace wizards—for solutions to problems not yet seen and for insights into what had never been done. He had no titles—beyond his Ph.D.s in quantum physics and mathematics and his degree in literature—and he worked for no one but himself. Like a whale trapped on land, in the physical world he flopped and gasped and was an object of pity or derision, but deep in the electronic waters of the cyberocean, he slid sleek and powerful. There he was king—Neptune—and lesser mortals paid homage.

Laughing happily, he flourished his finger like a duelist's sword and jumped to his feet. He punched the print command. As he spun a lopsided pirouette, the machine spat out the report. For Marty, there was nothing quite so satisfying as doing something no one else could. It was small recompense for a life lived alone, and in his quiet moments he occasionally considered that.

But in the end . . . the truth was he looked down upon the lead-footed, numb-headed folks who judged him while living "ordinary" lives and having "relationships." Good grief, despite his Asperger's syndrome, despite his need for drugs, he figured in the last fifteen years of seldom venturing beyond the walls of his bungalow, he had had more relationships than most people in a lifetime. What in heaven's name did the idiots out there think he had been doing? Geesh. What did they think E-mail was for? Dumb!

Grabbing the report, he waved it aloft like the head of a slain enemy. "Monster virus, none can defeat the paladin. And *I* am The Paladin! Victory is mine!"

A half hour later, footprints from the same FRMC terminal led him straight into the antiquated electronic network of the Iraqi government and to a series of reports a year ago concerning an outbreak of ARDS. He printed out those, too, and continued to prowl through the Iraqi cybersystem searching for reports of anything like the virus as far back as Desert Storm. But there was nothing else to find.

Sophia Russell's telephone records were a tougher challenge. He found no intruder footprints in the Frederick phone system. If there had been a record of an unaccounted-for call from Sophia Russell's line to an outside destination, it had been erased from inside the company and every trace removed.

All attempts to find Bill Griffin through college, medical, social security, or any other private or public part of his past had turned up the same message: Address unknown. So Marty launched into the FBI system, which he had penetrated so often his computer could almost do it on its own. His time was limited before they would trace him, because their Intruder Detection System (IDS) was one of the best. He popped in long enough to see that Griffin's official record showed termination for cause. If there were any secret arrangements, Marty found none— no clandestine reports, no pay vouchers, no code passwords, and nothing else to indicate Griffin was undercover. However, the record was flagged, and there was a notation: Griffin's listed address was no longer valid, the Bureau had no current address, and one should be obtained.

Boy, Griffin was really something. Even the FBI wondered where he was.

Far tougher than the FBI's firewall and IDS was the army intelligence system. Once Marty breached the firewall, he had to dash in, read the personnel file, and dash out. He found no current address. Marty scratched his head and pursed his lips. It seemed to him Griffin had not only wanted to vanish, but he had had the expertise to do it. Shocking.

That deserved some respect. Even though Marty had never personally liked Griffin, he had to hand it to him now. So he sat back, crossed his arms, and smiled, not touching his computer for a full thirty agonizing seconds. It was his way of giving the guy some respect.

Then with a flourish he opened a blank file dedicated to Bill Griffin himself. He was not accustomed to failure in the cyberworld, and it both annoyed and inspired him. Bill Griffin had blown him away. But this was not the end. It was the beginning! There was nothing quite so delicious as a new challenge from a worthy opponent, and Griffin was proving to be just that. So Marty grinned. He scratched his chin and willed his brain to leap into the stratosphere. To find a solution in his soaring imagination. That was what he could do off his meds—take flight.

But just as an idea began to form, he jumped, startled. His computer radiated a high-pitched tone and flashed a dazzling red signal:

INTRUDERS! INTRUDERS! INTRUDERS!

More excited than nervous, Marty pressed a key. This could be amusing. The screen revealed:

LOCATIONS A AND X

Eagerly he tapped a button, and two high-resolution monitors came to life on the wall above. At Location A, which was behind the bungalow, two men searched for a way to squeeze through the thick hedge. But it was too dense to be penetrated and too high to climb over. Marty watched their feeble attempts and hooted.

But Location X was another matter. He swallowed hard and stared: An unmarked gray van had stopped in his hidden driveway. Two muscled strangers stepped from it, both holding large semi-automatic pistols as their gazes swept his property. With a jolt of terror, Marty's catalog brain identified one gun as an old Colt .45 1911, while the other was a 10mm Browning of the type used now by the FBI. These intruders were not going to be easily scared off.

Marty's short, stubby body shuddered. He hated strangers and violence of any kind. His round face, so bright and excited seconds ago, was now pale and trembling. He studied the screen as the mechanical voice challenged the men in the front yard.

Just as he suspected, they decided to ignore the warning. They ran toward the front steps—an assault.

In an instant, Marty's mood improved. At least he could have fun for a little while. He snapped his fingers and bounced up and down in his chair as his automatic security system released a cloud of eye-stinging gas. The two men grabbed their faces. They jumped back, coughing and swearing.

Marty laughed. "Next time, *listen* when someone gives you good advice!"

In the rear, the second pair of strangers had stacked garbage cans from the neighbor's yard to climb up over the hedge. Marty watched intently. At just the right moment . . . just as they reached the top of the hedge . . . he tapped a key.

A barrage of heavy rubber bullets knocked them off. They fell hard, flat onto their backs in the neighbor's yard.

Marty had time only to chuckle, because the two in front had recovered enough to stumble through the gas and reach the front door.

"Ah, the pièce de résistance!" Marty promised.

He watched eagerly as a stream of Mace from the ports over the door sent the men staggering and howling back again. He clapped his hands. The short, burly one who seemed to be the leader recovered enough to lurch for the doorknob.

Marty leaned forward eagerly. The knob held a stun device. It sent a shock into the guy's hand. He screamed and jumped.

Marty chortled and spun in his chair to check the other pair. The two in the backyard showed resourcefulness. They had rammed their car through the hedge and were on their feet and moving forward again, crawling under the sweep of lasers.

Marty grinned as he thought about what waited for them: stun devices in the other doors and windows, and cages that would trap them if they got inside.

But all the defenses, diabolical though they were, were not lethal. Marty was a nonviolent man who had never had reason to expect serious danger. His security was aimed at pranksters, trespassers, and tormenters—against outsiders invading his peaceful isolation. He had constructed, invented, bought, and built a child's game of brilliant comic-strip mayhem and secret escape routes.

But none would, in the end, stop determined killers in a real world.

Clammy fear gripped his chest. His heart pounded. But being a genius had its advantages. He had designed a plan a dozen years ago for just this sort of emergency. He grabbed the remote control and the printouts for Jon, and then he rushed into the bathroom. He pressed a button on the remote, and the bathtub reared up against the wall. Another touch of the remote opened a trapdoor hidden under the tub. His chest tight with fear, he climbed down the ladder past the house's crawl space and into a well-lighted tunnel. With two clicks of his remote, the door closed above him and, out of his view, the tub lowered back into place.

Marty inhaled, relieved. In his rolling gait, he swayed and bumped along to another trapdoor overhead.

Seconds later he emerged in a nearly identical bungalow he also owned on the next street. This one was unmodified and empty. It was a deserted house with a perpetual FOR SALE sign and nothing in it except a telephone. Behind him, across the hedge between the bungalows, he could hear curses and yelps of pain. But he also heard the telltale noise of glass shattering, and he knew the attackers would soon be inside his house, searching for his escape route.

Afraid, he grabbed the phone and dialed.

Chapter Eighteen

Georgetown University was founded by Jesuits in 1789, the first Roman Catholic university in the United States. Handsome eighteenth- and nineteenth-century buildings stood among the trees and cobbled lanes, reminders of a time when science knew little of viruses, but education was beginning to be seen as a solution to the violent problems of modern society. Through the window of Georgetown's faculty lounge, Smith thought about this as he admired the old campus under the big trees.

He said, "So you're on the faculty here?"

"Associate professor of history." Marjorie Griffin shrugged sadly. "I suppose Bill never told you what I did. I was at NYU when we met. Then I applied down here."

"He never talked much about his private life," Smith admitted. "Mostly our work and shared past. The old days."

Absentmindedly she stirred her tea. "The few times we saw each other recently, it wasn't even that much. Something's happened to Bill over the last few years. He's become silent, moody."

"When did you last get together, Marjorie?"

"Twice in just the past few days. On Tuesday morning he appeared on my doorstep. And then again last night." She drank tea. "He was nervous, edgy. He seemed worried about you. When he came inside, the first thing he did was go to the front windows and watch the street. I asked him what he was looking for, but he didn't answer. Suggested a cup of tea instead. He had brought a bag of croissants from the French bakery on M Street."

"A spur-of-the-moment visit," Smith guessed. "Why?"

Marjorie Griffin did not answer at once. Her face seemed to sag as she studied the parade of students outside the windows on the cobbled lane. "Touching base, maybe. I hate to think he was saying good-bye. But that could've been it." She looked up at Smith. "I'd hoped you'd know."

She was, Smith realized almost with a shock, a beautiful woman. Not like Sophia, no. A calm beauty. A certain serenity in herself and in who she was. Not passive, exactly, but not restlessly seeking either. She had dark gray eyes and black hair caught in a French knot at the nape of her neck. An easy style. Good cheekbones and a strong jawline. A body between thin and heavy. Smith felt a stirring, an attraction, and then it was gone. It died before it could do more than appear in a flash, unexpected and unwanted, immediately followed by a sharp stab of sorrow. A throb of anguish that was Sophia.

"Two days ago, almost three now," he told her, "he warned me I was in danger." He described the meeting in Rock Creek park, the attacks on him, the virus, and the death of Sophia. "Someone has the live virus, Marjorie, and they killed Sophia, Kielburger, and his secretary with it."

"Good God." Her fine face redrew itself in lines of horror.

"I don't know who or why, and they're trying to stop me from finding out. Bill's working with them."

She covered her mouth with her hand. "No! That's not possible!"

"It's the only way he could've known to warn me. What I'm trying to figure out is whether he's undercover or with them on his own." He hesitated. "His closest friend in the FBI says he isn't undercover."

"Lonny Forbes. I always liked Lonny." She pressed her lips together and shook her head sadly. "Bill's grown harder. More cynical. The last two times I saw him, something was really bothering him. It seemed to me it was about something he's not proud of but won't stop doing because of the way the world is." She picked up her teacup, found it empty, and stared into it. "I'm just guessing about him, of course. I'll never marry again. I see a nice man now and then, but that's all it'll ever be. Bill was my great love. But his great love was his work, and somehow it failed him. What I do know is he feels betrayed. He's lost his faith, you could say."

Smith understood. "In a world with no values except money, he wants his share. It's happened to others. Scientists who sell out for big bucks. Put a monetary value on eradicating disease, curing ills, saving lives. Unconscionable."

"But he can't betray you," Marjorie said. "So he's torn apart by the conflict."

"He's already betrayed me. Sophia's dead."

As she opened her mouth to protest, Smith's cell phone rang. Throughout the faculty lounge, annoyed heads turned.

Smith grabbed the phone from his pocket. "Yes?"

It was Marty, and he sounded both excited and terrified. "Jon, I always said the world was unsafe." He paused and gasped. "Now I've proved it. Personally. There's a whole group of intruders. Well, four actually. They've broken into my house. If they find me, they'll kill me. This is your area of expertise. You've got to save me!"

Smith kept his voice low. "Where are you?"

"At my other house." He gave the address. Suddenly his voice broke. It shook with terror. "Hurry!"

"I'm on my way."

Smith apologized to Marjorie Griffin, scribbled his cell phone number for her, and asked her to call if Bill turned up again. He ran out of the lounge.

■

As Smith drove worriedly past Marty's house, he saw a gray van parked in the driveway. No one appeared to be in the van, and the high hedge and curtains hid the house's interior. He surveyed all around and saw nothing suspicious. There were the usual traffic noises. Smith scanned constantly for trouble as he continued on around the block and pulled into the driveway of a bungalow that was directly behind Marty's. In the front lawn stood a white metal FOR SALE sign rusting around the edges.

From the house's front window, a shade peeled upward, and Marty's frightened face peeked out just above the sill.

Smith ran to the front door.

Marty opened it, clutching a sheaf of papers and a remote control to his chest. "Come in. Hurry. Hurry." He stared fearfully past. "If you were Florence Nightingale, I'd be dead by now. What took you so long?"

"If I were Florence Nightingale, I wouldn't be here. We'd be in different centuries." Smith locked the door and scanned the empty room as Marty checked the front window. "Fill me in. Tell me everything that happened."

Marty dropped the window shade and described the four strangers, their weapons, and their attempts to break in. Meanwhile, Smith strode through the house, checking locks on doors and windows, and Marty followed in his rolling gait. The drapes and curtains were drawn, and the rooms were shadowy with sunlight and dust motes. The place was empty, and as secure as any ordinary house could be. Which was not very.

At last Marty finished his story with a stream of speculations.

"You're right," Smith said soberly, "they'll start searching the neighborhood soon."

"Swell. Just what I wanted to hear." Marty grinned weakly. It came out as a macabre grimace, but it was a brave try.

Smith squeezed his friend's shoulder, trying to keep the urgency from his voice. "How did they know about us, Marty? Did you tell anyone?"

"Not in a quadrillion years."

"Then they had to have followed me, but I don't see how." He quickly went through all the precautions he had taken to shake pursuit since he had left Frederick. "They couldn't have put a transmitter on the Triumph this time."

That was when he heard it . . . a noise that rose above the ambient sounds of the city. At first he could not place it. Then he knew what it was, and how they had followed him. His throat tightened. He strode to the front window, raised the shade, and looked out and up.

"Damn!" He slammed his fist against the wall.

Marty joined him, staring up at the helicopter hovering low to the south on a straight line with the pair of bungalows. As they watched, it banked in a sweeping turn north and came back around toward the house where he and Marty hid. Smith remembered hearing a chopper earlier when he had driven away from Marty's house.

He cursed and slammed the wall again. That was the answer—the Triumph. He knew he had shaken them before he pulled off the Interstate at Gaithersburg—there had been no way they could have bugged the Triumph that time. But how many restored—but battered from last night—'68 Triumphs could there be in the area? Not many, and probably not another on the interstate from Frederick to Washington early this morning. One of those choppers he had seen while eating breakfast in Gaithersburg that he had thought was monitoring traffic could have easily been something else entirely. All they had had to do was guess he would go into Washington and watch the Interstate for a Triumph. A license check would confirm it.

Pick him up at Gaithersburg. Follow him into Washington.

His Triumph had nailed him. Dammit!

Marty's voice was severe. "Okay, Jon. We don't have time for your bouts of anger. Besides, I don't want any holes in my walls unless *I* put them there. Tell me what you've figured out. Maybe I can help."

"No time. This is my area of expertise, right? You used to have a car. Do you still have it?" He had been falsely secure in his Triumph. Now his enemies would be falsely secure in relying on it to track him. Everyone had blind spots.

Marty nodded. "I keep it at a garage near Massachusetts Avenue. But Jon, you know I never go out anymore." He wandered into the next room and looked nervously out the window. He still carried his remote and the sheaf of papers as if they were talismans against danger.

"You do now," Smith told him firmly. "We're going to go out of here the front way, and—"

"J-J-Jon! Look!" Marty jabbed the remote like a pointer out the back window.

Instantly Smith was beside him, his Beretta in his hand. Two of the strangers had come through the hedge and now trotted toward the bungalow where Marty and Smith hid. The men were low to the ground, running with the careful urgency of men on the attack. And they were armed. Smith's pulse pounded. Beside him, Marty was rigid with fear. He put a hand on Marty's shoulder and squeezed as he crouched beside the window.

He let the pair get within fifteen feet. He slid up the window, aimed carefully, and fired the Beretta at each man's legs. His brain was rusty with years of inaction, but his muscle memory overcame the rust as smoothly as an oiled machine.

The two pitched forward onto their faces, moaning with pain and shock. As they crawled for the cover of a pair of old buckeye trees, Smith hurried to the living room.

"Come on, Marty."

Marty followed close behind, and they both looked out the window. As Smith had feared, the second pair was in front. One was the same burly man who had led the ambush two days ago in Georgetown. They had heard the shots, and the burly man had dived to the grass and pulled a Glock from his jacket. He landed hard on his chest, but held on to the Glock. The other man's reaction was thirty seconds too slow. He still stood on the brick path, his big old U.S. Army Colt .45 halfway up toward the house.

Smith missed his leg. But before the man could stumble back for the safety of the street, Smith's second shot drew blood from his shoulder and sent him sprawling.

Marty watched worriedly. "Good shooting, Jon."

Smith thought fast. His unexpected shots had put the two in the backyard out of action. But in the front, the leader was uninjured, and the second man had been only nicked. They would be careful now that they knew they faced lethal opposition, but they would not go away.

And the helicopter would send reinforcements.

His voice tense, Smith asked quickly, "Does your tunnel work from this end?"

Marty looked up. He nodded, understanding. "Yes, Jon. It'd be illogical if it didn't."

"Let's go!"

In the bedroom, Marty pressed his remote control. The box bed swung silently out of the way, exposing the trapdoor. Another electronic command opened it.

"Follow me." Holding his papers and the remote tightly, Marty slid into the brightly lighted shaft with its ladder that went through a crawl space and down into the concrete underground tunnel. As soon as he landed, he lurched out of the way.

A few seconds later, Smith's feet touched down next to him. "Impressive, Mart."

"Useful, too." He pressed a button on his remote. "This closes the trapdoor and puts everything back the way it was."

The two moved quickly along the bright tunnel. Finally they reached the other end, and Smith insisted on going up first. As he emerged into the small bathroom of Marty's home bungalow, he had a shock: A fifth man was crossing the hall into the living room.

Smith's pulse hammered. He listened. Then he realized the man was heading toward the bathroom.

He dropped back into the shaft. "Close it up!"

His round face anxious, Marty electronically closed the trap and lowered the bathtub. Seconds later they heard the man enter the bathroom, followed by the sound of a stream falling into the toilet.

Smith quietly told Marty what he wanted him to do.

Chapter
Nineteen

Beretta ready, Smith climbed up to wait on the top rung of the metal ladder. He took a deep breath as the trapdoor unlocked. But it was still weighted in place by the tub. As he raised his Beretta, the tub swung up against the wall, the trap sprang open, and the entire bathroom plus a section of the hall and living room came into view. Smith repressed a grim smile. The situation was better than he had hoped.

Ahead was the back of the man at the toilet. The guy's jaw dropped. Staring into the mirror, he had seen the bathtub rise like a white apparition into the air behind. The guy was not only stunned, he was exposed. He did not even have time to zip.

But he was a professional. So, fly hanging open, he grabbed his weapon from where he had laid it on top of the toilet tank and spun around.

"Good. But not good enough." With a mighty swing, Smith slammed his Beretta into the man's knee. He heard bone crack. The man dropped to the floor, groaning and clutching the knee. His weapon skidded toward the door.

Smith leaped up through the trap, snatched the gun, and grabbed the walkie-talkie from the back of the toilet tank. Now the man could not shoot or call for help.

"Hey!" the man bellowed. Pain stretched his narrow face. He tried to get up, but the crushed knee shot disabling pain, and he fell back onto the floor.

"Oh, my," Marty said as he clambered out. He hurried past him and into the hallway.

Smith followed, locking the bathroom door.

Marty wondered, "You didn't shoot him?"

He pushed Marty forward. "I crippled him. That was enough. It'll take three or four operations to repair that knee. The way he is, he can't hurt us and he's not going anyplace. Come on, Mart. We've really got to move."

As they crossed Marty's computer-filled office, he stopped for a moment, his face forlorn. He sighed, then he followed Smith to the front-door cage, which had been shot open.

Smith cracked open the front door and peered out. The gray van still stood in the driveway. He was tempted to hot-wire it, a skill he had learned from Bill Griffin as a teenager, but the helicopter still swung back and forth over the bungalows.

"Mart, we're going to Massachusetts Avenue and your car. Grab your meds."

"I don't like this." Marty stumbled back to his desk, picked up a small black leather case, and returned to Smith at the front door. "I don't like this at all." He shuddered. "The world is full of strangers!"

Smith ignored his complaints. Marty might fear people he did not know, but Jon figured he was far more afraid of dying. "Stay close to buildings, walk under trees, anything to hide. No running—that'd attract attention. With luck, the chopper up there won't spot us. If it does, we'll have to lose it when we reach your car. To be safe, I'm going to try to disable the van out there."

Marty suddenly raised a finger. He grinned from ear to ear. "I can handle *that!*"

"From here? How?"

"I'll fry its computer."

Smith never doubted Marty where electronics were concerned. "Okay. Let's see you do it."

Marty hunted in his desk drawers and produced a leather case about the size of a large camera. He aimed an aperture through the front doorway at the side at the van. He opened the lid, twirled some dials, and punched a button. "That should do it."

Smith stared suspiciously. "I didn't see anything happen."

"Of course you didn't. I used TED to destroy the on-board computer that controls engine functions."

"What the hell is TED?"

"Transient electromagnetic device. It works on RF—radio frequency. Think of static electricity, but stronger. I built this one myself and made it even more powerful than the usual. But the Russians will sell you an industrial-strength one. It comes in a briefcase and costs a hundred thousand dollars or so."

Jon was impressed. "Bring that thing along." He stepped outdoors. "Let's go."

Marty stood motionless just outside his doorway. He stared, stunned at the blue sky and green grass and moving traffic. He looked overwhelmed. "It's been a long time," he murmured and shivered.

"You can do it," Smith encouraged.

Marty swallowed and nodded. "Okay. I'm ready."

Smith in the lead, they ran from the porch and along the high hedge to where it joined the side hedge. Jon pushed through, and Marty followed. At the street, he stepped out and linked his arm with Marty's. They were just two convivial friends strolling along toward the avenue two blocks ahead.

Behind them the helicopter hung over the pair of bungalows. Busy Massachusetts Avenue was ahead. Once there, Smith hoped they could disappear among the throng of pedestrians flocking to the magnificence

of Embassy Row and the other historic buildings and institutions between Dupont and Sheridan Circles.

They did not make it. As they reached the second block, the chopper
roared closer. Smith glanced over his shoulder. The helicopter was
sweeping toward them.

"Oh, my." Marty saw it, too.

"Faster!" Smith ordered.

They ran down the side street, the helicopter following so low it was
in danger of trimming the trees. The draft from the mighty blades
blasted their backs. Then shots exploded from the chopper. Marty gave
a little scream. Bullets kicked dirt and concrete around them and
whined off into the air.

Smith grabbed his arm and shouted, "Keep running!"

They pounded on, Marty flailing like a combination of robot and rag
doll. The helicopter passed over and battled to bank and come back.

"Faster!" Smith was sweating. He pulled on Marty's arm.

The helicopter had completed its turn and started back.

But then Smith exulted. "It's going to be too late!" They tore onto
Massachusetts Avenue and plunged in among the crowds. It was Friday
afternoon, and people were returning from long lunches, making plans
for the weekend, and heading toward appointments.

"Oh, oh." Marty cringed against Smith, but he kept walking. His
round head swiveled, and his eyes were huge as he took in the multitude.

"You're doing great," Smith assured him. "I know it's tough, but
we're safe for a while here. Where's your car?"

Panting nervously, Marty told him, "Next side street."

Smith looked up at the helicopter that had made its turn and was
now hovering over the crowds and moving ahead slowly, trying to single
them out. He studied Marty in his customary tan windbreaker over a
blue shirt and baggy chinos.

"Take off your windbreaker and tie it around your waist."

"Okay. But they still could spot us. Then they'll shoot us."

"We're going to be invisible." He was lying, but under the circumstances it seemed the wisest course. Hiding his worry, he unbuttoned his uniform blouse and slipped out of it as they hurried along. He wrapped it around his garrison cap and tucked the bundle under his arm. It was not much of a disguise, but to eyes searching from a helicopter for two people in a crowd below, it might be enough.

They walked another block, the chopper closing in on them. Smith looked over at Marty, whose round face was miserable and sweating. But he offered a forced smile. Smith smiled back, even though he pulsed with tension.

The helicopter was closer. Suddenly it was almost above them.

Marty's voice was excited. "This is it! I recognize the street. Turn here!"

Smith watched the chopper. "Not yet. Pretend to tie your shoelace." Marty squatted and fussed at his tennis shoes. Smith bent and brushed at his trousers as if he had gotten dirt on them. People hurried past. A few threw annoyed glances at them for impeding the flow.

The helicopter passed over.

"Now." Smith pushed through the crowd first, creating a path for Marty. In a dozen feet, they were on a narrow side street that resembled an alley. Marty led him to a three-story, yellow-brick building marked by a wide garage door. There was an attendant's kiosk, but no cars were going in or out. Smith did not like the flat roof. The chopper could land up there.

Marty presented his identification to a stunned attendant who had clearly never laid eyes on the owner of the vehicle in question. "How long you taking it out for, Mr. Zellerbach?"

"We don't know for sure," Smith told the man, saving Marty from having to talk to the stranger.

The attendant scoured the ownership papers once more and led them up to the second floor, where a row of stored cars waited under protective canvas covers.

When he whipped the cover off the next-to-the-last one, Smith stared. "A Rolls-Royce?"

"My father's." Marty grinned shyly.

It was a thirty-year-old Silver Cloud, as gleaming as the day it had cruised out from under the hands of the long-forgotten craftsmen who built it. When the attendant started it up and rolled it carefully out from the row, its original Rolls-Royce engine purred so softly Smith was not sure it was actually running. There was not a squeak, squeal, knock, or rattle.

"There you are, Mr. Zellerbach," the attendant said proudly. "She's our belle. Best car in the house. I'm glad to see she's going somewhere at last."

Smith took the keys and told Marty to sit in the backseat. He left his uniform blouse off but put on his cap so he would look more like a chauffeur. Behind the wheel, he studied the dashboard instruments and gauges on the whorled wood and examined the controls. With a sense of awe, he slid the clutch into gear and drove the elegant machine out of storage and onto the side street. Almost anywhere in the nation the Rolls would stand out as glaringly as his Triumph. But not in New York, Los Angeles, or Washington. Here it was just one more expensive car carrying an ambassador, a foreign dignitary, an important official, or a CEO of some kind.

"Do you like it, Jon?" Marty asked from the backseat.

"It's like riding a magic carpet," Smith said. "Beautiful."

"That's why I kept it." Marty gave a satisfied smile and leaned back like an overweight cat against the seat, comforted by the close walls of the car. He set his papers and his black medicine case beside him and gave a little chortle. "You know, Jon, that guy in the bathroom's going to tell the others about my escape route, but they're never going to figure out how to make it work." He held up the remote control with a flourish. "Zounds! They're screwed!"

Smith laughed and glanced at the rearview mirror. The chopper circled helplessly a block away. He turned the grand machine onto Massachusetts Avenue. Inside the Silver Cloud, there was hardly a sound despite the heavy traffic.

He asked, "Are those papers printouts of what you were able to download?"

"Yes. I have good news, and I have bad news."

Marty described his cybersearch as they passed Dupont Circle and glided north, through the city to I-95 and onto the Beltway. As Marty talked, Smith remained tense and alert for anyone following. He had the constant sense they could be attacked again from any point at any time.

Then he looked into the rearview mirror at Marty with amazement. "You really were able to find the report from the Prince Leopold?"

Marty nodded. "And virus reports from Iraq."

"Amazing. Thank you. What about Bill Griffin and Sophia's phone records?"

"No. Sorry, Jon. I really tried."

"I know you did. I'd better read what you've got."

They were approaching the Connecticut Avenue exit at the extension of Rock Creek park in Maryland. Smith took the exit, drove into the park, and stopped the Rolls at a secluded meadow surrounded by a stand of thick trees. As Marty handed him the two printouts, he said, "They'd been deleted by the director of NIH's Federal Resource Medical Clearing House."

"The government!" Smith swore. "Damn. Either someone in the government or army's behind what's happening, or the people who are have even more power than I'd thought."

"That scares me, Jon," Marty said.

"It scares me, and we better find out which it is soon."

Muttering, he read the Prince Leopold report first.

Dr. René Giscours described a field report he had seen while doing a stint at a jungle hospital far upriver in Bolivian Amazonia years ago. He had been battling what appeared to be a new outbreak of Machupo fever and had no time to think about an unconfirmed rumor from far-off

Peru. But the new virus jogged his memory, so he checked his papers and found his original note—but not the actual report. His jottings to himself back then emphasized an unusual combination of hantavirus and hemorrhagic fever symptoms and some connection to monkeys.

Smith thought about it. What had caught Sophia's interest in this? There were few facts, nothing but the vague memory of an anecdote from the field. Was it the mention of Machupo? But Giscours made no special connection, did not suggest any link, and Machupo antibodies had shown no effect on the unknown virus. It did suggest the new unknown virus actually existed in nature, but researchers would assume that. Perhaps it was the mention of Bolivia. Maybe Peru. But why?

"Is it important?" Marty wanted to know, eager to help.

"I don't know yet. Let me read the rest."

There were three more reports—all from the Iraqi Minister of Health's office. The first two concerned three ARDS deaths a year ago in the Baghdad area that were unexplained but finally attributed to a hantavirus carried by desert mice drawn into the city by lack of food in the fields. The third reported three more ARDS cases in Basra who had survived. *All three in Basra.* Smith felt a chill. The exact same numbers had died and survived. Like a controlled experiment. Was that what the three American victims were, too, part of some experiment?

Plus there was the connection of the first three American victims to Desert Storm.

He felt a settling in his chest, as if now at last he had a clearer sense of direction. He had to go to Iraq. He needed to find out who had died and who had survived . . . and why.

"Marty, we're going to California. There's a man there who'll help us."

"I don't fly."

"You do now."

"But, Jon—" Marty protested.

"Forget it, Marty. You're stuck with me. Besides, you know deep down you like doing crazy things. Consider this one of your craziest."

"I don't believe thinking positively is enough in this case. I might freak out. Not that I'd want to, you understand. But even Alexander the Great had fits."

"He had epilepsy. You have Asperger's, and you've got medication to control it."

Marty froze. "Little problem there. I don't have my meds."

"Didn't you bring your case?"

"Yes, of course I brought it. But I have only one dose left."

"We'll have to get you more in California." As Marty grimaced, Smith restarted the Rolls and pulled onto the Interstate. "We'll need money. The army, the FBI, probably the police, and the people with the virus will be monitoring my bank accounts, credits cards, the works. They won't be monitoring yours yet."

"You're right. Since I value my life, I suppose I have to go along. At least for a while. Okay. Consider it a donation. Do you think fifty thousand dollars would be enough?"

Smith was stunned at the large sum. But when he thought about it, he realized money was meaningless to Marty. "Fifty thousand should do fine."

■

Over the roar of the rotors and the slipstream wind, Nadal al-Hassan shouted into the phone, "We have lost them." He wore dark sunglasses over his hatchet face. They seemed to absorb the sunlight like black holes.

In his office near the Adirondack lake, Victor Tremont swore. "Damn. Who is this Martin Zellerbach? Why did Smith go to him?"

Al-Hassan covered his open ear to hear better. "I will find out. What about the army and the FBI?"

"Smith's officially AWOL and connected to the deaths of Kielburger and the woman because he was the last to see them alive. Both the police and the army are looking for him." The distant roar of the helicopter in his ear made him want to shout as if he were there with al-Hassan. "Jack McGraw's staying on top of the situation through his source in the Bureau."

"That is good. Zellerbach's residence has much computer equipment. Very advanced. It is possible that is why Smith went there. Perhaps we could learn what he is looking for by analyzing what this Zellerbach was doing when we arrived."

"I'll send Xavier to Washington. Have your people watch the hospitals where all the victims were treated, especially the three survivors. So far the government hasn't revealed the survivals, but they will. When Smith hears about them, he'll probably try to reach them."

"I have already seen to it."

"Good, Nadal. Where's Bill Griffin?"

"That I do not know. He has not reported in to me today."

"Find him!"

Chapter Twenty

7:14 P.M.
New York City

Mercer Haldane, chairman of Blanchard Pharmaceuticals, Inc., could barely manage a smile as Mrs. Pendragon brought in the agenda for tomorrow's board meeting. Still, he bid her his customary cheerful goodnight. Safely alone again, he sat brooding in his white tie and tails. One of the quarterly dinners for the board was tonight, and he had an enormous problem that must be addressed first.

Haldane was proud of Blanchard, both of its history and its future. It was an old company, founded by Ezra and Elijah Blanchard in a garage in Buffalo in 1884 to make soap and face cream from their mother's original recipes. Owned and run by one or the other Blanchard, it had prospered and branched into fermentation products. During World War II, Blanchard was one of the few manufacturers selected to make penicillin, which elevated it to a pharmaceutical company. After the war, the company grew rapidly and went public with great fanfare in the 1960s. Twenty years later, in the early 1980s, the last Blanchard descendant handed over the operation of the company to Mercer Haldane. As CEO, Haldane ran Blanchard into the 1990s. Ten years ago, he had assumed the chairmanship as well. It was his company now.

Until two days ago, the future of Blanchard looked as rosy as its past. Victor Tremont had been his discovery, a brilliant biochemist with executive potential and creative flair. Haldane had nurtured Victor slowly, bringing him up through all the company's operations. He had been grooming Victor to succeed him. In fact, four years ago Haldane had promoted him to COO, even though he retained effective control. He knew Victor seethed under the constraint, that he was eager to run the company, but Haldane considered that a plus. Any man worth his salt wanted his own show, and a hungry man kept his competitive edge.

Tonight it was Mercer Haldane who seethed.

A year ago, a new auditor had reported accounting for research and development that seemed odd. The auditor was concerned, even nervous. It was impossible to follow funds for a project through to its conclusion. Haldane considered the man's worry nothing more than unfamiliarity with the intricacies of R&D in the pharmaceutical industry. But Haldane was also a cautious executive, so he had hired a second outside auditing firm to look more deeply.

The result was alarming. Two days ago, Haldane had received the report. In an intricate pattern of small, barely noticeable irregularities—overruns, shortfalls, paper transfers, borrowings, excessive supply and repair costs, pilfering, and spillage and leakage losses—almost a billion dollars appeared to be missing from the total R&D budget over a ten-year period. A billion dollars! In addition, a similar sum appeared to have been applied to a phantom R&D program Haldane had never heard of. The paper trail was exceedingly complex, and the auditors admitted they could not be absolutely certain of their findings. But they also said they were sure enough that they believed they should be granted permission to continue digging.

Haldane thanked them, told them he would be in touch, and immediately thought of Victor Tremont. Not for a second did he believe a billion dollars could be lost through tiny pinpricks, or that Victor would steal such a sum. But it was possible his hungry second-in-command could order a secret research project and try to keep it hidden from Haldane. Yes, he would believe that.

He made no immediate move. Victor and he would meet in his New York office before the private dinner he gave for the board at the quarterly meeting. He would brace Victor with what he knew and demand an explanation. One way or another, he would discover whether any secret program existed. If it did, he would have to fire Victor. But the project might be worth saving. If there were no such program, and Victor could not explain the lost billion, he would fire him on the spot.

Haldane sighed. It was tragic about Victor, but at the same time he felt an eagerness that made his blood rush. He was getting on in years, but he still enjoyed a good fight. Especially one that he knew he would win.

At the sound of his private elevator coming up, he crossed the luxurious office with its view south over the entire city to the Battery and the bay. He poured a snifter of his best XO cognac and returned to his desk. He opened a humidor, selected a cigar, lighted it, and took the first long, savory draw as the elevator stopped and Victor Tremont stepped out in his white tie and tails.

Haldane turned his head. "Good evening, Victor. Pour yourself a brandy."

Tremont eyed him where he sat behind the big desk smoking the cigar. "You're looking solemn tonight, Mercer. Some problem?"

"Get your brandy, and we'll discuss it."

Tremont poured a snifter of the fine old cognac, helped himself to a cigar, sat in a comfortable leather armchair facing Haldane, and crossed his legs.

He smiled. "So, let's not waste our valuable time. I have a lady to pick up for the dinner. What have I done wrong?"

Haldane bristled. He was being challenged. He decided to be blunt and put Victor in his place. "It seems we have a billion dollars unaccounted for. What did you do, Victor—steal it or divert it into some pet scheme?"

Tremont sipped his brandy, turned his cigar to study the ash, and nodded as if he had expected this. His long, aristocratic face was shadowy in the lamplight. "The secret audit. I thought that was probably it. Well, the simple answer is no . . . and yes. I didn't steal the money. I did divert it to a project all my own."

Haldane controlled his anger. "How long has this been going on?"

"Oh, I'd say ten years or so. A couple of years after that specimen-finding trip to Peru you sent me on when I was working in the main research lab. Remember?"

"A decade! Impossible! You couldn't have fooled me that long. What really—"

"Oh, but I could, and I did. Not alone, of course. I put together a team inside the company. The best men we have. They saw the billions that could be made on my concept, and they signed on. A little creative bookkeeping here, help from security there, some fine scientists, my own outside laboratory, a lot of dedication, some cooperation inside our federal government and military, and *voilà!*—the Hades Project. Conceived, planned, developed, and ready to go." Victor Tremont smiled again and waved the cigar like a magic wand. "In a few weeks—months at most—my team and Blanchard will make billions. Possibly hundreds of billions. Everyone will be rich—me, my team, the board, the stockholders . . . and, of course, *you*."

Haldane held his cigar frozen in midair. "You're insane."

Tremont laughed. "Hardly. Just a good businessman who saw an opportunity for gigantic profit."

"Insane and going to prison!" Haldane snapped.

Tremont held up a hand. "Calm yourself, Mercer. Don't you want to know what the Hades Project is? Why it's going to make all of us filthy rich, including you, despite your lack of gratitude?"

Mercer Haldane hesitated. Tremont was admitting he had used company funds for secret research. He would have to be terminated and probably prosecuted. But he was also a fine chemist, and legally the project did belong to Blanchard. Perhaps it would make a large profit. After all, as chairman and CEO, it was his duty to protect and enhance the company's bottom line.

So Haldane cocked his white head. "I can't see how it can change anything, Victor, but what is this brilliant coup of yours?"

"When you sent me to Peru thirteen years ago, I found an odd virus in a remote area. It was deadly, fatal in most cases. But one tribe had a cure: They drank the blood of a specific species of monkey that also carried the disease. I was intrigued, so I brought home live virus from victims as well as various monkeys' blood. What I found was startling, but rather elegantly logical."

Haldane stared. "Go on."

Victor Tremont took a long drink of the cognac, smacked his lips in appreciation, and smiled over the top of the snifter at his boss. "The monkeys were infected by the same virus as the humans. But it's a strange one. The virus lies dormant for years inside its host, rather like the HIV virus before it becomes AIDS. Oh, a small fever perhaps, some headaches, other sudden and brief pains, but nothing lethal until, apparently spontaneously, it mutates, gives symptoms of a heavy cold or mild flu for two weeks or so, and then becomes lethal to both humans and monkeys. However, and this was key, it strikes earlier and with far less severity in the monkeys. Many monkeys survive, and their blood is full of neutralizing antibodies to the mutated virus. The Indians learned this, by trial and error I expect, so when they fell ill they drank the blood and were cured. In most cases, anyway, if they got the right monkey's blood."

Tremont leaned forward. "The beauty of this symbiosis is that no matter how the virus mutates, the mutation always appears in the monkeys first, which means antibodies are always available for any mutation. Isn't that an exquisite bit of nature?"

"Stunning," Haldane said drily. "But I see no avenue to profit in your anecdote. Does this virus exist elsewhere where there's no natural cure?"

"Absolutely nowhere as far as we've been able to ascertain. That's the key to the Hades Project."

"Enlighten me. Please. I can't wait."

Tremont laughed. "Sarcasm. One step at a time, Mercer." He stood up and walked to the bar. He poured more of the chairman's fine cognac. Seated again, he crossed his knees. "Of course, we couldn't very well import millions of monkeys and kill them for their blood. Not to mention that not all monkeys carried the antibodies, and that blood would deteriorate rapidly anyway. So first we had to isolate the virus and the antibodies in the blood. Then we had to establish methods of large-scale production and provide a broad enough spectrum to accommodate some of the spontaneous mutations over time."

"I suppose you're going to tell me you did all this."

"Absolutely. We isolated the virus and were capable of production within the first year. The rest took varying lengths of time, and we finalized the recombinant antiserum only last year. Now we have millions of units ready to ship. It's been patented as a cure for the monkey virus, without mentioning the human virus, of course. That's going to appear to be a bit of luck. Our costs have been inflated and well tabulated, so we can claim a higher price to the public, and we've applied for FDA approval."

Haldane was incredulous. "You don't have FDA approval?"

"When the pandemic starts, we'll get instant approval."

"*When* it starts?" It was Haldane's turn to laugh. A derisive laugh. "What pandemic? You mean there's no epidemic of the virus to use your serum on? My God, Victor—"

Tremont smiled. "There will be."

Haldane stared. "Will be?"

"There have been six recent cases in the United States, three of which we secretly cured with our serum. More victims here are coming down with it, plus there have already been over a thousand deaths overseas. In a few days, the globe will know what it's facing. It won't be pretty."

Mercer Haldane sat motionless at his desk. Cognac forgotten. Cigar burning the desktop where the stub had fallen from the ashtray. Tremont waited, the smile never leaving his smooth face. His iron-gray hair and tan skin glowed in the lamplight. When Haldane finally spoke, his rigidity was painful to witness, even for Tremont.

But Haldane's voice was controlled. "There's some part of this scheme you aren't telling me."

"Probably," Tremont said.

"What is it?"

"You don't want to know."

Haldane thought that over for a time. "No, it won't play. You're going to prison, Victor. You'll never work again."

"Give me some credit. Besides, you're in as deep as I am."

Haldane's white eyebrows shot up in surprise. "There's no way—!"

Tremont chuckled. "Hell, you're in deeper. My ass is covered. Every order, every requisition, and every expenditure was approved and signed by you. Everything we did has your authorization in writing. Most of it's real because when you get in an irritable mood, you sign papers just to get them off your desk. I put them there, you scribbled your signature and shooed me out of the office like a schoolboy. The rest are forgeries no one's going to spot. One of my people has an expert."

Like a wary old lion, Haldane repressed his outrage at Tremont's underhandedness. Instead, he studied his protégé, assessing the potential value of what he had revealed. Grudgingly, Haldane had to agree the profits could be astronomical, and he would see to it that he got his share. At the same time, he tried to detect a flaw, a mistake that could lead to all their downfalls.

Then Haldane saw it: "The government's going to want to mass-produce your cure. Give it to the world. They'll take it away from you. National interest."

Tremont shook his head. "No. They couldn't produce the serum unless we gave them the details, and no one else has the production facilities in place. They won't try to take it anyway. First, because we'll have enough on hand to do the job. Second, no American government is going to deny us a reasonable profit. That's the name of the game we preach to the world, isn't it? This is a capitalist society, and we're simply practicing good capitalism. Besides, the spin is we're working around the clock to save humanity, so we deserve our reward. Of course, as I said, we've inflated our research costs, but they won't look too deep. The profits will be stupendous."

Haldane grimaced. "So there's going to be a pandemic. I suppose the only good thing about that is you've got the cure. Perhaps not so many lives will be lost."

Tremont noted the cynicism that Haldane had used to convince himself to capitulate. As always, Tremont had anticipated Haldane correctly. Now he looked slowly around the chairman's office as if memorizing every detail.

He focused on his former mentor again, and his face grew cool and remote. "But to make it all work, I need to be in charge. So at the board meeting tomorrow, you're going to step down. You're going to turn the company over to me. I'll be CEO, chairman of the executive committee, full control. You can stay on as chairman of the board, if you like. You can even have more contact with daily operations than any other board member. But in a year you'll retire with a very fat separation bonus and pension, and I'll take over the board, too."

Haldane stared. The combative old lion was fraying around the edges. He had not anticipated this, and he was shocked. He had underestimated Tremont. "If I refuse?"

"You can't. The patent is in the name of my incorporated group, with me as principal stockholder, and licensed to Blanchard for a large percentage fee. You, by the way, approved that arrangement years ago, so it's quite legal. But don't worry. There'll be plenty for Blanchard, and a big bonus for you. The board and stockholders will be ecstatic at the profits, not to mention the public-relations coup. We'll be the heroes riding to rescue the world from an apocalyptic disaster worse than the Black Plague."

"You keep stressing how much money I'm going to make. In or out. I see no reason to leave. I'll just run it myself and make sure *you* are financially rewarded."

Tremont chuckled, enjoying the vision of being a savior and making a fortune worthy of Midas at the same time. Then he turned his gaze grimly onto Haldane. "The Hades Project will be a stunning success, the biggest Blanchard has ever had. But even though on paper you approved it all, you really know nothing about it. If you tried to take over, you'd look like a fool at best. At worst, you'd reveal your incompetence. Everyone would suspect you were trying to take credit for my work. At that point, I could get the board and stockholders to kick you out in five minutes."

Haldane inhaled sharply. In his most terrifying nightmares, he had never expected this could happen. Events had him in an iron grip, and he had lost control. A sense of helplessness, of being a fish that thrashed inside an impenetrable net, swept over him. He could think of nothing to say. Tremont was right. Only a fool would fight now. Better to play the game and walk away with the loot. As soon as he decided that, he felt better. Not well, but better.

He shrugged. "Well, let's go and have dinner, then."

Tremont laughed. "That's the Mercer I know. Cheer up. You'll be rich and famous."

"I'm already rich. I never gave a damn about being famous."

"Get used to it. You're going to like it. Think of all the former presidents you can play golf with."

Chapter Twenty-One

4:21 P.M.
San Francisco, California

Using Marty Zellerbach's credit card, Smith and Marty arrived in a rented jet at San Francisco International Airport late Friday afternoon. Worried about Marty's need to refill his prescription, Smith immediately rented a car, drove them downtown, and found a pharmacy. The druggist called Marty's Washington doctor at home for authorization, but the doctor insisted on speaking directly with Marty. As Marty talked, Smith listened on an extension.

The doctor was stiff and strained, and he asked irrelevant questions. Finally he wanted to know whether Colonel Smith was with Marty.

With a jolt of adrenaline, Smith grabbed the receiver from Marty's hand and hung up both phones.

As the pharmacist gave a puzzled frown from behind the glassed-in counter, Smith explained to Marty in a low voice, "Your doctor was trying to hold you here. Probably for the FBI or army intelligence to arrive and arrest me. Maybe for the killers at the bungalow, and we both know what they'd do."

Marty's eyes widened in alarm. "The pharmacist gave the name of his drugstore and said where it was. Now my doctor knows, too!"

"Right. So docs whoever was listening in on the doctor's end. Let's go."

They rushed out. Marty's medication was wearing off, and they needed to save the last dose for the morning and the long drive ahead. Marty grumbled and stayed close to Smith. He put up with buying clothes and other necessities, and he grudgingly ate dinner in an Italian restaurant in North Beach that Smith remembered from a brief stint at the Presidio when it was an active army base. But the computer genius was growing more agitated and talkative.

At nightfall they took a room at the Mission Inn far out on Mission Street. Fog had rolled in, wrapping itself around picturesque lampposts and rising above bay windows.

Marty noticed none of the area's charm or the advantages of the small motel. "You can't possibly subject me to this medieval torture chamber, Jon. Who in heaven's name would be idiotic enough to want to sleep in such a foul dungeon?" The room smelled of the fog. "We'll go to the Stanford Court. It's at least presentable and almost livable." It was one of San Francisco's legendary grande dame hotels.

Smith was amazed. "You've stayed there before?"

"Oh, *thousands* of times!" Marty said in an enthusiastic exaggeration that warned Smith he was beginning to spin out of control. "That's where we rented a suite when my father took me to San Francisco. I was enthralled by it. I used to played hide-and-seek in the lobby with the bellmen."

"And everyone knew that's where you stayed in San Francisco?"

"Of course."

"Go there again if you don't mind our violent friends finding you."

Marty instantly flip-flopped. "Oh, dear me. You're right. They must be in San Francisco by now. Are we safe in this dump?"

"That's the idea. It's out of the way, and I registered under an alias. We're only here one night."

"I don't plan to sleep a wink." Marty refused to take off his clothes for bed. "They could attack at any hour. I'm certainly not going to be seen running down the street in my nightshirt with those beasts or the FBI pursuing me."

"You've got to get a good night's sleep. It's a long trip tomorrow."

But Marty would hear none of it, and while Smith was shaving and brushing his teeth, he hooked a chair under the knob of the only door. Then he crumpled a newspaper sheet by sheet and arranged the crushed papers in front of the door. "There. Now they can't sneak in on us. I saw that in a movie. The detective put his pistol on the bedside table, too, so he could reach it quickly. You'll do that with your Beretta, Jon, right?"

"If it makes you feel better." Smith came out of the bathroom, drying his face. "Let's get to bed."

When Smith slid under the covers, Marty lay down fully dressed on the twin. He stared up at the ceiling, his eyes wide open. Suddenly he looked to Smith. "*Why* are we in California?"

Smith turned off the bedside light. "To meet a man who can help us. He lives in the Sierras near Yosemite."

"That's right. The Sierras. Modoc country! You know the story of Captain Jack and the Lava Beds? He was a brilliant Modoc leader, and the Modocs were put on the same reservation as their arch enemies, the Klamaths." In the dim room, Marty launched into the excited reverie of his unleashed mind. "In the end, the Modocs killed some whites, so the army came after them with cannon! Maybe ten of them against a whole regiment. And . . ."

He related every detail of the injustice done by the army to the innocent Modoc leader. From there he described the saga of Chief Joseph and his Nez Percé in Washington and Idaho and their mad dash for freedom against half the army of the United States. Before he had finished reciting Joseph's heartrending final speech, his head jerked around toward the door.

"They're in the corridor! *I hear them!* Get your gun, Jon!"

Smith leaped up, grabbed the Beretta, and tried to speed quietly through the rumpled newspapers, which was impossible. He listened at the door. His heart was thundering.

He listened for five minutes. "Not a sound. Are you sure you heard something, Marty?"

"Absolutely. Positively." His hands flapped in the air. He was sitting upright, his back rigid, his round face quivering.

Smith crouched, trying to relieve his weary body. He continued to listen for another half hour. People came and went outside. There was conversation and occasional laughter. Finally he shook his head. "Not a thing. Get some sleep." He moved through the noisy newspapers to his bed.

Marty was chastened and silent. He lay back. Ten minutes later he enthusiastically began the chronological history of every Indian War since King Philip's in the 1600s.

Then he heard steps again. "There's someone at the door, Jon! Shoot them. Shoot them! Before they break in! *Shoot them!*"

Jon sped to the door. But there was no sound beyond it. For Smith, it was the final straw. Marty would be inventing wild dangers and re lating more stories about early America all night. He was reaching warp speed, and the longer he was off his medication, the worse it would be for both of them.

Smith got up again. "Okay, Marty, you'd better take your last dose." He smiled kindly. "We'll just have to trust we can get you more when we get to Peter Howell's place tomorrow. Meanwhile, you've got to sleep, and so do I."

Marty's mind buzzed and flashed. Words and images whipped through with incredible speed. He heard Jon's voice as if at a great distance, almost as if a continent separated them. Then he saw his old friend and the smile. Jon wanted him to take his drug, but everything within him railed against it. He hated to leave this thrilling world where life happened quickly and with great drama.

"Marty, here's your medicine." Jon stood beside him with a glass of water in one hand and the dreaded pill in the other.

"I'd rather ride a camel across the starry sky and drink blue lemonade. Wouldn't you? Wouldn't you like to listen to fairies playing their golden harps? Wouldn't you rather talk to Newton and Galileo?"

"Mart? Are you listening? Please take your meds."

Marty looked down at Jon, who was crouching in front of him now, his face earnest and worried. He liked Jon for many reasons, none of which seemed relevant now.

Jon said, "I know you trust me, Marty. You've got to believe me when I tell you we let you stay off your medication too long. It's time for you to come back."

Marty spoke in an unhappy rush. "I don't like the pills. When I take them, I'm not me. *I'm* not there anymore! I can't think because there's no 'I' to think!"

"It's rough, I know," Smith said sympathetically. "But we don't want you to cross the line. When you're off them too long, you go a little nuts."

Marty shook his head angrily. "They tried to teach me how to be 'normal' with other people the way they teach someone to play a piano! *Memorize* normality! 'Look him in the eye, but don't stare.' 'Put out your hand when it's a man, but let a woman put out her hand first.' Imbecilic! I read about a guy who said it just right: 'We can learn to pretend to act like everyone else, but we really don't get the point.' I don't get the point, Jon. *I don't want to be normal!*"

"I don't want you to be 'normal' either. I like your wildness and brilliance. You wouldn't be the Marty I know without that. But we've got to keep you balanced, too, so you don't go so far out into the stratosphere we can't bring you back. After we get to Peter's tomorrow, you can slide off the pills again."

Marty stared. His mind did cartwheels of numbers and algorithms. He craved the freedom of his unfettered thoughts, but he knew Jon was right. He was still in control, but just barely. He did not want to risk dropping off the edge.

Marty sighed. "Jon, you're a champ. I apologize. Give me the darn pill."

Twenty-five minutes later, both men were sound asleep.

12:06 A.M., Saturday, October 18
San Francisco International Airport

Nadal al-Hassan strode off the DC-10 red-eye from New York into the main concourse. The overweight man in the shabby suit who greeted him had never met him, but there was no one else on the New York flight who fit the description he had been given.

"You al-Hassan?"

Al-Hassan eyed the shabby man with distaste. "You are from the detective agency?"

"You got that right."

"What do you have to report?"

"FBI beat us to the drugstore guy, but all he knows anyways is there was two of 'em, an' when they left they took a taxi. We're checking the cab companies, an' so's the local cops and the FBI. Hotels, motels, roomin' houses, car rentals, an' other drugstores, too. So far nothin'. An' the cops an' FBI ain't doin' no better."

"I will be at the Hotel Monaco near Union Square. Call me the instant you find anything."

"You want us checkin' all night?"

"Until you find them, or the police do."

The slovenly man shrugged. "It's your money."

Al-Hassan caught a taxi to the newly renovated downtown San Francisco hotel with its small, elegant lobby and dining room decorated to look like a continental city in the 1920s. As soon as he was alone in his room, he phoned New York and reported everything the sloppy man had told him.

Al-Hassan said, "He cannot use army resources. We are covering all Smith's and Zellerbach's friends as well as everyone connected to the virus victims."

"Hire another detective agency if you have to," Victor Tremont ordered from his New York hotel room. "Xavier's found what this Zellerbach person was doing for him." He recited the discoveries in Marty's computer logs. "Apparently, Zellerbach found the Giscours memo, and he uncovered reports about the virus in Iraq. Smith has probably figured out we have the virus, and now he wants to know what we're going to do with it. He's no longer a potential threat, he's a menace!"

Al-Hassan's voice was a promise. "Not for much longer."

"Keep in touch with Xavier. This Zellerbach person tried to trace the Russell woman's phone call to me. We expect he'll try again. Xavier is monitoring Zellerbach's computer. If he uses it, Xavier will keep him online long enough to initiate a phone trace through our local police in Long Lake."

"I will call Washington and give him my cell phone number."

"Have you located Bill Griffin?"

Al-Hassan was quiet, embarrassed. "He has contacted no one since we assigned him to kill Smith."

Tremont's voice cracked like a whip. "You still don't know where Griffin is? Incredible! How could you lose one of your own people!"

Al-Hassan kept his voice low, respectful. Victor Tremont was one of the few heathens in this godless country he respected, and Tremont was right. He should have kept a closer eye on the ex–FBI man. "We are working to find Griffin. It is a point of pride with me that we find him quickly."

Tremont was silent, calming himself. At last he said, "Xavier tells me Martin Zellerbach was also looking for Griffin's most recent address, obviously for Smith. As you suggested, there is a connection somewhere. Now we have evidence of it."

"It is interesting that Bill Griffin has made no attempt to contact or approach Jon Smith. On the other hand, Smith visited Griffin's ex-wife yesterday in Georgetown."

Tremont considered. "Perhaps Griffin is playing both sides. Bill Griffin could turn out to be our most dangerous enemy, or our most useful weapon. Find him!"

7:00 A.M.
San Francisco Mission District

Marty and Smith were awake and checked out by 7:00 A.M. By 8:00 they had driven across San Francisco's glistening bay and were heading east on I-580. After Lathrop, they crossed to 99 and 120 and headed south through fertile inland farmlands to Merced, where they stopped to eat a late breakfast. Then they turned east again, straight toward Yosemite on 140. The day was cool but sunny, Marty was still calm, and as they reached the higher elevations the sky seemed to grow a translucent blue.

They climbed steadily to the three-thousand-foot Mid Pines Summit, picked up the rushing Merced River, and entered the park at El Portal. Marty had been watching quietly out the window. As they climbed two thousand feet beside the rapidly falling river and into the famed valley, his gaze continued to drink in the stunning mountain scenery.

"I think I've missed getting out," he decided. "Indescribably beautiful."

"And few people to interfere with the view."

"Jon, you know me too well."

They drove past the towering stream of Bridal Veil Falls, wreathed in its own rising mists, and the sheer cliffs of El Capitan. In the distance was legendary Half Dome and Yosemite Falls. They turned sharply onto the north fork of the valley drive and continued on Big Oak Flat Road to its junction with high-elevation Tioga Road, which was closed to all traffic from November to May and often far into June. They continued east through patches of snow and the magnificent scenery of the high country of the untamed Sierras. At last they headed down the eastern slope, the land growing drier and less lush.

As they descended, Marty began singing old cowboy tunes. The meds were wearing off. A few miles before Tioga Road reached Highway 395 and the town of Lee Vining, Smith turned onto a narrow blacktop road. On either side were parched, grassy open slopes with barbed-wire fences marking property lines. Cattle and horses grazed under trees whose black silhouettes stood stark against the gold-velvet mountains.

Marty burst into song: "*Home, home on the range, where the deer and the antelope play! Where seldom is heard a discouraging word and the skies are not cloudy all day!*"

Smith drove the car up dizzying switchbacks, crossed several streams on rickety wood bridges, and ended at the edge of a deep ravine with a broad creek roaring below. A narrow steel footbridge crossed the ravine to a clearing and a log cabin hidden among towering ponderosa pine and incense cedar. The snow-capped peak of thirteen-thousand-foot Mount Dana towered like a sentinel in the distance.

As Smith parked, Marty continued to fly through his mind, stimulated by the remarkable range of scenery—from ocean to mountains to cattle land. But now he realized they must be near their destination, and he would be expected to stay here. Sleep here. Maybe live here quite a while.

Smith came around and opened his door, and he climbed reluctantly out. He shrank from the footbridge, which swayed slightly in the wind. The ravine it crossed plunged thirty feet.

He announced, "I'm not putting a toe on that flimsy contraption."

"Don't look down. Come on, over you go." Smith pushed.

Marty clutched the handrails all the way. "What are we doing in this wasteland anyway? There's only that old shack over there."

As they started up the dirt trail toward it, Jon said, "Our man lives there."

Marty stopped. *"That's* our destination? I will not stay five seconds in anything so primitive. I doubt it has indoor plumbing. It certainly has no electricity, which means no computer. I must have a computer!"

"It also has no killers," Smith pointed out, "and don't judge a book by its cover."

Marty snorted. "That's a cliché."

"On with you."

When they reached the ponderosas, they plunged into the gloom under the thick branches that towered high above. The aroma of pine filled the air. Ahead through the tall trees the shack stood silent. Every time Marty looked at it, he shook his head in dismay.

Suddenly a high-pitched snarl froze them in their tracks.

A full-grown mountain lion sprang from a tree ahead and crouched ten feet away. Its long tail whipped, and its yellow eyes glared.

"Jon!" Marty cried and turned to run.

Smith grabbed his arm. "Wait."

A voice with an English accent spoke from somewhere ahead. "Stand quite still, gentlemen. Don't raise a weapon, and he won't hurt you. And perhaps neither will I."

Chapter Twenty-Two

From the low-roofed porch of the cabin, a lean man of medium build stepped out of the shadows holding a British Enfield bullpup automatic rifle. His words were addressed to Smith, but his gaze was fixed on Marty Zellerbach. "You said nothing about bringing anyone with you, Jon. I don't like surprises."

Marty whispered, "I'd be happy to leave, Jon."

Smith ignored him. Peter Howell was not Marty Zellerbach. His defenses *were* lethal, and you took them seriously. Smith spoke quietly to the man with the gun. "Whistle up the cat, Peter, and put down the armament. I've known Marty a lot longer than I've known you, and right now I need you both."

"But *I* don't know him," the wiry man said just as quietly. "There's the rub, eh? Are you saying you know all there is to know about him and that he's clean?"

"Nobody cleaner, Peter."

Howell studied Marty for a long minute, his pale blue eyes cool, clear, and as penetrating as an X-ray machine. Finally he gave a harsh sound somewhere between blowing air and clearing his throat. "*Ouish*, Stanley," he said softly. "Good cat. Go on with you."

The mountain lion turned and padded away behind the cabin, glancing back occasionally over his shoulder as if he hoped he would be called upon to pounce.

The lean man lowered the assault rifle.

Marty's eyes were bright as he watched the big cat move off. "I've never heard of a trained mountain lion. How did you do it? He even has a name. How deliciously wonderful! Did you know African kings used to train leopards to hunt? And in India, they trained cheetahs—"

Howell stopped him. "We should have our talk inside, you see. Never know whose ears are listening." He motioned with the Enfield and stood aside to let them precede him into the cabin. As Smith passed, the Englishman raised an eyebrow and nodded to Marty's back. Smith nodded affirmatively in return.

Inside, the cabin was larger than it appeared from the front and belied its rustic appearance. They stood in a well-appointed living room with nothing of the Western lodge about it except the enormous field-stone fireplace. The furniture was comfortable English country-house antiques mixed with men's-club leather chairs and military mementoes from most wars of the twentieth century. The wall space not taken up by guns, regimental flags, and framed photos of soldiers displayed several giant abstract expressionist paintings—de Kooning, Newman, and Rothko. Originals worth a fortune.

The room occupied the entire width of the cabin, but a wing, hidden from the front, extended at the left rear deep into the tall pines. The cabin was actually built in an L-shape, with most of it in the stem of the L. The first door off the hallway behind the living room proved to be a study with an up-to-date PC computer.

Marty let out a cry of joy. Peter Howell watched him dash for the computer, oblivious to anyone.

Howell quietly asked, "What is it?"

"Asperger's syndrome," Smith told him. "He's a genius, especially with electronics, but being around people is hell for him."

"He's off his medicines now?"

Smith nodded. "We had to leave Washington in a hurry. Give me a minute, then we'll talk."

Without a word, Howell returned to the living room. Smith joined Marty at the computer.

Marty looked up at him reproachfully. "Why didn't you tell me he had a generator?"

"The lion sort of took it out of my mind."

Marty nodded, understanding. "Stan-the-cat is a mountain lion. Did you know that in China they trained Siberian tigers to—"

"Let's talk about it later." Smith was not as confident of their safety as he had told Marty. "Can you try again to find out whether Sophia made or received special phone calls? And also locate Bill Griffin?"

"Precisely what I intended. All I need do is tie into my own mainframe and software. If your friend's equipment isn't as primitive as his choice of location, I'll be up and running in minutes."

"No one can do it better." Smith patted his shoulder and backed away, watching him hunch farther and farther over the keyboard as he entered the computer world that was all his own.

Marty muttered to himself, "How could this pipsqueak machine have so much power? Well, no matter. Things are surely looking up."

Smith found Peter Howell sitting before a fireplace, cleaning a black metal submachine gun. Beside him, a roaring fire licked and spat orange flames. It was a homey picture, except for the military weapon in the Englishman's hands.

Howell spoke without looking up. "Take a chair. That old leather one is comfortable. Bought it from my club when I saw I'd become something of a liability at home and that it might be wise to do a bunk to where I was less known and could watch my back better."

A shade under six feet, Howell was almost too lean under the dark blue-green plaid flannel shirt and heavy khaki British army trousers he wore stuffed into black combat boots. His narrow face had the color and texture of leather dried out by years of wind and sun. It was so deeply lined his eyes seemed sunk in ravines. The eyes were sharp but guarded. His thick black hair was nearly all gray, and his hands were curved brown claws.

"Tell me about this friend of yours—Marty."

Jon Smith sank into the chair and touched the high points of his and Marty's growing up together, the difficulties of Marty's young life, and the discovery that he had Asperger's syndrome. "It changed everything for him. The drugs gave him independence. With them, he could make himself sit through classes and then do the spade-and-shovel work necessary to get two Ph.D.s. When he's medicated, he can do the boring, nitty-gritty things that are necessary to survive. He changes lightbulbs, does his laundry, and cooks. Of course, he has plenty of money to hire people to do those things, but strangers make him nervous. He has to take the medicine anyway, so why not take care of himself?"

"Can't say I blame him. You said his medication was wearing off?"

"Yes. One way to tell is he talks in exclamation points, just as you heard. He lectures and enthuses and seldom sleeps and drives everyone nuts. If he stays off too long, he can zoom into never-never land and be so out of control he's dangerous to himself and maybe to others."

Howell shook his head. "I feel sorry for the young fellow, don't get me wrong."

Smith chuckled. "You've got it reversed. Marty feels sorry for *you*. And for me. Actually, he pities us, because we can never know what he knows. We can't conceptualize what he understands. It's everyone's loss that he's isolated himself to concentrate strictly on his computer interests, although from what I understand of what he's doing, other computer experts consult him from around the world. But never in person. Always by E-mail."

Howell continued to clean his weapon—a Heckler & Koch MP5, as lethal as it looked. He said, "But if he's mechanical and slow when he's on the drugs, and gaga when he's off, how does he manage to get anything accomplished?"

"That's the trick. He's learned to let himself go beyond the stage where the meds are working but not quite into the state where he's flying high and wild. He'll have a few hours a day in that in-between condition, and that's heaven for him. New ideas seize him with lightning speed. He's sharp, incisive, quick, and half out-of-control every minute. He's unbeatable."

Howell's creviced face looked up from the weapon. His pale eyes flickered. "Unbeatable at computers, is he? Well, now. That's something else again." He returned to the H&K submachine gun. It had been the weapon of choice of the British Special Air Service some years ago and probably was still.

"You always clean a gun when you have visitors?" Smith closed his eyes, resting after the long drive from San Francisco.

Howell snorted. "You ever read Doyle's *The White Company*? Quite good, actually. Much more interesting to me as a boy than Sherlock Holmes. Odd about that. The boy's the father of the man and all that." He appeared to think about boys and men for a moment before continuing. "Anyway, there's an old bowman in the book—Black Simon. One morning the hero asks him why he's sharpening his sword to a razor's edge, since the company doesn't expect any action. Black Simon tells him he dreamed of a red cow the nights before the major battles of Crecy and Poitiers, and last night he again dreamed of a red cow. So he was getting prepared. Of course, later that day, just as Simon expected, the Spanish attacked."

Smith chuckled and opened his eyes. "Meaning, when I appear, you'd better prepare for trouble."

Howell's weathered face smiled. "That's about it."

"Right as usual. I need help, and it's probably dangerous."

"What else is an old spook and desert rat good for?"

Smith had first met him during the boredom of Desert Shield when the hospital spent every day preparing and waiting for action that never came. But it came to Peter Howell. Or, to be exact, Peter and the SAS went to it. Peter had never said exactly where "it" had been, but one night he appeared at the hospital like a ghost who had arisen out of the sand itself. He had a high fever and was kitten-weak. Some doctors swore they had a heard a helicopter or a small land vehicle close by in the desert that night, but no one was sure. How he had arrived or who had brought him remained a mystery.

Smith realized instantly the unknown patient wearing British desert camos without rank or unit markings had been bitten by a venomous reptile. He had saved Peter's life with immediate treatment. In the following days, as Peter recovered, they came to know and respect each other. That was when Smith learned his name was Maj. Peter Howell, Special Air Service, and that he had been deep inside Iraq on some unnamed mission. That was all Peter would ever say. Since he was obviously far too old to be a normal SAS trooper, there had to be more to the story, but it was years before Smith gleaned the rest, and even then it remained hazy.

Simply put, Peter was one of those restless and reckless Brits who seemed to pop up in every conflict of the last two centuries, small or large, on one side or the other. Educated at both Cambridge and Sandhurst, a linguist and adventurer, he had joined the SAS in Vietnam days. When the action faded, he volunteered for MI6 and foreign intelligence. He had worked for one or the other ever since, depending on whether the wars were hot or cold, and sometimes for both at once. Until he grew too old for one, and outlived his usefulness to the other.

Now he had found a well-deserved retirement on the remote and sparsely populated eastern side of the Sierras. Or so it appeared. Smith had a suspicion his "retirement" was as murky as the rest of his life.

Now that Smith was AWOL, he needed the kind of help the SAS and MI6 could give. "I have to get into Iraq, Peter. Secretly, but with contacts."

Howell began to reassemble the H&K. "That's not dangerous, my boy. That's suicide. No way. Not for a Yank or a Brit. Not the way things are over there these days. Can't be done."

"They murdered Sophia. It has to be done."

Howell made a sound much like his recall of Stan the mountain lion. "Like that, eh? Care to explain this AWOL nonsense?"

"You know I'm AWOL?"

"Try to keep in touch, you see. Been AWOL a few times myself. Usually a good story behind it."

Smith filled him in on everything that had happened since the death of Major Anderson at Fort Irwin. "They're powerful, Peter, whoever they are. They can manipulate the army, the FBI, the police, perhaps even the whole government. Whatever they're planning, it's worth killing people for. I've got to know what that is and why they killed Sophia."

His submachine gun cleaned, oiled, and back together, Howell reached out a brown claw for a humidor. He filled his pipe. Deeper in the house they could hear Marty raving at his computer, shouting excitedly to himself.

His pipe lit, puffing slowly, Howell muttered, "With that virus, and no known cure or vaccine, they can hold the planet hostage. It has to be someone like Saddam or Khadafy. Or China."

"Pakistan, India, any country weaker than the West." Smith paused. "Or no country. Perhaps it's all about money, Peter."

As the aromatic pipe tobacco scented the room, Peter thought about it. "Getting you into Iraq could cost more than my life, Jon. The price could be an entire underground. The opposition against Saddam Hussein is weak in Iraq, but it does exist. While it bides its time, my people and your people are there to help build it up. They'll get you in if I ask, but they won't compromise the entire network. If you stumble into serious trouble, you'll be on your own. The U.S. embargo is ruining the lives of everyone except Saddam and his gang. It's killing children. You can expect little from the underground and nothing from the Iraqi people."

Smith's chest tightened. Still he shrugged. "It's a risk I have to take."

Howell smoked. "Then I better get cracking. I'll arrange all the protection I can. I wish I could go, too, but I'd be a liability. They know me too well in Iraq, you see."

"It's better I go alone. I've got a job for you here anyway."

Howell brightened. "Do tell? Well, I was becoming a trifle bored. Feeding Stanley has its limits as excitement."

"Another thing," Smith added. "Marty has to have his meds, or he'll soon be useless. I can give you the empty bottles, but we can't contact his doctor in Washington."

Howell took the bottles and vanished into the hall and on past the room where Marty raved. Smith sat alone, listening to Marty. Outdoors the wind blew through the majestic ponderosa pines. It was a comforting sound, as if the earth were breathing. He let himself relax wearily into the chair. He cut off his grief for Sophia and his feelings of worry and all the tension of whether he could find what he needed in Iraq, and whether he would survive if he did. If anyone could get him into that brutalized country, it was Peter. He was sure answers were there somewhere—if not among those who had died from the virus last year, then among those who had survived.

5:05 P.M.
Washington, D.C.

In the single large room of Marty Zellerbach's disordered bungalow off Dupont Circle, computer expert Xavier Becker watched in fascination as Zellerbach, accessing his huge Cray mainframe from some remote PC, probed through the computers of the telephone company with the delicate skill of a surgeon.

Xavier had never seen anything like the search-and-cracking software Zellerbach had created. The sheer beauty and grace of the man's work almost made him forget what he was there for.

It was all he could do to keep one step ahead of Zellerbach as he led the distant cracker through a maze of phony positive results to keep him online while the police up north in Long Lake village traced Zellerbach through the maze of relays across the world. Xavier sweated, worrying Zellerbach would switch the sequence of relay lines, which would mean they would lose him. But Zellerbach never did. Xavier could not understand the oversight by such a genius. It was as if Zellerbach had set up his system of relays to hide his location because he knew it was the right thing to do, not because he cared about the reasons behind it, and so never thought of switching the trail again.

A tense voice announced in his earphones, "Just a few more minutes. Hold him on, Xavier."

Jack McGraw at Long Lake sounded as if he were sweating as much as Xavier. Twice before they had almost had Zellerbach, when Xavier had led him in circles with phony data while he tried to locate Bill Griffin, and again when he accessed USAMRIID's computer to check on progress with the unknown virus. Each time Zellerbach had moved too fast for Xavier to hold him. But not this time. Maybe Xavier's false data was better now, or maybe Zellerbach was getting tired and losing his concentration. Whatever it was, another two or three minutes and . . .

"Got him!" Jack McGraw's voice exulted. "He's online outside some little burg in California called Lee Vining. Al-Hassan's near Yosemite. We're alerting him now."

Xavier switched off. He felt none of the security chief's jubilation as he watched Zellerbach still following the fake trail he expected to lead to the phone call the Russell woman had made to Tremont. Zellerbach's creativity was too beautiful to be sabotaged by his own carelessness. It made Xavier feel sad and confused. It looked as if Zellerbach had been carried away by his own enthusiasm, by a kind of naive ignorance of the existence of the Xavier Beckers or the Victor Tremonts of this world.

2:42 P.M.
Near Lee Vining,
High Sierras, California

Smith stepped into the computer room, and Marty's frustration greeted him like an atomic blast. "Zounds, zounds, zounds! Where are you, you chimera! No one defeats Marty Zellerbach, you hear? Oh, I know you're there! Fuck and damn and—"

"Mart?" Smith had never heard him swear. It must be another sign he was going over the edge. "Mart! Stop it. What's going on?"

Marty went on swearing. He pounded the console, unaware Smith was speaking or that he was even in the room.

"*Mart!*" Smith grabbed his shoulder.

Marty whirled like a wild animal, teeth bared. And saw Smith. He suddenly collapsed in upon himself, drooping limp in his chair. He stared up with anguish. "Nothing! Nothing. I've found nothing. Nothing!"

"That's okay, Marty," Smith said in a soothing voice. "What didn't you find? Bill Griffin's address?"

"Not a trace. I was so close, Jon. Then nothing. The phone calls, too. I'm in my computer, using my own software. Just another step. It's there, I know it! So close—"

"We knew it was a long shot. What about the virus? Anything new at Fort Detrick?"

"Oh, I had that in minutes. Officially, there have now been fifteen deaths and three survivals here in America."

Smith jerked alert. "More deaths? Where? And survivors? How? What kind of treatment?"

"No details. Had to break through a brand-new security wall to find what I did. The Pentagon has all its data shut down, except to me." He chortled. "No information to the public except through the military."

"That's why we didn't hear about the survivors. Can you locate them?"

"I haven't seen a whisper of who they are or where they are. Sorry, Jon!"

"Not at Detrick or the Pentagon?"

"No, no. Neither place. Terrible. I think those Pentagon bandits are keeping the information off-system!"

Smith thought rapidly. His first instinct had been to find the survivors and try to get close enough to interview them. It seemed like the easiest, most direct route.

The reason the government had shut down the information was probably to avoid panicking people—standard operating procedure—and the situation was likely a lot worse than fifteen deaths. Scientists would be studying the three survivors around the clock to find answers before going public. Which meant every possible American human and technological security would be assigned.

Inwardly he sighed, frustrated. No way was he or even Peter Howell going to get past that.

Besides, the survivors would be the first place army intelligence, the FBI, and the murderers would expect him to go. They would be waiting. He inhaled and nodded. There was no choice. The only survivors he had a chance to reach were in Iraq. That locked-down country did not expect him, and they did not have the technological wizardry of the U.S. government. His best and fastest hope of finding out what was behind all this was to go there.

Marty was saying excitedly, "There! Almost got you! Just another minute."

Smith came out of his reverie to see him screaming at the console, hunched toward the screen like a hunter who sees his prey only a few feet ahead.

Fear tightened Smith's chest. Suddenly the mechanics of what Marty was doing made terrible sense. He snapped, "How long have you been connected to your computer in Washington?"

Howell appeared in the doorway. His wiry body went rigid. "He's been online through his own computer?"

"How long, Mart?" Smith repeated tensely.

Marty came out of his thrilled trance. He blinked and checked the time on the screen. "An hour, perhaps two. But it's *fine*. I'm using a series of relays all over the world, just as we're supposed to. Besides, it's my own computer. I—"

Smith swore. *"They know where your computer is!* They could be in your bungalow right now, inside your computer, teasing you on! Was the trail through the telephone company there the first time you cracked in?"

"Heck, no! I located a whole new path. I found a new one for Bill Griffin, too, but that led nowhere. This one in the phone company keeps opening up to new avenues. I know I can—"

Peter Howell's voice was crisp. "Do they have people in California?"

"I'd bet the farm on it," Smith told him.

"His meds are on the way." Howell spun on his heel. "Your killers can trace the phone line to Lee Vining and to me. Not my real name, of course. They'll have to locate the cabin, get out here, find the road, and reach us. I'd say an hour at worst. With luck two. We'd be wise to be away in less than one."

Chapter
Twenty-Three

6:51 P.M.
New York City

Victor Tremont adjusted his dinner jacket and straightened his black tie in the mirror of his suite in the Waldorf-Astoria tower. Behind him, still stretched naked on the rumpled bed, was Mercedes O'Hara. She was beautiful—all curves and lush, golden skin.

She fixed her dark eyes on him in the mirror. "I do not like to be hung in the bedroom closet with the suits until you decide I am to be used again, Victor."

Tremont scowled into the mirror. Neither patient nor reserved, the tall woman with the cascade of red hair falling across her breasts had been a mistake. Tremont rarely made that misjudgment. In fact, he could think of only one other time. That woman had killed herself when he had told her he would never marry her.

"I have a meeting, Mercedes. We'll go to dinner when I get back. The table is reserved at Le Cheval, your favorite. If that doesn't suit you, leave."

Mercedes would not kill herself. The Chilean woman owned extensive vineyards and a world-renowned winery in the Maipo Valley, sat on the boards of two mining companies and in the Chilean parliament, and had been a cabinet minister and would be again. But like all women, she demanded too much of his time and sooner or later would insist on marriage. None understood he did not need or want a companion.

"So?" She continued to observe from where she reclined on the bed. "No promises? One woman is the same as another. We are all a nuisance. Victor can love only Victor."

Tremont found himself annoyed. "I wouldn't say—"

"No," she interrupted, "that would require for you to understand." She sat up on the bed, swung her long legs over the edge, and stood. "I think I am tired of you, Dr. Tremont."

He stopped adjusting his black tie and watched in disbelief as she strode to her clothes and dressed without looking at him again. A surge of unexpected anger took hold of him. Who did she think she was? Such disgusting arrogance. With a powerful effort he repressed his rage. He returned to arranging his tie and smiled at her in the mirror.

"Don't be ridiculous, my dear. Go and have a cocktail. Put on that green evening gown that makes you look so wonderful. I'll meet you at Le Cheval in an hour. Two at the most."

Dressed in the black Armani suit that made her red hair flame, she laughed. "You are such a sad man, Victor. And such a fool."

Before he could respond, she had walked out of the bedroom, still laughing.

He heard the outer suite door slam.

Rage swept down over him like a mountain avalanche, and he felt himself actually shake. He took two swift steps toward the open bedroom door. No one laughed at Victor Tremont. No one! A woman. He would . . . would—

His face burned as if he had a fever. His fists clenched at his sides as if he were still a schoolboy.

Then he gave a short laugh. What the hell was he doing? The stupid woman.

She had saved him the tedium of correcting his mistake. He had thought this one was intelligent, but, in the end, none was. With relief, he saw now there would be no dramatic and tearful scenes of abandonment. He would not have to give her any expensive farewell gifts. She would walk away with nothing. Who was the fool now?

Grinning broadly, he returned to the mirror, finished adjusting his tie, smoothed his dinner jacket, took one last appraising glance at himself, and turned to leave the room for his meeting. Before he reached the door, his private cell phone rang. He hoped it was al-Hassan with news of Jon Smith and Marty Zellerbach.

"Well?"

The Arab's voice was reassuring. "Zellerbach connected to his own computer to continue searching for the Russell woman's phone call to you. Xavier held him on long enough for McGraw to trace him to Lee Vining, California." There was a pleased pause. "I am there now."

"Where in God's name is Lee Vining?"

"On the eastern side of the Sierra Nevadas near Yosemite National Park."

"How did you know to go to such a place?"

"The FBI found the motel where they'd slept last night and then located where they'd rented a car. Smith had asked for a map of Northern California and if a certain road through Yosemite was open. We drove to the park, and when McGraw contacted us, we simply continued on to Lee Vining. They're at the phone number of a man named Nicholas Romanov, obviously a false name. We are on our way there."

Tremont inhaled, pleased. "Good. Anything else?" At last the annoyance of Lt. Col. Jon Smith was ending.

The Arab's voice dropped lower—confidential. Pride radiated in his words. "Yes, I have other news. Very good news that you will like and not like. My investigation of Smith has shown that this Marty Zellerbach is an old friend from his school days—and so is Bill Griffin."

Tremont growled, "So Griffin did warn Smith in Rock Creek park!"

"And undoubtedly has no intention of killing Smith. But he may not be overtly betraying us."

"You think he still wants the money?"

"I see no signs that say otherwise."

Tremont nodded, thinking. "Then we may be able to use him to our advantage. All right, you deal with Jon Smith and everyone with him." A plan was beginning to form in his mind. Yes, he knew exactly what to do. "I'll handle Griffin."

7:52 P.M.
Thurmont, Maryland

Bill Griffin smiled thinly. The white pizza delivery truck had passed Jon Smith's three-story, saltbox-style house three times in the last two hours. He was inside the dark house and had been since 6:00 P.M., after abandoning his all-day stakeout of Fort Detrick. The first time he had seen the pizza truck slow as it passed the house, it had caught his attention. Could it have been Jon checking to be sure the house was safe and unwatched? The second time, he was prepared with his night-vision binoculars and saw that the driver was not Jon. By the third time, he knew: One of al-Hassan's men was looking for Jon—and perhaps for him, too.

Griffin knew the Arab had been suspicious ever since Rock Creek park, but al-Hassan would not expect Griffin to be waiting inside the house. Griffin had been careful to leave no indications he was there. His car was hidden in the garage of an empty house three blocks away, and he had entered Jon's place by picking the lock on the back door. Since Jon had returned to neither Detrick nor Thurmont, Griffin was beginning to think he would not. Had al-Hassan already killed him? No, otherwise al-Hassan would not be sending men to look for either Jon or Griffin.

He moved swiftly through the dark shadows and into the study. Once the computer was up and running, he entered the password and encryption code for his secret Web site. He immediately saw the message from his old FBI partner, Lon Forbes:

> *Colonel Jonathan Smith is trying to find you. He also contacted Marjorie for the same reason. FBI, police, and army are looking for Smith: AWOL and sought for questioning in two deaths. Let me know if you want to talk to him.*

Griffin thought, and then he checked for anything else. This time he spotted the footprints of someone who had hacked into the site, which might mean a third person was searching for him. There was nothing on the Web site to tell a hacker where he was. Still, a third tracker made him uneasy.

He exited, shut down the computer, and returned to the rear door. When he was sure there was still no one surveilling the back of the house, he slipped away into the night.

8:06 P.M.
New York City

The four people who were gathered in a private room at the Harvard Club on Forty-fourth Street were nervous. They had known one another for years, occasionally on opposing sides and with conflicting interests, but now a shared attraction to money, power, and a view of the future they liked to call "clear-eyed" had brought them together in this room.

The youngest of the four, Maj. Gen. Nelson Caspar, executive officer to the chairman of the Joint Chiefs, held a low conversation with Congressman Ben Sloat, who was a periodic visitor to Victor Tremont's hidden Adirondack estate. General Caspar glanced every few seconds at the door to the room. Nancy Petrelli, secretary of Health and Human

Services, paced alone near the curtained windows in her cream-colored St. John's knit suit. Lt. Gen. Einar Salonen (Ret.), major lobbyist for the American military-industrial complex, sat in an armchair holding a book but not really reading. Neither General Caspar nor General Salonen wore their uniforms, preferring simple but expensive business suits for this clandestine meeting.

Their heads rotated almost in unison as the door opened.

Victor Tremont hurried in. "Sorry, gentlemen and lady"—a slight bow to the HHS secretary—"but I was held up by some business relating to our problem with Colonel Smith, which, I'm happy to say, is about to be settled."

A murmur of relief spread across the room.

"How did the meeting with Blanchard's board of directors go?" General Caspar rumbled. It was the question on everyone's minds.

Tremont perched on the arm of a leather couch, elegant in his dinner jacket and black tie. Assurance radiated from him, and he seemed to draw his four distinguished guests toward him like a magnet. He lifted his patrician chin and laughed. "I'm now in firm control of the entire company."

General Salonen's voice was loudest. "Congratulations!"

"Great news, Victor," Congressman Sloat agreed. "This puts us in the power position."

Secretary Petrelli admitted, "I wasn't sure you could pull it off."

"I had no doubt." General Caspar smiled. "Victor always wins."

Tremont laughed again. "Thank you. Thank you very much for your vote of confidence. But I must say I agree with General Caspar."

Now everyone laughed, even Nancy Petrelli. But her laughter had little humor in it. She went right to the critical point: "You told the board? The details?"

"Chapter and verse." Tremont crossed his arms, smiled, and waited. Teasing them.

The tension in the room grew electric. Their gazes were riveted on him.

"And?" Nancy Petrelli demanded at last.

"What did the goddamned board say?" General Salonen wanted to know.

Victor Tremont smiled broadly. "They jumped on the Hades Project like a dog on a bone." He gazed around the room at the relieved faces. "You could see the dollar signs flash in their eyes. I thought I was in Las Vegas, and they were slot machines."

"No qualms?" Congressman Sloat asked. "We don't have to worry about second thoughts? Bad consciences?"

Tremont shook his head. "Remember, we hand-picked all of them. We pooled our sources so we could choose for background, interest, and risk tolerance." His biggest problem had been getting the names past Haldane so they could be proposed and voted onto the board while old members retired or their terms expired. "Of course, now the question is whether we judged them accurately."

"Obviously we did," Congressman Sloat said with satisfaction.

"Exactly," Tremont said. "Oh, they were a little green around the gills when I laid out the possible deaths without our serum, and all the deaths that will unavoidably occur before it is approved for use on humans. But I explained that on the other hand the virus wasn't a hundred percent fatal without treatment, and they realized the deaths would extrapolate into not much more than a million or so worldwide if the government accepts our serum quickly."

Nancy Petrelli, ever the pessimist, said, "And if the government won't pay our price at all?"

A heavy silence dropped like a dark shroud over the small room. They looked uneasily away from the HHS secretary. It was a question that had been on all their minds.

"Ah, well," Tremont said, "we knew that risk from the start. It was the gamble we took to make the billions we're going to. But I doubt our government or any other government will see another choice. If they don't buy the serum, an awful lot of their people are going to die everywhere. That's the simple answer."

General Caspar nodded appreciatively. "Who dares, wins."

"Ah, yes. The motto of the SAS." Tremont nodded recognition to the general and added drily, "But I'd like to think we take our risks for much larger and more realistic rewards than a few medals and a pat on the back from the queen, eh?"

Tremont swung his leg as he watched the four wrestle with the enormity of it. *Conscience makes cowards of us all.* Shakespeare's words, or close enough, echoed through his mind. *But screw your courage to the sticking point, we shall not fail.* But it was not courage or Shakespeare that had made them accept the risk of the potential slaughter. Not at the beginning of the twenty-first century. It was power and wealth.

General Salonen said bluntly, "But none of us or our families will die. We have the serum."

They had all thought it, but only Salonen had the bravery or perhaps the insensitivity to say it. Tremont continued to wait.

"How long until it begins?" Nancy Petrelli asked.

Tremont considered. "I'd say in three or four days the reality of a pandemic will strike the global conscience like a bolt of lightning."

There was a murmur. Whether it was pity or greed it was hard to tell.

"When it does," Tremont continued, "I want each of you to emphasize the danger to humanity. Hit the panic buttons. Then we make our announcement of the serum."

"And ride to the rescue." General Caspar gave a coarse laugh.

All their doubts vanished as the four conspirators united in their vision of the goal they had dreamed of for so long. It was close. Very close. Just on the other side of the horizon. For the moment, any fear of an opposition, of Bill Griffin's potential treachery, or of Jonathan Smith's determined investigation flew from their minds.

"Beautiful," someone breathed.

Chapter
Twenty-Four

3:15 P.M.
High Sierras, California

"Oh, look!" Marty cried. "That's so *beautiful!*" He came to an abrupt halt in the hallway, turned, and his awkward body rolled and thumped into a dim, cavernous room near the back of Peter Howell's Sierra hideaway. He gazed transfixed at the opposite wall, his green eyes shining.

On the wall, about ten feet above the floor, transparent electronic maps glowed. Each nation was alight in a different color. Tiny blinking bulbs moved continuously across the maps. Rows of multicolored lights blazed after each name on a roster that hung next to the maps. Beneath it all, state-of-the-art computer equipment filled the wall. In the center of the room waited a leather-and-steel command chair. On either side of it stood a large globe and a file cabinet.

Smith studied the maps—Iraq, Iran, Turkey, and the parts of all three that formed the historic land of the Kurds. Then there was East Timor. Colombia. Afghanistan. Southern Mexico and Guatemala. El Salvador. Israel. Rwanda. The hot spots of tribal conflict, ethnic strife, peasant revolt, religious militancy, popular insurgency.

"Your control room?" Jon asked Peter.

"Right." Peter nodded. "Good to keep busy."

It was more than any one private citizen should—or could—have. Obviously, Peter Howell was still working for somebody.

Marty rushed toward the computer installation. "I knew your PC had far too much power to be ordinary. It must be connected to this Goliath. It's *gorgeous!* I want maps like yours for my bungalow. You're monitoring activities in these countries, aren't you? Are you linked directly to centers in each one? You *must* show me what *you're* doing. How the maps are linked. How—"

"Not now, Mart." Jon tried to be patient. "We're on our way out. We're evacuating, remember?"

Marty's face fell. "What's so important about leaving? I want to live in this room." The sullen expression vanished. His round face was as alight as the maps above. "That's what I'm going to do! It's perfect. The whole world will come to me here. I'll never have to leave or—"

"We're leaving right now," Jon said firmly, pushing him toward the door. "You could help us load, okay?"

"As long as we're here, I'll take my files." Peter grabbed a stack of brown files from the top of the free-standing cabinet. As he walked out the door, he pressed a finger against the frame. Jon heard a quiet *click*. "You two take what food you like from the kitchen to tide us over a day or so. We'll need weapons and ammo, and the whiskey, of course."

Jon nodded. "We have things in our car, too. How the hell do we carry it all?"

"Ah, trust me."

A low crooning sound came from the control room. Marty had slipped away from Jon and now sat in Peter's power chair before the wall-sized console. He rocked from side to side, his gaze locked on the shifting array of lights on the transparent wall maps. He was beginning to understand what they all meant, how they interconnected. It was intriguing. He could almost feel the lights pulse in rhythm with his brain—

Jon touched his shoulder. "Mart?"

"No!" He whirled as if bitten. "I'll never leave! Never! Never! Nev . . ."

Jon tried to hold him as he kicked and writhed. "He needs to go back on his meds, pronto," he told Peter.

Wild with rage, Marty lashed out with his fists, swearing incoherencies. Jon gave up and grabbed him in a bear hug, lifted him so that his feet were off the floor, and moved him away from the console as he continued to kick and shout.

Peter frowned. "We don't have time for this." He stepped forward and slugged Marty on the chin.

Marty's eyes widened, and then he collapsed in Jon's arms, unconscious.

Peter's wiry frame trotted back out into the hallway. "Bring him."

Jon sighed. He had a feeling Marty and Peter were not going to get along. He picked up Marty, who had a peaceful expression on his round face. He dropped him over his shoulder and followed the ex–SAS trooper and MI6 agent through the rear door in the kitchen into what turned out to be a garage.

Parked and waiting was a medium-sized RV.

"There's another road," Jon realized. "Of course, there has to be. You're not going to live anywhere where you know you're trapped."

"Right. Never have only one way out. It's a dirt road. Not on the map, not maintained well, but it'll do. Stash Marty in the RV."

Jon deposited Marty on one of the three bunk beds fastened in a stack in the back. The rest of the RV's interior was the usual—kitchen, dining nook, bath, all in miniature, except for the living room. That was the heart of the vehicle. It was a compact version of the map-and-computer center from the house, complete with wall maps, console, and tiny colored lights that came to life as Jon watched.

"Adding a final boost to the batteries," Peter said as Jon returned to the garage. The Brit had hooked up the RV to the house current.

For the next hour they carried food, whiskey, guns, and ammo from the house. While Jon packed it away, Peter vanished to make arrangements. Finally Marty moaned on the bunk and flopped one arm. At the same time, Jon heard the approaching engine of a low-flying aircraft.

He pulled out his Beretta and raced into the house.

"Relax," Peter told him.

They went out front to stand together and look up at the mountain sky. A single-engine Cessna swooped low and roared over the cabin. A small steel tube dropped from it into the clearing. Moments later, Peter returned with the tube.

"The little man's medicine."

Inside the RV, Jon sat the groaning Marty up on the bunk, gave him a pill and a glass of water, and watched him take the drug, grumbling the whole time. Then he lay back without a word and stared up at the RV's ceiling. He rarely spoke of his affliction, but sometimes Jon caught him in an unguarded moment like this, staring off as if wondering what other people felt and thought, what a 'normal life' was really all about.

Peter stuck his head inside the door. His face was grim. "We have company."

"Stay down, Mart." Jon patted his friend and hurried out into the garage.

Binoculars dangled from Peter's neck. He held his cleaned H&K MP5 in one hand, and with the other he tossed Jon the bullpup Enfield. His lined, perpetually tanned face had some kind of strange inner glow, as if who he really was—what he really liked, what made his blood course—had suddenly come alive.

Jon inhaled and felt the buzz of excitement and fear that he used to crave. Perhaps the killers had arrived. And he was ready to meet them. In fact, eager.

With Peter in the lead, they loped through the house and out onto the front porch. They stayed hidden behind bushes that rimmed the porch as they studied the steel footbridge that crossed the deep ravine and the five figures on the far side, who were investigating Jon's rental car.

Peter watched through binoculars. "Three are sheriff's deputies from the county. Two are wearing dark suits and hats and appear to be running the show."

"They don't sound like our killers." Jon took the glasses and focused. Three definitely were uniformed police of some kind, and the other two were doing the ordering. The two in suits stood apart talking to each other as if the police weren't there. One pointed at the cabin.

"FBI," Jon guessed. "They won't come over shooting. I'm just AWOL."

"Unless they're in cahoots with your villains, or unless the situation has changed. Best we take no chances. Let's give them something to think about."

Peter left Jon and disappeared back into the house. Jon continued to focus on the FBI men, who were instructing the deputies to stay back as they advanced. All five took out their weapons and, with the FBI in the lead, approached the bridge. The first FBI man carried an electric bullhorn.

They were only steps from the bridge when the five men came to an abrupt, astonished halt. Jon blinked, unsure himself. One second the footbridge had been there. The next, it vanished.

There was a slapping sound, and dust rose from the ravine in a hazy brown-and-white cloud.

The intruders' mouths fell open. They looked down, then up and across. The two cops ambled forward. Through the binoculars, Jon watched them grin and peer appreciatively down into the steep ravine again. It was a joke on the FBI. The men laughed.

Peter returned to crouch beside Jon. "Surprise them a trifle?"

"I'd say. What happened?"

"Electric legerdemain. The bridge has deucedly massive hinges on this side. When I release the gadgets that attach it at the far side, it swings down into the ravine, bounces against the wall, and comes to rest hanging straight down. A job putting it back, but a crew from Lee Vining will do that when I need them." He stood. "Anyway, that should hold them a half hour or so. It's a nasty climb down and up. Come on."

Jon chuckled as they trotted back through the house and into the garage, where Marty now sat on the RV steps looking tired and rueful. "Hi, Jon. Was I trouble?" His words were slow.

"You were brilliant as usual, but we're going to have to abandon our clothes again. The FBI's found us. They've got our car, and we're leaving fast."

"What can I do?"

"Get back inside and wait."

Jon stepped out back again. He found the Brit sitting cross-legged in the pine-needle duff under the trees. Sunlight shone through the pine branches, making intricate patterns on the Englishman and the golden mountain lion sitting on its haunches, facing him.

Peter spoke quietly. "Sorry, Stanley, but I'm off again. A nuisance, I know. So it's back to the missus and fend for yourself for a bit, I'm afraid. Hold the fort until I return, and I'll be back before you can say Bob's your uncle."

The big solemn cat, his tail lying quiet, had fixed its yellow eyes on Peter. It almost seemed to Jon the cat actually understood the words. Whatever it was—words or tone or body language—the cougar stepped close, reached out its neck, and gently nudged Peter on the nose.

"Good-bye, boy." Peter nudged back.

He stood. They exchanged a look, and the cat turned and bounded lightly off into the trees. Peter headed toward Jon.

"Will he be okay?" Jon wondered. "Can he survive alone?"

"Stan's only partly trained, Jon. Not tame. I'm not sure any cat is actually tame, but that's a different discussion. Stanley will tolerate and protect me and the cabin, but he actually lives something of a double life. He's got his territory, hunts as usual, mates, and has cubs, but for some reason has accepted me and my spread as part of his responsibility. He eats the food I give him as compensation for taking time off from the hunt, I think, not because he needs it. He'll be fine."

"He won't try to attack those cops out there?"

"Only if I told him to. Otherwise he'll avoid humans, as any lion will unless he's threatened. But he'll protect the place against other animals—bears, for example, who'd destroy it." Suddenly he raised his head, cocked an ear. "Right! They're in the ravine and starting up. Time to dust."

■

Moments later, loaded and electrically charged, the RV was bouncing away down the mountainside among the tall pines and cedars and the occasional black oak. Behind them, a series of muffled explosions sounded inside the cabin.

"*J-o-n!* What's that?" Marty's head swiveled.

"They're in the house!" Jon swore. "Damn."

"Hardly," Peter told them. "A little self-destruct device. Can't leave the control and computer room for them, can we? It's imploding now. Everything in there will be destroyed, but the rest of the house will be fine. Untouched. Clever, eh? Work of an old sapper I know gone electronic."

With winter late in the Sierras, white patches from early snowfalls sparkled among the trees. Exposed rocks and ruts from past rains jarred the RV. They made decent time as they swayed, dipped, and jounced down serpentine switchbacks.

Jon hung on. "Did you get me set up for Iraq?"

Peter reached into the pocket of the bush jacket he had put on over his flannel shirt. He handed Jon an envelope. "Printout's inside. Follow the instructions to the letter, or the trip will be over long before you know it. To the letter."

"I understand."

Peter glanced sideways. "There was talk of a task for me."

"What about me, Jon?" Marty asked from behind.

"You know what we have to do," Jon told them. "Find where the virus came from, how to treat it, who has it, what they plan to do with it, and who killed Sophia."

"And how to stop them," Peter said grimly.

"Especially how to stop them." Jon hung on as a deep pothole hurled them off their seats, shaking their bones. "Every Bio-Level Three and Four lab around the globe is working on the treatment, so we've got help there. But that still leaves the other questions. In reality, it's all one big one: Who has it? But information about any one of the others could lead to the final answer. I'm counting on Iraq as the best chance to discover where it came from and what they're planning to do with it."

"And the answer to who killed Sophia could also tell us the rest, too," Peter decided. "My assignment, right?"

"Yes. Yours and Marty's." He looked back. "You keep trying to pull up any missing phone calls, Mart, and locate Griffin. But hit and run this time. Don't stay on the same line long. Switch routes. Those are two important assignments."

Marty's face was guilty. "I'm sorry, Jon."

"I know." Jon paused. "We've got to have some way to stay in touch."

"The Internet," Marty said promptly. "But not regular E-mail."

"Right you are," Peter agreed. "But perhaps there's somewhere we can leave a message."

Jon smiled. "I know—right under their noses, where they'll never see it. We can use the Asperger's syndrome Web site."

Marty nodded enthusiastically. "That's great, Jon. Perfect."

They continued to discuss the site's Web ring and what kind of coded messages to leave until Peter suddenly shouted: "Hold fast! Bogies at ten o'clock!"

The RV gave a wild lurch to the right, swaying so far over for a second it rode on two wheels. A volley of shots exploded from the forest. Glass flew and metal ripped at the back of the RV. Marty cried out.

"Mart?" Jon looked back.

Marty sat huddled on the floor of the careening RV, clutching his left leg and trying not to be flung from side to side like a sack of flour. A bloody sack of flour. Jon could see a spreading pool of red on Marty's trouser leg, but Marty grinned feebly and said in a shaky voice, "I'm all right, Jon."

"Get a towel," Jon called back, "fold it and press it hard against the wound. If the bleeding doesn't stop soon, yell out."

He needed to stay in the cab where he could use Peter's Enfield if any of the attackers cut them off.

Peter was too busy to use a weapon as he turned the wheel with a vise grip, his pale eyes cool. The unwieldy vehicle bounced off the road through the trees and brush, miraculously hitting nothing as Peter guided it with the precision of an astronaut docking at a space station. Twice he plunged the massive vehicle through streams, kicking up sheets of water and tilting dangerously on rocks hidden beneath the surfaces.

On the road, two men ran with rifles trying to get a clear shot at the RV, but the bone-jarring, unpredictable lurches and bounces of the vehicle frustrated them. They dodged branches and leaped over rocks. Behind them, a gray SUV battled to turn on the narrow road so it could join the pursuit.

As the runners fell farther behind, Jon spotted a deep ravine looming straight ahead. "Peter! Careful!"

"Got it!" Peter slammed the brakes and pivoted in a half J-turn. The top-heavy vehicle threatened to flip over as it skidded sideways, sideswiped two giant boulders, and finally came to a shuddering stop barely feet from the chasm.

On the road, the runners were far back but closing in again. In the distance, the SUV had almost succeeded in turning.

Tension in the RV was thick. Jon stared down at the deep ravine and wiped sweat from his face.

"Here we go." Peter gunned the engine, and the big vehicle leaped ahead parallel to the ravine and straight toward the road.

Jon watched the two pursuing attackers, who were trying to short-cut the road by sprinting among the trees. "They're getting close!"

Peter gave the running men a quick glance. The ravine made a sudden sharp turn away, and he angled the RV out of the trees and onto the road once more. With a relieved grin, he jerked the clumsy vehicle around and roared away down the dirt road, kicking up clouds of dust.

A final fusillade rang out, and bullets slashed through the trees around the fleeing vehicle. Jon forced himself to take a long breath and relax his hands on his weapon. He checked the side-view mirror: The two men had been joined by a third, and they stood angry and frustrated, their weapons dangling at their sides, in the center of the dusty road.

Jon recognized the short, burly man who had joined the first two.

"It's them," he said angrily. "The people who've been trying to kill me." He looked at Peter. "There'll be more of them somewhere."

"Of course." Peter studied the rough road as the vehicle continued to shake and bounce. "Evasive strategy, I should say. Knowledge of the terrain. Trust the enemy to overrate the element of surprise."

Jon climbed back to Marty, hanging on to anything he could hold. But this time Marty was right—the flesh wound in his left leg was superficial. Jon applied antibiotic and a bandage. One of the RV's windows had been shot out and the outer shell ripped with bullet holes in three places, but nothing had penetrated, and nothing important was damaged, especially not the computer that was part of Peter's standard equipment.

He rejoined Peter up front, and five minutes later heard the sound of traffic.

"What do you think?" He scrutinized the dirt road ahead as it wound down among the trees. "Will they be waiting where we join the highway?"

"Or sooner. Let's disappoint them." Peter smiled his almost dreamy smile.

Ahead was a track that led off from the road to the left. Even narrower than the road they traveled, even more deeply rutted, it was only inches wider than the RV. But it was a road, not a trail.

Peter explained, "Fire road. Forest's full of them. Unmarked on any maps but the forestry service's and the fire district's."

"We're taking it?" Jon asked.

"The scenic route." With a short smile, Peter swung the RV onto it.

Pine branches brushed and scraped against the RV's metal sides. The noise was endless and unnerving, like fingers on a chalkboard. Fifteen minutes later, just as Jon was beginning to think he was going to lose his mind, he saw the end of the road.

"This it?" he asked Peter hopefully.

"What? Stop this lovely jaunt?" Peter turned the vehicle onto another fire road. "We're going downhill now, notice? Won't be long," he said cheerfully. "Buck up, lad."

This fire road was an equally tight squeeze. Overhanging branches continued to scratch the sides as Peter pressed the RV onward. Jon closed his eyes and sighed, trying to keep his skin from crawling. At least Marty was not complaining from the back. But then, Marty was on his meds. Thank God for at least that.

When they finally reached the highway, Jon sat up alertly. Peter paused the RV among the trees at the blacktop's edge. The horrible scratching and groaning stopped, and only the sound of the engine and the traffic marred the quiet beauty of the forest.

Jon peered around. "Any sign of them?" Traffic on the wide two-lane road in front of them was heavier than he'd expected. "This isn't 120."

"U.S. 395. The big one on this side. Should do. See anyone lurking?"

Jon surveyed both directions. "No one."

"Good. Neither do I. Which way?"

"Which way gets us to San Francisco faster?"

"To the right, and back on 120 through Yosemite."

"To the right then, and 120."

Peter's pale eyes twinkled. "Cheeky of you."

"Going back the way we came should be the last thing they'd expect us to do, and all RVs look alike anyway."

"Unless the ambushers read our plate."

"Take the plates off."

"Dammit, my boy. Should've thought of that." Peter pulled a screwdriver and a set of Montana license plates from the glove compartment and jumped out.

Jon grabbed his Beretta and followed. He stood watch as Peter lifted off the old one and screwed on a license from Montana. In the tranquil forest, birds sang and insects buzzed.

Minutes later, both men returned inside.

Marty was sitting at the computer. He looked up. "Everything okay?"

"Absolutely," Jon reassured him.

Peter put the RV into gear and said enthusiastically, "Let's bell the cat."

He rolled the lumbering vehicle onto the highway heading south. When the 120 intersection appeared, he turned onto it, and they climbed back uphill. A quarter of a mile later they passed two SUVs parked along the dense forest, one on each side of the dirt road that led from the back of Peter's property.

At one of the SUVs, a tall, pockmarked man with hooded dark eyes and wearing a black suit spoke into a walkie-talkie. He seemed agitated, and he stared up the mountainside in frustration. He hardly glanced at the battered RV with the Montana plates as it climbed up the highway toward Yosemite.

"Arab," Peter said. "Looks dangerous."

"My conclusion, too." Jon stared at the highway traffic. His voice was grave. "Let's hope I can find some answers in Iraq, and that you'll be able to track Bill Griffin and find out more about Sophia's death. Those erased phone calls could be critical."

They drove on. Peter turned on the radio. It droned news of an unknowing world, while the approaching darkness cast its long, ominous shadows over the white peaks of the high Sierras ahead.

Part Three

Chapter
Twenty-Five

8:00 P.M., Tuesday, October 21
The White House, Washington, D.C.

Like an accusation, the front page of *The Washington Post* lay on the big Cabinet Room oval table where the president had left it. Although none of the solemn cabinet chiefs who sat around the polished table and none of their assistants who packed the walls looked at the newspaper with its banner headline, everyone was painfully aware of it. They had awakened to find their own copies lying on their doorsteps, just as hundreds of millions of Americans had discovered similar terrifying headlines awaiting them. All day long the news had blared from their radios. On television, little else was discussed.

For days scientists and the military had kept the president and high officials informed, but not until now, when the so-called civilized world seemed to erupt with the news, had the full force of the growing epidemic hit home.

DEADLY PANDEMIC OF UNKNOWN VIRUS SWEEPS GLOBE

In the packed cabinet room, Secretary of State Norman Knight pushed his metal-rimmed glasses up on his long nose. His voice was sober. "Twenty-seven nations have reported fatalities due to the virus, a total so far of more than a half million. All began with symptoms of a heavy cold or mild flu for some two weeks, then it'd suddenly escalate into acute respiratory distress syndrome and death within hours, sometimes less." He sighed unhappily. "Forty-two nations are reporting sudden cases of what appears to be a mild flu. We don't know yet whether that's the virus, too. We've barely started counting those victims, but they're in the high millions."

A shocked hush greeted the secretary's figures. The packed room seemed to grow rigid.

President Samuel Adams Castilla's penetrating gaze traveled slowly over their faces. He was looking for clues into the minds of his cabinet chiefs. He had to know on whom he could count to remain steady and bring knowledge, wisdom, and the will to act. Who would panic? Who would be shocked into paralysis? Knowledge without the will to act was impotent. Will to act without knowledge was blind and reckless. And anyone with neither to offer needed to be dismissed.

Finally he spoke, keeping his voice composed. "All right, Norm. How many in the United States?"

The secretary of state's long face was topped by an unruly shock of thick white hair. "Beyond the nine cases early last week, the CDC reports some fifty more deaths and at least a thousand flulike cases that they're testing for the new virus right now."

"It looks like we're getting off light," said Admiral Stevens Brose, chairman of the Joint Chiefs. His voice was cautiously hopeful.

Too cautious and too hopeful, President Castilla reflected. It was strange, but he had noticed that military men were often the least willing to act on the instant. But then, they had seen the deadly consequences of ill-considered action more than most.

"That's so far," Nancy Petrelli, secretary of Health and Human Services, pointed out ominously. "Which doesn't mean we won't be devastated tomorrow."

"No, I suppose it doesn't," the president agreed, a little surprised by the HHS secretary's negative tone. He had always found her to be the optimistic type. Probably a measure of the terror this virus was instilling in people and governments. That alone emphasized the need for action—considered and meaningful action, yes, but *some* action, to mitigate the sense of helpless panic that could freeze everyone in its grip.

He turned to the surgeon general. "Anything new on where those six original cases contracted the virus, Jesse? A connection among them?"

"Aside from the fact that all were either in Desert Storm or related to someone who was, neither the CDC nor USAMRIID has been able to find anything."

"Overseas?

"The same," Surgeon General Jesse Oxnard admitted. "All the scientists agree they're stumped. They can see it in their electron microscopes, but the DNA sequence information so far doesn't offer any useful clues. It matches no known virus exactly, so they can only guess how to deal with it. They have no idea where it came from and nothing that'll cure or stop it. All they can suggest are the usual methods for treating any viral fever and then hope the mortality rate is no worse than the fifty percent we had in the first six cases."

"At least that's something," the president decided. "We can mobilize every medical resource in the advanced industrialized countries and send them all over the world. Medicines, too. Everything anyone needs or thinks they need." The president nodded to Anson McCoy, secretary of defense. "You put the whole armed forces at Jesse's disposal, Anse, everything—transports, troops, ships, whatever it takes."

"Yessir," Anson McCoy agreed.

"Within reason, sir," Admiral Brose warned. "There are some nations that might try to take advantage if we put too many resources into this. We could leave ourselves open to attack."

"The way it's going, Stevens," the president said dryly, "there might not be much left to attack or defend anywhere. It's a time for new thinking, people. The old answers aren't working. Lincoln said something like that in a crisis a long time ago, and we may damn well be approaching the same kind of crisis now. Kenny and Norman have been trying to tell us that for years. Right, Kenny?"

Secretary of the Interior Kenneth Dahlberg nodded. "Global warming. Environmental degradation. Destruction of the rain forests. Migration from rural areas all across the Third World. Overpopulation. It's all leading to the emergence of new diseases everywhere. That means a lot of deaths. This epidemic may be only the tip of the iceberg."

"Which means we've got to put everything into stopping it," the president said. "As must every industrialized country." Out of the corners of his eyes he saw Nancy Petrelli open her mouth as if to object. "And don't tell me how much it's going to cost, Nancy. That doesn't matter at this point."

"I agree, sir. I was going to offer an idea."

"Okay." The president tried to control his impatience. In his mind he was gearing up for action. "Tell us what's on your mind."

"I disagree that all scientists have nothing to suggest. My office had a call not an hour ago from a Dr. Victor Tremont, chairman and CEO of Blanchard Pharmaceuticals. He said he couldn't be absolutely certain, having never tested it against the new virus, but the description he's heard of the virus and its symptoms seems to closely match a monkey virus his company's been working with for some years." She paused for effect. "They have developed a serum that cures it most of the time."

There was a stunned moment. Excitement exploded in a cacophony of conflicting voices. They bombarded the HHS secretary with questions. They objected to the possibility. They thrilled at a cure.

Finally the president slammed his fist onto the table. "Hold it, dammit! All of you, *shut up!*"

The cabinet room almost vibrated with the abrupt silence. The president glared at each of them, allowing time for the room to calm. Tension was palpable, and the ticking of the clock on the mantel seemed as loud as thunder.

Finally, President Castilla returned his hard gaze to the HHS secretary. "Let's hear that again straight out and in fewer words, Nancy. Someone thinks they have a cure for this thing? Where? How?"

Nancy Petrelli glanced with considerable animosity toward her fellow cabinet members and the other advisers who were ready to jump on her again. "As I said, sir, his name is Victor Tremont. He's CEO and chairman of Blanchard Pharmaceuticals, a large international biomedical company. He says a team at Blanchard has developed a cure against a virus found in monkeys from South America. Animal testing has been highly positive, a veterinary use patent has been granted, and everything's under review by the FDA."

Surgeon General Oxnard frowned. "It hasn't been approved by the FDA even for animals?"

"Or ever tested on humans?" Secretary of Defense McCoy demanded.

"No," the HHS secretary said, "they had no intention of using it on humans. Dr. Tremont thinks this unknown virus may be the same monkey virus but contracted now by humans, and I'd say—considering the circumstances—we'd be idiots not to investigate further."

"Why would anyone develop a cure for a monkey virus?" the secretary of commerce wanted to know.

"To learn how to combat viruses in general. To develop mass production techniques for the future," Nancy Petrelli told them. "You've just heard Ken and Norman say emerging viruses are an increasing danger to the world with all the access to what were once remote areas. Today's monkey virus can be tomorrow's human epidemic. I'd say we can all appreciate that now, can't we? Maybe we should consider the possibility that a monkey-virus cure just might cure humans, too."

The hubbub erupted again.

"Too damn dangerous."

"I think Nancy's right. We don't have a choice."

Robert Ludlum and Gayle Lynds

"FDA would never allow it."

"What do we have to lose?"

"A lot. It could be worse than the disease."

And: "Does it sound a little funny to anyone else? I mean, a cure for an unknown disease just appearing out of nowhere?"

"Come on, Sam, they've obviously been working on it for years."

"A lot of pure research doesn't have a practical use at first, then suddenly it does."

Until the president again banged the table.

"All right! All right! We'll discuss it. I'll listen to any and all objections. But right now, I want Nancy and Jesse to go to this Blanchard Pharmaceuticals and check it out. We have a disaster on our hands, and we certainly don't want to make it any worse. At the same time, we could use a miracle right about now. Let's all hope to hell this Tremont knows what he's talking about. Let's do more. Let's pray he's right before half the world is wiped out." He stood up. "All right, that's it. We all know what we have to do. Let's do it."

He strode from the room with a far more positive stride and manner than he felt. He had young children of his own, and he was frightened.

■

In the soundproof backseat of her long black limousine, Nancy Petrelli spoke into her cell phone. "I waited until the situation appeared to be as grim as possible, as you suggested, Victor. When I saw that everyone was ready to concede all we could do was put on Band-Aids and hand out a lot of TLC, I dropped our bombshell. There was a lot of gnashing of teeth, but in the end I'd say the president's position is, basically, he's ready to take any help he can get."

"Good. Intelligent." Far away in the Adirondacks, Tremont smiled in his office above the placid and peaceful lake. "How is Castilla going to handle it?"

"He's sending me and the surgeon general up to talk to you and report back."

"Even better. We'll put on a science-and-humility show for Jesse Oxnard."

"Be careful about it, Victor. Oxnard and a few others are suspicious. With the president looking for anything positive, they won't do more than mutter, but give them any suggestion that something isn't right and they'll pounce."

"They'll find nothing, Nancy. Trust me."

"What about our colonel Jon Smith? Is he out of the picture?"

"You can count on it."

"I hope so, Victor. I really hope so."

She clicked off and sat in the dark limo, her manicured fingers tapping rapidly against the armrest. She was excited and afraid. Excited that everything appeared to be going exactly as planned, and afraid that something . . . some small chink they had forgotten or ignored or had not dealt with . . . could go wrong.

In his office, Victor Tremont looked out at the distant dark shadows of the high Adirondacks. He had reassured Nancy Petrelli, but he was having a harder time reassuring himself. After al-Hassan missed Smith and his two friends in the Sierras, all three had vanished. What he hoped was that they had gone into hiding and posed no further threat— that they were hunkered down, afraid for their lives.

But Tremont could take no chances. Besides, from every piece of information he had been able to learn about Smith, it seemed obvious to him that Smith was not the type to give up. Tremont would continue to keep everyone watching for him. Smith's chances of doing damage, or even surviving, were not good. Tremont shook his head. For a moment he felt a chill. A not-good chance with a man like Smith was not the same as no chance at all.

Chapter
Twenty-Six

8:02 A.M., Wednesday, October 22
Baghdad, Iraq

Once considered the cradle of civilization, the city of Baghdad sprawled on a dry plain between the Tigris and Euphrates Rivers. A metropolis of contrasts, it seemed to shudder in the morning light. From turquoise-tiled domes and minarets, *muezzin* wailed across the rooftops of the exotic city, calling the faithful to prayer. Women dressed in long *abayas* glided like black pyramids through the narrow byways of the old *suq* and toward the glassy, modern high-rises of the new city.

This ancient city of myth and legend had been invaded many times across the millennia—by Hittites and Arabs, Mongols and the British—and each time it had survived and triumphed. But after a decade of U.S.-led sanctions, that long history seemed irrelevant. Life in Saddam Hussein's shabby Baghdad was a day-to-day struggle for the basics—food, clean water, and medicine. Vehicles lumbered along palm-lined boulevards. Smog stank the sweet desert air.

Jon Smith had been thinking about all this as the taxicab had rushed him through the gray city streets. Now as he paid off the driver, he looked carefully around at a once-expensive neighborhood. No one appeared too curious. But then, he was dressed as a U.N. worker with an official U.N. armband and a plastic identification badge snapped to his jacket. Also, taxis were everywhere in this grim, embattled city. Driving a cab was one of the few occupations most middle-class Iraqis were already prepared to do: They still had at least one operating family car, and Saddam Hussein kept the price of gas low, less than ten U.S. cents a liter.

As the driver sped away, Smith surveyed the street again and warily strode across to what had once been the American embassy. The windows were shuttered, and the building and grounds were in disrepair. There was a sense of abandonment about the compound, but Jon pushed on through. He rang the bell.

The United States still had a man in Baghdad, but he was Polish. In 1991, at the end of the Gulf War, Poland assumed control of the imposing American embassy on P Street Northwest. Since then, even when U.S. bombs and missiles fell, Polish diplomats held forth from the embassy, representing not only their nation's interests in Iraq, but America's. From the great shuttered embassy, they handled passport questions, reported on local media, and occasionally passed sub-rosa messages between Washington and Baghdad. As in all wars, there were times when even enemies needed to communicate, which was the only reason Saddam Hussein tolerated the Poles. At any moment, the mercurial Hussein could change his mind and imprison them all.

The embassy's front door swung open to show a big man with a snub nose, thick gray hair, and shaggy eyebrows that were lowered over intelligent brown eyes.

He fit the description Peter had given Jon. "Jerzy Domalewski?"

"The same. You must be Peter's friend." The door swung open wider, and the diplomat's gaze took in the tall American with one savvy glance. In his midforties, he wore a brown suit that sagged as if it had gone too long between cleanings. He spoke in Polish-accented English. "Come in. No point in making ourselves into bigger targets than we already are." He closed the door behind Jon and led him across a marble foyer into a large office. "You are sure no one followed you?" He liked the level look in the stranger's dark blue eyes and the sense of physical power he radiated. He would need both attributes in perilous Baghdad.

Instantly Smith caught the whiff of fear. "MI6 knows what it's doing. I won't bore you with the circuitous route they used to get me into the country."

"Good. Do not tell me." Domalewski nodded as he closed the office door. "There are secrets no one should know. Not even me." He gave a small, wry smile. "Take a chair. You must be weary. That one with the arms is comfortable. Still has its springs." As Jon sat, the diplomat continued on to the window where he cracked open the shutter and stared outside at the morning. "We must be so careful."

Jon crossed his legs. Domalewski was correct: He was tired. But he also felt a pounding need to get on with his investigation. Sophia's beautiful face and the agony of her death haunted him.

Three days ago, he had arrived at London's Heathrow airport in the early hours of the morning dressed in new civilian clothes he had bought in San Francisco. It was the beginning of a long, grueling journey. At Heathrow, an MI6 agent sneaked him into a military ambulance that had whisked him to some RAF base in East Anglia. From there he had been flown to a desert airstrip in Saudi Arabia and picked up by a nameless and taciturn British SAS corporal dressed in long Bedouin robes who spoke perfect Arabic.

"Put these on." He tossed Jon robes identical to his. "We're going to take advantage of a little-known prewar agreement." It turned out he was talking about the Iraqi–Saudi Arabian Neutral Zone, which the two nations still maintained so their nomadic Bedouins could continue their historic trade routes.

In the sweltering robes, Jon and the corporal were handed from Bedouin camp to Bedouin camp by the Iraqi underground until on the outskirts of Baghdad the corporal surprised him with fake identity papers. Iraqi *dinars*, Western clothing, and a badge and armband for a U.N. worker from Belize. Jon's cover name was Mark Bonnet.

He had shaken his head, amazed at MI6's thoroughness. "You've been holding out."

"Hell, no," the corporal said indignantly. "Didn't know whether you'd make it. No point wasting good ID on a bloody corpse." He pumped Jon's hand in farewell. "If you ever see that arse Peter Howell again, tell him he owes us all a whopper."

Now Jon sat in the former American embassy, dressed like a typical U.N. worker in his brown cotton slacks, short-sleeved shirt, zippered jacket, and the all-important U.N. armband and badge. He had money and additional identification in his pocket.

"Do not take our concern personally," Domalewski was saying as he continued to study the street. "You cannot blame us for not being especially enthusiastic about helping you."

"Of course. But be assured—this may be the most crucial risk you've ever taken."

Domalewski nodded his shaggy head. "That was in the message from Peter. He also gave me a list of doctors and hospitals you wished to visit." The Pole turned from the window, his thick eyebrows raised. Again he considered the American. His old friend Peter Howell had said this man was a medical doctor. But could he handle himself if violence struck? It was true that from his high-planed face to his broad shoulders and trim waist, he looked more like a sniper than a healer. Domalewski considered himself an apt judge of people, and from everything he could see about this undercover American, perhaps Peter had been right.

Jon asked, "You've arranged meetings?"

"Of course. I will drive myself to some. Others you must handle yourself." The diplomat's voice became a warning: "But remember your U.N. credentials will be useless if you fall into the government's hands. This is a police state. Many citizens are armed, and anyone can be a spy. Hussein's private police force—the Republican Guard—is as brutal and powerful as the SS and Gestapo combined. They're always sniffing for enemies of the state, dissenters, or simply someone whose looks they do not like."

"I understand they can be random."

"Ah, so you do know something about Iraq."

"A bit." Smith nodded grimly.

Domalewski cocked his head, continuing to appraise the American. He went behind his desk and pulled out a drawer. "Sometimes the greatest danger is the very arbitrariness of it all. Violence here erupts in a heartbeat, often for no logical reason. Peter said you should have this."

He sat in an armchair next to Jon and held out another U.S. Army Beretta.

Smith took it eagerly. "He thinks of everything."

"As my father and I both found in our time."

"Then you've worked with him before."

"More than once. Which is why I am doing him the favor of helping you."

He had wondered why Domalewski had agreed. "Thanks to both of you."

"I hope you will still thank us tomorrow or the next day. Peter says you are adequate with the Beretta. Do not hesitate to use it if you must. However, remember any foreigner caught with a gun will be arrested."

"I appreciate the warning. I plan to avoid that."

"Good. Have you heard about the Justice Detention Center?"

"Sorry, no."

Domalewski's voice dropped, and horror infused his words. "The existence of the detention center was confirmed just recently. It is six stories deep into the ground. Imagine that—no windows for the world to look in, no exterior walls for the cries of the tormented to be heard through, and no hope of escape. Iraqi military intelligence built it under the hospital near the al-Rashid military camp south of here. They say Qusai, Saddam's insane son, supervised the design and construction himself. Military officers and personnel who displease Saddam have an entire floor of torture and execution chambers reserved for them. Other prisoners can be sent to a level where they officially do not exist. They cannot be asked about. Their names cannot even be mentioned. Those sad creatures are disappeared and lost forever. But for me, the worst part of the underground building . . . the most grisly and somehow savage . . . is on the bottom floor. There Saddam has not only dungeons but an appalling fifty-two gallows."

Jon repressed a shudder. "Good God. *Fifty-two gallows?* Mass executions. He hangs fifty-two at a time? The whole place sounds like a piece of hell. The man's an animal!"

"Exactly. Remember, it is better to use the gun than to be caught with it. At best, the confusion might give you a chance." He hesitated. He clasped his hands and looked up at Jon, his eyes dark with concern. "You are undercover, unofficial, and unprotected. Oh, yes, they would arrest you, and, if you were very lucky, they would kill you quickly."

"I understand."

"If you still wish to proceed, you have a lot of territory to cover today. We must leave immediately."

For a brief hallucinogenic moment, in his mind Smith saw Sophia's tortured face as she fought to live. The glistening sweat on her flushed cheeks . . . her silky hair matted down . . . her quivering fingers desperately reaching for her throat as she tried to breathe. Her pain had been excruciating.

As he studied the grave face of Domalewski, what he was really thinking about was the only woman he had ever loved and her terrible, inexplicable, needless, criminal death. For Sophia, he could handle anything. Even Iraq and Saddam Hussein.

He stood up. "Let's go."

Chapter
Twenty-Seven

10:05 A.M.
Baghdad

Alone in the backseat of the American embassy's only operating limousine, Jon looked out on the bustling city and noted with disgust one consistent feature—the photographs of Saddam Hussein. From towering billboards to wall-size posters to framed pictures in dingy storefront windows, Hussein with his thick black mustache and toothy smile was everywhere. Cradling a child. Heroically facing off against America's new president. Leading a family gathering or a businessmen's group. Proudly saluting goose-stepping troops.

In this once-legendary land of learning and culture, Hussein's steel-fisted rule was stronger than ever. He had turned his nation's state of war into the basis of his power, and the wretchedness of his people into patriotic pride. While he blamed the U.N.'s embargo—*"al-hissar"*—for causing a million of his people to die of malnutrition, he and his cronies had grown shamelessly fat and rich.

Jonathan's disgust only deepened when they reached the elegant Jadiriya suburb, where many of Hussein's courtiers, sycophants, and war profiteers had settled in splendor. As Jerzy Domalewski drove, they cruised past showy mansions, fine cafés, and glitzy boutiques. Polished Mercedeses, BMWs, and Ferraris lined the curbs. Servants in livery stood guard outside pricey restaurants. Poverty had been banished, but human greed was everywhere.

Smith shook his head. "This is criminal."

Domalewski was wearing a chauffeur's cap and jacket. "Considering what the rest of Baghdad looks like, entering Jadiriya is akin to landing on another planet. A very rich planet. How can these people stand to live within their selfish skins?"

"It's unconscionable."

"Agreed." The Polish diplomat stopped the limo in front of an attractive stucco building with a blue-tile roof. "This is it." The engine idling, he glanced back over his shoulder. His face was solemn and anxious. "I will wait. Unless, of course, you run out of there with the Republican Guards on your backside. I have only the smallest worry of this, you understand. Still, if such an unfortunate event should occur, please do not be insulted if all you see is the exhaust from this vehicle's tailpipe."

Smith gave a brief smile. "I understand."

The graceful building housed the offices of Dr. Hussein Kamil, a prominent internist. Smith stepped out into the warm sunshine, looked warily around, and strode through a line of date palms toward the carved wood door. Inside, the waiting room was cool and empty. Smith took in the rich rugs, draperies, and upholstered furniture. He studied the closed doors, wondering how safe he was and whether he would find answers here. Despite the doctor's apparent affluence, he was not doing as well as he might. Iraq's economic isolation showed in small ways. The draperies were faded and the furniture worn. The magazines on the side tables were five and ten years old.

One of the doors opened, and the doctor appeared. He was a man of medium height, in his early fifties, with a swarthy complexion and nervous, darting eyes. He wore a white medical coat over pressed gray trousers. And he was alone. No nurse. No receptionist. Obviously he had timed Smith's appointment to make certain no one would witness it.

"Dr. Kamil." Jon introduced himself by the fake name on his U.N. papers—Mark Bonnet.

The doctor inclined his head politely, but his voice was low and uneasy. "You have your bona fides?" He spoke English with a British upper-class accent.

Jon handed over the forged U.N. identification. Dr. Kamil had been told Jon was part of a worldwide team investigating a new virus. The doctor led him into an examination room where he studied the credentials as carefully as he would evidence of cancer.

As he waited, Jon looked around—white walls, chromed equipment, two wood stools, and a table painted white where the short stubs of pencils lay in a pottery bowl. The medical equipment showed the effects of years of use without replacement. Everything was clean and shiny, but there were empty stands where test tubes should be waiting. The white cloth that covered the examination table was thin and eaten with tiny holes. Some of the equipment was very out of date. That would not be the only problem this doctor—all the doctors of Iraq—faced. Domalewski had said many were graduates of the world's finest medical schools and continued to provide good diagnoses, but their patients had to find their own drugs. Medicine was available mostly on the black market and not for *dinars*. Only for U.S. dollars. Even the elite had trouble, although they were willing to pay astronomical sums.

Finally the doctor returned the paperwork. He did not invite Jon to sit, and he did not sit himself. They stood in the middle of the spartan, run-down room and conversed, two suspicious strangers.

The doctor said, "What exactly is it you wish to know?"

"You agreed to talk to me, Doctor. I assume you know what you wanted to say."

The doctor waved that off. "I cannot be too careful. I am close to our great leader. Many members of the Revolutionary Council are my patients."

Jon eyed him. He looked like a man with a secret. The question was whether Smith could find some way to convince him to reveal it. "Still, something's bothering you, Dr. Kamil. A medical matter, I'd say. I'm sure it has nothing to do with Saddam or the war, so it should be no danger to either of us to discuss it a moment. Perhaps," he said carefully, "it's the deaths from an unknown virus."

Dr. Kamil chewed on his lower lip. His ebony eyes were troubled. He glanced almost pleadingly around as if he feared the walls themselves would betray him. But he was also an educated man. So he sighed and admitted, "A year ago I treated a patient who died of sudden acute respiratory distress syndrome with hemorrhaging from the lungs. He had contracted what appeared to be a heavy cold two weeks *before* the ARDS."

Jon repressed excitement. They were the same symptoms as the victims in the United States. "Was he a veteran of Desert Storm?"

The doctor's eyes radiated fear. "Do not say that!" he whispered. "He had the honor of fighting with the Republican Guard during the *Glorious War of Unification!*"

"Any chance his death resulted from biological warfare agents? We know Saddam had them."

"That is a *lie!* Our great leader would never permit such weapons. If there were any, they were brought in by the enemy."

"Then could his death have been caused by the enemy's biological agents?"

"No. Not at all."

"But your patient was infected sometime during the war?"

The doctor nodded. His swarthy face was anxious. "He was an old family friend, you see. I gave him a complete physical every year of his life. You can never be too careful about health in a backward nation such as ours." The fearful eyes swept the room; he had insulted his country. "Not long after he returned to his normal life he began to show many symptoms of minor infections that failed to respond to normal treatment but disappeared anyway. Over the years, he had increasing fevers and brief flulike episodes. Then he developed the heavy cold and died abruptly."

"Were there other deaths in Iraq from the virus then?"

"Yes. Two more here in Baghdad."

"Also veterans from the war?"

"So I have been told."

"Was anyone cured?"

Dr. Kamil crossed his arms and nodded miserably. "I have heard rumors." He did not look at Jon. "But in my opinion, those patients simply survived their ARDS. Other than untreated rabies virus, no virus kills one hundred percent. Not even Ebola."

"How many survived?"

"Three."

Three and three again. The evidence was piling up, and Jon fought back both his excitement and his horror. He was uncovering information that pointed more and more to an experiment using human guinea pigs. "Where are the survivors?"

At that, the frightened doctor stepped back. "No more! I do not want you going elsewhere and having survivor data traced back to me." He yanked open the door of the examination room and pointed at another door across the hallway. "Go. Leave!"

Jon did not move. "Something made you want to tell me, Doctor. And it's not three dead men."

For a moment the doctor looked as if he could jump out of his skin. "Not another word! Nothing! Leave here! I do not believe you are from Belize or from the U.N.!" His voice rose. "One phone call to the authorities and—"

Jon's tension escalated. The terrified doctor looked as if he might explode, and Jon could not take the chance that he would be trapped in the consequences. He slipped out the side door and along an alley. With relief, he saw the embassy limousine still waited.

■

In his office, Dr. Hussein Kamil shook with fear and anger. He was furious to have put himself in this position, and he was afraid he would be caught. At the same time, this wretched situation offered an opportunity, if he dared take it.

He bowed his head, crossed his arms, and tried to quiet his tremors. He had a large family to support, and his country was disintegrating as he watched. He had the future to think of. He was tired of being poor in a land where plenty was to be had.

At last he picked up the phone. But it was not the authorities he dialed.

He inhaled. "Yes, Dr. Kamil here. You contacted me about a certain man." He steadied his voice. "He has just left my office. He carries the credentials of a U.N. employee from Belize. The name is Mark Bonnet. However, I feel certain he is the one you asked me to watch for. Yes, the virus from the Glorious War of Unification. . . . That was what he asked about. No, he did not say where he was going. But he was very interested in the survivors. Of course. I am most grateful. I will expect the money and the antibiotics tomorrow."

He dropped the receiver into its cradle and fell into his chair. He sighed and felt better. So much better that he allowed himself a faint smile. The risk was high, but the payoff was, with luck, more than worth it. By making this one call, he was about to become a rarity in Baghdad: He would have his own private supply of antibiotics.

He rubbed his hands. Optimism coursed through his veins.

The rich would crawl to him when they or their children fell ill. They would throw money at him. Not *dinars*, which were useless in this benighted land in which he had been imprisoned since the stupid Americans began their war and embargo. No, the wealthy sick would shower him with U.S. dollars. Soon he would have more than enough to pay for his family's escape and a fresh life somewhere else. Anywhere else.

7:01 P.M.
Baghdad

Night fell slowly across exotic Baghdad. A woman shrouded from head to toe in the ubiquitous *abaya* scuttled like a black spider beneath candlelit second stories and balconies on the narrow, cobbled street. In Baghdad's sizzling summers, these overhangs provided shade to the oldest sections of the city. But now it was a cool October night, and a swath of stars showed in the narrow opening above.

The woman glanced up only once, so concentrated was she on her two missions that lay ahead. She appeared old. She was terribly bent over, probably not only from age but malnutrition—and she carried a frayed canvas gym bag. Besides the body-cloaking black *abaya*, she wore a traditional white *pushi* that covered most of her face and revealed only her dark eyes, which were neither properly downcast nor idle.

She hurried past bay windows—*mashrabiyah*—with carved-wood screens that allowed viewing out onto the street but not in. At last she turned onto a winding thoroughfare lighted by wavering antique street lamps and filled with the babble of voices—struggling shopkeepers desperate to sell their few wares, would-be consumers with subsistence *dinars*, and barefoot children running and shouting. No one gave her more than a cursory glance. The place bustled in a final surge of energy as the traditional closing hour of 8:00 P.M. approached.

Then a trio of Saddam Hussein's feared Republican Guards in their distinctive dark-green fatigues and webbed weapon belts appeared.

She tensed as they approached. To her left, among the row of open-air stands steaming in the cool night air, was a farmer hawking fresh fruit from the countryside. A crowd had gathered, fighting over who could buy and at what price. Instantly she pulled *dinars* from her voluminous *abaya*, slid into the throng, and added her voice to those calling for the farmer's merchandise.

Her heart pounded as she studied the muscular guards from the corners of her eyes.

The three men stopped to watch. One made a comment, and another responded, secure in their weapons and well-fed existence. Soon they were laughing and sneering.

The woman sweated as she continued to beg the farmer for fruit. Around her, other Iraqis glanced nervously over their shoulders. While most resumed their clamor, some slunk furtively away.

That was when the guards chose their victim: A baker with an armload of bread loaves piled high, his face tucked behind to hide, had backed off and was skirting the crowd. The woman did not recognize him.

With hard gazes, the trio surrounded the baker, their pistols drawn. One knocked away the loaves. Another crashed his gun across the baker's panicked face.

Hidden in the woman's canvas bag was a gun. Every fiber of her wanted to pull it out and kill the brutal guards. Hidden by her *pushi*, her face flushed with rage. She bit her lip. She wanted desperately to act.

But she had work to do. She must not be noticed.

There was an abrupt hush on the busy street. As the baker fell, people averted their gazes and moved away. Bad things happened to anyone who attracted the attention of the mercurial guards. Blood poured from the fallen man's face, and he screamed. Sickened, the woman watched two of the guards grab his arms and drag him off. He had been publicly arrested, or perhaps he was simply being harassed. There was no way to know. His family would use whatever clout they had to try to free him.

A full minute passed. Like the lull before a sudden desert storm, the night air seemed heavy and ominous. There was little relief knowing the volatile guards had chosen someone else. Next time, it could be you.

But life went on. Sound returned to the winding street. People reappeared. The farmer took the money from the woman's palm and left an orange. With a shiver, she dropped it next to the gun in her canvas gym bag and sped off, uneasily scanning all around while in her mind she still saw the terrified face of the poor baker.

At last she turned onto Sadoun Street, a commercial thoroughfare with high-rises taller than all the minarets on the far bank of the Tigris. But this wide boulevard now contained few upscale goods and even fewer buyers who could afford them. Of course, no tourists came to Baghdad anymore. Which was why when she finally entered the modern King Sargon Hotel, she found a vast emptiness. The once-magnificent lobby with its obsidian and chrome had been designed by Western architects to combine the culture of the ancient kingdoms with the most up-to-date conveniences of the West. Now, in the shadows of poor lighting, it was not only scruffy but deserted.

The tall bellman with large dark eyes and a Saddam Hussein mustache was whispering angrily to the bored desk clerk. "What has the great leader done for us, Rashid? Tell me how the genius from Tikrit has destroyed the foreign devils and made us all rich. In fact, so rich my Ph.D. adorns this worn-out bellman's suit"—he pounded his chest in outrage—"in a hotel where nobody comes, and my children will be lucky to live long enough to have no future!"

The clerk responded gloomily, "We will survive, Balshazar. We always have, and Saddam will not live forever."

Then they noticed the bent-over old crone standing quietly before them. She had arrived softly, like a puff of smoke, and for a moment the desk clerk felt disoriented. How could he have missed her? He stared, catching a brief glimpse of sharp black eyes over the *pushi*. Quickly she lowered her gaze in the presence of men not her husband.

He frowned.

She made her voice humble and frightened, and she spoke in perfect Arabic: "A thousand pardons. I have been sent to be given the sewing for Sundus."

With the sound of her fear, the desk clerk recovered his disdain and jerked his head toward a service door behind him. "You should not be in the lobby, old woman. Next time, go around to housekeeping. The back is where you belong!"

Murmuring words of apology, she dropped her head and brushed past the Ph.D. bellman named Balshazar. As she did, her unseen hand slid a folded paper into the pocket of his frayed uniform.

The bellman gave no indication of it. Instead, he asked the haughty desk clerk, "What about the electricity? What is the schedule for its being turned off tomorrow?" Unconsciously he laid a protective hand over the pocket.

As the woman disappeared through the service door, she heard the rise and fall of the men's voices resume. Inwardly she sighed with relief: She had successfully completed her first mission. But the danger was far from over. She had one more crucial errand.

Chapter
Twenty-Eight

Baghdad

A sharp wind off the desert blew through nighttime Baghdad, sending home shoppers on Sheik Omar Street. The spicy scents of incense and cardamom were in the brisk air. The sky was black, and the temperature was dropping. The bent old woman in the black *abaya* and face-hiding *pushi* who had carried the message to the King Sargon Hotel threaded among pedestrians and past plywood stalls where used parts and Iraqi ingenuity for repair flourished. These days, many of the city's once comfortable middle-class manned these lowly stalls where everything from herbs to hot foods and used plumbing pipes were sold.

As the woman approached her destination, she stared, appalled. Her heart thudded against her ribcage. She could not believe her eyes.

Because the crowds had thinned, he stood out more than he would have under ordinary circumstances. Tall, trim, and muscular, he was the only northern European on the street. He had the same dark blue eyes, raven-black hair, and cool, hard face she remembered with such pain and anger. He was dressed casually in a windbreaker and brown trousers. And despite the U.N. armband, she knew he was no U.N. worker.

She would have covertly studied and analyzed him if he had been any European, an unusual sighting in today's Iraq. But this man was not just anyone, and for a split instant she stood paralyzed in front of the workshop. Then she quickly continued inside. Even the most experienced observer would have seen nothing in her manner but the slightest of hesitations. Yet her shock was profound.

What was he doing in Baghdad? He was the last person she expected or wanted to see: Lt. Col. Jonathan Smith, M.D.

■

On edge, Jon surveyed the street of plywood stalls and narrow repair shops. He had been slipping into medical offices and the storerooms of clinics and hospitals all day, talking to nervous doctors, nurses, and former medics from the war. Many had confirmed there had been six ARDS victims last year with the symptoms of the deadly virus Jon was investigating. But none could tell him about the three survivors.

As he strode along, he shrugged off a feeling he was being watched. He scrutinized the lamp-lit street with its faded bazaar shops and men in long loose shirts—*gallabiyyas*—who sat at scarred tables drinking glasses of hot tea and smoking water pipes. He kept his face casual. But this section of old Baghdad seemed an odd place to meet Dr. Radah Mahuk, the world-famous pediatric physician and surgeon.

Still, Domalewski's instructions had been specific.

Jon was getting desperate. The famed pediatrician was his last hope for the day, and to stay in Baghdad another twenty-four hours would increase his danger exponentially. Any of his sources could report him to the Republican Guard. On the other hand, the next informant might be the one to tell him where the virus had originated and what bastard had infected the Iraqis and Sophia.

Every nerve on edge, he paused outside a workshop where bald tires dangled from chains on either side of a low, dark door. This gloomy tire-repair shop was where Domalewski had sent him. According to the diplomat, it was owned by a formerly well-to-do Baghdad businessman who was bitter because his burgeoning company had been ruined by Saddam Hussein's unnecessary wars.

The store's seedy appearance did nothing to relieve Jon's suspicions. He glanced at his watch. He was on time. With a last look around, he stepped inside.

A short, balding man with rough skin and the usual thick black mustache stood behind a battered counter, reading a piece of paper. His thick fingers were stained with tar. Nearby, a woman wearing the usual fundamentalist black robes was shopping through tires.

"Ghassan?" Jon asked the man.

"Not here." The Iraqi answered indifferently in heavily accented English, but the gaze that swept over Jon was shrewd.

Jon lowered his voice and glanced back at the woman, who had moved closer, apparently to examine a different group of tires. "I have to talk to him. Farouk al-Dubq told me he has a new Pirelli." It was the coded signal Jerzy Domalewski had relayed to Jon. It should activate no outside interest because Ghassan's booming company on Rashid Street had specialized in the best new tires from around the world, and everyone knew he was a connoisseur.

Ghassan raised his brows in approval. He gave a brief smile, crumpled the piece of paper between his work-worn hands, and said heartily in much better English, "Ah, *Pirelli*. An excellent choice in tires. In the back. Come." But as he turned to lead Jon, he muttered something in Arabic.

Suddenly, the hairs on the back of Jon's neck stood on end. He spun just in time to see the woman in the long black *abaya* slide like a shadow out the front door.

He frowned. His gut told him something was wrong. "Who—?" he began.

But Ghassan was speaking urgently to him. "Please hurry. This way."

They ran from the empty front through a thick-curtained doorway and into a cavernous storage room with so many piles of worn-out tires that they nearly blocked the rear entrance. One stack reached the ceiling. On the lowest mound near the room's center sat a middle-aged Iraqi woman cradling a baby. Fine wrinkles creviced her cheeks and high forehead. Her charcoal eyes focused on Jon with curiosity. She wore a long print dress, a black cardigan sweater, and a white cowl wrapped over her head and around her neck. But Jon's gaze was on the moist, feverish face of the baby. As it whimpered, he hurried toward it. Obviously the infant was sick, and all Jon's medical training demanded he help, whether or not this was a trap.

Ghassan spoke to the woman in rapid Arabic, and Jon heard his fake U.N. name mentioned. The woman frowned and seemed to be asking questions. Before Jon could reach the child, a violent crash sounded from the shop's front. Someone had kicked open the door. He froze, tense. Booted feet thundered, and a voice bellowed in Arabic.

A bolt of adrenaline shot through Jon. They had been betrayed! He pulled out his Beretta and whirled.

At the same time, Ghassan yanked out an old AK-47 assault rifle from the center of a pile of threadbare Goodyear tires and snapped, "Republican Guards!" He handled the AK-47 with a familiarity that told Jon this was not the first time he had used the powerful assault rifle to defend himself or his store.

Just as Jon started toward the noise, Ghassan ran in front to block him. Radiating hot rage, Ghassan jerked his head back at the middle-aged woman with the sick infant. "Get them out of here. Leave the rest to me. This is *my* business."

The resolute Iraqi did not wait to see what Jon would do. Determined, he sprang to the open archway, shoved the muzzle of his AK-47 through the curtain, and opened fire with a series of short bursts.

The sound was thunderous. The plywood walls rocked.

Behind Smith, the woman cried out. The baby screamed.

Beretta in hand, Jon raced back through the stacks of tires toward them. The woman was already up with the baby in her arms, hurrying toward the rear door. Suddenly a fusillade of automatic fire from the front blasted into the storage room. Ghassan fell back and jumped behind a pile of tires. Blood poured from a wound on his upper arm. Jon pulled the woman and baby down behind a different stack of tires. Bullets thudded into the storage room and landed in the hard tires with radiating *thunks*. Rubber exploded into the air.

Behind his stack of tires, Ghassan was excitedly muttering his prayers: "Allah is great. Allah is just. Allah is merciful. Allah is—"

Another burst of violent automatic fire ripped the room. The woman ducked over the child to protect it, and Jon arched himself over both as wild bullets exploded bottles and jars on the shelves. Glittering shards of glass sprayed the storage area. Nuts, bolts, and screws that had been in the containers shot out like shrapnel. Somewhere an old toilet flushed spontaneously.

Jon had seen this before—the stupid belief of ill-trained soldiers that brute firepower would subdue all opposition. The truth was, it would do little damage to a target entrenched or under cover. Through it all, Ghassan's frenzied voice continued to pray. As gunfire erupted again, Jon sat back on his heels and looked worriedly down at the woman, whose face was white with fear. Smith patted her arm, unable to reassure her in her own language. The baby cried, distracting the woman. She cooed soothingly down to it.

Abruptly, there was silence. For some reason, the Republican Guards were holding their fire. Then Jon knew why. Their booted footsteps hammered toward the curtained archway. They were going to rush the storage room.

"Praise Allah!" Ghassan leaped excitedly up from behind his pile of tires. He was grinning maniacally, and fire burned in his black eyes. Before Jon could stop him, he charged through the curtained doorway, his AK-47 blazing.

Screams and grunts from beyond the curtain echoed through the shop. The sound of scrambling and diving for cover. Then a sudden silence.

Jon hesitated. He should get the woman out of here, but maybe—

Crouched low, instead he ran toward the curtained archway.

Another violent fusillade burst out beyond the curtain.

Jon hit the floor and crawled forward. As he reached the curtain, the barrage stopped. He held his breath and peered under the bottom of the dangling curtain of beads. As he did, a single rifle, like a small voice in the wilderness, tore out another series of defiant bursts. Ghassan lay behind a corner of the shop counter. He had the Republican Guards pinned down. Smith felt a surge of admiration.

Then he saw the Guards crawling through the shop to get behind where Ghassan held out. There were too many of them. The brave Iraqi could not survive much longer. Jon wanted desperately to help him. Maybe the two of them would be able to at least gain the time for everyone to escape.

Then he heard the vehicles outside on the narrow street.

They were bringing up reinforcements. It would be suicide.

He looked back at where the woman watched him. She held the baby and seemed to be waiting to see what decision he made. Ghassan had told him to save her. He was sacrificing his life not only to defend his business but to make certain she and the child escaped. Plus, Jon had a mission to complete, one that could save millions of people from a horrible death. Inwardly he sighed as he accepted the fact that he could not save Ghassan.

Once he decided, he did not wait. As the ear-splitting sounds of gunshots continued, Jon yanked open the splintered rear door. The screams of the injured in front echoed through the bullet-riddled shop. He gave the woman a reassuring smile, took her hand, and peered out into a dark alley so narrow and deep, even the wind had little room to blow. He tugged, pulling her behind, and slid out into the passageway.

Cradling the infant close in one arm, she followed as they ran two doors to the left. And froze.

Military vehicles screeched to a stop at both ends of the alley. Soldiers jumped out and pounded toward them. They were caught. Trapped in the Republican Guards' snare.

Chapter Twenty-Nine

1:04 A.M., Wednesday, October 22
Frederick, Maryland

Specialist Four Adele Schweik awoke with an abrupt start. Next to her ear pulsed the sharp, unnerving alarm from the sensor she had planted in the Russell woman's office a half-mile away at USAMRIID. Instantly alert, she turned off the annoying blast, jumped from bed, and activated the video camera she had also installed in the distant office.

In her dusky bedroom, she sat at her desk and stared at the monitor until a figure dressed in black appeared in Russell's office. Apprehensively she studied the intruder. He—or she—looked like an alien invader, but he moved with the fluidity of a cat, and a swift purpose that told Schweik he had broken into guarded buildings before. The figure wore an antiflash hood with respirator and a black flak vest. The vest was state-of-the-art—it would stop cold the bullets of most pistols and submachine guns.

As stiffly alert in her nightgown as she was in her daytime uniform, she stayed before the glowing screen long enough to be certain of the intruder's intention: He was conducting a thorough search of Sophia Russell's office. In a rush of adrenaline she yanked off her nightgown, dressed in her camos, and raced out to her car.

■

In a darkened RV a block from the entrance to Fort Detrick, Marty Zellerbach glared unhappily at his computer screen. His face was pinched with worry, and his soft body slumped in exaggerated despair. He had taken his Mideral seven hours ago, and as its effects had faded he had finished a brilliant program to automatically switch relay routes randomly, assuring no one could trace his electronic footprints ever again.

But that achievement had not led to success in either of his two main objectives: Sophia Russell's other phone calls, if they existed, remained stubbornly erased, and Bill Griffin's tracks had been too well covered.

He needed to find a creative solution, which was a challenge he would welcome under different circumstances. But now he was anxious. There was so little time, and the truth was . . . he had been working on both problems all along, and he still had no breakthrough on either. Plus there was the fact that he was frightened for Jon, who had willingly vanished into Iraq. And—as much as he distrusted people in general— he had no desire to see vast quantities of them erased, which was sure to be their fate if the virus was allowed to continue its rampage.

These were the moments he had spent his life avoiding: His well-honed self-interest had just collided with his deepest, darkest secret.

No one knew he harbored a streak of altruism. He never hinted at it and certainly would never admit it, but he actually thought kindly of human babies, old people with cantankerous dispositions, and adults who quietly did charity work without being paid. He also gave away his entire yearly trust income to a variety of worthy causes around the world. He made plenty to cover his living expenses by solving cyber-problems for individuals, companies, and the government, and he always had that pleasant savings account from which he had drawn fifty thousand dollars for Jon.

He sighed. He could feel the nervous edginess that told him he was close to needing another pill. But his mind ached to escape into the unknown where he could be his liberated, exciting self. As he thought that, bright colors flashed somewhere ahead on the horizon, and the world seemed to expand in ever-larger waves of possibilities.

This was that fertile time when he was close to losing control, and there was every reason he should. He had to figure out how to check Sophia Russell's phone logs for accuracy, and he desperately needed to find Bill Griffin.

Now was the time!

Relieved, he leaned back, shut his eyes, and happily launched himself into the starry world of his vast imagination.

Then a cold, hard voice that seemed to come from nowhere shocked him: "Should I have been the enemy, you would be dead."

Marty jumped. He yelled, "Peter!" He turned. "You idiot! You could've given me cardiac arrest sneaking up like that!"

"Sitting duck," Peter Howell grumbled and shook his head morosely. "That's what you are, Marty Zellerbach. Must be more alert." He was reclining in a lounge chair, still dressed in the all-black uniform of an SAS counterterrorist commando. His gray antiflash hood lay in his lap. He had returned from his uneventful mission inside USAMRIID and reentered the RV without disturbing the air.

Marty was too angry to play the old spy's game. He longed for all this aggravation to end so he could return to his quiet bungalow where the most annoying event of the day was the arrival of the mail.

His lip curled in a sneer. "The door was locked, you moron. You're nothing but a common burglar!"

"An *un*common burglar." Peter nodded sagely, ignoring Marty's pitying glare. "If I were the usual bumbling second-story man, we wouldn't be having this chat."

After they had left Jon Smith at San Francisco International Airport, they had taken turns driving the RV cross-country, sleeping and eating in it so they could make the best time. Peter had shouldered the vast majority of the driving and the shopping to lessen Marty's complaining. Plus he had had to teach Marty to drive again, which had tried his patience. Even now he looked at the electronics genius and was not quite sure how the soft little man could feel superior, since he appeared to be so handicapped in daily life. Besides, he was bloody irksome.

Marty groused, "I hope to heaven you achieved better results than I."

"Alas, no." Peter's leathery face grimaced. "I found nothing of consequence." Once they had reached Maryland, he had decided the wisest course was to start at the beginning with Sophia's lab and office, to be sure Jon had missed nothing. So he had parked the RV where it was now, donned his SAS commando gear, and slipped into Fort Detrick. He sighed. "Marty, my boy, I'm afraid we're going to need your unearthly electronic skills to dig into the poor lady's past. Can you break into her personnel file here at Detrick?"

Marty brightened, raised his hands above his head, and snapped his fingers as if they were castanets. "You have but to ask!" Moving with great speed, he tapped keys, watched the monitor, and minutes later sat back, crossed his arms, and shot a Cheshire-cat smile at Peter. "Tadah! Personnel file for Sophia Lilian Russell, Ph.D. Got it!"

Peter had been watching from the shadows, worrying as soon as Marty began talking in exclamation points. Thin and wiry, he slid across the RV's living room to lean over the computer monitor.

He said quietly, "Jon thinks there was something in the deleted report you recovered from the Prince Leopold Institute that Sophia considered important. That's why the report was erased and the page of her comments cut from her logbook." He looked into Marty's shining green eyes. "What we need is anything that could tie into that report."

Marty bounced up and down on his chair. "Not a problem! I'll print out the entire file." Electric energy seemed to shoot from his pores, and a self-satisfied smile wreathed his face. "Got it! Got it!"

Peter clamped a hand on his shoulder. "Better take your Mideral pill, too. Sorry. Know you don't like 'em. Buck up, though. What we're about to do is a task for the boring part of both of our brains. At least you can medicate yours."

■

With Sophia's file in front of them, Peter read the Prince Leopold report aloud as Marty checked it against the personnel file. Marty moved line by line, his mind working methodically, while Peter read and reread the report. The Mideral was a wonder drug, and its quick-acting effect had slowed Marty's speech and enabled him to sit quietly through the onerous task. He was acting like a courtly but gloomy gentleman.

As dawn approached, they had still found no link between Sophia's past activities and current contacts at USAMRIID.

"Right," Peter acknowledged. "Take a step back. Where did she do her postdoc work?"

Marty peered at the file. "University of California."

"Which one?"

If Marty had been off his meds, he would have thrown up his hands in despair at how poorly Peter was informed. Instead he simply gave a shake of his head. "Berkeley, of course."

"Ah, yes. And they say we Brits are snobs. Can you crack that august institution, or do we have to drive all the way back to the West Coast?"

Marty raised his brows at Peter's idea of levity. He said in a measured, irritatingly slow voice, "Tell me, Peter, do we dislike each other as much when I'm off my meds?"

"Yes, my boy. We certainly do."

With dignity, Marty inclined his head. "Thought so." He sat at his computer, and ten minutes later Sophia's transcript at Berkeley was in his hands.

Peter read aloud the Prince Leopold report again.

Marty checked the transcript. "No names that match. No fieldwork.

Her entire program was in human genetics, not virology." He sat back, and the transcript slid off his knee. "It's hopeless."

"Nonsense. As we Brits say, 'We've not yet begun to fight.' "

Marty frowned. "That was John Paul Jones *against* the British."

"Ah, but technically he was still a Brit when he said it."

Marty gave a gimlet smile. "You're still trying to hold on to the colonies?"

"Always did hate to give up a good investment. Very well, where did she do her doctoral studies?"

"Princeton."

"Crack away."

But the transcript of her doctoral studies showed her work to be far too extensive and lacking in detail to help. Her dissertation had no connection to viruses. Instead, she had researched the gene cluster that held the genetic mutation responsible for the missing tails of Manx cats.

Marty pointed out, "She took extensive field trips. That could be useful."

"Agreed. Is a graduate adviser listed?"

"Dr. Benjamin Liu. Emeritus. He still teaches an occasional course, and he lives in Princeton."

"Right," Peter said. "I'll crank up this heap. We're off."

8:14 A.M.
Princeton, New Jersey

Sunrise illuminated the autumn colors of trees and bushes as Peter and Marty drove north. They traded off driving to sleep and crossed the Delaware Memorial Bridge south of Wilmington and sped up the Jersey Turnpike past the bustling metropolises of Philadelphia and Trenton. When they entered Princeton, the sun was bright, and the tree leaves were vibrant shades of red, gold, and tangerine.

It was an old town, Princeton, a scene of battle during the Revolutionary War when the British headquartered here. It still retained the tree-lined streets and grassy meadows, the old houses and classic university buildings, and the elegant and peaceful atmosphere in which high learning and tranquil lifestyles were most comfortably pursued. The famed university and the historic town were symbionts, neither succeeding fully without the other.

Dr. Benjamin Liu lived on a side street heavily planted in maple trees whose leaves burned flame red, as if on fire. The sedate, three-story frame structure was shingled in that eastern seaboard wood color that is neither dark brown nor dark gray but somewhere in between, earned by years of bravely facing the elements.

Dr. Liu himself had a well-weathered face. Far from the cliché of an inscrutable Chinese courtier, he was tall and muscular, with the eyes and white drooping mustache of an ascetic Mandarin but the jutting chin, full cheeks, and ruddy complexion of a New England whaling captain. He was a fine blend of Chinese and Caucasian, and the walls of his study helped to show why. Hanging there were two portraits that appeared to be his parents. One was a tall, athletic, blond woman wearing a yachting cap and carrying a fishing rod, while the other showed a distinguished gentleman in the traditional robes of a Mandarin Chinese elder seated on the bow of a ship. On one side of the photographs hung mounted game fish, while on the other were displayed historic Chinese court badges of rank.

Dr. Liu had just finished his breakfast. He waved them to seats in the study. "So how can I help you? You spoke on the phone of Sophia Russell. I remember her well. A great student. Not to mention a hell of a looker. She was the only time I was tempted to dare the fates with a teacher-student affair." He sank into a wing-back chair. "How is she, anyway?"

On his meds, Marty began one of his slow, methodical answers. "Well, Sophia Russell is—"

Peter gave in to impatience. "Right, Marty. My job here." He focused on the retired professor. "She's dead, Doctor Liu. Sorry to be so blunt, but we're hoping you can help. She died from the new virus."

"Dead?" Dr. Liu was shocked. "When? I mean, is it possible?" He looked from Peter to Marty and back to Peter. He shook his head, slowly at first, then vigorously. "But she was so . . . young." He hesitated as if seeing Sophia's vitality. Then the rest of what Peter had said penetrated. "The new virus? It's a global disaster! I have grandchildren, and I'm frightened to death. It could wipe out half the species. What are we doing to stop it? Can anyone tell me?"

Peter's voice was reassuring. "Everyone's working around the clock, Professor. It's what Dr. Russell was researching."

"Researching? So that's how she got the virus?"

"Perhaps. It's one of the things we're trying to ascertain."

The professor's face was set in grim lines. "I can't imagine I can be of any help, but I'll try. Tell me what you want."

Peter handed the one-page report to the professor. "This is from the Prince Leopold Institute of Tropical Diseases. Please read it and tell us if anything in there ties in with Dr. Russell's studies at Princeton. Classes, field trips, research, friends, any bloody thing that occurs to you."

Professor Liu nodded. He took his time reading. He stopped often to think and remember. An old clock on the mantel of the study ticked loudly. He read the report again. And again.

Finally, he shook his head. "I see nothing here that strikes me as relating to Sophia's work or studies. She concentrated on genetics and, as far as I know, never took a field trip to anywhere in South America. Giscours didn't study at Princeton, and Sophia didn't study in Europe. I see no way they could've met." He pursed his lips and glanced down at the report again. He raised his head. "But you know, I do recall . . . yes, a trip. In her undergraduate years. Not viruses, though." He hesitated. "Damn, it's only something she mentioned in passing at an informal gathering." He sighed. "I'm not going to be able to tell you more than that."

Marty had been listening closely. Even when he was on his medication and his brilliant mind was tethered, he still tested smarter than ninety-eight percent of the human populace. Which increased his annoyance with Peter Howell. So just to prove he could, he forced himself to ask quickly: "Where was she an undergraduate?"

The professor looked at him. "Syracuse. But she wasn't studying biology then. So I don't see how that trip could possibly relate to Giscours and his report."

Peter opened his mouth to speak, but Marty jumped in: "Something had better." He felt a sudden chill and looked at Peter.

Peter gave a grimace of understanding. "It's our last chance."

■

Specialist Four Adele Schweik sat in her small Honda watching the house. The heavy man, Maddux, sat in the passenger seat beside her. She had spotted the black-clothed intruder leave Fort Detrick and get into the RV parked on the street, and then she had followed them to Princeton. Now she needed to get back to her post at USAMRIID.

She told Maddux, "That's his RV over there. He looks and acts dangerous. Be careful. He's with another man who should give you no trouble. You can pick them up when they come out."

"You reported to Mr. al-Hassan?"

"There wasn't time."

Maddux nodded. "Okay, go. We'll take over."

He stepped out of the car and hurried to his van. Schweik drove away without another glance at him or the RV.

Chapter
Thirty

9:14 A.M.
Long Lake Village, New York

The Adirondack mountain air was sweet and fresh, and the sun that morning cast long, damp shadows from the tall pines onto Blanchard Pharmaceuticals' sprawling complex. Inside the brick headquarters, Surgeon General Jesse Oxnard was impressed. He and HHS secretary Nancy Petrelli had finished a tour of Blanchard's labs and production facilities, conducted personally by Victor Tremont himself. The surgeon general had known of the company, of course, but it had always maintained a quiet profile, and he had had no idea of its great size or worldwide presence.

The two government officials met with senior staff over coffee and then rejoined Tremont in his grand, half-timbered office. A wall of windows overlooked the forested lake that gave the town its name. They settled into chairs beside Tremont's fireplace where wood burned in a comforting glow, and they listened attentively as Tremont enthusiastically described the origin of the promising experimental serum.

"... our microbiology people came to me with the proposal more than a decade ago, because at the time I was in charge of R&D. They predicted more and more diseases would emerge as Third World nations became more accessible and their populations burgeoned. In other words, fewer locations would be remote enough to confine deadly outbreaks. The industrial world would have no defenses against these plagues, which could be even more devastating than HIV-AIDS. My people hoped by working with some of the more obscure ones we'd learn not only valuable science but develop serums for hitherto incurable diseases. One of the viruses they concentrated on was fatal to a certain species of monkey that was an especially close genetic relative to humans. We developed a recombinant antiserum cocktail against that virus, and developed the biotechnology to produce the antibodies in bulk as a feasibility study on mass production techniques for the future." He gazed earnestly at the pair. "It's the study I phoned you about, Secretary Petrelli. Now maybe that effort may help the world. At least, I certainly hope so."

Jesse Oxnard was not sure. He was a big, robust man with heavy jowls and a thick mustache. He frowned. "But this development . . . this serum . . . is still essentially in the research stage. Isn't that so?"

An understanding smile spread across Tremont's tanned, aristocratic face. The firelight reflected in his iron-gray hair as he shook his head. "We're past both the animal-testing and the primate-testing stages. In fact, we've shown the serum cures the virus in affected monkeys. And, as I said, purely as a scientific study, we developed the facilities and techniques to produce it in bulk. In fact we have millions of doses already on hand. That's what prompted us to get the patent and apply for FDA approval for veterinary use."

Nancy Petrelli watched the effect all this was having on the surgeon general, while at the same time she marveled at Victor Tremont's smooth telling of the concocted story. She almost believed it herself. Which reminded her to cover her back when dealing with Victor. She never let herself think he was her friend. At first he had needed her initial investment, and later he wanted her influence as a congresswoman and then as secretary of HHS. That was as warm and fuzzy as it got with Victor.

Nancy was a realist. She wore her silver hair short and efficient. She dressed in feminine but businesslike St. John's knits. And she never gambled unless she figured the odds were greatly in her favor. She was backing Victor Tremont and his high-class, high-powered con game because she believed he would pull it off. She was also well aware his crimes would be compounded by mass murder if he was caught, so she had decided to distance herself from any hint that she might have known what he was actually doing. At the same time, she fully expected him to triumph and make her rich.

As much for her own benefit as Oxnard's, she said, "Monkeys aren't people, Dr. Tremont."

Victor glanced quizzically at her and agreed: "True. But in this case, they are very close genetically and physiologically."

"Let me make certain I understand this." Surgeon General Oxnard stroked his mustache. "You can't be sure the serum will cure people."

Tremont answered solemnly, "Of course not. We won't know until it's actually tested on humans. But considering the situation, I think we need to try."

The surgeon general frowned. "That's a huge obstacle. In fact, it's entirely possible we may discover the serum may cause harm."

Tremont knit his fingers together and stared down at his hands. When he looked up, he said earnestly, "Well, one thing seems almost certain—millions will die if we don't find a cure for this horrible virus." He shook his head as if in an agony of indecision. "Don't you think I've wrestled with this exact problem? It's why I hesitated for two days to come forward. I had to be comfortable in my own mind I was doing the right thing. So the answer is yes, I'm convinced there's a very good chance our serum will cure this terrible epidemic. But how can I guarantee it won't create a greater suffering until it's tested?"

All three silently contemplated the dilemma. Jesse Oxnard knew he could not possibly recommend Tremont's serum for use without thorough testing, but at the same time he recognized he would look bold and decisive if it saved millions around the globe from certain death.

Nancy Petrelli continued to concern herself with herself. She knew the serum would work, but she had learned the hard way to never go out on the end of a political limb. She would position herself solidly on the side of caution and join the minority that would, in the end, she was sure, be overruled in Victor's favor.

Meanwhile Victor Tremont was worrying about Jon Smith and his two friends. He had heard no news about them from al-Hassan since the fiasco in the Sierras. As he thought that, he brought himself back to the present. He had a brave gesture in mind that he hoped would convince the surgeon general and, through him, President Castilla. But he had to time it just so.

As he looked up at Petrelli and Oxnard and their clouded faces deep in thought, he knew the time had come.

He must break the impasse. If he could not convince Surgeon General Oxnard, it was possible everything he had striven for over the past dozen years would be lost.

Inwardly he nodded grimly. He would not lose. He could not. "The only way to be sure is to test it on a human." He leaned toward them, his voice commanding and grave. "We have isolated small quantities of the lethal monkey virus. It's unstable, but it can be preserved for a week or so." He hesitated as if wrestling with a great moral question. "There's only one way to proceed. And please don't try to stop me—there's too much at stake. We must think of the greater good, not just what we as individuals risk." He paused again and inhaled. "I'll inject myself with the monkey virus—"

Surgeon General Oxnard flinched. "You know that's impossible."

Tremont raised a hand. "No, no. Please let me finish. I'll inject myself with the virus, and then I'll take the serum. The monkey virus may not be exactly the same as the one that's spreading, but I believe it's close enough that we'd see any adverse side effects when I self-administer the serum. Then we'll know."

"That's absurd!" Nancy Petrelli exclaimed, playing the devil's advocate. "You know we can't possibly allow you to do that."

Jesse Oxnard hesitated. "You'd actually do that?"

"Absolutely." Tremont nodded vigorously. "If it's the only way to convince everyone that our serum can stop what is rapidly becoming a horrible pandemic."

"But—" Nancy Petrelli began, playing out her opposition.

The surgeon general shook his head. "It's not for us to decide, Nancy. Tremont is making a magnificent humanitarian offer. The least we can do is respect that and put his suggestion before the president."

Petrelli frowned. "But, dammit, Jesse, we have no assurance the two viruses and the serum will interact the same way in the human body." She saw Tremont again frown at her curiously, as if he doubted he had heard her accurately. "If Dr. Tremont is going to offer himself as our guinea pig, he should be infected with the real virus. Or, at least, we should test the two viruses to see if, perhaps, they are identical."

Inside, Tremont seethed with rage. What the hell was she doing? She knew damned well the serum wasn't 100 percent effective—no serum or vaccine was. He had this contingency covered, yes, but she didn't know that. Outwardly he continued to nod. "She's right, of course. That'd be best. But taking the time to compare viruses would be an unnecessary delay. I assure you I'm quite willing to be infected with the real virus. Our serum will cure it. I'm certain."

"No." The surgeon general slapped his knees in disagreement. "There's no way we can let you do that. But the families of the victims are already clamoring to be helped, so it makes more sense to ask them if they'd be willing to let their sick relatives try it. That way we'll find out what we need to know and maybe save a doomed life, too. Meanwhile, I'll have Detrick and the CDC compare the viruses."

Petrelli objected, "The FDA will never approve."

Oxnard countered, "They will if the president tells them to."

"The director would probably resign first."

"That's possible. But if the president wants the serum tested, it will be."

Nancy Petrelli appeared to think about this. "I'm still against using the serum without the usual series of thorough tests. However, if we're going to go ahead, then it does make more sense to try to save someone who's already sick."

The surgeon general stood up. "We'll call the president and present both suggestions. The sooner we start, the more lives we'll have a chance to save." He turned to Victor Tremont. "Where can we phone in private?"

"I have a line in the conference room. Through that door." Tremont nodded to a door in the right wall of his office.

"Nancy?" Jesse Oxnard asked.

"You make the call. No need for both of us. Tell him I concur in everything."

As the surgeon general hurried out and closed the door, Victor Tremont swiveled in his chair to bestow a cold smile on the Health and Human Services secretary. "Covering your ass at my expense, Nancy?"

"Giving Jesse the negative to work against," Nancy Petrelli shot back. "We agreed I'd do the nay-saying, so he focuses on the positive, the advantages."

Tremont's tones gave no indication of his anger. "And a really good job it was, too. But, I think, more than a little self-protection, too."

Petrelli bowed to him. "I learned from a master."

"Thank you. But it does show a shocking lack of faith in me."

She allowed herself a curt smile. "No, only in the vagaries of chance, Victor. No one has ever found a way to outwit chance."

With that thought, Tremont nodded. "True. We do our best, don't we? Cover all possible contingencies. For example, I would insist we conduct the tests, and I assure you the virus would be harmless before it reached me. But there's always that little residue of chance left, isn't there. A risk for me."

"There's risk for all of us in this project, Victor."

Where the discussion would have taken them, Nancy Petrelli never found out. At that moment the door from the conference room opened, and Surgeon General Oxnard reentered the room, a great bear of a man with a relieved smile.

He said, "The president says he'll talk to FDA, but meanwhile we're to start looking for volunteers among the victims. The president is optimistic. One way or the other, we're going to test this serum and beat back this godawful virus."

•

Victor Tremont laughed long and loud. Yes! He had done it. They were all going to be rich, and it was only the beginning. At his desk, he smoked his Cuban cigar, drank his single-malt scotch, and rocked with laughter in private celebration. Until his cell phone rang in the bottom drawer.

He yanked open the drawer and snatched up the phone. "Nadal?"

There was a brief delay of wireless phoning from a long distance. Then there was the self-satisfied voice: "We have located Jon Smith."

This was proving to be his day. "Where?"

"Iraq."

Momentary doubt assaulted Tremont. "How did he ever get inside Iraq?"

"Perhaps the Englishman from the Sierras. I have found it impossible to learn anything about him. There is no certainty Howell is his correct name any more than Romanov. That leads me to believe he has much he wishes to be unknown."

Tremont nodded angrily. "Probably MI6. How did you locate Smith?"

"One of my contacts—a Dr. Kamil. I assumed Smith would be trying to find our test cases, so I alerted all the doctors I knew. Not that many are practicing now in Baghdad. Kamil reported Smith wants to know about the survivors as well."

"Damn! He can't be allowed to find that."

"If he does, it will not matter. He will never leave Iraq."

"He got in."

"He did not then have Saddam's police and the Republican Guards looking for him. Once they know the American intruder is there, they will seal their borders and hunt him down. If they do not kill him, we shall."

"Dammit, Nadal, make sure you do this time!" Tremont snarled, and remembered their other problem. "What about Bill Griffin? Where is he?"

Already humbled by Tremont's anger, al-Hassan's face grew stonier. "We are watching everywhere Jon Smith has been, but Griffin appears to have vanished from the earth."

"That's just perfect!" In a rage he punched the cell phone's off button and glared unseeing across the office.

Then the day's triumphs returned to make him smile. No matter what Jon Smith found in Iraq, and despite Griffin, the Hades Project was going forward according to plan. He sipped his whiskey and his smile broadened. Even the president was on board now.

10:02 A.M., Fort Irwin, Barstow, California

The man had followed Bill Griffin's rented Toyota pickup from Fort Irwin. He stayed at a safe distance, never too close or too far back, on the two-lane road and then on Interstate 15. He was waiting for him to land somewhere relatively permanent. A place where Griffin would return and where he would sleep. Griffin knew the man would have followed him all the way to Los Angeles if necessary until he was certain Griffin would remain in one place long enough for backup to arrive.

Now from behind the curtains of the Barstow motel room, Griffin saw the man get out of his Land Rover and head toward the motel office. An ordinary man in a nondescript brown suit and open-necked shirt. Griffin had never seen him before. He would have been surprised if he had. Still, he recognized the almost imperceptible bulge of a pistol under the man's suit coat. The man would check whether Griffin—or whatever name the customer in unit 107 was using—was registered for the night. Then he would make his phone call.

Griffin grabbed one of the motel's bath towels. He raised the rear window, climbed out, and circled behind the units to where he could see into the office. His stalker was showing a fake badge or official ID to the motel clerk. The clerk studied the register, nodded, and turned the register so his questioner could view it.

Griffin trotted to the man's Land Rover and slipped into the backseat of the high vehicle, crouched down, and waited. Quick footsteps hurried to the Rover, and the front door jerked open.

As it slammed shut, Griffin raised up, a silenced Walther PPK 6.35mm in his right hand, the bath towel in the other.

The man was dialing his car phone.

In a single motion, Griffin dropped the towel around the man's head and fired once. The man's head snapped back. With the towel Griffin caught most of the blood and brain matter. He quietly lowered the slumped body. Sweating, he got out, pushed the body into the passenger seat, and climbed behind the wheel.

Far out in the desert, he buried his stalker. Then he drove back into Barstow and left the car locked on a side street. Tired and angry, he walked to his motel, checked out, and drove toward Interstate 15. At Fort Irwin he had learned that Jon Smith had been interested in Tremont's "government scientists" and Major Anderson's service in Iraq during Desert Storm. When he reached Interstate 15, he turned the pickup toward Los Angeles and its international airport. He had decisions to make, and the best place to do that was on the East Coast.

Chapter
Thirty-One

8:02 P.M.
Baghdad

The bent woman in the black *abaya* was a block away from the used-tire shop when she heard the first fusillade. She paused next to an old man who sat cross-legged on the street, his palm outstretched as he begged. She gazed down at him with empty eyes, while her brain assured her she was not required to return to the shop to find out what the shooting meant.

But then she heard the explosive blasts of gunfire again.

When she had left the shop, her mission was over. She had made certain the undercover American doctor had made contact. At that point, she left, as she was supposed to. An armed attack had not been part of the plan. Nor had the man who had turned out to be the undercover doctor. She tensed. She might be many things, but one thing she was not was cavalier with her orders. She took tremendous pride in her work. She was thorough, responsible, and utterly reliable.

She looked down at the Iraqi beggar once more. She dropped *dinars* onto his palm. Her long *abaya* flapping around her legs, she moved as swiftly as her bent shape allowed back toward the tire shop.

•

In the Baghdad alley, the dark shadows were the only protection for Smith, the woman, and the baby. He pulled them close against the shack, which prevented them from being seen easily. The gunfire inside drowned out normal city sounds, but still Jon listened and watched. Through the gloom, he studied both ends of the alley. He could just make out what appeared to be a dozen Republican Guards. They were approaching carefully, their weapons first. They moved with certainty and stealth, Saddam Hussein's prized killers.

Still, he gave the woman a reassuring smile as she gazed anxiously up at him in the moonlight. "Be right back," he whispered. He knew she would not understand, but perhaps the sound of a human voice would help her to maintain her equilibrium as she cradled the baby protectively to her chest.

His pulse throbbing at his temples, Jon rolled to the left and pulled on the first door latch. Locked. Then the second. Locked again.

The Republican Guards drew closer.

He reversed course and slid past the woman. He tried a third door. Also locked.

Frustrated and worried, he drew her away from the tire shop to the building next door and tugged on her arm until she crouched beside him, low against the wall where it met the old stones of the alley. He wanted them to be small targets. He could see nothing else he could do—he was going to have to fight their way out.

His chest tight, he gripped his Beretta and continued to watch the stealthy shadows draw closer. Sweat gathered under his clothes despite the cool night air. The gunfire inside the tire shop had stopped. For a moment he thought about Ghassan and hoped he had survived; then he wiped away all thoughts of anything but the danger in the alley.

He concentrated. The only sound was the rhythmic pad of the soldiers' feet as they approached. He breathed deeply, keeping himself calm. He remembered Jerzy Domalewski's warning that it was better to shoot and risk death than be caught alive with the gun. He had to make every shot count, because it was not only his life at risk but the woman and child's, too. He would open fire as soon as the killers were close enough to make it impossible to miss. He needed to hit as many as possible, as quickly as possible.

He wished fervently he had more than his pistol as they closed in. He raised the Beretta. At just that moment, the baby let out a wail, instantly followed by a series of piercing cries. The sounds reverberated along the alley as the woman tried vainly to quiet the child.

Now the Guardsmen knew where they were. Smith's chest tightened into a knot. Instantly bullets bit into the wall. Wood splinters shot out, sharp as needles. The woman lifted her head, her eyes white with fear. As the baby screamed, Smith slid in front of them, firing left and right at the soldiers in the shadowy night alley.

Suddenly a voice snarled, "Get ready. Don't move until I tell you!" It was a woman's voice speaking in American English, and it came from the tire shop's rear entrance, where the bullet-riddled door hung half open on one hinge.

Before Jon could react, a long black *abaya* flowed out the doorway and into the gloom, immediately followed by two pale hands with short, blunt fingernails expertly clutching an Uzi submachine gun. The featureless woman balanced the weapon back against her bent body with impressive ease. She squeezed the trigger and sprayed the Republican Guardsmen in both directions.

As the woman turned left to concentrate fire, Jon stayed low on his heels so he was beneath her bullets and still protecting the Iraqi woman and baby. While she was left, he wheeled right and picked off two of the thugs with his Beretta as they raced across the alley. When she turned right, he aimed left. By rotating their fire from one end of the

alley to the other, in five minutes all the attackers had gone to ground—
dead, wounded, or just saving their hides. Shocked grunts and cries
echoed along the dark passage. But there was no more sound of feet
and no significant movement.

The *abaya*-clad woman barked, "Inside! Both of you."

Jon felt a jolt. There was something oddly familiar about the
woman's voice.

But that would have to wait. He pulled the woman with the baby
back inside the tire storage room, and they ran after the bent woman
as she limped past the tattered curtain and into the front, where blood
had splattered the walls and pooled on the floor. There Ghassan and
four Guardsmen lay dead against opposite walls. The metallic scents of
blood and death stank the air. Jon's throat tightened. Ghassan must
have killed the four soldiers before dying of a mortal wound to the chest.

"Ghassan!" The Iraqi woman gasped.

The woman in the *abaya* spoke rapid Arabic to the woman with the
baby as she swiftly pulled off the *pushi* and *abaya*. Asking questions,
she removed the harness that had kept her bent over. With relief, she
straightened to her full five feet nine inches. Jon watched, fighting
shock, as she adjusted the U.N. armband on her tweed jacket, smoothed
her gray skirt, and stuffed the *pushi* and *abaya* into a compartment
hidden under the false bottom of her gym bag. She had accomplished
her transformation in less than a minute, at the same time carrying on
a conversation with the woman.

But that was not what had frozen Jon. It was the disguised woman's
appearance.

She had the same striking gold hair as Sophia's, although it was short
and curled around her ears. She had the identical curved, sexy lips, the
straight nose, the firm chin, the glowing porcelain skin, and the dusky
come-hither look to her black eyes, although right now her gaze was
hard and bright as she seemed to be asking the Iraqi woman a final
question. It was Sophia's sister, Randi.

Smith inhaled sharply. "Christ, what are you doing here?"

"Saving your ass!" Randi Russell snapped without even looking at him.

Jon barely heard her. His heart felt as if it were breaking all over again. He had not remembered how much the two sisters had looked alike. Studying Randi now made his skin crawl, but at the same time he could not tear his gaze away. He held on to the shop counter and felt his heart rage. He blinked. He had to get over this quickly.

Her final question answered by the woman with the child, Randi Russell turned on Smith. Her face was cool marble. Not at all the face of Sophia. "The Guards' backups will be here any minute. We're going out the front. That's the most dangerous part, but it's safer than the alley. She knows the back streets better than I, so she'll lead. Keep your Beretta hidden but handy. I'll bring up the rear. They'll be looking for one European man and two Iraqi women, one wearing an *abaya*."

Jon forced himself back to the present. He understood. "The survivors in the alley will report us."

"Exactly. They'll describe what they saw. Let's hope my change of appearance will confuse the new team enough to hesitate. They hate Europeans, but they don't want an international incident, either."

Jon nodded. He felt his cool reserve return.

They slipped out of the store into the dark night. This was just a mission, he told himself, and Randi was just another professional. With a practiced sweep, his gaze took in the street. Instantly he saw two of them: A military vehicle parked at the far end. It looked like a Russian BRDM-2, an armored car with a 25mm gun, coaxial machine guns, and antitank missiles. A second armored car was lumbering along the street toward them, a lethal behemoth frightening pedestrians out of its way.

"They're looking for us," Jon growled.

"Let's go!" Randi said.

The woman carrying the infant hurried off, and within twenty feet slipped into a space between buildings so constricted one person could barely fit. Spiderwebs caught at his face as Jon ran along the narrow passage behind her. Alert and on edge, Beretta ready, he glanced back frequently at Randi to make certain she was all right.

At last they reached the end and stepped out onto another thoroughfare. Randi hid her Uzi back inside her gym bag, and Smith slid his Beretta beneath his jacket and into his waistband. The woman and child stayed ahead, while Jon and Randi strode along together, following at a discrete distance. It was natural—two European U.N. workers out for the evening. But it left Jon with a queasy feeling, as if the past had just slammed into the present and left him aching and forlorn. He kept pushing back the pain of Sophia's death.

Randi growled, "What in hell are you doing in Baghdad, Jon?"

He grimaced. The same old Randi, as subtle and understanding as a cobra. "Same as you, obviously. Working."

"Working?" Her blond eyebrows raised. "On what? I haven't heard of any sick American soldiers here for you to kill."

He said, "There seem to be CIA agents here, though. Now I know why you're never at home or at your 'international think tank.'"

Randi glared. "You still haven't said why you're in Baghdad. Does the army know, or are you off on another of your personal crusades?"

He spoke a half-lie: "There's a new virus we're working on at USAM-RIID. It's a killer. I've had reports of cases like it in Iraq."

"And the army sent *you* to find out?"

"Can't think of anyone better," he said lightly. Obviously she hadn't heard he had been declared AWOL and was wanted for questioning about General Kielburger's death. Inwardly, he sighed. She must not have heard about Sophia's murder, either.

Now was not the time to tell her.

The streets grew narrow again, with windowed overhangs that shone with yellow candlelight. The shops in these dark streets were little more than cubes set inside thick, ancient walls—not high enough in which to stand erect, and just wide enough for most adults to spread their arms. A single vendor squatted in each entrance, hawking meager goods.

The woman with the baby finally turned into the rear entrance of a run-down but modern building—a small hospital. Children lay sleeping and moaning on cots that rimmed the walls in the entryway and in the wards on either side. The woman carrying the feverish baby led Jon and Randi past crowded treatment rooms, all with child patients. This was a pediatric hospital, and from what Smith could assess, it had once been up-to-date and thoroughly outfitted. But now it was dilapidated, with its equipment in various stages of disrepair.

Perhaps this was where he was to meet the famous pediatrician. Because they were in such different fields of medicine, he had no personal knowledge of him. He turned back to Randi. "Where's Dr. Mahuk? Ghassan was supposed to take me to him. He's a pediatric specialist."

"I know," Randi told him quietly. "That's why I was in the tire shop—to make sure Ghassan made safe contact with an undercover agent—obviously, with you. Dr. Mahuk is a vital member of the Iraqi underground. We'd expected you to have your meeting there in Ghassan's store. We thought it'd be safer."

The middle-aged woman with the baby stepped into an office with a desk and examining table. Gently she laid the baby on the table. As the infant whimpered, she picked up a stethoscope that was curled on the desk. Jon followed the woman, while Randi paused to look carefully up and down the dingy corridor. Then she stepped inside the office and closed the door. There was a second door, and she moved swiftly across worn linoleum to it. Warily she opened it onto a ward. Children's voices and cries rose and fell. Her face sad, she shut this door, too.

She took out her Uzi. Resting it in her arms, she leaned back against the door.

As Jon stared, her expression hardened and grew watchful, the utter professional. She was guarding not only the Iraqi woman and baby but him, too. It was a side of Randi he had never seen. As long as he had known her, she had been fiercely independent, with a compelling sense of self-confidence. When he had first met her seven years ago, he had found her beautiful and intriguing. He had tried to talk to her about her fiancé's death, about his sense of guilt, but it had been no use.

Later, when Smith had gone to her condo in Washington to try to apologize again about Mike's death, he had discovered Sophia. He had never been able to penetrate Randi's rage and grief, but his love for Sophia had made it less necessary. Now he would have to tell Randi about Sophia's murder, and he did not look forward to it.

Inwardly he sighed. He wanted Sophia back. Every time he looked at Randi, he wanted her back even more.

The Iraqi woman smiled up at Jon as he helped her unwrap the blanket around the baby. "You will please forgive my deception," she said in perfect English. "Once we were attacked, I was concerned you might be captured. It was better you not know that I am the one you seek. I am Dr. Radah Mahuk. Thank you for your help in saving this little one." She beamed down at the child, then bent over to examine it.

Chapter Thirty-Two

9:02 P.M.
Baghdad

Dr. Radah Mahuk sighed. "There is so little we can do for the children. Or, for that matter, for any of the sick and injured in Iraq."

On the examining table, which had been repaired with nails and tape, the pediatrician listened to the chest of the baby—a little girl. She checked the baby's eyes, ears, and throat and took her temperature. Jon guessed she was about six months old, although she looked no more than four. He studied her thinness and the translucency of her fevered skin. Earlier he had noted the eyes were an ivory color and veinless—indicating a vitamin deficiency. This baby was not getting enough nourishment.

At last Dr. Mahuk nodded to herself, opened the door, and called for a nurse. As she handed the infant over, she stroked the little girl's cheek and gave instructions in Arabic: "Bathe her. She needs to be cleaned. But use cool water to help bring down the fever. I will be out shortly." Her lined face was worried. Weariness had collected in blue circles under her large dark eyes.

Randi, who had understood the doctor's orders, asked in English, "What's wrong with her?"

"Diarrhea, among other problems," the pediatrician answered.

Jon nodded. "Common, considering the living conditions. When sewage seeps into drinking water, you get diarrhea and a lot worse."

"You are right, of course. Please sit down. Diarrhea is common, particularly in the older parts of the city. Her mother has three other children at home, two with muscular dystrophy." She shrugged wearily. "So I told her I would take her little girl to see what I could do. Tomorrow morning, the mother will come and want her back, but she does not get enough to eat to produce milk to nurse. But perhaps by then I will find some good yogurt for the baby."

Dr. Mahuk pushed herself up onto the edge of the examining table and sat. Her legs dangled from beneath the simple print dress. She wore tennis shoes and white anklets. In Iraq, life for most people was basic, and this doctor, whose work had been published widely, who once had traveled the globe to address pediatric conferences, was reduced to nostrums and yogurt.

"I appreciate your taking the risk to talk to me." Jon sat in a rickety chair at the desk. He looked around the spartan office and examination room. A worried sense of urgency made him edgy. Still, he smoothed his features and kept his voice casual. He was grateful the pediatrician wanted to help, and he was frustrated from his long day.

She shrugged. "It is what I must do. It is right." She unwound her white cowl and shook out her long dark hair. As it fell in a cloud around her shoulders, she appeared younger and angrier. "Who would have thought we would end like this?" Her dark eyes snapped. "I grew up during the early promise of the Ba'ath Party. Those were exciting days, and Iraq was full of hope. The Ba'ath sent me to London for my medical degree and then to New York for training at Columbia-Presbyterian Hospital. When I returned to Baghdad, I founded this hospital and became its first director. I do not want to be its last. But when the Ba'ath made Saddam president, everything changed."

Smith nodded. "He sent Iraq into war with Iran almost immediately."

"Yes, it was terrible. So many of our boys died. But after eight years of blood and empty slogans, we finally signed a treaty in which we won the right to move our border a few hundred meters from the center of the Shatt al-Arab to its eastern bank. All those wasted lives for a minor border dispute! Then to add insult to injury, we had to return all the land to Iran in 1990 as a bribe to keep it out of the Gulf War. *Insanity.*" She grimaced. "Of course, after Kuwait and that terrible war came the embargo. We call it *al-hissar*, which means not only isolation but encirclement by a hostile world. Saddam loves the embargo because he can blame all our problems on it. It is his most powerful tool to stay in power."

"Now you can't get enough medicine," Jon said.

The pediatrician closed her eyes with angry frustration. "Malnutrition, cancers, diarrheas, parasites, neuromuscular conditions . . . diseases of all kinds. We need to feed our children, give them clean water, and inoculate them. Here in my country, every illness is a death threat now. Something must be done, or we will lose our next generation." She opened her dark eyes. They were moist with emotion. "That is why I joined the underground." She looked at Randi. "I am grateful for your help." She whispered insistently, "*We must overthrow Saddam before he kills us all.*"

Through the door against which she leaned, Randi Russell could hear the low voices of doctors and nurses, whose soft words were too often all they had to give to the sick and dying children. Her heart went out to them and this tragic country.

But at the same time, turmoil raged inside her. As she kept guard against more trouble from Saddam's elite forces, she gazed at the two doctors who continued deep in conversation. From the examination table where she sat, Radah Mahuk's dusky face was tormented. She was a key player in the shaky opposition group the CIA was financing and had sent Randi and others to help strengthen. At the same time, Jonathan Smith slouched in a low chair, apparently relaxed. But she knew him well enough to guess his casual demeanor hid vigilant tension. She thought about what he had told her—he was here to investigate some virus.

Her gaze hardened. Smith's tendency to be a loose canon could jeopardize Dr. Mahuk and, through Dr. Mahuk, the resistance. Suddenly uneasy, she adjusted the Uzi in her arms.

"That's why you agreed to talk with me?" Smith asked Dr. Mahuk.

"Yes. But we are all watched, hence the subterfuge."

Jon smiled grimly. "The more subterfuge, the better the CIA likes it."

Randi's unease rocketed to the surface. "The longer you're together, the more danger to everyone. Ask what you came to ask."

Jon ignored her. He focused on Dr. Mahuk. "I've already learned a great deal about the three Iraqis who died of an unknown virus last year. They'd been in southern Iraq on the Kuwait border at one time or another near the end of the Gulf War."

"So I was told, yes. A virus unknown in Iraq, which is strange."

"The whole thing is strange," Smith agreed. "One of my sources says there were also three survivors last year. Do you know anything about that?"

This time it was Dr. Mahuk who had to be prompted.

"Doctor?" Randi said.

The pediatrician slid off the table and padded to the door that was closed on the main corridor. She opened it quickly. No one was outside. She looked left and right. At last, she shut it and turned, her head cocked as she listened for intruders. "To even speak of the deaths and survivals is forbidden," she said in a strained voice. "But, yes, there were three survivors. All in Basra, which is in the south, too, as you must know. Close to Kuwait. It sounds to me as if you may have formed the same theory I have."

Jon said grimly, "Some kind of experiment?"

The pediatrician nodded.

He asked, "All three survivors were also in the Gulf War, stationed near the Kuwait border?"

"Yes."

"It's odd that all those in Baghdad died, while the ones in Basra survived."

"Very odd. It was one of the aspects that drew my attention."

Randi studied the pair. They were talking cautiously around an issue she did not quite understand but sensed was momentous. Their gazes were focused on each other, the tall American man and the small Iraqi woman, and the intellectual tension was palpable. At the moment, as they probed their mutual quest, the outside world had receded, which made them more vulnerable—and Randi more alert.

Jon asked, "Can you explain why those in Basra survived, Dr. Mahuk?"

"As it happens, yes. I was in the Basra hospital, helping to treat the victims, when a team of doctors from the U.N. arrived and gave each an injection. They not only improved, four days later they showed no ill effects from the virus. They were healed." She paused and deadpanned, "It was remarkable."

"That's an understatement."

"It is." She crossed her arms as if she had just felt a chill. "I would not have believed it had I not seen it."

Smith jumped up and paced around the room. His high-planed face was deep in thought; his blue eyes cold, glittering, and outraged. "You know what you're telling me, Doctor? A cure for a fatal and unknown virus? Not a vaccine, but a *cure?*"

"That is the only reasonable explanation."

"Curative antiserum?"

"That would be the best possibility."

"It would also mean those so-called U.N. doctors had the material in quantity."

"Yes."

Jon's words spilled out in a rush: "A serum in quantity for a virus that first broke out in Iraq's six cases last year and then mysteriously reappeared a little more than a week ago in six more cases halfway around the world, in America. And all twelve victims had served on the Iraq-Kuwait border during the war or had a transfusion from someone who'd served on the border."

"Precisely." The pediatrician nodded vigorously. "In two countries where the virus had never existed."

The two medical doctors faced each other across a great silence, both reluctant to say the next sentence.

But Randi could. "It's not remarkable. It's not even a miracle." They turned to stare at her as she spoke the unspeakable: "Someone gave all of them the virus."

It sickened Jon. "Yes, while only half were given the serum. It was a controlled, lethal experiment on humans who were uninformed and gave no consent."

The pediatrician paled. "It reminds me of the depraved Nazi doctors who used concentration camp inmates for guinea pigs. Obscene. Monstrous!"

Randi stared at her. "Who were they?"

"Did any of those doctors with the serum tell you their names, Dr. Mahuk?" Jon asked.

"They gave no names. They said helping the men could get them into trouble with our regime and with their supervisors in Geneva. But I am sure they were lying. There was no way they could have entered Iraq and worked at that particular military hospital without the government's knowing."

"How, then? A bribe?"

"A large bribe in some form to Saddam himself, I would guess."

Randi asked, "You don't think they were from the U.N. at all, do you?"

The pediatrician shook her head nervously. "I should have seen the natural conclusion before. It is the problem with today. Just to live is a battle, and so we miss the overall picture. The answer to your question is yes, I believe they were not from the U.N., nor were they practicing doctors. Instead, they acted like research scientists. Plus, they arrived quickly, as if they *knew* who was going to be sick and when."

It fit Jon's idea that the twelve victims were part of a test begun at the 167th MASH at the end of the Gulf War. "Did they give any hint about where they'd come from?"

"They said Germany, but their German was textbook, and their clothes weren't European. I think they were Americans, which, a year ago, would have made it even more dangerous for them to enter Iraq without the approval of Saddam himself."

Randi frowned. She adjusted the Uzi. "You have no thoughts about who could have sent them?"

"All I remember is their speaking once among themselves about excellent skiing. But they could be referring to many, many places."

Jon paced, contemplating research scientists from America who had a quantity of serum to cure the new virus. Suddenly he realized: "I've spent the day asking about the six who had the virus a year ago. What about since then? Have there been more cases in Iraq?"

Dr. Mahuk compressed her lips in shocked sorrow. She had devoted her life to healing, and now the world seemed to be exploding in a sickness beyond anyone's control. Anger and pain and outrage laced her voice as she told them, "In the past week, we have had many new victims of ARDS. At least fifty have died. We are not sure of the exact number, and it changes by the hour. We are only beginning to investigate whether it is the unknown virus, but I have little doubt. The same symptoms are there—the history of small fevers, the heavy cold or mild flu for a few weeks, and the sudden ARDS, the hemorrhaging and death within hours. There have been no survivors." Her voice broke. "None."

Smith whirled from his nervous pacing, stunned by the large number of deaths. Compassion filled him. Then he realized . . . this could be the answer: "Were these victims also in the Gulf War? Or from the Kuwait border?"

Dr. Mahuk sighed. "Unfortunately, the answer is not that simple. Only a few were in the war and none was from near Kuwait."

"Any contact with the original six of a year ago?"

Her voice was discouraged. "None at all."

Jon thought of his beloved Sophia and then of General Kielburger, Melanie Curtis, and the 167th MASH from ten years before. "But how could fifty people unknowingly be injected with the virus simultaneously—especially in a sealed-off nation like yours? Were they from one single area? Had they been abroad? Did they have contact with foreigners?"

Dr. Mahuk did not answer immediately. She peeled away from her listening post at the door. She fished in a skirt pocket and took out what looked like a Russian cigarette. As she paced across the room to the examining table, she lit it, tense and nervous. The pungent barnyard aroma characteristic of Russian tobacco filled the spartan office.

At last she said, "Because of my work with the virus victims last year, I was asked to study the new cases. I looked for all the possible sources of infection you mentioned. But I found none. I also found no connection among the victims. They appeared to be a random sampling of both sexes, all ages, occupations, ethnic groups, and geographic regions." She inhaled again, letting the smoke out slowly as if still forming her thoughts. "They did not appear to have infected each other or their families. I cannot say whether that is significant, but it is curious."

"It's consistent. Everything I've found so far indicates the virus has almost no contagious factor."

"Then how are they getting it?" Randi had been following the conversation closely. Although she had no degree in chemistry or biology, she had had enough science courses to be aware of some of the fundamentals. What the two doctors were talking about . . . were deeply worried about . . . was an epidemic. "And why only Iraq and America?"

she asked. "Could it be the result of some biological warfare weapon from Desert Storm hidden here in Iraq?"

Shaking her head, Dr. Mahuk walked to the chipped metal desk in the corner. Her cigarette smoke followed like a brown ghost. She took a sheet of paper from a drawer and handed it to Jon. Randi instantly joined him, shifting the Uzi out of the way so she could lean closely. Appalled, they read a computer printout of a *Washington Post* front page:

DEADLY PANDEMIC OF UNKNOWN VIRUS SWEEPS GLOBE

The story reported twenty-seven nations had fatalities of more than a half million. All the illnesses began with a cold or flu for some two weeks, then abruptly escalated into ARDS, hemorrhaging, and death. In addition, forty-two nations reported cases in the high millions of what appeared to be a heavy common cold. It was still unknown whether all or any of those had the virus.

The news took Jon's breath away. Cold fear swept through him. A *half million dead! Millions sick!* "Where did you get this?" he asked.

Dr. Mahuk stubbed out her cigarette. "We have a secret computer at the hospital. We took that off the Internet this morning. Obviously, the virus is no longer confined to Iraq and America or to the Gulf War. I do not see how the cause could be a biological weapon in my country. The high number of deaths is ghastly." Her voice broke. "That is why I knew I must speak to you."

The ramifications of the news story and the pediatrician's revelations shook Jon again. Quickly he reread the article, thinking about what he had learned. Dr. Mahuk had ruled out nearly every possible contact with the outside; still, the virus had exploded into a worldwide epidemic. Two weeks ago, every one of the victims had been alive except the original three in Iraq from a year ago. The velocity of the virus's current expansion was inconceivable.

He looked up from the printout. "This is out of control. I've got to get home. If there really are people in America with a serum, I've got to find them. By now, some friends of mine may have information, too. There's no time to lose—"

Suddenly Randi stiffened. "Wait."

Holding up her Uzi, she raced across the room to the door that opened onto the corridor. Smith was instantly at her side, his Beretta drawn. She was tense with nervous awareness.

Suddenly from the corridor a harsh voice, snarling in Arabic, became clear. Smaller, frightened voices answered. Heavy boots thudded authoritatively down the hall in the direction of the small examination room.

Jon looked at Dr. Mahuk and asked urgently, "The Republican Guards?"

She pressed quaking fingers to her lips and listened to the words. At last she shook her head and whispered, "The police." Her dark, expressive eyes were pits of fear.

Randi tore across the room to the other door. With her curly blond hair and long, svelte figure in the clinging skirt and jacket, she looked more like a runway model than a seasoned CIA agent. But Jon had seen her risk her life and succeed in a superb defense against the Republican Guards back in the alley behind the used-tire shop, and now she radiated that same kind of intelligent physicality.

"Police or guards. Doesn't matter. They'll try to kill us." Randi's head swiveled, her dark gaze summoning them to her. "We'll have to leave through the ward. Hurry!" She yanked open the door, looked back, and motioned Jon and Dr. Mahuk to go through first.

It was a mistake. The police were waiting for them on the other side. It was a trap, and they had fallen into it.

A uniformed Iraqi policeman lunged and tore the Uzi from Randi's hands before she could react. Three others poured into the room, AK-47 assault rifles leveled. As Jon tried to raise his Beretta two more policemen burst through the corridor door and fell on him wrestling him to the floor. They were caught.

Chapter
Thirty-Three

9:41 P.M.
Baghdad

Dr. Radah Mahuk stood motionless, her back to the wall, unable to move. She was brave but not foolhardy. Her job was to heal the sick, and she could not do that if she was killed. Nor could she try to save her country if she was consigned to the notorious Justice Detention Center. Like the dead Ghassan, she was a soldier in a sacred cause, but she had no gun, and she knew no self-defense. Her only weapons were her brain and the trust she had built among her countrymen. Free, she would be able to continue to help her people and perhaps the Americans, too. So she pressed back behind the counter, willing herself to be invisible. Sweat beaded up on her forehead.

Two more uniformed policemen entered from the corridor more warily, their gazes darting right and left, their weapons ready for any emergency. Behind them, a slender man dressed in a tailored uniform strolled into the room holding an Iraqi-made Beretta *tariq* pistol.

For the moment, no one was looking at Dr. Mahuk. She was not important, at least not yet. Terrified and heartsick, she slipped away into the hall and walked as slowly and unobtrusively as she could to locate a telephone.

In the room, the tailored officer smiled at Jon and said in lightly accented English, "Colonel Smith, yes? At last. You have been most difficult to find."

He inclined his head to Randi with exaggerated politeness. "And this lady? I do not know her. Perhaps the CIA? It is rumored your nation finds us so fascinating that you must constantly send undercover spies to measure the temperature of our love for our leader."

Jon's chest was tight with anger. They had been careless. Damn!

"I don't know her," he lied. "She's part of the hospital staff." It sounded lame even to his ears, but it was worth a shot.

The officer laughed in disbelief. "A European lady is a member of *this* hospital? No, I do not think so."

Angry with herself, worried for the underground organization, and frantically thinking of what they could do, Randi shot Jon a surprised look, grateful for his attempt.

But then the officer stopped smiling. He flourished his *tariq*. It was time to move his prisoners to wherever they were to be taken. He gave a command in Arabic, and the police pushed Randi and Jon out into the corridor. Doors quietly clicked shut ahead in the passageway as the terrified hospital personnel tried to keep themselves and their charges out of harm's way. The two Americans were marched out through a silent, empty corridor.

Randi watched nervously everywhere for Radah Mahuk, and when she saw no sign of her, she breathed deeply, relieved. Abruptly one of the policemen shoved the muzzle of his gun into her back, hurrying her along, a painful reminder of the danger of their situation. She broke out in fresh sweat, afraid.

The police paraded the Americans out into the star-studded night where an old Russian truck with a canvas-covered squad carrier waited at the curb, its motor rumbling. Billowing exhaust from the tailpipe of the old motor curled upward, silver white in the cold moonlight. Around them, the night sounds of the city were close and menacing. The police lowered the truck's tailgate, raised the canvas, and pushed the two Americans into the rear.

The interior was moist and dark, and there was a nauseating stink of diesel. Randi shivered and stared anxiously at Jon.

He gazed back, trying to hide his fear. His voice was wry: "And you complain about *my* crusades."

She gave a weak smile. "Sorry about that. Next time I'll plan better."

"Thanks. My disposition's improved already." He warily studied the interior. "How do you think they found us?"

"I don't see how they could've tracked us from the tire shop. My guess is someone in the hospital turned us in. Not every Iraqi agrees with Dr. Mahuk's revolutionary ideas. Besides, the way things are in this country, people will turn on you in the hope of gaining a little favor with the police."

Two of the Baghdad cops clambered up into the truck. They aimed their big Kalashnikovs at the Americans and indicated by waves of their hands and grunted words that the pair was to move deeper into the truck, far from the tailgate. Pretending defeat, Jon and Randi scrambled farther inside and settled behind the truck's cab on a plank seat. The two armed men took positions next to the tailgate on either side of the truck, guarding the only exit. They were about ten feet from their prisoners—within easy firing range.

The officer with the *tariq* pistol stood in the opening at the truck's rear. "*Au revoir* for now, my new American friends." He smiled at his idea of humor. But he aimed his weapon at them ominously as he ordered the tailgate locked into place.

Jon demanded, "Where are you taking us?"

"A playground. A weekend getaway. A resort, if you will." The Iraqi grinned under his mustache. Then his voice grew flinty and his eyes narrowed. "In truth? The Justice Detention Center. If you do what you are told, perhaps you will live."

Jon tried to hide a surge of fear as he remembered Jerzy Domalewski's description of the six-story underground torture and execution
complex. He exchanged a look with Randi, who sat close on his left.
Her face was expressionless, but he saw her hand tremble. She knew
about the detention center, too. That hellhole was not survivable.

The canvas flap dropped, and they were cut off from the outside.
The two guards sat back, their rifles pointed at the prisoners. There
were sounds in front as the officer and other police climbed into
the cab.

As the truck lurched away, Jon was silent. Because of him, Randi had
been caught. He had no illusions about what they would do to a CIA
spy, especially a female one. And how was he going to get word to
USAMRIID and the Pentagon to tell them what he had learned about
the virus and cure?

He said quietly, "We have to get out of here."

Randi nodded. "The detention center doesn't thrill me either. But
our guards are armed. Lousy odds."

He gazed through the inky shadows at the two Iraqis, whose faces
were fixed in watchful stares. Besides assault rifles, they had holstered
pistols on their hips.

They bounced onto a street so narrow that the truck's canvas sides
scraped the stone walls.

They had to act before it was too late. He turned to Randi.

"What?" she asked.

"Are you feeling ill?" he suggested.

She pursed her lips. Then she understood: "As a matter of fact, I
feel a terrible stomach cramp coming on."

"Groan loudly."

"Like this?" She moaned and grabbed her stomach.

"Hey!" Smith called to the guards. "She's sick. Come help her!"

She doubled over and shouted in Arabic, "I'm dying! You've got to
help!"

The guards exchanged a look. One raised his eyebrows. The other laughed. They hurled words Jon did not understand. Randi groaned again.

Jon stood, his back bent below the canvas top, and took a step toward the guards. "You've got to—"

One shouted at him, while the other fired his rifle. The shot blasted so close past Smith's ear that the sharp whine seemed to pierce his brain. As the bullet exited out the top of the canvas roof, the two guards motioned him roughly back.

Randi sat up. "They don't believe us."

"No kidding." Jon fell onto the seat, his hand over the ear, his head ringing. "What were they saying?" He closed his eyes, willing the throbbing pain to go away.

"That they'd done you the favor of missing. Next time, we're both dead."

He nodded. "Figures."

"Sorry, Jon. It was worth a try."

The truck was turning from narrow street to narrow street, following a twisting route. Its sides continued to rasp occasionally against buildings. She could hear the cries of shopkeepers open long after they should have closed in the hope of one more sale, perhaps their only sale of the day. Sometimes there were the disembodied, scratchy sounds of prewar radios. Everything told her they were staying in the older parts of Baghdad.

She whispered, "They're driving too slowly and staying on the back streets. That's not logical. The Baghdad police go wherever they want. Keeping a high profile is part of the job, but these men are avoiding major thoroughfares."

"You think they're not police?" He dropped the hand from his ear. The pain was receding.

"They have the uniforms and the high-powered Russian weapons. If they're not police, they'll be dead if they're caught. I don't know who else they could be."

"I do."

As he said that, the past week came rushing back, and something happened that he had been fighting: Randi disappeared, and Sophia took her place. His heart ached with every fiber at the sight of her again. Sophia's beautiful black eyes shone out at him, surrounded by the smooth, pale skin and the long, cornsilk hair. Her full lips spread in a sweet smile, showing tiny white teeth. She had that indefinable beauty that was so much more than flesh and bones. It radiated from an inner core of decency and vitality and intellect that transformed mechanics into aesthetics. She was gloriously beautiful in every way.

For one moment of madness, he truly believed she was alive. Just by reaching out, he could gather her into his arms, smell the scent of her hair, and feel the beat of her heart against his. *Alive.*

He dug deep inside himself, searching for strength.

And made himself blink.

He shook his head to clear it. He had to quit lying to himself. He was looking at Randi.

Not Sophia.

They were in grave danger. He had to face the truth. His stomach felt hollow, like an elevator falling too fast. It was possible neither of them would survive. He could delay no longer.

He had to tell her about Sophia. He had to say the words because if he did not, he was going to slip over into some other world where he could pretend forever Randi was Sophia. He could not allow his emotions to continue these cruel games.

Because it was not just his future at risk. It was Randi's, too, and tens of millions of people who could die from the virus. He could hear Sophia's voice inside his mind: "*Shape up, Smith. Just because you decide to live doesn't mean you don't love me. You've got a job to do. Love me enough to get on with it.*"

Randi was studying him. "You were going to say who you think the police are."

He inhaled again, pulling oxygen and sanity into his body. "At the time, I didn't notice. But when they first attacked, their leader said my real name. Not the cover name I'd been going around Baghdad using. I don't see how else he could've known I was Colonel Jon Smith except that he—all of them—were hired by the people with the virus. They've been trying to stop me from investigating ever since—"

He made himself see her, not her sister. But as he did, her face tightened as if she realized he was going to tell her something terrible, something that affected her intimately. One more thing she might never forgive him for.

He said gently, "Randi, I have terrible news. Sophia's dead. They murdered her. The people behind all this did it."

Chapter
Thirty-Four

Randi jerked erect. For a moment Jon had the sensation she had heard something else . . . not his voice or words. Her face was frozen. The muscles seemed to atrophy. But she gave no other outward sign she had received the devastating news that her sister had been murdered.

In the shocked silence, he felt the truck's every bump and lurch. Their lives depended on it, so he forced himself to pay attention. The truck's speed was increasing. Buildings seemed farther away, and the sounds of voices and radios receded. They must be on a wider street. He noted traffic sounds and bits of conversation from the truck's cab, but that was all.

His pulse throbbed guiltily at his temples. "Randi?"

Suddenly her face collapsed. Tears streamed down her cheeks, but she remained erect and motionless. She had heard the words, but she could not understand the meaning. Pain seared through her. Sophia? Dead? Murdered? She rejected them. Impossible. How could Sophia be dead?

Her voice was wooden through her tears. "I don't believe you."

"It's true. I'm sorry. I know how much you loved her, and she loved you."

Guilt overwhelmed her. His words were hammer blows. *I know how much you loved her.*

She had not seen Sophia in months. She had been too busy, too involved in her job. Other people needed her more. She had thought there would be plenty of time later to be close and really enjoy each other again. When they had both done what they had to do.

When Jon Smith no longer took up so much of Sophia's life.

It felt as if her heart were shattering. Angrily she used the fingers of both hands to wipe away her tears.

"Randi?"

She heard his voice. Heard the truck . . . with a sudden hollowness below the wheels. Her mind quickly shifted, and as if from a great distance she realized they were crossing a bridge. A long bridge with the sound of the truck echoing off water beneath. She heard the rush of open air around them. The far-off cries of men who were night fishing. The bray of a donkey.

And then with an aching rush, she remembered. *Sophia.* She crossed her arms, trying to hold herself together, and she looked at Jon. There was devastation in his face. His grief looked so deep it could never be erased.

That face was not lying: Sophia was dead.

Sophia was dead.

She inhaled sharply, trying to control herself. Her sister's face kept flashing into her mind. At the same time, she was looking at Jon Smith. She had just begun to think she could trust him. She wanted to believe he had nothing to do with it, but she could not help her suspicions.

His blind arrogance back when he had been treating Mike had led to Mike's death. Had he killed her sister just as he had killed Mike?

"How?" she demanded. "What did you do to her?"

"I wasn't there, not when it happened. I was in London." He told her everything, from the time he met Bill Griffin to his discovery of the missing page and the needle mark in Sophia's ankle. "It was the virus

Sophia was trying to identify, classify, and trace to its source. The same virus I followed here to Iraq. But her death was no accident. The virus isn't that contagious. She would have had to have made a very careless mistake. No, they infected her with it because she had uncovered something. They murdered her, Randi, and I'm going to find out who they are and stop them. They won't get away with it. . . ."

As he talked on, she closed her eyes, thinking about how much Sophia must have suffered before she had died. She fought back a sob.

Jon continued, his voice low and earnest, ". . . They murdered our director and his secretary, too, because I'd told them someone had the live virus and was using it on people. Now we have a global epidemic. How the new victims contracted the virus I don't know, or how someone cured a few. But I've got to find out. . . ."

He was still talking over the rumble of the truck, which was driving faster. The noises of the city had been left behind, and now it seemed as if they were in open country. There was only the occasional roar of a vehicle passing in the other lane.

Another surge of tears overcame her. He put an arm around her shoulder, and she pushed him away. She wiped her face with her sleeve.

She would not cry anymore. Not here. Not now.

". . . They're powerful," he was saying. "Obviously, they've been here in Iraq. Maybe they still are. Which is one more reason to think they sent these 'police.' The people behind the virus seem to reach everywhere. Even into our government and the army itself. High up into the Pentagon."

"The army? The Pentagon?" She stared at him in disbelief.

"There's no other explanation for USAMRIID's being taken out of the loop, shut down, and the lid clamped on. And then all the records that were erased through the NIH's FRMC terminal. I was getting too close, and they had to stop me. It's the only explanation for Kielburger's death. He was calling the Pentagon to tell them what I'd discovered when he vanished. He and his secretary disappeared and were found dead hours later. Now they're looking for me, too. I'm officially AWOL, plus I'm wanted for questioning in the deaths of General Kielburger and his secretary."

Randi repressed a bitter comment. Jon Smith, the man who had killed her great love, was telling her the U.S. Army was somehow involved in her sister's death and he had run from them in the noble cause of pursuing his investigation. How could she believe him? Trust him? His whole story sounded like some kind of enormous fabrication.

Yet any American who came to Iraq now risked his life. She had seen his courage as he had tried to protect Dr. Mahuk from the Republican Guards before he had even known she *was* Dr. Mahuk. Then there was the virus itself. If he had been the only one to tell her about it, she would be doubtful. But Dr. Mahuk was also a source, and she trusted Radah Mahuk.

As she was contemplating all this, she heard the truck cross another long bridge. Again there was the familiar hollow sound below, echoing from water.

What water? She came totally alert. "How many bridges have we crossed?"

"Two, as I recall. About fifteen, twenty miles apart. This is the second one."

"Two." Randi nodded. "That's what I counted. There should be a third soon."

She took a deep, shuddering breath. And another. They were all gone—her father, mother, and now her sister. First her parents in a boating accident off Santa Barbara ten years ago. And now Sophia. She wiped her eyes again as they waited, silent in their shared grief.

The truck drove onto a third bridge, and instantly she was back in the present. In the moment. At work. Right now it was her only balm.

In a charged whisper, she told him, "We must've crossed the Tigris in the middle of Baghdad. Then the second bridge had to be over the Euphrates. The third must be the Euphrates again. We're not going south. We're going *west*. If the land goes into a slow climb, we'll know we're heading into the Syrian Desert and eventually to Jordan."

Impressed, Jon stared past Randi at the two policemen, who were talking quietly. Their rifles rested in their arms, the muzzles pointed casually toward their prisoners. It had been a long time since he had tried to break away.

He said, "Tell them I'm stiff. That I'm just going to stretch."

She frowned, puzzled. "Why?"

"I've got an idea."

She seemed to study him again. At last she nodded. "Okay." She spoke humbly in Arabic to the two heavily armed men.

One responded in a bark, and she uttered more words.

At last she told Jon, "He says it's all right, but only you can stand. Not me." She gave a grim smile.

"Figures."

He got up to his feet and arched his back as if his limbs had gone to sleep. He could feel the policemen's intense gazes from the tailgate area. When they turned away, bored again and half asleep, he put his right eye to a long tear in the slope of the canvas roof. He looked out and up.

Suddenly the harsh voice of one of the policemen snarled.

Randi translated. "Sit, Jon. You've just been busted."

Smith fell back to the bench, but he had seen what he wanted: "The north star. We *are* going west."

"The Justice Detention Center is south."

"So I was told. Besides, that had to be miles back. They're not taking us to jail, and they're not taking us to the center. You have any weapons they didn't find?"

Her brows raised. "A small knife inside my thigh."

He looked down at her sedate gray skirt and nodded. She would be able to reach it quickly.

With an abrupt lurch, the Russian truck slowed and threw them forward. Another lurch sent them against the cab in front. It slammed

Randi into Jon. She quickly pushed away. The vehicle stopped. Voices talked roughly. Suddenly there were noises of men climbing from the cab and walking forward, talking.

In the truck's rear, the two policemen went into a crouch, AK-47s at the ready.

She cocked her head, listening to the Arabic words. "I think the officer and one of his men got out of the cab."

Jon shook his shoulders to relieve the strain. "Is it a checkpoint?"

"Yes."

Silence. Then laughter. More laughter, a slapping of backs, some boot clicking, and the two policemen climbed back into the front of the truck. The engine ground gears and bumped forward, gathering speed.

Randi's voice was low and thoughtful, "From what I could hear, the Republican Guard stopped them, and they had no trouble convincing them they're legitimate police. The Guards even seemed to know the officer by name."

"Then they *are* the police?"

"I'd say so, and that means they're probably moonlighting for your American friends. If we're both right, then whoever's behind all this has not only power but big money. The only good thing about our situation is we're not in the detention center. Still, there are six of them, all highly armed."

The corners of Jon's mouth turned up in a half smile, but his blue eyes were cold. "They haven't got a chance."

She frowned. "What do you have in mind?"

He whispered, "The pair who're guarding us were close to dozing off before the Republican Guard stopped the truck. With luck, the motion and monotony will lull them again and put them into a kind of trance. Let's pretend to nap. It could make them sleepy, too."

"We can't wait long. They haven't brought us out here to enjoy the desert air."

They sat in silence, eyes closed, heads drooping as they simulated sleep. They shifted positions from time to time the way sleeping people did. As his head nodded and he let out an occasional low snore, Jon watched the guards with his peripheral vision.

Miles passed. The guards' desultory conversation quieted and slowed as the truck rocked on into the night. Smith and Randi grew drowsy themselves. Then they heard a light snore that was not one of Jon's.

"Randi." His voice was husky.

One of the policemen had slumped back against the canvas side. The other's head had fallen forward, and he was nodding, fighting sleep.

Soon they would have the chance for which they had hoped—prayed, to be precise.

Jon pressed his index finger to his lips then pointed for Randi to crawl along the left side of the truck bed while he would crawl along the right. Randi nodded. They turned over onto their stomachs and rose to their knees. As the truck continued to rock, they slipped forward in the dim light.

Abruptly the truck made a sharp turn. Everyone was thrown hard to the right as it left the road for what felt like a rutted trail. The heavy vehicle jounced and shook with teeth-rattling vibrations. Disappointed, Smith resumed his slumped position against the wall, and Randi settled quickly back into her old spot as the two Iraqis, instantly awake, complained to one another.

"Damn," she muttered.

The truck slowed, but the damage was done. There was no way they could jump these alert guards and survive.

Jon swore. They had lost their best opportunity so far—maybe their last.

With another abrupt lurch, the truck slowed again, throwing them forward. As it lumbered to a stop, someone in the cab shouted angrily. An answering shout came from out in the night. Suddenly the motor of another vehicle roared. Headlights swept across the darkness and focused on the truck's canvas side, eerily illuminating the interior where Jon and Randi listened.

It was in Arabic. "What are they saying?" Jon asked.

"We've got more visitors." Randi listened to the voices. "And our friendly police aren't all that happy about it."

"Who is it this time?"

"I'm not sure. It could be Republican Guards again. Maybe something spooked them back at the checkpoint, and they've got a new batch of questions."

"Terrific. Then we're in even worse trouble." Jon wiped sweat from his face.

Suddenly Randi whispered urgently, "That last voice! It was speaking Arabic all right, but it wasn't *Iraqi* Arabic."

Inside the truck, the two policemen had gone into wary crouches, their AK-47s up. They radiated vigilance. Something out there frightened them. They exchanged low words and reached for the canvas flap that covered the rear.

Their backs were facing Jon and Randi.

Without hesitation, Jon breathed, "Let's do it."

He flung himself forward, trusting Randi to do the same. He tackled the policeman on the left, yanked him backward, and slammed his fist into the man's right temple. As he dropped to the floor unconscious, Jon wrenched away his AK-47.

At the same time, Randi pulled up her skirt, grabbed the knife from her thigh, and leaped at the second guard. Just as he whirled in his crouch to help his friend, Randi jammed the knife into his arm. He screamed, dropped his rifle, and grabbed the wound.

Randi thrust her knee up, connecting with his chin. His neck snapped back, and he sprawled onto his back unmoving, atop the other uniformed policeman.

As Randi swept up the AK-47, automatic fire exploded outside. It was as loud and surprising as thunder. Shouts and cries echoed across the desert night. There was the sound of running feet and more gunfire. It was a battle. The sounds were coming closer, and the fighting would soon be upon them.

Chapter Thirty-Five

6:32 P.M.
Long Lake Village, New York

At his desk in his corner office, Victor Tremont pushed aside the report on which he was working, rubbed his eyes, and again checked his Rolex. He tapped his fingers on the edge of the massive desk. He was tense, on edge. There had been no word from Nancy Petrelli or the surgeon general, and more than nine hours had passed since he had heard from al-Hassan. The end of more than a dozen years of risky work was coming to a triumphant conclusion, and he was too close to being one of the richest men in the world for anything to go wrong now.

Restless and concerned, he arose, clasped his hands behind his back, and paced across the plush carpeting to his wall of windows. The lake stretched into the distance like a silver crater in the final fade of sunlight. He could almost smell the thick pines on both sides as they darkened from blue to purple and now black. House lights blinked on like a scattering of emerging stars. He looked right and left to view the sprawling, heavily landscaped industrial complex that was Blanchard

Pharmaceuticals, as if to reassure himself that it was all there. That it was real. That it was his.

His intercom buzzed. "Mr. al-Hassan has arrived, Dr. Tremont."

"Good." He returned to his desk and composed his face. "Send him in."

Nadal al-Hassan's pockmarked features were triumphant. "We have Smith."

Excitement surged through Tremont. "Where?"

As al-Hassan came to a stop before the desk, his cadaverous frame leaned forward like a greyhound about to pounce on a rabbit. He smiled. "In Baghdad. The policemen I bribed 'arrested' them."

"*Them?*" This was even better than he had hoped. "Zellerbach and the Englishman are there, too?"

Al-Hassan's smile faded. "Unfortunately, no. He was accompanied by some CIA agent. A woman we believe was working underground there."

Inwardly, Tremont swore. An additional complication. "Whatever Smith has learned, she'll know by now. Destroy her. What about the other two?"

"We will have them soon. Zellerbach and the Englishman were discovered early this morning by our person inside USAMRIID—"

"This *morning?*" Tremont scowled angrily. "Why wasn't I told?"

Al-Hassan dropped his gaze. "Our agent at Detrick was alone at first and too involved following them. When Maddux and his men took over, they were kept so busy simply maintaining contact with this Howell that they had no chance to call. I received the full report only an hour ago. I have castigated him and impressed on him the need to keep me completely informed." Al-Hassan described Peter Howell's break-in search, Marty Zellerbach's downloading of Sophia's file, and the pair's subsequent trip to Princeton. "Maddux reports they have driven north and are now outside Syracuse."

Tremont paced across his office, thinking. Then he understood: "Zellerbach and Howell must be backtracking Sophia Russell's history." He paused, furious. "They could learn about her undergraduate trip to Peru and, from that, about her relationship with me." He glared, controlling his anger. He prided himself on his understanding of human nature, and as he stared at the Arab he reminded himself that this enigmatic man from another land was all that stood between him and discovery by Jonathan Smith and his allies. Inwardly he nodded: Yes, he had to make certain al-Hassan succeeded in destroying Smith. Suddenly he an idea: "You should have stopped them long ago, Nadal. You've *failed* me."

Just as Tremont had hoped, the hatchet-faced al-Hassan winced. The Arab stood motionless and silent, not quite able to speak, and Tremont had a sense of the man's discomfort, almost humiliation, because he had failed. This was exactly the reaction on which Tremont had been counting.

Al-Hassan's voice was flinty. "It will not happen again, Dr. Tremont." He straightened, and respect radiated from him. "I have a plan." He left the office as silently as death itself.

8:21 P.M.
Near Syracuse, New York

Dressed again in his black SAS uniform but without the hood or equipment belt, Peter pensively mulled everything over as he drove the big RV along the dark highway toward the distant twinkling lights of Syracuse. Behind him, Marty worked intently on the computer. The virus's sudden explosion across the world terrified both men. They must find something that clicked with the Prince Leopold report in Syracuse, or Marty had to turn up Sophia's missing phone calls or Bill Griffin's hideout.

They had heard nothing from Jon. This did not surprise Peter, but it concerned him. It could mean Jon was in trouble and unable to get back to the embassy in Baghdad, or it could mean nothing at all.

Soon after they had left Princeton, Peter had the uneasy sense they were being followed. To be certain, he had driven a circuitous route on secondary roads from New Jersey into New York. Well inside the state, he entered the thruway. If there had been a tail, he figured he should have exposed or lost it by now. Still, the uneasiness would not leave. These people were experienced and skillful.

Twice he pulled off at rest stops to search the RV's exterior for a tracking device. He found none. But the concern persisted, and he had learned long ago to trust his feelings. That was why he exited the thruway early to take the slower but less traveled back roads into Syracuse itself.

For the first five miles he saw only occasional lights behind, and those vehicles had driven straight on when he pulled off to watch. He had changed direction more than once, going west for a time, then south, then east, then back north, and finally west again toward the city. Now he was driving through the outer suburbs. Since he had still seen no evidence of surveillance, he began to relax.

The sky was starry and black, with charcoal clouds low and ominous beneath the moon. To their right, a woodsy state park extended along the road, its split-rail fence like ghostly broken bones in the night. The park appeared to be densely forested, with picnic tables and fireplaces dotting open areas. There was little traffic at this hour.

Then from out of nowhere a gray pickup passed the RV at high speed. It pulled in front, its brake lights instantly glowed blood red, and it slowed, forcing Peter to hit his own brakes. Peter instantly checked his rearview mirror. High headlights were closing in fast. It had to be another truck or SUV. Right on the RV's tail.

Peter called out, "Hold on, Marty!"

"What are you up to now?" Marty complained.

"Pickup in front. SUV or pickup in back. Bastards think they're going to trap us like chopped liver in a sandwich."

Marty's round face flushed pink. "Oh." He instantly locked down the computer, tightened his seatbelt, and gamely grabbed the table, which was bolted into the RV's frame. He steeled himself and sighed. "I suppose I'm actually growing accustomed to these emergencies."

Peter pumped the brake and yanked the steering wheel right. The left wheels tilted up like a yacht in a high wind. Marty let out a surprised yell. The RV skidded on the two others, landed hard, and tore into the lighted picnic grounds. Behind them, brakes shrieked and rubber burned. The high headlights bounced across grass, roared over a sapling, and blasted through brush to emerge again on the park road. The gray pickup was close behind.

Marty watched through the windows, his heart palpitating with fear. Still, he was riveted by the spectacle. Although the Englishman was intellectually inferior, he had an uncanny ability where anything physical, particularly violence, was concerned.

Ahead, the road forked. Peter swerved the RV right. He was racing the bouncing, swaying pickup through the darkness. Abruptly the road curved back toward the lighted picnic area.

"Bloody damn!" he swore. "Road's a loop." The high headlights were behind them, and the gray pickup was driving toward them from ahead. "Trapped again!" He reached behind his seat and pulled out his Enfield bullpup. "Get to the back door and use this!"

"Me?" But Marty caught the assault rifle as Peter tossed it to him.

"When I say, just point and pull the trigger, my boy. Imagine it's a joystick."

The creases on Peter's leathery face were deep canyons of worry, but his eyes were glowing. He hit the brake again, yanked the wheel, and ran the RV off the road into a grove of trees that extended thick into the darkness. As soon as he skidded the big vehicle to a stop, he jumped from the seat, pulled out his H&K submachine gun, grabbed two cases of clips, handed the SA80 rounds to Marty, and hurried with his own clips and submachine gun to a side window.

The RV's nose was deep in the trees, and the side door also faced the woods. This meant the vehicle presented a solid side to the attackers while Peter and Marty could still fire from both the rear door and the small side windows.

Marty was examining his weapon, prodding it as he muttered to himself.

Peter asked, "Got it figured out?" The one good thing about the annoying fellow was he had turned out to be as smart as Jonathan Smith had claimed.

"There are some things I never wanted to learn." Marty looked up and sighed. "Of course, I understand this primitive machine. Child's play."

The car behind the headlights was a large black SUV. It had stopped on the road. The gray pickup was driving slowly across the grass toward the RV.

Peter shot out the front tires of the pickup.

The pickup sagged to a stop. For a time nothing moved.

Then two men pitched out like rag dolls from the pickup and dove under it. At the same time, automatic fire blasted from the SUV and slammed into the RV's side with loud screeches of tearing metal.

"Down!" Peter shouted as the RV rocked from the gunfire's impact.

Marty dove head first, and Peter crouched against the side wall.

When there was a pause, Marty looked around. "Where are the bullet holes? We should look like a sieve."

Peter grinned. "Had some serious plate put on this buggy. Thought you knew that from the ruckus in the Sierras. Good thing, right?"

A new fusillade hammered against the armored steel sides. But this time, it smashed windows and tore curtains, too. Glass shards sliced through the air and embedded themselves into appliances. Bits of cloth floated down like snow.

Marty had wrapped his arms over his head. "Obviously you should have considered putting plate on the windows."

"Steady," Peter said quietly. "They'll become weary after a bit and stop to see if we're still alive. Then we'll just spoil their little party, eh?"

Marty sighed and tried to calm the terror in his veins.

After another minute of the violent barrage, the firing died away. The cessation of sound seemed to create a vacuum in the lighted park. The birds were silent. No small animals scurried through the underbrush. Marty's face was white with fear.

"Right," Peter said cheerfully. "Let's have a look-see."

He raised up to peer out a corner of the shattered window above him. The two men from the gray truck were standing in the shelter of their vehicle holding what looked like Ingram M11 submachine guns. They stared across the swath of lighted grass to the RV. As Peter watched, a short, heavy man in a cheap gray suit, his face glistening with sweat, stepped out of the big SUV. His weapon was a Glock pistol. He motioned with his arm, and two more well-armed men climbed from the SUV. With another motion he ordered the group to spread out and close in on the RV.

"Right," Peter said again, softly this time. "Marty, take the two on the right. I'll take the left. I doubt any of them will charge into fire, so don't worry about your aim. Just point in their direction, squeeze the trigger, and let it rip. Ready?"

"My degradation increases."

"Good man. Here we go."

Chapter Thirty-Six

Inside the heavily equipped RV, the tension was electric. Still some twenty yards away, the five armed men and the short, square leader were rapidly closing in on Peter and Marty. The attackers progressed carefully, their gazes constantly roaming. They carried their weapons with the sureness of experience. Even in the distance, menace radiated from their walks.

"Now!" Peter fired a careful burst at the leader, while Marty let loose with everything.

As Marty's barrage shredded leaves and pine needles, ripped bark, and sawed through small branches, Peter's target grunted, clutched his right arm, and fell to his knees. Marty continued to spray bullets. The noise was deafening.

"Hold it, Marty! That's enough."

The echoes of the furious volleying reverberated through the park. The four men and their wounded leader crawled wildly for the shelter of firepits, benches, brush, and trees. Once under cover, they opened fire again at the RV. Bullets whined through the open window above Peter's head and thudded into the opposite wall. Selective this time, they were looking for targets.

Peter crouched low. "They won't hit us dead on again because of our firepower, but at the same time they won't go away. They've probably left a driver in the SUV. It's only a matter of time before one of us is hit, we run out of ammo and they get us, or the police come and arrest us all."

Marty shivered. "Too bad the police are out of the question. Many aspects of the idea are appealing."

Peter nodded and grimaced. "They'd want to know what we were doing with highly illegal weapons and a command post in the RV. If we tell them about Jon, they'll check, find he's wanted, and toss us into the slammer to wait for the army and FBI. If we don't tell them, we'll have no explanation, and they'll lock us up with our villainous friends out there."

"Logical. You have a solution?"

"We must split up."

Marty said firmly, "I will not be abandoned to those cutthroats and murderers."

Peter's eyes glinted out from the shadows. In his black commando clothes, he was difficult to see. "I know you don't think I'm too swift, my boy, but do remember this is how I've made my living since before you were an irritating twinkle in your father's eye. Here's the plan: I shall slip out the front door where they won't see me. You will then blast away to cover me. Once clear, I will circle to the left and make so much noise they'll believe a brigade is escaping. When they're convinced we've both quit the RV, they'll pursue me with their entire force. At that point, you'll be able to safely crank up this packhorse and do a fast bunk. Clear?"

Marty pursed his lips. His round cheeks expanded in thought. "If I stay with the RV, then I can keep checking for contact from Jon while I pursue Sophia's phone calls and look for Bill Griffin. Obviously, I'll have to find someplace to hide the RV. When I do, I'll post my location at the Asperger's syndrome Web site, just as we discussed."

"You're quick, my boy. There are certain aspects to dealing with a genius I like. Give me a minute to get into position, then fire away until your magazine's empty. Remember, a full minute."

Marty studied the weather-worn face with the craggy features. He had grown accustomed to seeing it. Today was Wednesday, and they had been together constantly since Saturday. During the past five days, he had been hurled into more terrifying and hair-raising experiences than in his entire life, and with far more at stake. He supposed it was natural he had grown accustomed to having Peter around. For an instant he had a strange emotion: Regret. Despite all the Englishman's annoyances, Marty would miss him. He wanted to tell him to be careful.

But all he could manage was, "It's been strange, Peter. Thanks."

Their gazes connected. Quickly both turned away.

"I know, my boy. Me, too." With a wink, Peter crab-walked to the front of the RV and fastened on his equipment belt.

Marty gave a brief smile and took position again at the rear door. Nervously he waited while giving himself a stern lecture that he could indeed pull this off.

The incoming fire had all but ceased, probably while the attackers figured out a new plan. As soon as Peter slipped out of the RV and melted into the deep shadows of the moonlit woods, Marty counted out a minute in his head. He made himself breathe slowly and evenly. When the minute was up, he gritted his teeth, leaned out, and opened fire with the bullpup. The gun reverberated in his hands and shook his entire body. Frightened but determined, he kept up a steady stream of fire across the night and into the dark trees. Peter was depending on him.

From their cover, the attackers returned a fusillade. The RV rocked from the hail of bullets.

Sweat popped out on Marty's face. He kept squeezing the trigger as he fought back fear. When the magazine was empty, he hugged the gun to his chest and carefully peered around the corner of the doorway. He saw no movement anywhere. He wiped his palm across his forehead, getting rid of a layer of sweat, and let out a long stream of relieved air.

As another minute passed, he clumsily changed magazines. He sat back. Two minutes passed. His skin began to crawl with tension.

Then he heard what sounded like somebody trying to be quiet among the trees far off to his left. Peter! He cocked his head, listening.

A warning voice from one of the attackers carried across the picnic grounds: "They're escaping!"

Almost at once, heavy fire from what seemed like two or three rifles raked out of the forest on the left, the direction in which Peter had said he would go.

On the picnic grounds, the men from the pickup and SUV frantically found new hiding spots as gunfire continued from this new direction.

Then the firing ceased. It sounded as if several people were running away to the left through the forest.

"After them!" a different voice shouted from the picnic area.

Energy jolted Marty. That was what he had been waiting for. He watched as men from the truck ran off to the left. At the same time, someone turned on the SUV's engine, drove it in a wide U-turn, and headed off to the left also. Everyone was chasing Peter, just as he had predicted.

Guiltily, Marty rolled and bumped his way into the RV cab. He was safe while Peter was out there, a hare to their hounds. Still, he knew Peter was right—this was the rational way to handle this grave situation.

The keys were in the ignition. He took a long breath to calm his resisting nerves and started the engine. He was worried not only about whether he would ever be able to uncover the vital information Jon needed; more to the point was whether he could drive Peter's RV safely away from the park. But when the oversize motor's power surged up through his hands and into his body, he had an idea: He closed his eyes and put reality on hold. Suddenly he was inside a Galaxy-rated starship, piloting it singlehandedly into the dangerous Fourth Quadrant. It was a forced trip, because he was still under the influence of his Mideral. Still, stars, planets, and asteroids flashed past the starship's bulkhead windows in rainbows of light. He was gloriously in control, and the unknown beckoned.

His eyes snapped open. *Don't be silly*, he told himself with disgust, *of course you can drive this gravity-bound RV. It's virtually an anachronism!*

With a surge of confidence, he threw the RV into reverse, hit the accelerator, sped backwards, and scraped a tree. Undeterred, he looked over both shoulders, checked the rearview and side-view mirrors, and saw nobody. He yanked the steering wheel, turned the RV around, and blasted it out of the forest like toothpaste from a tube. At the same time, he watched for trouble, just as Peter had taught him. His glittering green gaze examined shadows and obstacles, checking everywhere that could be cover for their attackers.

But this part of the park was quiet. Heaving a sigh of relief, he rocketed the RV past the picnic grounds and onto the highway heading north to Syracuse.

■

Crouched in a concrete drainage ditch at the edge of the park, his submachine gun ready to fire, Peter Howell saw his RV rushing north on the highway. He grinned with admiration. That exasperating little bastard Marty had risen to the occasion yet again.

He rubbed a hand over his grizzled chin and refocused his attention. He breathed deeply, inhaling the earthy scents of the damp ditch but also the fragrant trees on the higher ground and the myriad creatures that inhabited it. At the same time he listened and scrutinized with every fiber of his body. His senses were alert, on fire. He could hear and sense the attackers moving toward him on foot and in the SUV on the road that crossed the drainage ditch. It was time to get himself away.

He unhooked two cylindrical black canisters from his belt, laid them side by side on the parapet of the bridge, and drew his 14-round Browning Hi-Power 9mm pistol from his open combat holster. The pistol in his right hand and the H&K MP5 in his left, he raised his eyes to look down the road.

They were advancing in a wide line. The SUV was behind, its headlights outlining the bloody fools. He needed them closer together. So when they were still some fifteen yards away, he opened fire with both guns, moving quickly from side to side to simulate shooting by more than one person.

They zeroed in on him and returned fire. He fell back, as if retreating. Encouraged, they ran toward him in a tighter semicircle, while he grabbed the canisters and shimmied toward them on his belly. As soon as they were just thirty feet away, he lifted his shoulder and hurled the first canister. The magnesium-based stun grenade exploded with a great flash and bang directly in the center of their semicircle, only a foot or two from most of them.

All went down. Some screamed and clutched their heads. Others were simply stunned and momentarily out of action. Which was all Peter needed.

He was up instantly, speeding around their left flank. The thousands of rounds fired in the SAS Close Quarters Battle House, perfecting the skill to rapidly score head hits while running at full speed, never left you. He squeezed off two fast shots, easily destroying the SUV's headlights, and then he threw the second stun grenade. It landed in their midst. Since they still had not recovered from the first, it was not only physically but psychologically devastating. Within minutes, as they still tried to gather their wits, Peter was a hundred yards off in the distance, trotting softly but swiftly away toward the highway and Syracuse.

■

As he closed in on the city, Marty slowed the RV, looking for somewhere to hide it and himself. He was beginning to think this time he had outsmarted himself. Where could you hide something as big and obvious as a recreational vehicle, especially one in which many of the windows had been destroyed and bullet holes had battered the sides? Behind him on the state highway a line of cars was piling up. Horns honked, making him nervous as he anxiously scanned all around for safety.

Finally, he pulled onto the shoulder so the backed-up cars and trucks could rush past in an angry roar. Worried, he drove back onto the highway and resumed his search. Then he saw an intriguing sight: On either side of the highway were car dealerships with brightly lighted showrooms and lots full of vehicles. There was everything from inexpensive compacts to luxury sedans and sports cars. Miles of them. It was giving him an idea. He craned to look ahead. Would he find—?

Yes! Like a miracle, a vast, lighted open area stretched off to the right. It was a new and used recreational vehicle sales lot and repair facility.

He thought of the old children's riddle: Where do you hide an elephant?

The answer, of course, was in a herd of elephants.

Chortling with glee, Marty turned into the main gate and drove to the back until he found an empty space. He pulled in and turned off his motor. It was late, so the dealer would have to close soon. With luck, no one would find him here at night.

10:27 P.M.
Syracuse, New York

Professor Emeritus Richard Johns lived in a restored old Victorian on South Crouse Avenue below the university's hill. In his living room, lovingly furnished by his wife with antiques of the same period as the house, he studied the man who had knocked on his door so late and wanted to know about Sophia Russell. There was something about the stranger that frightened Johns. An intensity. A suppressed violence. He wished he had never allowed him inside.

"I'm not sure what more I can tell you, Mr.—?"

"Louden. Gregory Louden." Peter Howell offered a smile as he reminded the professor of the false name he had given on the doorstep. Then: "Dr. Russell thought highly of you." He was dressed in coveralls and a trench coat he had bought from a curious trucker who had given him a ride into Syracuse. From there, he had caught a taxi to the professor's house near the university, which had so far turned out to be a waste of time. The man was nervous and had been able to remember only that Sophia had been an excellent student and had a few close friends, but he could name none.

Johns reiterated, "I was simply chair of her major department and had her in a few classes. That's all. I heard she switched her field of study in grad school."

"She was studying anthropology with you, wasn't she?"

"Yes. An enthusiastic student. We were surprised that she left the major."

"Why did she?"

"I have no idea." Johns knitted his brows. "Although I do recall that in her senior year she took the absolute minimum requirements for anthro. She studied a lot of biology instead. Too late to declare a different major by then, of course, unless she planned to stay on another year or two."

Peter stopped pacing. "What happened in her junior year to interest her in biology?"

"I have no idea about that either."

He remembered the Prince Leopold report had mentioned Bolivia and Peru. "What about field trips?"

The professor frowned. "A field trip?" His gaze focused on Peter as if he had suddenly remembered something. "Of course. We have a summer departmental trip for majors between their junior and senior years."

"Where did Sophia go?"

The professor's frown deepened. He leaned back, thinking. At last, he decided, "Peru."

Excitement made Peter's pale blue eyes luminous. "Did she talk about it when she got back?"

Johns shook his head. "Not that I remember. But everyone who goes has to write a report." He stood up. "I should have it here." And just like that he casually walked out of the room.

Peter's heart thudded against his chest excitedly. At last, he had gotten what seemed to be a break. He moved to the edge of his chair as the professor talked to himself in the next room. Drawers opened and slammed closed.

Then a triumphant "Ah-ha!"

Peter jumped to his feet, as Johns returned, thumbing through a stapled document. "When I was chairman, I kept them all. They are a useful body of work to draw from for motivating the lower-year classes."

"Thank you." The words were inadequate. Barely suppressing his eagerness, Peter took the undergraduate paper and sat in the closest chair. He read through it, and . . . there it was. He blinked, not quite believing his eyes. Then he read again, memorizing each word: "I encountered a fascinating group of natives called the Monkey Blood People. Some biologists from the States were studying them when we passed through. It seems like a fascinating field. There are so many illnesses in the tropics that it could be a life's work to help cure them."

No names. Nothing specific about the virus. But had she remembered Peru when she was given the unknown virus to work with?

Peter stood up. "Thank you, Professor Johns."

"Is that what you wanted?"

"It just might be," Peter said. "May I keep it?"

"Sorry. Part of my archives, you know."

Peter nodded. It did not matter; he had committed it to memory. He said a quick good-bye and headed out into the dark, cold night, which for the first time seemed friendlier. He trotted uphill toward the university, where he knew he would find a pay phone.

Chapter
Thirty-Seven

12:06 A.M., Thursday, October 23
Wadi al-Fayi, Iraq

The Syrian Desert was cold and silent, and the stink of diesel seemed oppressive inside the canvas-covered truck. Next to the tailgate, Jon and Randi listened for more gunfire. Behind them lay the two unconscious policemen who had been guarding them, while outside some new, unknown force besieged them.

Tense and alert, Smith dropped into a crouch, cradling his confiscated AK-47. He pulled Randi down next to him. She swung her Kalashnikov around so she was ready to shoot, too. They peered outside through cracks where the canvas flap closed against the sides of the truck.

"All I can see are streaks of fire and moving silhouettes," he said, disgusted. Sweat coated his face. Time seemed to pass with aching slowness.

"That's what I see, too. The light from the other truck's too glaring."

"Damn!"

They dropped the flap. Abruptly, the noise of fighting ceased. The cold night was menacingly quiet. The only sound was the raspy breathing of the two Iraqi guards lying unconscious on the floor in the eerie glow from the headlamps of the other vehicle.

Jon looked at Randi, who turned just at that moment. He frowned. She shook her head. Her face was pinched. He saw fear in her eyes, then she moved her gaze.

His chest tightened. Only the truck's canvas walls and their confiscated Kalashnikov rifles stood between them and whatever peril waited outside.

He told her, "We'll open fire. We've got no choice."

"As soon as they're close enough."

From the desert, a voice bellowed in Arabic at them, "Everyone has surrendered! Throw out your guns and follow with your hands up!"

Quickly Randi translated for Jon. She added grimly, "Sounds like the Republican Guard."

Smith nodded. In the hovering silence, his gaze narrowed. He was not going to just sit and wait to be executed. He inched back the flap. In the slit he could see a trio of black silhouettes, their guns aimed at the truck where he and Randi hunched.

"I can get three," Jon decided. "Perfect targets. Problem is, who are they? And where are the others?"

She rose up and peered out through the narrow opening above his head. The heat of her body warmed the chill around him.

"We may have to kill them anyway," she said grimly. "We've got to get this information about the virus out of Iraq. Concentrate on their legs. What's a few shattered femurs compared to what's at stake?"

He nodded sober agreement and slid the nose of his AK-47 out. He wrapped his finger over the trigger, prepared to fire, and—

Suddenly, a voice boomed: "Russell!"

Jon and Randi stiffened. They gazed at each other, shocked.

"Are you in there, Russell?" the voice yelled in English. Very American English. "If you and the U.N. guy have taken out the guards, give me a shout. Otherwise, you're not likely to leave there without a lot of birdshot in your carcasses!"

Randi inhaled with excitement. She squeezed Jon's shoulder. "I know who he is, thank God." She raised her voice. "Donoso? Is that you, pig breath?"

"No one else, little lady."

"We almost killed you, you fool!"

Jon spoke in a low, quick voice. "Don't tell them who I really am. Use the U.N. cover. He already believes it, or he wouldn't have identified me that way. If the U.S. Army gets its hands on me for being AWOL . . ." He let the words hang in the air. He knew she understood the inevitable result: He would be stopped from pursuing the people who had killed Sophia. "Randi? Will you do that?"

She turned her angry, blazing eyes onto him. "Of course."

He had to trust her, which suddenly made him very nervous. Together they raised the canvas that overlay the tailgate. Jon shot her a worried look as a short, swarthy man in desert camos came around from the side. He had the firm face and bunched muscles of someone religious in his fitness training. Carrying a cocked 9mm Beretta, he peered beyond them and their Kalashnikovs to the wounded policemen sprawled in the back of the truck.

He grinned approval. "Nice job. Two less for us to deal with."

Smith and Randi jumped down, and Randi pumped Donoso's hand. "Always interesting, Donoso. This is Mark Bonnet."

Jon exhaled, relieved, as she introduced him under the alias.

She gave him a polite smile, then returned to focus on Donoso. "Mark's here with a medical mission. Mark, meet Agent Gabriel Donoso. How the hell did you find us, Gabby?"

"Doc Mahuk called as soon as they grabbed you. Then one of our assets picked up the truck crossing the Tigris." His gaze swept the night. "I'd love to catch up on old times, but someone could've heard the gunfire. We'd better do a fast fade." He peered speculatively at Jon. "U.N. medical mission, huh?"

"CIA, I take it." Jon shook his hand and smiled. "My personal appreciation for the CIA grows by the instant."

Donoso nodded sympathetically. "Looks like you two have had a rough time."

As Donoso led them around the truck, Jon saw an old Soviet BMP-1 troop carrier whose sides had been stenciled with Republican Guard markings. Ruts showed where it had first been angled to block the road. Now its headlights shone directly onto the canvas-covered police truck. Sitting on the light desert soil with their backs against it were the surviving Baghdad policemen and their officer, who was bleeding from a shoulder wound and no longer sported his *tariq* pistol. Standing sentry were two CIA agents who might easily pass for Iraqis.

"Do you know what they were planning to do with us?" Smith asked Donoso.

"Yup. Get you deep out in the middle of nowhere, kill you, and hide your corpses where not even the Bedouins would dream of looking."

Jon raised his eyebrows. He exchanged a look with Randi. It was no surprise.

Donoso said, "I need those Kalashnikovs, Mr. Bonnet. Both of them, little lady."

As Randi and Jon handed over their weapons, Randi explained to Jon, "Donoso's an unrepentant male chauvinist pig. He knows better, but he just doesn't care. So he calls me little lady, or girlie, or sweetie-pie, or any other demeaning cliché he can dredge up from his rather ordinary redneck background."

Donoso grinned widely. "She sticks to 'pig breath.' She's got great legs but a limited imagination. Let's go. Into the carrier."

"A limited imagination? Hey, I'm the one who saved your butt in Riyadh. Where's your respect?"

He grinned sheepishly. "Whoops. That occasion slipped my mind." He added their AK-47s to a pile of other weapons taken from the Iraqi policemen. "See your guns in there?"

Jon quickly located his Beretta, while Randi dug around until she uncovered her Uzi. Donoso nodded approval and scrambled up into the carrier. Smith and Randi followed.

As they found places to sit, Jon nodded back at the prisoners. "What are you going to do about the Iraqis?"

"Nothing," Donoso told him. "If they so much as hint about being out here on their own in a police truck, they'll get a fast trip to Saddam Hussein's gallows. No way are they going to breathe a word about what happened."

Smith understood. "Which means they'd better have their own guns when they get back to headquarters."

Donoso nodded. "You got it."

While the prisoners glared up sullenly, the old troop carrier spun its treads into the parched soil and took off. Its speed increasing, the driver directed the big machine down the center of the narrow road that led deeper into the hard, rocky landscape. The moon was sinking in the west, while stars glimmered brightly above. Far ahead on the horizon were dry, rolling hills, black against an even blacker sky.

But Jon was watching behind. At last the Iraqis ran across the sand to the pile of guns and their truck. Now that the carrier was out of rifle range, they were safe to flee. Seconds later, their canvas-covered vehicle disappeared, raising mushroom clouds of light soil as it rushed back to Baghdad and, perhaps, survival.

"Where are we going?" Randi wanted to know.

"Old World War One outpost the Brits built," Donoso answered promptly. "It's nothing but ruins now. A few tumbledown walls and desert ghosts. A Harrier will pick you up there at dawn and fly you out to Turkey."

"They don't want me to stay on, pig breath?" Randi wanted to know.

Donoso shook his head with disgust. "No way, baby girl. This cute little caper has compromised you and damn near the whole operation." His voice rose, and he glared again at Jon. "Hope it was worth it."

"It was," Jon assured him. "You have a family?"

"As a matter of fact, I do. Why?"

"That's how important it is. With luck, you've just saved their lives."

The CIA agent looked at Randi. When she nodded, he said, "Works for me. But you'll have some fast talking to do at Langley, kiddo."

Randi asked, "You're sure a Harrier can take both of us?"

Donoso was all business. "Stripped, no missiles, one pilot. Not comfortable, but it can be done."

The lumbering carrier continued on through the windswept desert. Moonlight shone down, casting an unearthly silver cloak over the rocky *wadi*. Meanwhile, everyone's eyes were alert. Without ever discussing it, their gazes surveyed all around, watching uneasily for more trouble.

■

The ruins were on the north side of the road. From the carrier, Smith studied them. The remnants of stone walls emerged like worn, gray teeth from the desert. Skeletal brush had blown against some, while a clump of thorny tamarisk grew nearby, indicating water flowed somewhere under the salty surface of this forbidding landscape.

Donoso ordered a man to stand guard in the Russian BMP, and the rest of the crew settled against the walls, wrapped in lightweight blankets to wait out the starry night. The dry air smelled of alkali, and everyone was weary. Some fell quickly asleep, their low snores lost in the sound of a whispering wind that rustled the tamarisk and kicked up little tornadoes among the loose particles on the desert floor. Neither Randi nor Jon was among the sleepers.

He was studying her where she lay in shadows against the old wall. His head resting on a rock, he watched emotion play her face as if it were a musical instrument. He remembered that about Sophia, too. What she felt, she showed. Not a particularly demonstrative man, he had enjoyed that gift. Randi was more guarded than Sophia, but then Randi was a professional operative. She had been trained into sanity-saving unemotionality in her job. But not tonight. Tonight he could tell she was feeling the burning loss of her sister, and he felt deeply for her.

Grieving, Randi closed her eyes, overwhelmed by sorrow. In her mind, she could see her older sister clearly—the slender face, the softly pointed chin, and the long, satin hair pulled back into a ponytail. When the image of Sophia smiled, Randi fought back tears and hugged herself. *I'm so sorry, Sophia. So sorry I wasn't there.*

But suddenly a treasure trove of memories appeared from the past, and Randi went eagerly toward them, hoping for solace: Breakfasts were the best. She could smell again the comforting aroma of Maxwell House coffee and hear the cheerful chatter of their parents as she and Sophia ran downstairs to join them. Evenings brought picnics and panoramic sunsets across the Pacific Ocean so brilliant they pierced the soul. She remembered the fun of hopscotch and Barbie dolls, their father's silly jokes, and their mother's kind hands.

But what had dominated their childhoods had been the sisters' uncanny resemblance. From their earliest years, people remarked on it, while she and Sophia had taken it all for granted. They had been blessed with an unusual combination of genetic factors that had resulted in both being not blue-eyed, but brown-eyed blondes. Very dark brown eyes, almost black. Their mother had found it fascinating. So her daughters could view a parallel to their unusual coloring in nature, she had planted black-eyed Susans along the front of their hacienda in Santa Barbara, California. Every summer the cream-colored petals with the rich dark centers had erupted in fragrant color.

All of that had ignited Sophia's first interest in science, while the hacienda's breathtaking views of the Channel Islands and the immense Pacific had awakened in Randi a hunger to know what lay beyond the horizon. Her family had two homes—the one in Santa Barbara and another on Chesapeake Bay in Maryland. A marine biologist, their father had traveled back and forth regularly, and she, her sister, and their mother had occasionally accompanied him.

Who knew at what point other lives became important? For Randi, it began with the constant feeling of being new herself, not only during the trips from coast to coast but to the Sea of Cortés, the Mediterranean, and the other distant locations that attracted her father's excited attention. Soon she grew comfortable exploring the unknown and meeting unfamiliar people. Then she enjoyed it. Finally she craved it.

A gift for languages had sent her on full scholarship to Harvard for bachelor's degrees in Spanish and government and then to Columbia for a master's in international relations. Everywhere she went, she took additional language courses until she was fluent in seven. It was at Columbia that the CIA recruited her. She had been a natural—the tweed and contacts of an Ivy League education plus the wanderlust of a gypsy. But she had turned out to be a lackadaisical operative, doing only an adequate job while avoiding the tough assignments . . . until Mike died in Somalia.

Untouched by bullet or knife, an invisible virus had felled him in an ugly, painful end. Even now it brought a catch to her throat and a searing regret for what might have been.

That was when the inequities of life began to strangle her. Everywhere she looked, people were hungry, imperiled, lied to, or repressed. It outraged her. She had turned inward, and her work became the center of her life. Once she no longer had Mike, the only thing that mattered was making the world a better, safer place.

But she had not made the world safer for Sophia.

She inhaled, trying to calm her emotions. She forced herself to focus. She had a goal. She knew she would never be able to like Smith and probably never to really trust him, but that no longer mattered.

She needed him.

She rose quietly, her blanket wrapped around her. She gazed around at the sleeping men. Carrying her Uzi, she crept across to where Jon lay. She stretched out beside him. He turned his head to look at her.

"You all right?" he asked quietly.

She ignored the kindness in his voice. She whispered, "Let's get one thing straight. I understand intellectually you didn't mean to kill Mike. Lassa is hard to tell from malaria at first, and it could've killed him anyway. But it might not have if you'd diagnosed it in time and gotten help."

"Randi!"

"Shhh. I don't know that I'll ever be able to forgive you. You were too cavalier. Presumptuous. You thought you knew it all."

"I was arrogant, yes. But I was mostly ignorant. So are most army doctors when it comes to rare tropical diseases." He sighed wearily. "I was wrong. Fatally wrong. But it wasn't from not caring or being careless. I just didn't know. It's not an excuse, it's an explanation. Lassa is still mistaken for malaria. I tried to tell you Mike's death was the reason I transferred to USAMRIID, so I could become an authority on infectious diseases. It was the only way I could make up for what had happened— make sure it never happened again to another army doctor. I'm so sorry he died, and I deeply regret the role I played in it." He gazed at her. "Death is damnably final, isn't it?"

She heard the pain in his voice and knew he must be thinking about Sophia again. Part of her wanted to forgive him and put it all behind her, but she could not. Despite his contrition and efforts to make amends, he could still be the same old cowboy, galloping heedlessly through life as he pursued his private interests.

But right now that was irrelevant. "I have a proposition for you."

He crossed his arms over his blanket and frowned. "Okay. Let's hear it."

"You want to find out who killed Sophia, and so do I. I need your scientific knowledge to help me track the people behind the virus. You need my contacts and other abilities. Together we make a good team."

He studied her face, so like Sophia's. Her voice was Sophia's voice, but her toughness was her own. To work with her was appealing . . . and dangerous. He could not look at her without remembering Sophia and feeling a raw rush of pain. He knew he had to go on with his life, but with Randi around, would he be able to? She looked so much like her sister, they could have been identical twins. He had loved Sophia. He did not love Randi. And to work with her could cause him endless grief.

So he said, "There's nothing you can do for me. This isn't a good idea. Thanks, but no thanks."

She said roughly, "This isn't about you or me. This is about Sophia and all the millions of people out there who are going to die."

"It *is* about you and me," he corrected her. "If we can't work together, neither of us will accomplish a damn thing. Whatever chance I have of getting to the bottom of this will evaporate in arguments and hard feelings." His voice lowered and he growled. "Understand this. I don't give a flying leap what you think of me. All I care about is Sophia and stopping her killers. You can continue on the rest of your life still hauling around your precious load of anger if that's what you want. I don't have time. I've got something far more important to do. I'm going to stop this scourge, and I don't need you to help me do it."

He had taken her breath away. She was silent, stunned that her rage at him showed so much. Also, she felt guilty, which she was not ready to admit. "I could turn you in. Right now, I could go to Donoso, whisper in his ear, and he'd have the military police waiting for you when we land in Turkey. Don't look at me like that, Jon. I'm just laying out the alternatives. You say you don't need me, and I say you do. But the truth is, I don't play dirty with people I respect, and I respect you for everything I've seen in Iraq. Which means even if you and I can't work out something, I'll say nothing to Donoso." She hesitated. "Sophia loved you. That's important, too. I may never get over Mike's death, but that won't stop me from working cooperatively with you. For instance, do you have any idea what you're going to do once I get us into the United States?"

Smith scratched his chin. All of a sudden the potential had shifted. "You can get me into the United States?"

"Sure. No problem. I'll be offered a transport or some other military flight back home. I'll take you with me. Those U.N. credentials are perfect."

He nodded. "You think you can get your hands on a computer with a modem, too, before we arrive?"

"Depends. For how long?"

"With luck, a half hour. There's a Web site I need to check to find

out where to meet my friends. They've been investigating certain aspects of the situation while I've been gone. Assuming they survived, of
course."

"Of course."

She stared at him, relieved and surprised at his pragmatism. He was
a lot more complicated than she had suspected. Also a lot more decisive.

She was almost ready to apologize when he said, "You're tired. I can
see it in your face. Get some sleep. We've got a busy day tomorrow."

He had ice in his veins. But that was what she needed. Without ever
saying so, he had agreed to work with her. As she turned away and closed
her eyes, she said a silent prayer that they would succeed.

Part Four

Chapter Thirty-Eight

5:32 P.M., Wednesday, October 22
Washington, D.C.

At last count, nearly a million had died worldwide. Tragically, hundreds of millions were ill with the symptoms of a heavy cold that could be the first onslaught of the deadly virus no one had a scientific name for yet. Hysteria swept across the hemispheres like the four horsemen of the Apocalypse. In the United States, hospitals were flooded with the ill and the frightened, and the loss of confidence over the past few days had driven down the stock market by a shocking fifty percent.

In President Castilla's private office in the White House Treaty Room, a row of colorful Kachina dolls with feather headdresses and leather loincloths stood on the marble mantelpiece. As he studied them, he could almost hear the heavy, rhythmic stamp of Indian feet and the hortatory medicine chants to save the world.

He had left the frantic West Wing to find respite in his home office so he could polish an important speech he was scheduled to deliver to a dinner of Midwest party leaders in Chicago next week. But he could not write. The words seemed trivial.

Would any of them even be alive next week?

He answered his own question: Not unless some miracle stopped the raging pestilence that had been loosed upon the world, and that would take more than the dances and chants of Kachinas, real or imaginary.

He pushed the legal pad and its offending words away. He was about to stand and leave the room when a heavy knock sounded on the closed door.

Samuel Adams Castilla stared at it. For a second, he held his breath. "Come in."

Surgeon General Jesse Oxnard entered, not running but walking very fast. Behind him, HHS Secretary Nancy Petrelli trotted to keep up. White House Chief of Staff Charles Ouray strode in after her. Bringing up the rear was Secretary of State Norman Knight, who carried his metal-rimmed reading glasses as if he had just pulled them from his nose. He looked solemn and uneasy.

But Surgeon General Oxnard's heavy jowls quivered with excitement. "They're out of danger, sir!" His thick mustache pumped up and down as he continued, "The volunteer virus victims . . . Blanchard's serum *cured* them. Every last one!"

Nancy Petrelli was triumphant in a baby-blue knit suit: "They're re-covering rapidly, sir. All of them." She nodded her silver head. "It's like a miracle."

"Thank God." The president slumped back into his chair as if he had suddenly gone weak. "You're absolutely sure, Jesse? Nancy?"

"Yessir," Nancy Petrelli assured him.

"Absolutely," the surgeon general enthused.

"What's the status at Blanchard?"

"Victor Tremont is waiting to be told to start shipping the serum."

Charles Ouray explained, "He's waiting for the FDA to approve it." The White House chief of staff's voice had an ominous tone. He crossed thick arms over his round paunch. "Director Cormano over there says that'll take at least three months."

"Three months? God in heaven." The president reached for his phone. "Zora, get me Henry Cormano over at the FDA. Right now!" He returned the handset to its cradle. He stared at it, outraged. "Are we all to perish under our own stupidity?"

The secretary of state cleared his throat. "The FDA is there to protect us from the mistakes of overeagerness and fear, Mr. President. That's why we have the agency."

The president's lips turned down with irritation. "There's a time to know when the fear is so big and so real that the protection is irrelevant, Norm. When the caution is more dangerous than the possible mistake."

The phone buzzed, and President Castilla snatched it.

"Cormano—" he began and then sat in smoldering silence, foot tapping impatiently, as the FDA director stated his case. At last the president snapped, "Okay, Cormano, hold it. What can happen that's worse than what *is* happening? Uh-huh. Dammit, it's horrible now." He listened for another angry minute. "Henry, listen to me. Really listen. The rest of the world *will* approve this serum now that it's cured victims of a virus you scientists can't even tell me where it came from. You want Americans to be the only ones continuing to die while you 'protect' them? Yes, I know that's unfair, but it's what they'll say and it's true. Approve the serum, Henry. Then you can write a long memo blasting me with why you didn't want to and what a goddamned ogre I am." He paused to listen, gave up, and shouted, "No! Do it *now!*"

Castilla slammed the phone into its cradle and glared at everyone in the Treaty Room until his gaze settled on the surgeon general.

He barked, "When can they ship?"

Jesse Oxnard shot back, "Tomorrow afternoon."

"They'll need to pay their costs," Nancy Petrelli pointed out. "Plus a reasonable return on investment. It's what we agreed to, and it's fair."

"Money will be wired tomorrow," the president decided, "right after the first batch leaves their lab."

"What if a nation can't pay?" Nancy Petrelli asked.

"Advanced nations will have to cover the impoverished nations' costs," the president told them. "It's been arranged."

Secretary of State Knight was shocked. "The pharmaceutical company wants money up front?"

Chief of Staff Ouray scowled. "I thought this was *pro bono*."

The surgeon general shook his head, chiding them. "No one provides vaccines or serums for nothing, Charlie. You think the flu vaccine we want everyone in the nation to have every winter is free?"

Nancy Petrelli explained, "Blanchard incurred enormous expense developing the biotechnology and facilities to produce the antiserum in quantity to see if it could be done so we'd have such facilities in the future. They expected to recoup over a long period. But now we need it all and fast. They're way out on a financial limb."

"I don't know about this, Mr. President," Norman Knight worried. "I guess I have some reservations about 'miracles.' "

"Especially when they don't come cheap," Ouray added, an edge of sarcasm in his voice.

The president slammed his fist onto his desk, jumped up, and paced into the center of the room. "Dammit, Charlie, what's the matter with you? Haven't you been listening these last few days?" He prowled back behind his desk and leaned over it, facing them. "*Almost one million dead!* Untold millions who could be dying any day. And you want to argue about dollars? About a reasonable return for stockholders? In *this* country? We *preach* that economic view as the only right and fair way, dammit! We can end the scourge of this awful virus right now. This minute. And it'll be fast and cheap compared to what we spend every year fighting flu, cancer, malaria, and AIDS." He spun on his heel to peer out the Treaty Room window as if looking out on the entire planet. "It could really *be* a miracle, people!"

They waited unspeaking, awed by the righteous rage of their taciturn leader.

But when he turned to face them again, he had calmed himself. His voice was quiet and compelling. "Call it God's will, if you like. You cynics and secularists are always doubting the unknown, the spiritual. Well, there are more things on heaven and earth, gentlemen and lady, than are dreamed of in your philosophies. If that's too highbrow for you, how about 'Don't look a gift horse in the friggin' mouth'?"

"It doesn't appear it's going to be exactly a gift," Ouray said.

"Oh, for God's sake, Charlie. Give it up. It's a miracle. Let's enjoy it. Let's *celebrate*. We'll have a big ceremony accepting the first shipment up there at Blanchard's headquarters in the Adirondacks. A beautiful setting. I'll fly there, too." He smiled as the ramifications struck him. At last there was good news, and he knew exactly how to use it. His voice rose again, but this time in excited anticipation. "In fact, let's bring all the world leaders in by closed-circuit TV. I'll give Tremont the Medal of Freedom. We're going to stop this epidemic in its tracks and honor those who've helped us." He gave a wicked grin. "Of course, it's not too shabby for our political aspirations either. After all, we've got to think of the next election."

5:37 P.M.
Lima, Peru

Amid the gilt and marble of his office, the deputy minister smiled.

The important Englishman said, "Everyone who goes into Amazonia needs a permit from your ministry, correct?"

"Very true," the deputy minister agreed.

"Including scientific expeditions?"

"Especially."

"These records are open to the public?"

"Of course. We are a democracy, yes?"

"A fine democracy," the Englishman agreed. "Then I need to examine all the permits granted twelve and thirteen years ago. If it's not too much trouble."

"It is no trouble at all," the deputy minister said cooperatively and smiled again. "But, alas, the records from those years were destroyed during the time of a different government."

"Destroyed? How?"

"I am not certain." The deputy minister spread his hands in apology. "It was a long time ago. There was much turmoil from unimportant factions that wished a coup. Sendero Luminoso and others. You understand."

"I'm not certain I do." The important Englishman smiled, too.

"Ah?"

"I don't recall an attack on the interior ministry."

"Perhaps when they were being photocopied."

"You should have a record of that."

The deputy minister was unperturbed. "As I said, a different government."

"I will speak with the minister himself, if I may."

"Of course, but, alas, he is out of the city."

"Really? That's odd, since I saw him only last night at a concert."

"You are mistaken. He is on vacation. In Japan, I believe."

"It must have been someone else I saw."

"The minister is unremarkable in appearance."

"There you are, then." The Englishman smiled as he stood and bowed slightly to the deputy minister, who returned a pleasant nod. The Englishman left.

Outside on the wide boulevard of the elegant old city famed for its colonial architecture, the Englishman, whose name was Carter Letissier, flagged down a taxi and gave the address of his Miraflores house. In the taxi, his smile evaporated. He sat back and swore.

The bastard had been bought. And recently, too. Otherwise, the minister would have allowed Letissier to waste his time in the files only to discover the records really *were* missing. Instead, the records must not have been destroyed yet. But Letissier also knew they would be gone by the time he could get an appointment with the minister. He glanced at his watch. The ministry was closing. Given the normal lazy habits of Peruvian deputy ministers, the records would not actually disappear until tomorrow morning at the earliest.

■

Three hours later, the grand offices of the Ministry of the Interior were dark. Armed with his 10mm Browning semiautomatic, Carter Letissier broke in dressed completely in black and wearing the black boots and antiflash hood with respirator of the British SAS counterterrorist commando. At one time he had been a captain of the 22nd SAS Regiment, a proud and memorable period in his life.

He went directly to the filing cabinet he had learned contained Amazonian documents, found the section on permits, and extracted the folders for the two years he needed. He erected and flicked on the minute lamp he had brought with him. Under it, he opened the folders and photographed the pages with his minicamera. As soon as he had finished, he returned everything to where it belonged, collapsed his light, and slipped back out into the night.

In his private darkroom in the Miraflores house, Letissier, now a well-known importer of cameras and equipment to Peru, developed the film. When the negatives were dry, he made large prints.

Grinning, he dialed a long series of numbers and waited. "Letissier here. I have the names of those who led scientific teams to the location you wished in the years you wished. You have paper and pencil ready, Peter?"

Chapter Thirty-Nine

10:01 A.M., Thursday, October 23
Syracuse, New York

The old industrial city of Syracuse was nestled in the autumn-colored hills of central New York state, a land of rolling farmland, ample rivers, and independent-minded people who enjoyed the great outdoors from the safety of their sprawling lakeside metropolis. Jonathan Smith knew all this because his grandparents had lived here, and he had visited them yearly. A decade ago, they had retired to Florida, where they had fished, surfed, and happily gambled until first his grandmother had died of a heart attack, and then within three months his grandfather had followed, too lonely to go on.

Jon gazed out the window of the rented Oldsmobile that Randi was driving. As they sped along, she shifted lanes, preparing to leave Interstate 81 going south to join Route 5 east toward where they hoped to find Marty. From here he could see familiar landmarks in the central city—the historic brick Armory, the Weighlock Building, and Syracuse University's recent Carrier Dome. He was glad the old buildings were still standing, an affirmation that there was some sort of continuity in this precarious world.

He was tired and tense. It had been a long trip from the Iraqi desert to Syracuse, New York. As Gabriel Donoso had promised, a Harrier jet had picked them up and flown them to Incirlik Air Base in Turkey. There Randi had finessed a ride on a C-17 cargo jet. Once aloft, she had sweet-talked the copilot out of his notebook computer, and Jon had tapped into the Internet to search OASIS, the Asperger's syndrome Web site. Finally he had found Marty's message on the ABCs of Parenting page, part of the Web site's extended Web ring:

> *Coughing Wolf,*
>> *A riddle: Who is attacked, separated, stays home with Hart's erroneous comedy 5 ways east, is colored lake green or thereabouts, and whose letter is stolen?*
>
>> *Edgar A.*

"That's the message?" Randi had read it over his shoulder skeptically. "Your name's not even on it. And there sure as hell isn't any 'Zellerbach' mentioned."

"I'm Coughing," he explained. "Think: Smith Brothers cough drops. My uncle who treated Marty swore by them. Marty and I joked about it all the time. Horrible-tasting black things. And what does a wolf do?"

"Howls." She rolled her eyes. "Howell. Unbelievable. That's really stretching it."

He smiled. "That's why we agreed to address our messages to each other that way. We figured they'd expect us to use E-mail to communicate, but going through the Asperger's site gave us a place to hide out, as long as we came up with some kind of personal code. For Marty and me, since we grew up together, it's no problem. We have a lot of shared history to draw on."

"So he fashioned this message from allusions the three of you would understand but with any luck they wouldn't." She crouched next to him. "Okay, I'm hooked. Translate it."

"The first two things are obvious: Marty and Peter were 'attacked,' and had to 'separate.' But Marty 'stayed home.' That is, he's in the RV someplace and may still not know where Peter is."

"Clear as a bell," she said with more than a little sarcasm. "So where are Mr. Zellerbach and the RV?"

"In Syracuse, New York, of course."

She frowned. "Enlighten me."

" 'Hart's erroneous comedy.' "

"That tells you he's in Syracuse?"

"Absolutely. Rogers and Hart's Broadway musical *The Boys from Syracuse* was based on Shakespeare's *The Comedy of Errors*. So, Marty's in the RV somewhere in or near Syracuse."

"And 'five ways east?' "

"Ah! That was particularly clever of him. I'll bet we'll find him on some kind of Highway 'five' on the 'east' side leading into Syracuse."

She was doubtful. "I'll believe it when I see it."

They had landed at Andrews Air Force Base outside Washington and caught a ride over to Dulles, where they had eaten breakfast and bought new clothes—simple dark trousers, turtlenecks, and jackets. They had discarded what they had worn in Baghdad and boarded a commercial flight for Syracuse. They had been watchful the entire morning, their gazes never ceasing to look for anyone too curious. For Jon, the entire trip had been one of fighting off tension between the two of them. He was getting over the shock of looking at Randi and thinking for a moment she was Sophia. But still, the fact was unchangeable: The face, voice, and body were so close that it kept his pain simmering. He was amazed that they worked together as well as they did, and he was grateful for her help in getting him out of Iraq and back into the United States.

A half-hour ago they had landed at Hancock International Airport northeast of Syracuse, where Randi had rented the Oldsmobile Cutlass.

Now they were on Route 5—there was no Interstate 5—watching both sides of the road as they skirted the city.

" 'Colored lake green,' " he read. "Something on this highway refers to the color green, and it involves a lake. A landmark. Maybe a motel."

"If you've interpreted the gibberish right," Randi pointed out, "we could pass something like that a hundred times and not notice."

He shook his head. "I'll know. Marty wouldn't give us anything that hard to figure out once we'd gotten this far. Keep driving."

They cruised through the suburb of Fayetteville, still searching for the final references in the message. They were growing discouraged. They passed country clubs, malls, car dealerships, used-car lots, and all the other satellite businesses of the citified suburb that had once been a country town. Nothing rang a bell.

Suddenly Jon froze. Then his arm shot out and he pointed. "There!" On their left was a pole sign at the entrance to a large park: GREEN LAKES STATE PARK. "Both 'lake' and 'green.' " His voice was excited. "The message says 'or thereabouts,' so he's got to be holed up somewhere nearby."

Randi's gaze was on the traffic as she expertly moved from lane to lane so they could keep their slower speed without interfering with the flow. "Looks as if you've been right so far. Let's see if I can help. Okay, now it refers to a letter that's been stolen and the message is signed 'Edgar A.' " She drummed her fingers on the steering wheel. "What strikes me is Edgar Allan Poe's 'The Purloined Letter.' Does that help?"

Jon was staring off into the distance, trying to put himself in Marty's place. Marty was an electronics wizard, but he also enjoyed arcane information and trivia. "That's it! So where's a missing letter best hidden? In a letter rack, of course, with other letters where no one will notice. The best place to hide something is in plain sight."

"Then your friend is saying he's hidden where we can see him. What the hell does that mean?"

"He's talking about the RV, not about himself. Turn the car and go back the way we came."

Annoyed at his bossiness, Randi pulled off into a side street, U-turned, and spun back onto the road toward Syracuse itself. "Did you see something earlier?"

Smith's blue eyes were alight. "Remember those car dealerships lining the road on the other side of Fayetteville? I think one of them was an RV lot."

Randi began to laugh. "That's just dumb enough to be where he is."

Watching carefully, they drove through Fayetteville once more. The city seemed longer, more chaotic. Jon was getting impatient.

Then he saw it. "That's it. On the right." His voice was compressed excitement.

She said, "I see it."

Ahead spread a mammoth lot crammed with a variety of recreational vehicles, new and used. Sunlight played across them, and the metallic vehicles glowed. There was no showroom, only a wood-sided sales office where a man wearing sunglasses and a polyester suit sat in a lawn chair in front, reading a newspaper.

"Doesn't look busy. That could be a break for us." Randi drove past, turned the corner, and parked in the shade of a large flaming maple.

Jon decided, "We'd better scout it on foot to be safe."

They walked back, alert for surveillance. Cars and trucks continued along the busy road. No one sat inside parked vehicles. The few pedestrians strode past without paying much attention. No one leaned against the buildings across the street, pretending to be waiting for someone while in reality they were on watch. From where they walked, they could see the man sitting in front of the sales office. About forty feet distant, he turned the page of his paper, engrossed.

Everything appeared normal.

Jon and Randi exchanged a look and quietly stepped over a loose chain that fenced the lot. They slipped between two RVs and searched the packed area. They sped past row after row of campers, trailers, and RVs. Smith was beginning to think he had been wrong, that this was not where Marty had gone to ground. Finally they reached the last line of vehicles, which backed up to a stand of sycamores, maples, and oaks. A breeze rustled through the woods, disturbing the mounds of colored leaves that had already fallen.

"Jesus." He let out a long, shocked breath. "There it is." Peter's RV was at the very back among a long row of dusty used vehicles that appeared to have been for sale a long time. Its metal sides had been ripped up by what had to have been gunfire, and several of its windows were shot out.

"Wow." Randi took a deep breath. "What happened to it?"

Jon shook his head worriedly. "Doesn't look good."

No one was in sight. They split up, and, weapons in hand, reconnoitered. When they saw nothing suspicious even in the woods, they approached the trashed vehicle.

"I don't hear anything inside," Randi whispered.

"Maybe Mart's sleeping."

He reached to try the door, and it opened in his hand as if it had been closed so hurriedly that the latch had failed to catch.

They jumped back, their weapons ready. The door swung back and forth in eerie silence. No one appeared. After another minute, Smith climbed up into the living room. Behind him, Randi aimed her mini-Uzi around the interior, her fierce black gaze sweeping it.

Jon called softly, "Mart? Peter?"

There was no answer.

Jon padded forward across the cramped interior. Randi, her back to him, advanced in the other direction toward the driver's cab. A box of Cheerios, Marty's favorite dry cereal, stood beside a bowl on the kitchen table. The spoon was still in the bowl, as was a puddle of congealing milk. One bunk had been slept in. It was a jumble of sheets and blankets. The computer was on, but opened only to the desktop, and the bathroom was empty.

Randi returned. "No one up front."

"No one anywhere," Jon said. "But Marty was here not long ago." He shook his head. "I don't like it. He hates to go out in public or to risk contact with strangers. Where could he have gone? And why?"

"What about your other friend? The MI6 person?"

"Peter Howell. No sign of him either."

They studied the silence and emptiness. There was a sense of abandonment. Jon was at a loss and very worried about Marty and Peter.

Randi was peering at the interior, at the bullet holes that had eaten up sections of the walls and destroyed some of the hanging maps. "There was one hell of a battle, from the looks of it."

He nodded. "My guess is Peter must have had armor sheeting built in under the RV's metal skin. Look at where the shots landed. The only way the bullets got inside was through the windows."

"And the fire fight obviously wasn't here. We'd have seen signs outside."

"Agreed. Marty, Peter, or both escaped in the RV and were hiding out here."

"We'd better search more thoroughly."

Jon sat at the computer to look for what Marty had been working on, but Marty had applied some kind of password that blocked him. For a half hour he tried to break through. He keyed in the name of Marty's street in Washington, his birth date, the names of his parents, the name of the street where he had grown up, their elementary school. They were all traditional sources for passwords, and Marty had probably used them in the past. But not now.

Smith was shaking his head in discouragement when Randi called out. He turned quickly.

"Look! Now we know who has the serum!"

She was sitting on the small sofa, all long legs and blond dishevelment. As she leaned forward, her blond curls fell toward her eyes, and her pink lips were pursed in thought. He could see her long dark lashes even across the room. Her twill trousers had pulled up a little, and her slender ankles showed above her tennis shoes. Her breasts were outlined high and round under her tight white turtleneck. She was beautiful. With the intense expression on her face, she looked so like Sophia, and for a moment he regretted agreeing to work with her.

Then he pushed it all away. He knew he had made the right decision, and they had to get on with it. "What have you got?"

She had been going through the piles on the coffee table. She held up a copy of *The New York Times* so he could see the front-page banner headline:

BLANCHARD PHARMACEUTICALS HAS CURE

He crossed the room in three long steps. "I recognize the company name. What does the article say?"

She read aloud:

> At a special press conference last night, President Castilla announced that preliminary tests showed a new serum had cured a dozen victims of the unknown virus that is sweeping the world.
>
> Originally developed to cure a monkey virus found in a remote area of Peru, the serum was the result of a decade-long research-and-development program into little-known viruses at Blanchard Pharmaceuticals that was initiated by its CEO and chairman, Victor Tremont.
>
> "We are grateful for the foresight Dr. Tremont and Blanchard showed in investigating unknown viruses," the president said last night. "With their serum, we are optimistic we will be able to save many lives and stop this terrible epidemic."
>
> Twelve nations have placed orders for the serum and others are expected to make formal requests shortly.
>
> President Castilla said he would attend a ceremony at 5:00 P.M. today honoring Tremont and Blanchard at the company's headquarters in Long Lake. The ceremony will be broadcast around the world. . . .

Jon and Randi stared at each other.

"The article says it was a decade-long project," he said.

"You're thinking about Desert Storm."

"You bet I am," he said angrily. "Nineteen ninety-one. Maybe they had nothing to do with infecting the twelve victims. This is a monkey virus, and we can't be sure it's the same virus that we've been working on, even though the serum apparently cures it. But I've got to wonder. Now they come forward with a *serum?* Very convenient."

"Too convenient," she agreed. "Especially since we know three were cured last year in Iraq and three here just last week. But as far as we know, it's a different virus."

"Suspicious as hell."

She said, "You don't believe it's a different virus."

"As a scientist, it's such a remote possibility that the only alternative that comes to mind is some madman from the company stole it and decided to play God. Or Satan, if you will."

"But how did the epidemic break out? Awfully good timing that Blanchard happens to have a serum that works on monkeys and apparently on people. How could Blanchard or anyone *know* it'd break out now, or ever?"

He grimaced. "I've been wondering the same thing."

They stared at each other in silence.

That was when they heard a faint sound behind the RV. A twig snapped.

Randi swept up her Uzi, and Jon pulled the big Beretta from his waistband. In the cramped RV, they listened intently. No more twigs broke, but there was a light rustle of something moving among fallen leaves.

It could have been the wind or an animal, but Randi did not believe it. Her chest tightened. "One," she estimated. "No more."

Jon agreed, but: "It could be a scout sent ahead, the rest watching. Maybe from the trees back there."

"Or a diversion, and the others out front."

The sound ceased. There was nothing but the distant traffic.

"You take the back," he said. "I'll take the front."

He flattened against the wall next to a front window, inched to the edge, and looked out toward the door and studied the row of used RVs. He saw no movement.

"Quiet back here," Randi whispered as she scrutinized the woods that formed the back perimeter of the lot.

"There're too many blind spots," he decided. "We'll have to go out."

Randi nodded. "You go left. I'll go right. I'll lead."

"*I'll* lead." He raised the Beretta and reached to fling open the door.

Suddenly there was a loud click and a scraping of wood on wood behind them.

They whirled like a pair of synchronous swimmers at the Olympics, their weapons ready.

Surprised, they watched four squares of the large geometric pattern on the vinyl floor swing up, instantly followed by a Heckler & Koch MP5 submachine gun.

Jon instantly recognized the weapon. "Peter!" He forced himself to relax the finger on his trigger. "It's okay, Randi."

She frowned and stared suspiciously as the lined, leathery face of Peter Howell emerged as far as his shoulders. He wore a trench coat over his black commando clothes.

Instantly he pointed the H&K at Randi. "Who?"

Jon said, "Randi Russell. Sophia's sister. She's CIA. It's a long story."

"Tell me later," Peter said. "They've got Marty."

Chapter Forty

10:32 A.M.
Lake Magua, New York

Marty's head rotated as he gazed around the windowless room with its dank basement smell and single cot. He concentrated hard to see it. Where he sat tied to a chair with thin nylon rope, his mind was floating in a luminescent cloud above everyone's heads, dazzling and airy and all-knowing. He loved the feeling of floating, his heavy body so light he seemed effervescent. Part of him knew he had been too long between doses of Mideral, but the rest of him did not care.

He was annoyed. "You must realize all this is absolutely ridiculous at your ages. Cops and robbers! Really! I assure you I have much more important matters to attend to than sitting here answering your stupid questions. I demand you take me back to the pharmacy instantly!"

His voice was firm, even arrogant, and in the chair in the basement room of Victor Tremont's grand lodge he drew himself up defiantly. These people would not intimidate him! With whom did they think they were dealing? Zounds, the rascals and poltroons would soon know that it was unwise, even dangerous, to attempt to do battle with him!

"We do not play games, Mr. Zellerbach," Nadal al-Hassan said coldly. "We will know where Smith is, and we will know at this moment."

"No one can know where Jon Smith is! The world cannot contain him or me. We fly through a different time, in another universe. Your puny world does not have enough gravity to hold us. We are infinite! *Infinite!*" Marty blinked up at the pockmarked Arab. "My goodness, your face. How terrible. Smallpox, I should guess. You're lucky to have survived. Do you know how many died over the centuries from that dreadful scourge? How long and at what cost it has taken the world to eradicate the disease? There are still two or three test tubes of it in deep freezers. Why—"

Marty rambled on as if sitting at his ease in some armchair and discoursing with a group of students on the history of viral diseases. "There's a new virus breaking out right now. It's deadly, Jon tells me. He says he thinks someone actually has it and is killing people with it. Can you imagine?"

"What else does Jon say about this virus?" Victor Tremont asked, smiling and friendly.

"Oh, a great deal. He's a scientist, you know."

"Perhaps he knows who has it? What they plan to do with it?"

"Well, I assure you, we—" Marty stopped and his eyes narrowed. "Ah, you are trying to trick me! *Me!* You fools, you cannot outwit The Paladin! I will speak no more." He clamped his lips tightly together.

Exasperated, al-Hassan muttered an Arabic curse and raised his fist.

Victor Tremont put out a hand. "No. Not yet. The medicine he got at the pharmacy where Maddux found him is Mideral, one of a new family of central nervous system stimulants. With what you learned from his doctor, we know he has a type of autism. From his behavior, I'd say he's off the medicine and irrational."

"Then can we learn nothing about where Jonathan Smith is?" al-Hassan asked.

"On the contrary. Administer his Mideral. Within twenty minutes, he will calm and come crashing back to reality. If his condition is Asperger's syndrome, he may be exceptionally intelligent. But the Mideral will slow him down and make him a little dull. At the same time, he'll be able to recognize he's in danger. We should be able to get what we need from him then."

Marty sang loudly. He barely noticed when al-Hassan untied one of his hands and gave him a pill and a glass of water. He stopped to swallow the pill then resumed singing as al-Hassan tied him again.

Victor Tremont and the Arab watched as his vocalizing slowly faded, his arrogant pose slumped against the ropes, and his feverishly bright eyes turned quiet.

"I think you can question him now," Tremont said.

Al-Hassan smiled his wolf smile and walked around to face Marty. "So, let us begin again, Mr. Zellerbach, eh?"

Marty looked up at the lean, dour Arab. He cowered on the chair. The man was too close, and he looked evil. The other man—the tall one—stood on Marty's other side. He was too close as well, and too menacing. Marty could smell them. Strangers. He could barely breathe. He wanted to make them go away. Leave him alone.

"Where is your friend Jon Smith?"

Marty quavered in the chair. "Ir-Iraq."

"Good. He was in Iraq. But he is now back in America. Where will he go now?"

Marty blinked up at them as they leaned closer, eager. He remembered posting the message to Jon on the Web site. Maybe Jon had already found it and was heading toward the RV. He fervently hoped so.

He felt his teeth grind. No! No, he would not tell them. "I—I don't know."

The Arab muttered another curse and swung his fist. Marty screamed with fear.

Pain exploded in his head, and a great wave of black rolled over him.

"Damn." Victor Tremont knotted his fists. "He's unconscious."

"But I did not strike him with that much force," al-Hassan protested.

Tremont scowled with disgust. "We'll have to wait until he comes to and try something less physical."

"There are ways."

"But with him, it will be tricky not to kill him. You saw how excitable he is."

They stared in frustration at the silent Marty, whose head hung limply forward, his body lashed to the chair.

"Or," Victor Tremont began to smile. He paused as his shrewd mind worked on an idea. "I have a much better way to find what we need to know." He nodded. "Yes, a much better idea."

10:35 A.M.
Syracuse, New York

Peter Howell peeled off his trench coat to reveal his black commando suit. His pale gaze surveyed the bullet-spattered interior of his high-tech RV. Brief sadness showed on his lined face, and then it was gone, overtaken by complete concentration as he walked rapidly through it, checking.

"What happened to Marty?" Jon stared at the Englishman's back as he turned from the driver's seat. "Do you know where they've taken him?"

"Spotted him at a chemist's a few blocks from here. Pharmacy to you Yanks. There were three." Peter's wiry body bristled with energy as he strode toward them. "The leader was that short, heavy fellow we saw back at the ambush on the dirt road in the Sierras."

Randi said, "That means the people with the virus have him?"

Jon grimaced. "That's what it means. Poor Mart."

"Will he talk?" Randi asked.

"If he had, I'd think they'd be here by now," Peter said.

"But he will?"

"He's not strong," Smith admitted. He described Asperger's syndrome.

"That little fellow is a lot tougher and shrewder than one would imagine, Jon," Peter decided. "He'll find a way not to crack."

"Not forever. Not many can. We've got to get him out of there."

"Do we know where he is?" Randi asked Peter.

Peter shook his head. "Unfortunately, I was on foot and unable to follow the car they took him away in."

"How did you figure out where to find him?" Jon asked.

"Located the RV from his message about an hour ago." Peter reported how he had found the RV empty, just as they had. But he had also found drafts of a fake doctor's prescription printed out from the computer. "Marty must've forged a prescription for his Mideral. He was almost out of his pills last night when we separated." He described the gunfight in the park.

Jon shook his head. "How do you think they found you?"

"I figure they must've been tailing us all the way from Detrick just looking for the most agreeable moment to attack. I thought I'd shaken any possible pursuit, but it would seem they're quite good." His gaze settled on bullet holes that had pocked a map of Third World countries and shook his head. "I went looking for the closest chemist's shops. I got to the third one just as Marty came out and those three seized him."

"No indication on the car who they were?"

"None, I'm afraid."

"Then the only way we're going to find him is to find *them*."

"Right. A serious problem. I may have a solution, but first fill me in quickly about Iraq."

Smith hit the high points of his investigation in Baghdad until the Republican Guards' attack in the tire shop.

The Englishman's wrinkles expanded in a wide grin at Randi. His gaze swept over her in appreciation. "The CIA is improving the quality of its agents, miss. You're a welcome change over the usual sobersides in their three-piece suits. Just a garrulous old man's opinion, mind you."

"Thanks. You're not so bad yourself." Randi smiled back. "I'll be sure to pass on your recommendation to the director."

"You do that." Peter turned to Jon. "What happened next?" His face went quickly sober again as he listened to what they had learned from Dr. Mahuk in the pediatric hospital, and how they had been captured by the Baghdad police who had apparently been in the pay of whoever was behind the virus.

"So three victims were cured in Iraq, too?" The Englishman swore. "A diabolical experiment. Don't like to think about the money and power that can actually accomplish anything in that closed-off country. Of course your trip confirmed the virus's roots in the Gulf War." He paused. "My turn. Got a little piece of news that blows the lid off this whole nasty business. I believe I know what Sophia discovered that was so important in Giscours's report from the Prince Leopold Institute."

Jon inhaled, excited. "What?"

"Peru. It was Peru all along." He described Sophia's field trip there twelve years before as an anthropology student from Syracuse. With that small piece of information, he had contacted a former associate in Lima, who had secured a list of scientists who had trekked into the Peruvian Amazonia that same year.

Smith asked instantly, "You have the list?"

A grin of satisfaction spread across Peter's brown, leathery face. "Does a fox find the heather? Come, children."

As he stalked to the kitchen table, he pulled out two folded sheets of paper from somewhere inside his black commando outfit. He lay them out, flicked on the overhead light, and the three of them bent over, quickly reading the names.

Peter explained, "There were a lot more in Amazonia that year, but not at the same times as Sophia."

The fourteenth leaped out at both Jon and Randi.

"That's it!" Randi said. *"Victor Tremont."*

Smith nodded grimly, "CEO and chairman of Blanchard Pharmaceutical. The president's going to give him a medal today for saving the world with his serum. The great humanitarian, working his company around the clock to produce it while he sells it only at cost."

"Bloody hell." Peter shook his head. "Believe that, and you'll believe we Brits acquired our empire to bring civilization to the natives."

"We already knew Blanchard had the serum," Randi said, thinking about the newspaper story. "Now it seems Tremont himself brought the virus from Peru."

Jon nodded. "And because he's a scientist, he could've recognized the potential of a serum for such a deadly virus and somehow managed to infect a few people during Desert Storm. He must've known it wasn't very contagious and that it was slow-acting, lying in the body for years like HIV."

"Good God," Peter breathed. "So he started his secret testing on humans in Iraq ten years ago, when he had no guarantee he'd ever develop a serum to cure them when the virus went into its last fatal stages? He's a monster!"

"Maybe it's worse than that. It's very convenient for the virus to break out now." Jon's eyes were icy blue. "Somehow he made the pandemic start so he could cure it and make a fortune in the process."

Shocked silence filled the RV. Smith had spoken the words they had not wanted to hear. But it was the truth, and the implications hung in the air like a sharp ax waiting to fall.

Randi finally said, "How?"

"I don't know," Jon admitted. "We've got to check Blanchard's records. Damn, I wish Marty were here."

"Perhaps I can substitute," Peter said. "I'm pretty fair with a computer, and I've been watching him use his own special programs for days."

"I tried, but he was using a password."

Peter gave a grim smile. "That I know, too. Typical of Marty's odd sense of humor. The password is Stanley the Cat."

10:58 A.M.
Long Lake Village, New York

In the deep recesses of whatever honesty and integrity he had left, Mercer Haldane had suspected what Victor Tremont had never admitted: Somehow Victor had *caused* the pandemic that was sweeping the world. Now, as he looked down through his office window at the platform and giant TV screen that were being assembled for this afternoon's ceremony, he could keep silent no more. God in heaven, the president himself was coming to send off the first official batch of serum as if Blanchard and Victor were Mother Teresa, Gandhi, and Einstein rolled up into one.

For days the moral battle had raged inside him.

Once he had been an honorable man and had taken great pride in his integrity. But somewhere along the line of building Blanchard into a world-class pharmaceutical giant, he realized now he had lost his way. The result was that Victor Tremont was to receive America's revered Medal of Freedom for what could be the most despicable act the globe had ever seen.

Mercer Haldane could not tolerate that. No matter what would happen to him . . . even though he would probably have to take the blame . . . so be it. He had to stop this tragic farce. Some things were more important than money or success.

He reached for his phone. "Mrs. Pendragon? Please get the surgeon general's office in Washington. I believe you have the number."

"Of course, sir. I'll put the call through immediately."

Mercer Haldane leaned back in his executive desk chair to wait. He rested his neck against the cool leather and put his hands over his eyes.

But another wave of doubt assaulted him. With a shock, he remembered again he could go to prison.

Lose his family, his position, his fortune. He grimaced.

On the other hand, if he said nothing, Victor would make a great deal of money for all of them. He knew that.

He shook his white head. He was being a fool. Worse, a sentimental old fool. What did all those faceless millions really matter? They would die one way or another anyway, and the way life was, most would not expire from natural causes but from disease, hunger, war, revolution, earthquake, typhoon, accident, or an angry lover. There were too many people anyway, especially in the Third World, and the overpopulation increased geometrically every year.

The result was nature would strike back anyway, as it always did, with famines, plagues, wars, and cosmic disasters.

What did it matter if he and Victor and the company grew wealthy on the deaths of millions?

He sighed, because the truth was . . . it mattered to *him*.

A person controlled his fate. He remembered what the Prussians said: A man's worth began only when he was willing to die for his principles.

Mercer Haldane had been trained on principles. At one time, he had cherished them. If he still had a soul to save, the only way he could do it was to stop Victor Tremont.

Inwardly he continued his war, his eyes closed, his neck against the chair pillow. As the conflict raged on, he felt ever more weak and miserable. But in the end, he knew he was going to tell the surgeon general everything. He had to. He would pay any cost to know he had done the right thing.

When he heard the door open, he uncovered his eyes and swung around in the chair. "Is something wrong with the connection, Mrs. Pendragon?"

"Lost your nerve, Mercer?"

Victor Tremont stood in the office. He was a towering figure in his expensive business suit and polished kid shoes. His thick, iron-gray hair glowed in the overhead lights, and his distinctive face with its aquiline features and faintly haughty expression glowered down on Haldane. He radiated the kind of self-assurance that commanded boardrooms with the ease of a great maestro before a world-class orchestra.

Haldane lifted his old eyes to gaze at his former protégé. He said evenly, "Found my conscience, Victor. It's not too late for you to rediscover yours. Let my call to the surgeon general go through."

Tremont laughed. "I believe it was Shakespeare who wrote a conscience was a luxury that made cowards of us all. But he was wrong. It makes us victims, Mercer. Losers. And I have no intention of being either." He paused and scowled. "A man is either the wolf or the deer, and I plan to do the eating."

Haldane raised his hands, palms up. "For God's sake, Victor, we *help* people. Our goal is to relieve suffering. 'First, do no harm.' We're in the *healing* business."

"The hell we are," Tremont said harshly. "We're in the money business. Profits. That's what counts."

Haldane could contain himself no longer. "You're an egotistical freak, Victor!" he exploded. "A *fiend!* I'll tell the surgeon general everything. . . . I'll —"

"You'll do nothing," Tremont snapped. "That call's never going to go through. Mrs. Pendragon knows a winner when she sees one." He slid his hand inside his jacket and withdrew a dark, lethal Glock 9mm pistol. "Nadal!"

Mercer Haldane's old heart pounded. Sweat suddenly bathed him as a tall, pockmarked Arab entered the room. He, too, carried a large pistol.

Paralyzed with fear, Mercer stared from one to the other, speechless.

Chapter Forty-One

11:02 A.M.
Lake Magua, New York

The Christmaslike odor of pine needles permeated the spacious living room of Victor Tremont's lodge. Through the windows, the lake reflected crystalline blue surrounded by the thick green forest. Near the giant fireplace where flames licked high, Bill Griffin sat in a leather club chair. His stocky body gave every appearance of being relaxed. As usual, his brown hair hung limp and unruly to his jacket collar. He crossed his legs and lighted a cigarette.

He smiled a slow smile at Victor Tremont and Nadal al-Hassan and explained calmly, "The trouble was, all of us were working at cross-purposes. Ever since you gave me the order to eliminate Jon Smith, I've been watching three places at once—his house in Thurmont, the Russell woman's condo in Frederick, and Fort Detrick. No wonder you had a hard time contacting me."

It was all a lie. He had been hiding in a walk-up apartment in Greenwich Village that belonged to a woman friend from the old days in New

York. But when he had seen the news story about the president's honoring Blanchard Pharmaceuticals and the orders that were rolling in for the serum, he had known he had to return to make certain he received his fair share.

And there was still the issue of Smith. "I'd expected to take out Smith when he left Detrick," he explained, "but I couldn't get a decent opportunity, and after that night he never showed up again at any of the other places. He vanished into thin air. Maybe he gave up or took leave. Or went somewhere to grieve for the woman." He hoped that was true, but knowing Jon, he doubted it.

Victor Tremont stood looking out the picture window at the trees as the sun reflected scattered bursts of light on the lake's surface. His voice was thoughtful. "No. He hasn't taken leave to mourn."

Nadal al-Hassan sat one hip of his emaciated frame onto the arm of the high sofa that faced the fireplace. "In any case, it is irrelevant now. We know where he is, and he will soon be no more problem."

Griffin's cheeks widened in another smile. "Hell, that's a relief." He added almost as an afterthought, "Maddux on him?"

Tremont left the window and bent to his humidor to extract a cigar. He offered the humidor to Griffin, who lifted his cigarette and shook his head. Nadal al-Hassan, as a strict Muslim, did not smoke.

As Tremont lighted the cigar, he spoke over his hands and the rising smoke and aroma: "Actually, Maddux has captured one of Smith's friends. A computer geek named Martin Zellerbach. We'll soon make Zellerbach divulge where Smith is hiding in Syracuse."

"Smith is in Syracuse?" Griffin seemed alarmed. He gazed accusingly at al-Hassan. "That close to us? How the hell did he get so near?"

Al-Hassan's voice was mild. "By checking back through Russell's life and education. She did her undergraduate work at Syracuse."

"Where she was studying when she went on the trip to Peru?"

"I'm afraid so."

"Then he knows about us!"

"I don't think so. At least, not yet."

Griffin's voice rose. "But, dammit, he will. I'll stop him. This time, I'll—"

Tremont interrupted, "You needn't worry about Smith. I have another job for you. Jack McGraw is up to his nostrils preparing security for the president. The ceremony this afternoon is, of course, a great honor, but it was a last-minute decision. Everyone's scrambling. Plus there are all the media people to deal with. We don't want any interlopers crashing the party. You have FBI experience, so you should be the one to coordinate with the Secret Service."

Griffin was puzzled. "Of course. You're the boss. But if you're still worried about Smith, then I think—"

"That won't be necessary." Al-Hassan's voice was definite. "We have it taken care of."

"How? Who?" Griffin glanced doubtfully at the Arab while inwardly he worried.

"General Caspar has managed to plant a CIA agent with Colonel Smith. She is Russell's sister, and she has a strong personal hatred for him from some old insult. She has been told Smith is a grave danger to the country. She will have no qualms about eliminating him." Al-Hassan studied Griffin. "I think we should consider the task completed. For us, Smith is dead."

Bill Griffin's face remained unchanged. He took a long drag on his cigarette.

Then he nodded, feigning satisfaction tinged with doubt to be consistent with the stance he had taken since he had discovered Smith was a target. They had suspected him since the night he had warned Jon. His failure to kill him had deepened their distrust. Now they had captured Zellerbach, whom he remembered from high school as a genius, but also as weak and easily frightened. Sooner or later, Marty would break and betray Jon. Plus they had planted Sophia Russell's sister, Randi. That was especially bad. He had heard Jon speak about how much the woman hated him. She would be capable of killing. Any CIA field agent had to be.

With Marty's capture and the infiltration of Randi Russell, Tremont and al-Hassan had their problems under control. Or so they thought.

Griffin stood up, a stocky man with a bland face. "Sounds like the perfect assignment for me. I'll get right on it."

"Good." Tremont gave him a dismissive nod of the head. "Use the Cherokee. Nadal and I'll take the Land Rover after we finish our business here. Thanks for coming in, Bill. We were worried about you. Always a pleasure to see you."

But as Griffin exited, Tremont's expression changed. His gaze cold, he watched the traitor disappear out the door.

■

Bill Griffin drove the Jeep Cherokee off the road and parked in a dense stand of oaks and birch trees. As he pulled brush around the Cherokee to camouflage it from the road, his mind was a maelstrom of conflict. Somehow he must reach Jon and warn him about Randi and Marty. But at the same time, he did not want to lose everything he had worked for since he had met Victor Tremont and joined the Hades Project two years ago. He was entitled to his share of the good things along with all the other thieving bastards who ran this world. More than entitled after his years of service to the goddamn ungrateful cheats and liars who ran the Bureau and the country.

But he would not let them kill Jon. That far he would not go.

He waited among the trees, watching the rustic lodge and the matching outbuildings. Insects buzzed. The aroma of sun-warmed forest duff scented the air. His pulse began to race.

After fifteen minutes, he heard the Land Rover. With relief, he watched it pass where he hid and disappear southeast among the trees. Tremont and al-Hassan would reach the main country road after a few more miles and drive on into Long Lake village to prepare for the ceremony. That did not give him much time.

Urgency swept through him as he drove back to the lodge, parked behind the staff wing, and hurried to a cyclone-fenced enclosure at the edge of the woods, out of sight of the lodge. He unlocked the gate and whistled softly. The large Doberman appeared silently from inside a wood doghouse. His brown coat shone in the mountain light. His sharply pointed ears periscoped forward as his intelligent eyes never strayed from Griffin.

Griffin stroked the dog behind his ears and spoke quietly. "Ready, boy? Time to go to work."

He headed out of the enclosure, the big dog trotting softly behind. He relocked the gate, and they moved swiftly toward the lodge. He watched everywhere. The three-man outside security team should be no problem, since they knew him. Still, he would rather not take the chance. At a side door of the lodge, he breathed deeply and gazed around one more time. Then he opened the door, and he and the Doberman entered. The house was eerily quiet, a massive wood coffin. Almost everyone had left for the celebration at Blanchard headquarters in Long Lake village, with the exception of a few technicians in the big lab on the second floor. Tremont would not stash a prisoner on the lab floor.

The rest of the lodge should be empty, except for Marty and perhaps an armed guard to watch him. He bent to the Doberman. "Sweep the area, boy."

The Doberman vanished among the corridors, as silent as fog rolling across a moor. Griffin waited, listening to the relaxed chatter of two of the security men who had paused outside a window as they made their individual rounds.

Two minutes passed, and then the Doberman was back, circling and eager to lead Griffin to what he had found. Griffin followed the pacing animal along a hallway lined with doors to guest rooms that had once been the retreats of the nineteenth-century wealthy, who had played here at returning to nature. But the dog stopped at none. Instead, he continued on past the gleaming kitchen, strangely silent and empty because the cooks and scullery staff had been given the afternoon off to attend the festivities in Long Lake village.

At last the dog stopped before a closed door. Griffin tried the knob. It was locked.

His skin prickled with nerves. The enormous empty house was enough to make anyone edgy, but now Griffin was about to open a door he had never seen beyond. Glancing right and left, he drew a small case from his jacket pocket and extracted a set of narrow picklocks. He worked skillfully through three of them. Finally the fourth opened the lock with a quiet click.

Griffin pulled out his pistol and turned the knob. The door swung open silently, its hinges well oiled. Inside was a faint smell of mold. He felt around the wall until he found a light switch. He flicked it on, and an overhead lamp illuminated stairs that disappeared down into a cellar. Griffin gave a hand signal and closed the door. The Doberman raced down to continue its mission, nails tapping on the wood stairs.

As Griffin waited, he stared uneasily down into the darkness. The dog was back in seconds, indicating for Griffin to follow.

Griffin found another light switch midway down. This turned on a series of overhead lights that illuminated a large cellar with open storage rooms filled with cardboard banker's boxes. Each box was neatly labeled with the names of files, sources, dates—the history of a scientist and businessman. But the dog's interest was at the only closed door. He circled warily in front of it.

His gun ready, Griffin pressed his ear against the door. When he heard nothing, he looked down at the dog. "A mystery, eh, boy?"

The dog lifted his muzzle as if in agreement. Right now the animal was merely watchful and alert, but if Griffin should need him, he would instantly turn into a killer.

Using his tools again, Griffin unlocked the door, but he did not open it. The basement area seemed like a sepulchre. It increased his disquiet. His veins rushed with an urgency that he act, but prudence had taught him long ago to never expect the expected. He did not know what waited on the other side of the door—whether it was an armed squad, a madman, or simply nothing. Whatever it was, he would damn well be prepared.

Again he listened. Finally he put the picklocks away, gripped his weapon firmly, and pressed open the door.

The room was a dark, shadowy cell with no windows. A rectangle of light spilled in from the hallway. Ahead, a mounded figure lay on the only piece of furniture—a narrow cot shoved against the far wall. There was an open pot on the floor, and the unpleasant odor of urine rose from it. The whole place gave off an air of danger and sadness. Griffin quickly signaled the Doberman to guard the doorway and sped softly to the bed. A small, rotund man was sleeping under a wool blanket.

He whispered, "Zellerbach?"

Marty opened his eyes. "What? Who?" His speech was slow; his movements stiff.

"Are you all right? Are you injured?" Griffin supported his shoulders until Marty was sitting upright. For a moment, he thought Marty had been hurt and then that he was disoriented by sleep. But as the fellow shook his head and rubbed his eyes, Griffin remembered the Marty Zellerbach he had known in high school. He was Jon's other close friend—the crazy, supercilious bastard who was always getting Jon into fights and arguments. Not crazy or arrogant, they found out later, but sick. Some kind of autism.

He swore silently. Could the guy tell him what he needed to know?

He tried, "Bill Griffin, Marty. Remember me?"

Marty stiffened in the shadows. The cot creaked. "Griffin? Where have you been? I've been searching for you everywhere. Jon wants to speak to you."

"And I want to speak with him. How long have you been here?"

"I don't know. It seems like a long time."

"What did you tell them?"

"Tell?" Marty remembered all the questions. The blow to his head and the blackness. "It was terrible. Those men are deviants. They enjoy other people's pain. I was . . . unconscious." His heart thundered as he thought back to the wretched experience. It seemed to have happened only minutes before, as fresh in his mind as an open wound. But the events were muddy, too. Confused. He shook his head, trying to clear it. He knew a lot of the problem was he had been on his meds. "I don't think I told them anything."

Griffin nodded. "I don't think you did either." If he had, they would have captured or killed Jon by now. But then, the Russell woman could have killed Jon already, too. "I'm going to get you out of here, Marty. Then you can take me to Jon."

Marty's round face was anguished as he admitted, "I'm not sure where he is."

Griffin swore. "Wait. Okay, think. Where could he be? You must've arranged somewhere to meet. You're some kind of genius. Geniuses always think of things like that."

Marty was suddenly suspicious. "How did you find me?" He had never liked Bill Griffin. Bill had been a loudmouth and know-it-all back when they had been in school together, even though—at least in Marty's opinion—Bill was really just above average. Plus, Bill had vied with Marty for Jon's attention. Marty cringed back against the wall. "You could be one of them!"

"I *am* one of them. By now, Jon knows it, too. But he's in a lot more danger than he thinks, and I don't want him killed. I've got to help him."

Marty wanted to help Jon, too, which made him want to trust Griffin. But could he? How could he be sure?

Griffin studied Marty. "Look, I'm going to get you out of here safely. Will you believe me then and tell me where you were supposed to meet Jon? We'll go there together."

Marty cocked his head. His gaze grew sharp and analytical. "All right." It was a simple matter, he told himself. If he decided he did not trust Griffin, he would simply lie.

"Good. Come on."

"Can't. They chained me to the wall." Forlornly, Marty held up his hands and shook his right leg. Thin, strong chains were attached to brackets on the wall. Each was secured by a powerful padlock.

"I should've suspected something like this when they didn't leave someone behind to guard you."

"It's been unpleasant," Marty admitted.

"I'll bet." He got out his picklocks once more and quickly opened the padlocks.

As Marty rubbed his wrists and ankles, Griffin whistled low for the Doberman.

The dog padded toward them, his back nose high and sniffing.

"Friend," Griffin said to the dog and touched Marty. "Good. Protect."

With amazing patience, the usually nervous Marty swung his legs off the cot and sat quietly as the powerful Doberman smelled his clothes, his hands, and his feet.

As the big animal stepped back, Marty asked, "Does he have a name?"

"Samson."

"Suits him," Marty decided. "A big bruiser of a dog."

"That he is." Griffin ordered, "Scout."

Samson trotted out into the corridor, looked both ways, and angled off toward the stairs.

"Come on," Griffin said.

Griffin helped Marty until he was out of the room, and then Marty shook him off. With Griffin in the lead and Marty half-running in his usual rolling gate, they moved quickly up the stairs and through the deserted corridors to the rear door where Griffin had parked his car. Marty's brain was working at full speed now, and his emotions were ratcheted to a fine pitch. He had mixed emotions about Bill Griffin, but at least Griffin had gotten him out of that disgusting dungeon.

As Griffin paused at the door, Marty grabbed his arm and whispered, "Look. A moving shadow." He pointed out the small side window.

The Doberman's head was up, alert, his ears rotating as he listened. Griffin gave a hand signal that told the Doberman to stay. At the same time, he pulled Marty down. They hunched together on the floor.

Griffin spoke in a husky whisper. "It's just one of the security guards. He was clocking in at a key station. He'll be gone in three minutes. Okay?"

"You don't have to ask my permission, if that's what you mean," Marty said tartly. He was definitely feeling better.

Griffin raised his eyebrows. He pulled himself up and looked out the window. He nodded to Marty. "Let's go." As soon as Marty was on his feet, Griffin pushed him outside. The Doberman ran ahead toward the red Jeep Cherokee. Bill pulled open the door, and Samson leaped in. Marty clambered aboard while Griffin slid behind the steering wheel.

As Griffin turned on the motor, he ordered, "Get down on the floor."

Marty had been through enough emergencies in the past week that he no longer objected when someone who understood the unfathomable world of violence told him what to do. He crouched on the floor in the back. Samson sat above him on the seat. Marty reached out a tentative hand. When the muscular dog dipped his head and slid his nose under it, Marty smiled and patted the warm muzzle.

"Nice doggie," he cooed.

Griffin drove swiftly away, breathing deeply with relief. Another security guard waved as he sped out of the compound, and he waved back. It had been less than twenty minutes since he had returned, and he felt confident no one would remember his earlier departure. Now he concentrated on one goal: reaching Jon before Randi Russell could kill him.

"Okay, we're out. Now where do we go?"

"Syracuse. I'll tell the rest when we get there."

Griffin nodded. "We'll have to fly. Rent a car there."

But in his haste and relief, he had forgotten about the vital third guard, who had been hidden in a stand of poplars. As the guard watched the Cherokee disappear down the road, he spoke quietly into a cell phone. "Mr. Tremont? He's taken the bait. He's busted that Zellerbach guy out, and they're driving out of here. Yes, sir. We planted the tracking device, we've got the airport covered, and Chet's waiting at the country road."

Chapter Forty-Two

1:02 P.M.
Syracuse, New York

"Dammit all!" Peter Howell's wiry frame was bent over his computer as he stared in frustration at the glowing monitor. "There's precious little in Blanchard company's files about the veterinarian serum *or* the monkey virus. What there is looks bloody completely on the up-and-up." As the wind blew through the RV's broken windows, he ran his gnarled brown hand through his gray hair in disgust.

"Nothing about tests on humans?" Smith was sitting on the sofa nearby, his arms crossed over his chest, his legs extended. He had been dozing as Peter had searched for information. The Beretta was tucked into his belt, easily reachable.

"Or Iraq?" Beside him, Randi stretched. She had been sleeping, too, until Peter's loud curse had jerked her awake. Suddenly she was aware of Jon and how closely they were sitting together. She adjusted her weight, tactfully putting more space between them. Her Uzi was beneath the sofa, just behind her heels. When she tapped back, she could feel its comforting hardness.

"Not a syllable," Peter growled as he continued to stare intently at the screen. "I suppose it's possible we're on the wrong track—that Blanchard's clean as a boatswain's whistle and they don't have the virus. That their serum is simply what it looks like—a fortuitous coincidence."

"Oh, please." Randi shook her head in disbelief.

"That doesn't explain the initial twelve human test subjects," Jon said. "Whoever set that experiment in motion ten years ago had the virus then and the serum last year to cure the Iraqis and then, last week, the three Americans."

They considered some other explanation for the experiment.

"There must be another set of records." Peter rotated in his chair. He gave them a baleful look and scratched his leathery cheek.

"Unless they just didn't keep written records," Randi suggested.

"Impossible," Smith disagreed. "Research scientists have to keep notes, results, speculations, every piece of paper, each bit of an idea, or they can't move forward in their work. Besides, their supervisors have to monitor progress, set goals, and go after funding, and their bookkeepers have to keep accurate financial accountings."

"But scientists don't have to put everything on a computer," Randi said. "They could do it by hand, too."

Jon shook his head. "Not today. Computers have become a research tool in themselves. For projections, for simulated reactions, for statistical analysis . . . everything would take years otherwise. No, there have to be real records on a computer somewhere."

"I'm convinced," Peter agreed, "but where, eh?"

"We need Marty." It was Smith's turn to swear. His navy blue eyes were dark with frustration.

Randi said reasonably, "We can try other ways. Let's drive to Blanchard, break in, and search their files on site. If there's anyone around, we'll 'convince' them to talk nicely with us, too."

"Great," Jon began, "I'm sure we haven't broken *every* law yet. There must be some we've missed."

Suddenly there was frantic knocking on the RV door. The vehicle shuddered with it.

"Must be getting old." Peter snapped up his H&K MP5. "Missed hearing anyone approach."

Instantly Randi and Jon became a blur of movement as they pulled out their weapons.

"Jon!" The voice outside was thin, familiar, and commanding. "Jon! Open the darn door. It's *me.*"

"Marty!" Smith jumped to the entryway and cracked open the door.

For the moment, Marty's round, chubby body was athletic. He pushed the door back, leaped inside, and grabbed Jon by both arms. "Jon! At last." He hugged him and stepped quickly back, embarrassed. "I was beginning to think I'd never see you again. Where in heaven's name have you been? Are you uninjured? Bill rescued me, so I decided it was safe to bring him to you. Is that okay?"

"Trap," Peter barked. He swung the MP5 around so it pointed at Griffin, who had stepped quietly inside.

The ex–FBI man stood alone with his back against the closed door in his windbreaker and trousers, his arms hanging loosely from his broad shoulders. His hands were empty, but his stocky body was rigid and alert. His long brown hair was greasy, as if he had not washed it in days, and his brown eyes had an empty look that chilled Jon.

Randi instantly backed Peter with her Uzi.

"No!" Smith yelled, stepping in front of Griffin. "Hold it, both of you. Marty's right. This is Bill Griffin. Put down the guns." He swung around to face Griffin. "You alone?"

"We're alone," Marty assured them. "Bill says he has to warn you, Jon. You're in bigger danger than ever."

"What danger?"

Randi and Peter, still watchful, had slowly lowered their weapons. The moment their weapons were down, Bill Griffin dipped his hand inside his jacket pocket and pulled out a 9mm Glock.

"Her." Griffin pointed the deadly instrument at Randi's heart, his hollow eyes focused on her. "She's CIA. Sent by General Nelson Caspar to assassinate you, Jon."

"What?" Randi's pale brows arched in outrage. Her blond head whipsawed from Griffin to Smith. "That's a lie!" Then she glared at Griffin. "How *dare* you? You're working for *them*, but you come in here and accuse me?"

Jon held up his hand. "Why would the exec of the chairman of the Joint Chiefs want me killed?"

"Because he's working for the same people I am."

"Tremont and Blanchard Pharmaceuticals?"

Bill nodded. "It's what I was warning you about back in Rock Creek park."

Jon stared at him. "But you didn't warn anyone else." His high-planed face radiated rage. "So they killed Sophia."

"That's the world we live in," Griffin said bitterly. "There are no good guys. No one believes in right and wrong anymore. It's get what you can for yourself. So now I'm going to get mine. I'm owed that much."

Jon looked away, forcing himself to remain composed. Sophia was dead. He couldn't bring her back. He would always carry the pain, but maybe he could learn to live with it better. He made his voice quiet. "No one's owed anything, Bill. And you're wrong about Randi. She couldn't have been sent to kill me. Impossible, considering the circumstances of how we met. In fact, she saved my life." He shot her a smile and was surprised to see her Ice Queen face soften. "She wants to stop what Tremont is doing as much as I. Who told you Caspar sent her to kill me?"

As Bill Griffin listened to Jon, he had a strange feeling. Almost as if he had missed some important piece in the puzzle of life. He was not sure exactly what it was, only that for a few lucid moments he recognized the loss and that he had never been able to find the directions that would lead him back to what was gone. So now as he studied Jon, saw him shudder for control as he was reminded again of Sophia's death, he felt loneliness and regret. Perhaps he had been too hasty in taking care of himself. Maybe he should have warned Sophia. He could have warned others, too—

And then he stopped himself. How far could he go? Certainly he was not prepared to save the world. But maybe this one last time he could do something for Jon to make up for what had happened to his fiancée.

So he told him, "Victor Tremont is behind everything. His number-one gun is Nadal al-Hassan. They—" But as he said the names, a warning bell rang loudly inside his head. He thought about Tremont's lodge and how empty—and safe—it had been when he had broken in to find Marty. How conveniently they had escaped.

How easily he had passed the sentries.

His gaze moved quickly to Marty. "Did Tremont or any of the others give you something to carry?" he growled. "Think! Any buttons, coins, pens, maybe a comb?"

Jon turned on Griffin. "You're thinking—?"

Bill ordered Marty, "Search your pockets. Maybe they slipped you something without your even knowing it. It could've been any of them. Maybe Maddux?"

At first Marty had not realized what they were asking, and then it became clear. "You're worried they bugged me!" Instantly he turned his pockets inside-out onto the coffee table in the living room. "I don't remember anything, but I was unconscious after the pockmarked man hit me."

His plump hands, which were so naturally agile on a keyboard and clumsy almost everywhere else, worked with speed. The former FBI agent watched with an itching urgency that made him want to rip every piece of clothing off Marty so he could make certain he was clean.

Instead, he ordered, "Take off your belt, Marty. Quick."

Jon added, "Your shoes, too."

As Marty stripped off his belt and threw it at Jon to examine, fury rose in a red tide from Bill Griffin's throat to his neutral face. "They told me a lie they knew I'd have to try to warn you about, Jon. Then they let me break Marty out, so he'd take me to you because they didn't learn anything from him. Two birds with one stone. They must've suspected me since Rock Creek park. I should've—"

The sharp bark of a dog carried from outside the RV. A single bark and no more.

Bill froze. His face went slack. "They're outside. Al-Hassan and his men."

"How do you know?" Randi slid along the wall to the corner of a front window with its glass still intact. She peered carefully around.

"The dog," Jon realized. "The Doberman you had in the park."

Bill nodded. "Samson. He's trained for attack, scouting, sentry duty, you name it."

"I see them," Randi whispered. "Looks like four. They're hiding among the row of RVs in front of us. One's a tall Arab."

"Al-Hassan," Bill said. His voice was deathly quiet.

Peter made a clucking sound with his tongue against the roof of his mouth. He murmured, "Here's how they got to us." He held up a tiny tracking transmitter he had taken from the hollowed-out heel of Marty's shoe. "Darling little bug, isn't it?" He shook his head with disgust, flung the device out the back window, and snapped up his submachine gun.

Randi was still on watch at the window. "I don't see any police or military."

"What does it matter?" Bill said harshly. "I led them here, and they've got you. Stupid. I was stupid!"

"Hardly," the Englishman said calmly. "It's going to take a lot more bloody work than they've put out to get us." He reached for the light fixture on the wall over the kitchen table, pressed a button on its side, and there was a popping sound as four vinyl squares, indistinguishable from the others covering the floor, lifted up in the middle of the living room. His wiry frame moved lightning-fast across the floor to the exit. "Never leave a single way out, friends. Jon, would you do the honors?"

Jon raised the trapdoor and dropped through.

"You next, my boy," the Englishman told Marty.

Marty nodded glumly, peered down at the asphalt, and let his feet fall through. The big Doberman was lying quietly under the RV, his large dark eyes scanning the open area and the woods behind where the RV was parked. In the deep shadow beneath the vehicle, Marty crawled quickly out of the way as Randi Russell, Bill Griffin, and Peter Howell landed, one after the other. The watchful Doberman raised his nose at Marty, and Marty slid closer. As Samson resumed his sentry duty, Marty crouched next to him and ran his hand over the handsome animal's sleek back. Strangely, he felt no fear. Then he raised his gaze to look around at the wheels of other RVs and the thick tree trunks of the forest. He saw no feet, and for a wild moment he had the hope that maybe al-Hassan and his killers had given up and gone home.

Bill Griffin called the dog and spoke softly. "Friends, Samson. Friends."

He had the dog smell each of them.

Then, with Jon in the lead, they crawled to the end of the RV that was closest to the woods. There were only about fifteen feet between them and safety.

"That's it." Peter nodded toward the trees. "We can hide there and figure out what to do next. When I say 'go,' jump up and run as if the hounds of hell are on your tails. I'll cover you." He patted his H&K.

But then shapes moved out from the forest line.

"Flatten!" Smith growled and dropped onto his face.

As the four others fell, a fusillade swept across the open area, whining and ricocheting off the side of the RV. They scrambled back, searching for cover behind the tires.

Bill Griffin raised his voice. "How many?"

"Two." The Englishman's eyes were narrow slits as he searched the woods. "Or three," Jon countered, breathing hard.

"Two or three," Randi echoed, "which means one or two are still in front."

"Yeah." Bill Griffin looked around at their tension and fear and at the brave lights in their eyes. It was true even of Marty with his odd condition and even odder mind. Marty was not the same prissy, whiny nuisance he remembered. Marty had grown up. As he thought that, he felt a terrible tear rip through something old and painful inside. At the same time, he felt a shift. Maybe it was the sourness from all the years of working for men with pinched minds. Or perhaps it was simply that he had never fit into this world which made so much sense to others. But probably the truth was he did not care a damn about anything or anyone anymore, not even himself.

He desperately wanted to care again. Now he saw it—why he had risked so much to save Jon. By doing that, he had had a hope of saving something good within himself. Thinking that, his blood seemed to course more vigorously. His mind grew incredibly clear. A sense of purpose swept through him as strong as he remembered from the old days when he and Jon were young and the future lay ahead.

He knew what to do.

Knew with every fiber in his body. With all his disappointment.

Exactly what he must do to retrieve himself.

Without warning, he crawled quickly out from under the RV, surged to his feet, and with a sharp guttural sound charged straight toward where the attackers crouched at the edge of the woods. The Doberman followed.

"Bill!" Jon shouted. "Don't—"

But it was too late. The stocky man's legs pumped and his long hair flew behind as he pounded toward the trees, firing his Glock. He was excited and immensely relieved, and he did not give a damn anymore about anything but redeeming himself. With bared fangs, the Doberman sprang toward one of the attackers on Bill's left.

Jon, Randi, and Peter leaped out with their weapons to follow. It was over in seconds.

By the time Jon reached him, Bill Griffin lay on his back on dry weeds at the edge of the woods. Blood bubbled up from his chest.

"Jesus," Peter breathed as his canny gaze swept the trees and RVs, looking for more trouble.

Ten feet away the short, heavy man who had led the attack on Jon in Georgetown that first day was crumpled in a lifeless heap. A second man lay dead of a gunshot to his head. A third man had sprawled back, his throat torn open, while the Doberman paced the woods in search of others.

"No sign of the man Bill called al-Hassan," Peter noted quickly. "He could still be out front."

"If he's alone, he probably won't try anything by himself," Randi agreed, her Uzi ready. Her voice softened and she looked down. "How is he, Jon?"

"Help me."

As Peter stood watch, his H&K fanning all around, Randi helped Jon carry Griffin into the shelter of the trees, where they laid him on a bed of dry leaves.

"Hold on, Bill." His throat tight, Jon crouched down. He tried to smile at his old friend.

Peter backed up to join them in the forest, holding his position as sentry.

Jon's voice was gentle. "Bill, you damn fool. What were you thinking? We could've handled them."

"You . . . don't know that for sure." He tugged Jon down by the collar. "This time . . . you could've got yourself killed. Al-Hassan is out there . . . somewhere. Waiting for reinforcements. Leave . . . get out of here!"

His grip was strong, but then pink foam appeared on his lips.

"Take it easy, Bill. I'm just going to take a look at your wounds. We'll be fine—"

"Bullshit." Griffin gave a weak smile. "Go to the lodge . . . Lake Magua. Horrible . . . horrible—" His eyes closed, and he breathed shallowly.

"Don't talk," Jon said anxiously as he ripped open Bill's shirt.

His eyes opened. "No time . . . Sorry about Sophia . . . Sorry for everything." His eyes widened as if seeing into a vast darkness.

"Bill? Bill! Don't do this!"

His neck went limp, and his head dropped back. In death, the bland face seemed suddenly younger, somehow more innocent. The features that had so easily fit into so many different roles smoothed out to show a strong bone structure with definite cheekbones and chin. As Jon looked numbly down, somewhere a bird began to sing. Insects hummed. The sunlight through the trees was warm.

Smith went into action. He felt the carotid artery. Nothing. Frantically, he put his hand on the bloody chest. But there was not even a whisper of a beat. He sat back, crouching next to his friend. Pain swept through him. First Sophia and now Bill.

Suddenly the Doberman appeared. He stood over Bill, guarding him. He nudged Bill's head and made what sounded like a low moan in his throat. Marty murmured something and stroked the Doberman's back.

Smith closed Bill's eyes and looked up. "He's gone."

"We've got to leave, Jon." Peter's voice was kind but definite. He handed him a colored kerchief from one of the webbed belt pouches on his commando uniform.

As Jon wiped blood from his hand, Randi said, "I'm sorry, Jon. I know he was your friend. But more of them will be here soon."

When Smith did not get up immediately, Marty said, "Jon!" His voice was sharp. "Let's go. You're scaring me!"

Smith stood and gazed around at the battered RV and the dead bodies. He breathed deeply, controlling his grief and rage. He glanced once more at Bill Griffin.

Victor Tremont had a lot to answer for.

He moved into the woods. "We'll work our way back to the car through here."

"Good idea." Randi took the lead.

"Come on, Samson," Marty called.

The dog lifted his head. Then he nudged his dead master's shoulder. He made a low sound in his throat again and prodded Bill one last time.

When there was no response, he gave a final look around as if saying good-bye. He trotted silently into the woods, following.

Randi's long body angled left. With sure footsteps, she forged a path through the underbrush and around the trees. Jon and Marty came behind with Peter and the Doberman bringing up the rear. Peter's H&K swept from side to side.

Jon looked at Marty. "You know anything about this 'lodge' Bill was talking about? Lake Magua?"

"It's where they chained me in a room."

"You know where it is?"

"Of course."

Suddenly Peter's voice sounded over their conversation. "Bogies at six o'clock. They're coming after us. I'll keep them busy. Go!"

"Not without you!" Smith refused.

"Don't be stupid. You've got Tremont to finish off. I can take care of myself."

At the sounds of feet approaching through the trees, the big Doberman stopped its loping trot and spun back to join Peter. He spoke low to the dog, then looked back at Smith.

"Go on. Now! Samson and I will cover your tails and buy you time. Hurry!" He gazed down at the dog. "You understand hand signals, boy?" He lowered his hand to his side and made a swift motion. Instantly the dog raced off into the woods to scout. Peter nodded, satisfied. "See, I won't be alone."

"He's right," Randi agreed. "It's what Bill would've wanted."

Jon was frozen for a second. His high-planed face with the dark blue eyes looked ominous in the shadowy forest. His long, muscular body was tensed, ready to spring. Bill had just died, and now Peter was volunteering to stay behind where his risk of being killed, too, was enormous. Jon had devoted himself to saving lives, not taking them. And now, because of circumstances, he was caught in what seemed a hopeless loop of death.

He studied Peter's wrinkled, weathered face and the sharp eyes that had one message: *Go. Leave me alone. This is what I do.*

Smith nodded. "Okay. Marty, you follow me. Good luck, Peter."

"Right." Already the Englishman had turned, his gaze searching the forest behind as if his whole life were focused on this moment.

Jon stared a second longer. Then he, Marty, and Randi sped away through the timber. Behind them a long burst of gunfire sounded, followed by a cry of pain.

"Peter?" Marty's voice rose with worry. "Do you think he's hurt? Maybe we should go back?"

"It was his H&K's fire," Jon assured him, although he was not sure.

Marty nodded uncertainly, remembering the endless days of too-close contact in the RV and Peter's tart humor and irritating habits. "I hope you're right. I . . . I've grown to like Peter."

Grimly they continued on. The woods were quiet now, shocked as sporadic gunfire sounded. Each shot seemed to pierce Smith to the quick. Then there was silence. That was worse. Peter could be lying in his own blood somewhere, dying.

At last they emerged on a quiet residential street that paralleled Route 5. Grave and wary, they hid their weapons inside their clothes, trotted right, and turned onto the street where Jon and Randi had parked their rented car under the maple tree.

They split up and approached the car cautiously.

But no one was around, and no one tried to stop them. Marty heaved a sigh and climbed into the backseat. Jon slid into the driver's seat, Randi jumped into the front passenger seat, the mini-Uzi on her lap, and they headed for the Thruway. An hour later they arrived at the Oriskany-Utica airport, where they rented a light plane and flew into the vast wilderness of Adirondack State Park.

Chapter Forty-Three

3:02 P.M.
Lake Magua, New York

Victor Tremont's timbered lodge loomed enormous through the trees below. Here at the back of it, a narrow brick drive led from an oversize timbered garage deep among the trees. Three heavily armed men patrolled. On the far side of the lodge a pristine lake was nestled in the forest of pine and hardwood trees. Large white clouds hovered above, and the long light of the late-afternoon sun cast dark shadows across the wooded slopes.

Taking it all in from a rise in the forest behind the lodge were Jon, Randi, and Marty. They lay on their stomachs on the thick carpet of duff under dense pines as they carefully analyzed the lodge's layout and the bored actions of the trio of guards.

"I hope Peter is all right," Marty worried quietly as he peered ahead, not sure exactly what he was supposed to be looking for.

"He knows what he's doing, Mart," Smith answered as he recorded the sentries' routes.

Then Jon peered over at Randi, seeing her face intent on the scene below. She was stretched out on his other side and had been quietly listening.

She gave him a sympathetic smile.

With that troubled exchange, the three turned their full attention back to planning how to break into Tremont's mountain castle. One of the bored and yawning guards circled the log-and-frame building every half hour, checking doors and cursorily sweeping the grounds with a gaze that would have seen nothing that was not immediately obvious. The second man sat relaxed in a chair, smoking and enjoying the late October sunlight, his old M-16A1 assault rifle across his lap. The third was comfortably ensconced in a civilian Humvee beside the small clearing for a helipad fifty yards to their right, his rifle jutting up beside him.

"They haven't had any intruders for years," Jon guessed. "If ever."

"Maybe there isn't anything to guard," Randi said. "Griffin could've been lying to us. Or just mistaken."

"No. He saved us, and he knew he was dying," Smith insisted. "He wouldn't lie."

"It's happened, Jon. You yourself said he'd gone wrong."

"Not that wrong." He turned to Marty. "When they had you locked up here, Mart, what do you remember of the layout inside?"

"A big living room and a lot of small rooms. A sun room and kitchen. Places like that. They questioned me in a room downstairs. It was empty except for a chair and a cot, and when I woke up I was in a basement storage room chained to a wall."

"That's all you can tell us?" Randi asked.

"I didn't exactly get a vacation brochure of the place," he said huffily. Then he grimaced. "All right. I'm sorry. I know you didn't mean anything. Well, I did see some people in white coats, like doctors. Most wore white pants, too. They were going upstairs to the second floor, but I don't know to where exactly."

"A laboratory?" Randi wondered.

"A *secret* lab." Jon's voice was low but charged. "That's it—one of the things Bill could've told us. A secret lab for research and development. The records of the experiment on the twelve victims from the Gulf War and whatever else they've been doing should be here. That's probably why nothing showed up on the Blanchard company computer. They never put anything there."

"Some other company name and password, maybe," Randi theorized.

Jon said, "We'd better get in there and find out for sure. Marty, stay here. You'll be safer. If you see or hear anyone, fire a single shot to warn us."

"You can count on it." Marty hesitated, his round eyes widening with shock. "I can't believe I said that. Especially that I said it enthusiastically." He was gripping the Enfield bullpup in his plump hands with nervous distaste. He had taken a new dose of meds and was still calm, but the effect would wear off soon.

Jon and Randi decided to delay until the guard completed his next circuit and rejoined the one at the front for a relaxed smoke. Then they would take out the one in the Humvee in the clearing to the right, where the afternoon sun sent long, cool shadows through the tall trees.

They did not have long to wait. After a few minutes, one of the two at the front stood and vanished behind the lodge. Ten minutes later he reappeared, this time coming around the building's far side. He gave a cursory scan of the forest and grounds, logged in at the key station next to the main rear entrance, and finally circled back to the front to rejoin his companion.

Only the guard in the Humvee remained on this side of the big lodge.

"Now," Jon said.

They slipped through the pines to the clearing. Out of sight of his colleagues, the guard in the Humvee was dozing in the warm sunshine, slumped in the driver's seat.

"You want to work around behind the Humvee, Randi?" Jon suggested. He could feel his pulse begin to pound behind his ears. "I'll watch from here and cover you. When you get there, give me a signal, and I'll distract him from this side. If he wakes up too soon and hears you, I'll take him out."

"I'll wave a hankie." She gave a short smile. "Well, a Kleenex." She was relieved to be in action again.

Her heart pumping, she melted among the trees until she was out of Smith's view. He crouched in the shadows just inside the forest. Beretta ready, he watched the dozing guard and waited. Five minutes passed. Then he saw a flash of white directly behind the parked Humvee. The guard stirred, moved in his seat, but did not open his eyes. As the man settled in once more, Jon loped straight toward the squat, open vehicle.

But just as Jon was halfway across the clearing, the guard's eyes snapped open. He grabbed his M-16. Randi materialized behind him. Her pale hair was a wreath of sunlight around her head, and her beautiful face was stony with concentration. Her body moved with the fluidity of a feral cat as she sprinted silently to the topless Humvee, ran up over the back, balanced one foot on the top of the backseat and the other on the rollover rail, and pressed her Uzi down into the back of the guard's head. It took Jon's breath away. He had never seen a woman move like that.

Her voice was cold and clear. "Release the rifle."

The guard hesitated a second as if calculating his chances, then slowly lay the rifle on the seat beside him. He placed his hands flat on his thighs in plain sight, like someone who knew the proper procedure for being arrested.

"Good decision."

Jon reached the Humvee and removed the M-16. He and Randi marched the guard back to where Marty waited. The three worked quickly together. Marty ripped the man's shirt into strips. Jon and Randi used the guard's belt and the strips of cloth to gag and tie him hand and foot. Trussed up, unable to speak, he lay on a bed of pine needles, shooting angry looks.

Smith took the guard's ring of keys. "The two others out front won't expect us from inside the lodge."

"I like that." Randi nodded, approving the plan.

He looked at her a little longer than necessary, but she did not seem to notice.

Marty sighed. "I know what you're going to tell me. 'If you see anything, shoot.' Gad. And to think two weeks ago I'd never even held a gun. I'm *devolving*."

They left Marty shaking his head as he guarded the disabled sentry and trotted down the slope to a side rear entrance of the lodge. The scent of pine was aromatic but somehow cloying.

As Randi stood guard, Jon found the right key and unlocked the door. They stepped warily inside a small foyer where sunlight beamed down from clerestory windows and more shone ahead at the far end of a hall. Closed doors lined the hallway, and there was the faint odor of good cigars as they padded toward the second source of light.

"What's that?" Randi stopped, her athletic shoes motionless on the parquet floor.

Smith shook his head. "I didn't hear anything."

She was frozen there, her even features pursed in concentration. "It's gone. Whatever the sound was, I can't hear it now."

"We'd better try all the doors."

She took one side, and he the other. They turned every knob.

"Locked." Jon shook his head. "They look as if they might be guest rooms or offices."

"We'd better leave them until later," Randi decided.

They passed a staircase that rose to a landing and turned. They could see nothing above the landing. They continued on, listening. The odor of cigars increased. Edgy, Jon's gaze swept everywhere. At last they stood at the timbered entry to a cavernous living room decorated with rustic wood-and-leather furniture, brass-and-wood lamps, and low wood tables. It had to be the big room Marty had described. Across it extended a wall of windows through which sunlight flooded. There was also an enormous stone fireplace in which coals glowed, warming the room against the October chill. The expanse of windows looked out to the lake through the dense trees, and in the middle of the wall were double front doors that opened out to a covered porch.

Without speaking, the silent pair slipped together across the room, stood beside the doors, and surveyed the porch. Beyond the porch, on the lawn off to the left, were the two remaining guards relaxing in Adirondack chairs, smoking and chatting, their rifles across their knees. They were gazing out at the valley where the colors of autumn had turned the sweep of hardwood trees to rich golds and reds among the green pines.

She was watching the sentries. "They're perfect targets," she murmured.

"Lazy idiots. They think because Tremont is gone they can do what they want."

"If it comes to shooting," Randi whispered, "I'll take the one on the right, you take the one on the left. With luck, they'll surrender."

"That's what we want." Smith nodded in agreement. He was getting used to working with her. In fact, he was enjoying it. Now, if they could just do it well enough to survive . . . "Let's go."

They eased the doors open and padded out onto the porch as the two men talked and smoked in their chairs. The sun was hard and flinty as Jon's gaze locked onto the guards sitting directly below, unknowing.

The taller guard flicked his cigarette onto the grassy lawn and stood. "Time to do another turn around the property." Before Jon or Randi could move, he saw them. "Bob!" he called in alarm.

"Lay down your weapons," Jon commanded.

Randi's voice was tense. "Do it slowly. So no one makes any mistakes."

Both men froze. One was completely on his feet but only half-turned to face them, while the other was merely halfway out of his chair. Neither's weapon was pointed at Jon and Randi, while Jon and Randi had the guards completely covered. It was a surprise ambush that had worked, and there was no doubt in anyone's minds that unless the sentries wanted to commit suicide, they would do exactly as told.

"Shit," one muttered.

∎

The timbered grounds were quiet as Smith locked the three tied-up sentries in an outbuilding behind the garage. Marty stood in the shadows next to it, while Randi was out of sight, monitoring the lodge for any activity. Marty's round face was worried, and his green eyes had a dark look, as if he were in a world he had never wanted to know anything about. His plump body seemed desolate in his baggy pants and jacket.

He looked up at Jon. "You want me to stay here?" he asked, as if he knew the answer.

"It's safer, Mart, and we need someone to be sentry. I don't know what we're going to find in the lab. If something happens to us, you've got a chance to make it by escaping into the woods."

Marty nodded soberly. His fingers twitched on the bullpup as if he longed for a keyboard instead. "It's okay, Jon. I know you'll be back for me. Good luck. And if I see anything"—he gave a brave smile—"I'll be sure to fire once."

Smith clamped a hand on his shoulder in encouragement.

Marty patted Jon's hand. "I'll be okay. Don't worry about me. You'd better go."

∎

Weapons in hand, Jon and Randi met at the side door of the lodge they had used before. They exchanged a long look, and some kind of recognition passed between them. Jon moved his eyes away, and Randi found herself wondering nervously what was happening to her.

Inside the lodge, they paused at the foot of the staircase in the long hall. There had been no gunshots fired outdoors, and they hoped that whoever was at work upstairs had no idea the sentries had been taken and the lodge invaded. The whole point of this stealthy attack was to accomplish what they needed as quickly and efficiently as possible—and to emerge alive and intact.

Warily, they padded up the stairs, rounded the landing, and continued on up. As they neared the top, there was still silence.

And then they saw why. A thick glass door with heavy glass panels on either side was set back from a small foyer area. Beyond the glass was a vast, gleaming laboratory with offices and rooms around its perimeter. Off to the side was what looked like a "clean room" devoted to experiments that had to be conducted in an atmosphere free of contaminants. Another room held an electron microscope. All labs had the same sense about them—orderliness touched with an aura of controlled chaos that came from papers, test tubes, Bunsen burners, glass beakers, flasks, microscopes, file cabinets, computers, refrigerators, and all the other paraphernalia that was so vital to scientists in their pursuit of codifying the unknown. This one also had what looked like a next-century spectrometer.

But what riveted Jon's gaze, what gave him both a sinking sensation and a jolt of triumph, was a heavy door in the center of one wall marked by the glaring red trefoil symbol of a biohazard. It was the door to a Level Four Hot Zone laboratory installation. A secret Level Four.

"I see four people," Randi whispered.

Jon kept his voice even. "Time to introduce ourselves."

They pushed in through the door, their weapons in front of them.

Chapter Forty-Four

Two of the technicians looked up. As soon as they saw the guns, fear shot into their faces. One of them moaned. At the sound, the other two looked up. They blanched. Without saying a word, Jon and Randi had all four's attention.

"Don't shoot!" begged the oldest of the two men.

"Please. I have children!" said the younger of the two women.

"No one's going to be hurt if you just answer a few questions," Smith assured them.

"He's right." Randi pointed her Uzi at what looked like a small conference room off the lab. "Let's go in there and have a warm and friendly chat."

In their white uniforms, the four technicians filed into the room and, when told, took chairs at the Formica-topped conference table. They ranged in age from mid-forties to mid-twenties, and they had the look of people who put in regular days. These were no wild-eyed, pasty-faced scientists who lived in their labs weeks at a time when wrapping up a project. They were ordinary people with wedding rings and photos of extended families on their workbenches. Technicians, not scientists.

Except the older of the two women. She had short gray hair and wore a long white lab coat over street clothes. She had been silent and watchful since they had entered. Some kind of scientist or supervisor.

Sweat bathed the high forehead of the older, balding man. His gaze had been on the guns, but now he looked up at Randi. "What do you want?" His voice was shaky.

"Glad you asked," she told him. "Tell us about the monkey virus."

"And the serum that happens to cure a human virus, too," Jon said.

"We know it was brought from Peru twelve years ago by Victor Tremont."

"We also know about the experiments on the twelve soldiers in Desert Storm."

Randi asked, "How long have you had the serum?"

"And how did the epidemic start?"

Hearing the rapid-fire questions, the older woman's gray features pinched. Her faded eyes grew defiant. "We don't know what you mean. We have nothing to do with any monkey virus or serum."

"Then what do you work on here?" Randi demanded.

"Antibiotics and vitamins mostly," the supervisor told her.

Smith said, "So why the secrecy? The remoteness? This lab doesn't show up in any of Blanchard's documents."

"We don't belong to Blanchard."

"Then whose antibiotics and vitamins are you working on?"

The supervisor flushed, and the others looked terrified again. She had said more than she had wanted to. "I can't tell you that," she snapped.

Randi said, "Okay. Then we'll look at your files."

"They're computerized. We don't have access. Only the director and Dr. Tremont do. When they get back, they'll put an end to you and all this—"

Jon's anger was rising. Whether they knew it or not, they had helped murder Sophia. "No one's going to come back anytime soon. They're too busy getting medals, and your three guards are dead outside," he lied. "You want to join the guards?"

The supervisor glared at him, stubbornly silent.

Randi tried to control her rage. "Maybe you think because we've been polite so far that we won't kill you. You're right, we probably won't. We're the good guys. But," she added cheerfully, "I have no problem with causing considerable pain. Mistakes do get made. You hear me clearly?"

That got their attention. At least the attention of the other three. They hurriedly nodded.

"Good. Now, which of you is going to tell us the name of the company you work for and the computer passwords?"

"And," Smith added, staring at the supervisor, "why you need a Level Four lab for vitamins and antibiotics?"

The supervisor's face paled, and her hands trembled, but she intensified her glare of intimidation at the other three.

But the smallest and oldest man ignored her. "Don't try that, Emma." His voice was weak but determined. "You're not in charge here anymore. They are." He looked at Jon. "How do we know you won't kill us anyway?"

"You don't. But you can be sure the odds are far better that if anyone's going to be hurt, it's going to be now. Later, we're going to be too busy bringing down Victor Tremont."

The older man stared. Then he nodded soberly. "I'll tell you."

Jon looked at Randi. "Now that things are handled here, I'll get Marty."

She gave a brisk nod. As she held her Uzi on the four lab workers, her mind was on Sophia. She was closing in on Sophia's killer. She was going to make them pay, no matter what she had to do.

"Talk," she told the older lab technician. "Talk fast."

■

Marty was sitting against a tree near the shed, the Enfield bullpup lying across his lap. He was humming to himself. He seemed to be studying sunbeams that danced in a shaft of yellow light through the trees. To look at him where he leaned back, his short legs stretched out on the pine needles, his ankles crossed, he could be an imp from some long-ago fairy tale without a problem in the world. Unless you noticed his eyes. That was where Smith's attention was fixed as he approached silently, cautiously. The green eyes were almost emerald in color and troubled.

"Any problems?"

Marty jumped. "Darn it, Jon. Next time make some noise." He rubbed his eyes as if they hurt. "I'm happy to report I've seen or heard no one. The shed's been quiet, too. But then there's not a lot any of those three can do, considering how well we tied them. Still, I don't think I'm cut out for guard work. Too boring and too much responsibility of the wrong kind."

"I see the problem. Feel like some computer sleuthing instead?"

Marty immediately looked more cheerful. "At last. Of course!"

"Let's go into the lodge. I need you to search some of Tremont's files."

"Ah, Victor Tremont. The one behind it all." Marty rubbed his hands.

Once inside, they were moving past the row of closed and locked doors when Smith heard a sound. They were almost in the same place in the hall where Randi had thought she had heard something.

He stopped and grabbed Marty's arm. "Don't move. Listen. Are you picking up anything?"

They stayed that way, slowly rotating their heads as if by movement alone they could enhance their hearing.

Jon spun around. "What was that?"

Marty frowned. "I think someone's shouting."

The sound came again. It was a voice, but muffled and far away. A man's voice.

"It's this one." Jon pressed his ear to one of the doors. It appeared to be thicker, sturdier than the others, and the lock was a heavy deadbolt. Someone was shouting but barely audible somewhere on the far side.

"Open it!" Marty said.

"Give me the bullpup." With the big assault rifle, he shot out the lock.

Screams of terror sounded above their heads from the laboratory, but the door swung open. They entered cautiously. There was a second door almost at once. Smith shot this one open, too, and they found themselves in a large, well-furnished living room. There was a kitchen through an archway, a formal dining room, a wet bar, and a corridor that probably led to bedrooms. The noise, clearly shouting now, was coming from the corridor.

"You stay back and cover me, Mart."

Marty did not bother to protest. "Okay. I'll do my best."

As Jon warily entered the corridor, whoever was calling must have heard enough to convince him someone was on the way. Banging started behind the third door.

Jon tried it. Locked. "Who's in there?" he called out.

"Mercer Haldane!" the furious voice bellowed. "Are you the police? Have you captured Victor?"

"Stand back," Jon called again. He used his Beretta on the simple room lock.

The door blasted open, and a short bantam-rooster of an older man with a mane of unruly white hair, thick white eyebrows, and a clean-shaven but choleric face sat in an armchair in what looked like a master bedroom. He was handcuffed and chained to the wall at the ankle but not gagged.

"Who the devil are you?" the old man demanded.

"Lt. Col. Jonathan Smith, M.D. Someone your people have been trying to murder."

"Murder? Why, for the love of—" The old man stopped. "Ah, yes, Victor. I knew he was worried about . . . M.D. you say. Don't tell me: CDC? FDA?"

"USAMRIID."

"Fort Detrick, of course. So have you caught the bastard?"

"We're trying."

"You'd better try faster. He's getting that damned medal at five o'clock. Probably the money a minute or so later, and no telling where he'll be by six o'clock. A long way from here, if I know him."

"Then you'd better help us."

"Just ask."

"You think he created the virus epidemic?"

"Of course he did. Are you a numbskull? That's why he locked me in here. What I don't know is how he did it."

Jon nodded. "Figures. Watch yourself. I'm going to shoot this leg chain off."

Mercer Haldane crunched with fright. Then he shrugged. "I hope your aim's good. I intend to live long enough to bring Victor down to his knees."

Smith shot out the chain lock and helped the old man up. "My other associate's in the lab. We're trying to locate Tremont's research records."

"He must have his illicit records hidden. I tried to find them, too."

Jon patted Marty on the back. "You didn't have my secret weapon."

■

When Jon and Marty strode into the laboratory with the short old man red-faced and angry under a shock of white hair, Randi was waiting for them. She had locked the four lab technicians in the conference room.

"What was all the shooting? You nearly gave me a coronary."

Jon introduced Mercer Haldane and asked, "What did the technician tell you?"

"They work for Tremont and Associates. The password into their computer is Hades."

Marty made a beeline to the nearest terminal, Haldane on his heels.

Marty's face was almost relaxed, so happy was he to be returning to a world he understood. Without looking at Haldane, Marty handed him his bullpup, sat, flexed his fingers, and went to work. Haldane rolled a stool over so he could sit next to him. Jon followed and took the bullpup Enfield away from the former CEO. He was not about to trust him.

Smith quietly explained to Randi, "Mercer Haldane is the former chairman and CEO of Blanchard. Last week Tremont forced him out and took over."

"How could he do that?"

"Old-fashioned blackmail, he says. But I think he was bought off, too. A cut of the Hades Project. That's what Tremont named the virus and serum project. He kept it hidden from Haldane and Blanchard for more than a decade."

"A perfect name for the horror they're causing. What else did he tell you?"

"Just about what we'd figured. Tremont found the virus in Peruvian Amazonia and brought it back to Blanchard along with a crude native cure: the blood of monkeys that had survived the disease and were full of neutralizing antibodies. Some Indians down there drink the blood, and it saves a lot of them every year. Tremont set up his secret team with company money and personnel, and they did most of the work here to isolate the virus and develop their antiserum by cloning the genes that made the antibodies. Then the bastard used DNA repair enzymes to introduce a few subtle mutations into the viruses to make it become virulent progressively earlier."

"That's all he could tell you?" She was disappointed.

"Yes. Except he's sure Tremont's caused this pandemic somehow."

The shout of rage echoed through the lab. "Useless! It's all nothing!"

Marty was glaring at Haldane and the conference room where they had locked up the technicians. "There's nothing in the files of Tremont and Associates. It's all routine junk about antibiotics and vitamins and hair spray! That technician lied to us."

"No," Haldane realized. "That's Victor. It's a dummy company.

These people are technicians. He used them but told them nothing. They think they're working for Tremont and Associates. The Hades password is his idea of a joke on anyone accessing his computer."

Jon nodded. "That sounds like the kind of man who could run an experiment on humans in the Gulf War. But the real stuff has to be in there somewhere, Mart. Keep hacking. We've got to know."

Marty sounded discouraged. His meds had not worn off yet. "I'll try, Jon. Only I really need my own—"

They heard a sudden sound outside the windows of the secret laboratory. Like a seasoned team, Jon and Randi dashed to look out. A car was approaching on the mountain road, a cloud of dust spinning out from the tires.

Adrenaline jolted Smith. "Mart! Haldane! Watch those technicians."

Jon and Randi tore across the laboratory, out through the door, and down to the landing. Side by side, they dropped flat where they could see anyone below who passed through the corridor from the living room or the side door. Randi looked over at Jon, at his blue eyes so intense, at his wide face with the hard chin, his swept-back black hair. His expression was granite.

"Now what?"

"We'll know soon." He did not look at her. He did not have to. He could feel her presence like a reassuring friend.

Two car doors closed. Footsteps rapidly approached the house. A voice spoke low and urgent.

Chapter Forty-Five

3:32 P.M.
Lake Magua, New York

Rapid footsteps, soft and light, padded swiftly along the corridor from the back door.

"What the—" Randi began.

Before Jon could answer, the big Doberman, Samson, appeared at the bottom of the stairs. He looked up at the landing, bared his fangs, and bunched his powerful muscles to attack.

Smith stood up, his Beretta behind his back. "Samson, sit!"

Puzzled, the dog cocked his head. Jon repeated the command, and suddenly the animal seemed to identify him as one of the "friends" Bill Griffin had ordered him to sniff under the RV. Slowly he sank back on his haunches, still staring up.

Jon raised his voice. His face was eager. "Peter?"

The lean and leathery ex-SAS strolled into view, again wearing the trench coat buttoned over his black commando suit. "Who else? You don't think Samson would go over to the enemy, do you?" He and the Doberman climbed the stairs.

Randi jumped up. "Perish the thought. Good to see you, Peter."

Smith's smile was broad. For a moment he looked ten years younger. "We've been worried."

"No sentries outside. That your handiwork?"

Jon said, "Yes. Everyone else is at the ceremony, I expect."

Randi added, "Except for four lab techs we've got locked up. And the former head of Blanchard, who's helping Marty at the computer."

Randi stopped, and she and Jon stared at Peter, whose left arm was dangling straight down, useless. Blood had dried on Peter's left wrist and hand beneath the long trench-coat sleeve.

"You're wounded! How bad? Let me look at it," Jon ordered.

"Pinprick."

"Goddamn it, come up here and take off your coat."

He held the laboratory door open as Peter sighed and topped the stairs, Samson at his side.

"Marty," Randi called as they entered. "Peter's here."

Marty spun in his chair as Peter walked in. A smile of welcome wreathed his round face. The Englishman allowed himself a return smile. He and Marty stared at each other a long moment.

Finally Peter said, "Mustn't worry about me, my boy. Remember the old man's been through worse than this on more continents than he cares to name. Now get yourself back to work." There was affection in his voice.

Marty's green eyes twinkled. He gave a short nod and returned to his chair. As he told Mercer Haldane about Peter, the Doberman appeared at Marty's side. Marty patted him, and the dog sighed and laid tiredly at his feet.

The Englishman said quietly to Jon, "Don't fuss. I've stopped bleeding. I'll be fine until I reach the docs."

"I *am* a doc, you crazy Brit. Everything else about you may be working, but your memory's going south."

Peter gave a wry grimace and laid the H&K submachine gun on a lab bench. Jon helped him off with his trench coat. Underneath, he wore only his commando trousers and webbed belt. His chest was naked. Bullets had struck him in the side and arm. He had wrapped what looked like pieces of a torn sheet around the wounds.

As Peter unwound the cloth, Randi got the older male technician from the conference room. He produced an extensive first-aid kit. The wound in the upper chest below the armpit had gone cleanly through the flesh around an upper rib. It appeared to have cracked the rib, but touched nothing vital. The arm injury was a shallow tunnel through muscle. The bleeding had all but stopped. Jon washed the wounds, applied antibiotic, rebandaged each one properly, and insisted Peter take at least aspirin.

Smith told him, "You need a hospital, but that will hold you for now."

"Good as new," Peter declared. "Tell me what you've found."

"We're pretty sure this is where Tremont and his associates did most of the actual work. Marty and Haldane are trying to bust into the records now. Tremont pushed Haldane out only last week. Blackmail, he says, but I suspect he settled for a big cut of the billions they'll all make. Then his conscience started bothering him."

"It'd be pleasant if conscience bothered more people," Peter observed. "Shall we see what progress they've achieved?"

"Not a damn thing." Randi shook her head with discouragement. "Marty's still loosening up from his meds and having trouble figuring how the records are entered. This system's unconnected to Blanchard's mainframe, so Haldane's stumped."

Randi was leaning over Marty and Mercer Haldane as Marty manipulated the keyboard and Haldane sat beside him, interpreting what he found.

"Tell the boy," Peter said, wincing as the simple act of speaking tweaked his wounds, "he had best hurry. Samson and I injured the enemy but we by no means put them out of action. That Arab we saw back in the Sierras appears to be the boss, just as Griffin said. He escaped unharmed with at least two of his men. The rest won't be active anytime soon, if ever."

"Could they have followed you?" Randi wanted to know.

"Think not. But it's likely they'll eventually decide Griffin or Marty informed us of this lodge and that we're here. They could arrive with reinforcements any minute."

Jon said, "You hear that, Mart?"

"I've tried everything I know," Marty snapped testily. "Now I'm working to establish an untraceable link with my computer so I can use my own programs. Give me another few seconds."

Both the testiness and the quickening of his speech showed his meds were almost gone, and they waited as patiently as they could.

"Someone better go down and watch," Smith realized. "Not you, Peter."

"Samson can go. He'll be a better lookout than any of us."

As Peter sent the dog off, Marty shouted, "I'm connected!"

"Thank God," Randi said fervently.

"All right, let's start a search for the company that operates this computer." Marty worked the keyboard, and the screen began to flash permutations too fast for them to see. Finally on the screen appeared the logo and name of Blanchard Pharmaceuticals, Inc.

"That means Victor registered the machine to us, and we pay for it," Haldane said. "An unexplained extra computer system was one item the accountants found they couldn't trace to any authorized research program."

Marty played across the keyboard. The screen continued to flicker through a series of computations. Finally a name flashed on: VAXHAM Corporation.

"What the devil is VAXHAM?" Haldane wondered.

Marty was leaning forward, concentrating. He clicked on VAXHAM, and it lit up with a long series of directories. One was "Laboratory Reports." He punched in and scrolled rapidly through the dated entries all the way back to the very first one: January 15, 1989. Jon leaned over his shoulder.

"Wow," Jon breathed. "A report of the first restriction enzyme mapping of the monkey virus from Peru! Now we're getting somewhere." Smith pulled up a stool. He studied the restriction map of the virus and in his mind compared it to the same mapping of the one that had killed Sophia that he had studied at USAMRIID. He let out a long whistle and looked up. "No surprise, but at last we have confirmation. They're almost identical—in fact, they may be identical. The monkey virus and the one killing people are the same."

Randi said angrily, "Victor Tremont knew it all along."

Each year listed a summary of the technical findings for virus and serum. They showed a steady lessening of the incubation time in victims before the final fatal outbreak and the steady increase in serum effectiveness on the virulent stage—at least in a petri dish and later in monkeys. Again it was confirmation of what they had guessed. But Marty could find no data about the Iraq experiments nor how the virus had suddenly spread like a contagion across the world from remote Peru— or from Victor Tremont and his VAXHAM Corporation.

"The last directory is blocked by a password," Marty announced. Then he sneered, "Complacent fools, they think they can keep out Zellerbach the Magician!"

He raised his hands as if he were a concert pianist and attacked the keyboard. Using his own software, he sent the screen into a paroxysm of kaleidoscopic words, questions, commands, and images. It took a matter of seconds.

"There!" Marty chortled. "How absurdly commonplace."

A single short phrase appeared on the screen: *Lucifer at Home.*

"Hades," Jon groaned.

"People," said Marty pompously, "are both unimaginative and predictable."

He entered the password. The first documents that appeared were a meticulous series of financial spreadsheets and summary reports covering every year from 1989 to the present. The corporate officers were listed: Victor Tremont, with some 35 percent of the stock, and George Hyem, Xavier Becker, Adam Cain, and Jack McGraw with 10 percent each.

In his heightened state, Marty saw the connection instantly: "VAX-HAM. With Tremont, an acronym of first and last names: Victor, Adam, Xavier, Hyem and McGraw, with an extra 'A' to make it look like a word."

"Those are some of the best people in the company." Haldane was aghast. "All of them head departments, and McGraw's security. No wonder they could get away with so much for so long."

Major stockholders were listed: Maj. Gen. Nelson Caspar and Lt. Gen. Einar Salonen (Ret.). "There's your army connection," Randi told Jon. She shook her head with disgust.

"Also the government," Haldane said furiously. "Nancy Petrelli. She's Health and Human Services. And there's Congressman Ben Sloat."

Marty was still searching. "These seem to be year-by-year statistics of progress on the project. Reports of operations, I guess." He paused. "Here are data about antibiotic shipments."

Jon and Haldane leaned closer.

Haldane was surprised. "Those are Blanchard antibiotics. All of them. And the figures appear to be our total shipments for each year."

Puzzled, they read on until Smith suddenly inhaled sharply. He stood up, radiating rage. "That's it!" His face was tight, his high cheekbones prominent under the harsh overhead fluorescent lights. His dark blue eyes had blackened into bottomless pits. He seemed to be fighting disbelief, violence, and grief.

Mercer Haldane looked up, and Randi turned to stare.

"What is it, my boy?" Peter had been sitting off to the side, weary and in pain, but the look on Jon's face had snapped him out of his exhaustion.

Jon's voice was arctic. "Marty, print it out. All of it. Start with the corporate progress reports. And do it fast!"

"Jon?" Randi was watching his drawn face and empty eyes. He was worrying her. "What does it mean?"

Everyone focused on him. The lab was silent as his gaze slowly took in the test tubes, microscopes, and benches where so much despicable work had been done over the past decade. His chest burned, and his stomach felt as if a Mack truck had just slammed into it. He began to talk.

Chapter
Forty-Six

Jon's voice was hoarse, and he spoke slowly, as if he had to make certain he was precise in each word. "Those antibiotic shipments of Blanchard's tell the story. Remember when I explained that the virus isn't very contagious? So that led me to the question of how so many millions of people could get so terribly sick and die at about the same time. The answer is what we guessed—Victor Tremont." He hesitated. His hands balled into fists at his sides. He growled, "The bastard shipped the virus across the world in all of Blanchard's antibiotics. Antibiotics that were meant to cure people were also infecting them with an untreatable, deadly illness." His eyes were haunted. "Tremont and his gang set it all in motion ten years ago. The Hades Project. For a decade he's been contaminating Blanchard's antibiotics to infect millions *even though he knew he might never have a cure when the virus went into its fatal stages!*"

"Bloody hell," Peter said, his voice unbelieving.

Jon went on as if he had not heard. "They sent the virus out to create an epidemic that'd start ten years later, working to change the virus so that every year it would mutate into its lethal stage earlier and earlier. All so it would turn lethal to millions and millions this year, and they could cure it and make billions of dollars in profit. That was before they could know whether they'd ever have a serum, or that it'd be effective enough, or that it'd be stable and could be even shipped. They condemned millions of people to certain death on the gamble they could make them pay to save their lives."

Randi shook her head, shocked. "It was all so Blanchard and Tremont could make billions of dollars. Get rich. Live well." Her voice broke. "That's why Sophia died. She was in Peru and must've met Tremont there. That's the missing phone call. When she started studying the unknown virus, she remembered something, and she called Tremont. No wonder he had to stop her investigation."

Jon looked at Randi as tears slid down her cheeks. His eyes grew moist and his throat thickened. She reached out and took his hand. He nodded and squeezed hers.

Haldane stood up, trembling with the horror of it. "Great Lord. I never imagined anything so obscene. All those poor sick people who needed our antibiotics. Trusting science and medicine to ease their suffering. Trusting Blanchard."

Jon turned on the former CEO in fury. "How much were *you* going to make, Haldane, before your sudden change of heart?"

"What?" Haldane blinked at him. His wrinkled face became as angry as Jon's. "Victor forged my name. He tricked me! He made it look as if I'd approved everything. What was I supposed to do? He had me cornered, powerless. He was going to take my company. I deserved something! I—" He stopped as if hearing his own words, and he fell back down onto the stool. His voice dropped in shame. "I didn't know then what he'd done, how horrible the consequences would be. When I saw what it meant, I couldn't stay silent." He laughed a derisive laugh at himself. "Too little, too late. That's what they'll say. As greedy as the rest, he found too little conscience, too late."

"Sounds about right," Jon said in revulsion. He turned his back on Haldane to face Peter and Randi. "We've got to—"

"Jon!" The cry was so loud and appalled that everyone whirled to its source. All but forgotten in the horror of the revelation, Marty had continued working the keyboard and peering at the screen. "They never stopped. Oh, no, no, *no*. They've not only put the virus in the antibiotics every year since, *they're still doing it!* It says here a shipment of contaminated medicine will go out today at the same time as the first antiviral serum shipment!"

A thunderous silence filled the room. They looked at one another— Jon, Randi, Marty, Peter, and Mercer Haldane—as if they had not heard correctly. Could not have.

Jon's voice was stunned. "He's creating a pandemic that will go on and on."

Randi added, "And make a nuclear bomb seem like a child's toy."

Peter's pale blue eyes pierced the lab. He gripped his injured arm as if the pain had suddenly increased. "Then we must mess up the arsehole's plans."

"We'd better hurry." Marty was still reading from the computer screen. "Blanchard will have a little over two billion dollars in payments wired electronically from many countries as well as America the instant the first shipment leaves the plant." He swiveled around. His eyes snapped with outrage. "And your Victor Tremont appears to have recently opened a bank account in the Bahamas. Probably in case of an unexpected emergency, wouldn't you think?"

"So if we don't stop him today," Randi said, "another shipment of the virus goes out, and Tremont probably flies the coop with a billion dollars or so."

"But how?" Mercer Haldane groaned, seeing any chance for redemption in the pages of history vanishing. "Victor gets the medal, and the shipment goes out in an hour! And the president will be at Blanchard with the secret service and FBI and every policeman the state and village can spare."

Jon nodded. "The president!" A plan was forming in his mind. "That's how we stop Tremont. We show the president what he's done."

"If we can get to him," Randi said.

"With the proof on paper," Peter added.

"And someone whom he'll believe," Jon finished. "Not a discredited scientist like me, AWOL from the army and wanted for questioning."

"Or a CIA agent who's probably been branded as rogue by now, too," Randi agreed glumly.

Marty, who was still printing out the records of the Hades Project, said over his shoulder, "May I suggest Mr. Mercer Haldane, former chairman of Blanchard Pharmaceuticals, who, at least on paper, appears to be one of the heinous conspirators?"

Everyone stared at the white-haired executive. He nodded enthusiastically, seeing a chance to reclaim his self-respect. "Yes. I like that. I want to tell the president *everything*." Then his eagerness faded. "But Victor would never let me get close."

"I'm not sure anyone could personally reach the president today," Randi agreed.

Jon pursed his lips, thinking. "Which leaves us back where we started. But we've got to stop Tremont some damn way."

"And very soon," Peter warned. "That bloody al-Hassan and his troops could show up here any second. Then where are we?"

"Who else will be at the ceremony?" Randi wondered. "The surgeon general? Secretary of state? The president's chief of staff?"

"They'll be just as well guarded," Smith knew. "Besides, Tremont's people will see to it we don't get close. Tremont's security uses violence as their tool of choice. In some ways, they're a worse obstacle than the secret service."

Randi ruminated, "I wish some of those foreign leaders were going to be there in person. We might have a chance to—"

"Wait." Jon suddenly had another idea. He sat on the stool next to Marty. "Mart, can you break into a closed-circuit TV transmission?"

"Sure. Once I broke into a CNN transmission." He laughed, remembering the prank. "Of course, that was only a local cable station, and I was in another studio in the building. I don't know about a national cable company. What's the company? What are the computer codes? Of course, I'd need a TV camera here, too."

Mercer Haldane suggested, "There's a local studio in Long Lake village."

"They'll be routing the feed through there," Randi objected. "There'll be technicians everywhere."

"We'll go in shooting if we have to. Could you tap into the cable from there, Mart?"

"I think so."

"Okay, that's what we'll do."

Peter was doubtful. "The whole village is going to be crawling with police tripping on each other's shoes."

Movement at the perimeter of the room drew their attention. The older male technician who had brought the medical kit to Jon was walking slowly toward them. They had forgotten to lock him back into the conference room. His face was drained of color.

"I didn't know any of what you've just found out. All I do is routine analysis." He held out a hand as if asking forgiveness. "I've taken Blanchard antibiotics myself. I have a family who—" He swallowed. "They've taken them, too, off and on over the years. I . . . maybe you should know Mr. Tremont has a small TV studio in the lodge. He had it installed to connect to the plant and to the local studio for making publicity and inspirational videos and live broadcasts. It's state-of-the-art. I can show you where it is."

"Marty?" Jon asked.

"I'll probably need more time from there." He was doubtful.

After the first shock of Tremont's monstrous plan had begun to wear off, Smith's mind had been clear and precise. Now it seemed as if his faculties had never been sharper. He checked his watch and barked orders. "We've got forty minutes. Randi, we're going to the ceremony to try to give the printouts of all the records to the president. If we can't get near, at least we can cause a disturbance and give Marty more time." He turned to Peter. "You and Samson stay here to protect Mart and Haldane. Haldane, once you're on camera, you're going to give the speech of your life."

"I will." The former CEO nodded. "You can count on it."

Pale from his wound, Peter murmured, "Piece of cake."

"Take the lab technician to show you where the TV studio is, and we'll leave the three others locked up. We'll take the M-16s in case we need to make a lot of noise. All set?"

Everyone nodded. For a brief moment they gazed around at each other, as if for reassurance. Then they were a blur of action as they ran out of the lab. Peter, Marty, and Haldane followed the technician into the rear corridor. Jon and Randi sprinted outside to their rented car.

■

Randi drove fast along the mountain road in the late-afternoon sunlight. It was a shock to see how normal and beautiful the world looked. Less than a half mile from the lodge, they saw dust clouds rising ahead.

"Pull off!" Jon snapped.

Tires screeching, she sped the car off the road into the tall pines. A branch ripped off an outside mirror. With her Uzi and one of the M-16s, and he with the other two M-16s, they leaped out of the car and ran back fifty feet. As they turned to look through the trees, they saw three SUVs racing along the road.

"There he is." Jon recognized the lean Nadal al-Hassan from the Sierras in the front seat of the lead SUV. "No surprise."

"Al-Hassan," Randi agreed, remembering him from outside Peter's battered RV.

"Shoot at them with everything we have so they'll think there's a lot of us, but don't hit the tires."

"Why the hell not?" Randi demanded.

"We need to make them follow us and leave the lodge alone."

Using both hands, they dodged from side to side and fired their weapons. They hit mostly air but still caused enough damage to send all three vehicles careening off the road. As soon as the tires of the third SUV skidded to the side, Jon and Randi loped back to their car. Randi pulled out onto the road again and, as they sped past al-Hassan and his men, they saw one of the three SUVs had its front tires shot out. It was out of commission, abandoned in the trees.

"Damn!" Jon swore.

"Peter and Samson will handle them if they have to."

The two other SUVs had smashed windows but no major damage. They bumped back onto the road. As they watched in the rearview mirror, two men ran from the disabled vehicle and clambered aboard the others as they turned to chase Jon and Randi toward the county highway, a mile and a half ahead.

"Stay ahead until we hit Long Lake village," Smith said. "Keep them chasing us."

"Piece of cake," Randi replied in Peter's voice, smiling grimly.

Chapter Forty-Seven

4:52 P.M.
Long Lake Village, New York

The sun was low in the mountain sky, and it was one of those beautiful afternoons in the Adirondacks that sent shivers of pleasure into the souls of any nature lover. Rich autumn colors showed in the leaves of the towering hardwoods. The pines seemed to grow straight up to the blue sky. The air was crisp and clean. Daisies were still in bloom. Outside on the lawn in the center of the sprawling complex that was Blanchard Pharmaceuticals' headquarters, an audience of dignitaries sat in white folding chairs at the back of the raised platform, waiting eagerly for the formalities of this notable occasion to begin. Before the platform stood an animated crowd.

As he waited in the tent erected to protect him, President Samuel Adams Castilla contemplated the festivities with satisfaction. Composed of local citizens of the rural region, representatives from most nations on earth, and editors, columnists, and reporters from all the major news media everywhere, the audience was everything a president who had an election to win could have wanted. This historic ceremony being telecast to every corner of the world and, more important, to the American people should assure his reelection by a landslide.

Next to him stood Victor Tremont, whose gaze moved slowly across the surging throng. His thoughts were far less sanguine. He was consumed with an uneasy foreboding, as if his father stood over his shoulder saying again, *"No one* can have everything, Vic." He knew there was no realistic basis for such defeatism, but he could not seem to shake off the worry. That infernal Smith and the stupid Russell woman's CIA sister had once again escaped the best efforts of al-Hassan and his men. They had vanished, and Tremont had heard nothing from al-Hassan since.

Despite his confidence that he had prepared for any emergency, it concerned him, and he studied the crowd for a sign of the pair. He wished to God he had never taken that phone call from Sophia Russell. Why had she remembered that momentary encounter more than a dozen years ago? Chance. The completely unforeseeable element in everything.

But it would not stop him.

He was just reanalyzing all his actions when the first blaring brass bars of "Hail to the Chief" began.

"We're on," the president said with relish. "This is a grand moment, Dr. Tremont. Let's make the most of it."

"Agreed, Mr. President. And thank you again for the honor."

Ushered by the secret service, he and the president stepped out. Applause began with a trickle and quickly grew thunderous. The two men smiled and waved. Following instructions given him earlier, Tremont hung back so the president could march first toward the platform. He followed, trying to memorize the details of this exciting occasion. The platform was decorated with yards of red, white, and blue bunting. The podium was fronted by the presidential seal in blue and gold. Behind the platform rose a towering closed-circuit TV screen so everyone could view the dignitaries from around the world who would participate with live speeches.

The president first, they mounted the stairs to continuing applause. The six rows of seated dignitaries sprang to their feet to greet the president. There were all the members of the cabinet, including a beaming Nancy Petrelli; the chairman of the Joint Chiefs with his executive aide, Maj. Gen. Nelson Caspar; the New York congressional delegation; and the ambassadors of fifty nations.

At the podium, Surgeon General Jesse Oxnard, his massive head and mustache dominating everything, clapped with the others. At last he stepped to the podium to make introductions.

5:30 P.M.

Jon and Randi stood among the crowd a few yards apart and near the back.

They had managed to evade their partly disabled pursuers and arrive in Long Lake a half hour ago, where they had searched along the packed sidewalks for ways to change their appearances. At last they had found an outdoor clothing store, then a toy store and a drugstore on the main street, which was one of the few highways that crossed the Adirondack Wilderness. They bought supplies at all three and used public restrooms to change. When they finally emerged, he was darker-skinned and looked as if he belonged in this mountain region. He wore bulky hunting pants, a plaid hunting coat, and a ragged black mustache detached from a child's mask. She was in a mousy gray dress, flat heels, hair darkened with shoe polish, and a straw hat.

There were enough foreign observers and journalists to distract everyone's attention, so most people gave them only a few curious glances. Still, from around the periphery and up on the platform itself, the secret service, FBI, and Blanchard's security people continually scanned the hordes, alert to any intrusion.

Jon and Randi shifted locations frequently. They kept their heads down and quiet, friendly smiles on their faces. They made certain their muscles appeared relaxed.

Once the band struck up "Hail to the Chief" and everyone was riveted as President Castilla and Victor Tremont strode toward the platform, Randi moved closer to Jon to whisper, "The woman with the short silver hair wearing the knit business suit is Nancy Petrelli, and the general in the second row behind Admiral Brose is Nelson Caspar."

"I expect Ben Sloat and old General Salonen are here somewhere, too."

Their plan was simple: Work their way far enough forward to get the president's personal attention, and they would try to shout out their story. To wave their documents. To accuse Tremont and his cohorts to their faces with everyone as witnesses, and maybe to make one or more of them panic and reveal themselves. At least, to convince the president to hear. After all, this was a public gathering.

That was at the best.

At the worst, they wanted to give Marty a chance to break into the closed-circuit broadcast so Mercer Haldane could confirm everything they claimed.

But first, they had to slip through the crowd without attracting the sharp eyes of the hundreds of public and private security who were watching for interlopers, troublemakers, terrorists . . . and them.

5:09 P.M.
Lake Magua

Muttering wildly to himself in the small TV studio, Marty worked feverishly at the computer in the state-of-the-art control room.

"Where are you, you *beast!* I know you're in there somewhere. Give me the code name and the password, damn you! Once more, the telephone company is . . . ."

Mercer Haldane waited out in the studio with the four technicians and a series of blowups of the computer records. Behind them was a photographic backdrop of an Adirondack woodland scene, the high peaks of Whiteface and Marcy in the distance. Haldane's cheeks were sweating. He continually mopped them as he watched Marty through the control room window. He glanced often and nervously at his watch.

". . . All right, *yes!* I have you. I'm into the telephone company. Now the line into the local TV cable station. Come on . . . *come on* . . . I know you want me to find you . . . yes, that's it . . . *damnation!* . . ."

At the studio door, Peter kept guard on the corridor, listening for any sounds of warning from Samson. He also glanced from time to time at his watch while he observed Marty's frantic efforts.

". . . Ah-*ha!* Got you. Now, the control room. Here we go . . . here we . . . Zounds and putridity! You won't stop me . . . you *can't* . . ." Sweat dripped from Marty's face, and his fingers pounded the keyboard as he frantically searched for the key into the system.

5:12 P.M.
Long Lake Village

As the surgeon general continued to talk, extolling the virtues of Victor Tremont and the wisdom of the president, Jon and Randi edged forward in parallel paths, slowly converging again as they advanced. Jon saw Victor Tremont's pockmarked killer, Nadal al-Hassan, in deep conversation with a man who looked as if he were the chief FBI agent present. Al-Hassan's arm swept over the crowd as he held a sheaf of photos in his lean hand. Jon did not have to guess whom the photos pictured. He repressed a worried groan.

The surgeon general's introduction ended, and the president stepped to the podium. His face was solemn as his gaze slowly traversed the faces in the audience and turned to do the same to all the dignitaries seated behind him. He continued on in a full circle across the vigilant backs of the secret service and Tremont's security team until he again faced the rapt crowd.

"These are terrible times," he began. "The world suffers. Millions die. And yet we are here to celebrate. And it is entirely fitting that we should do so. The man we come to honor will go down in history not only as visionary but as a great humanitarian. He . . ."

As the president continued in rousing, cadenced tones, Jon and Randi moved inexorably forward, sometimes only a few steps, other times several feet at a time. They were careful to make no one angry. To attract no undue attention. And to appear to be enthralled with the president's speech as it came quickly to its peroration: ". . . It is my eternally grateful pleasure to present the nation's highest civilian award to Dr. Victor Tremont, a giant sun that will soon shed light on this great darkness into which we have all been plunged."

Attempting to appear solemn but honored, humble but strong, while suppressing his real response of a loud, triumphal laugh, Victor Tremont moved toward the podium with what came out as a grotesque grimace. The medal was presented and accepted with a modest embarrassment, and the giant TV screen sprang to life with the image of the British prime minister towering over them all.

5:16 P.M.

Nadal al-Hassan's mirrored black eyes slowly traversed the surging crowd. His face was expressionless, and his dark, narrow head moved like a praying mantis as his cold gaze paused on a face that resembled one or the other of his quarries, on a shoulder that looked familiar, on a military posture among the packed throng.

They would be here, he was sure. Smith had proved to be a far more resourceful and dangerous adversary than he had ever expected. He had little faith in the state or local police of this rustic town, in McGraw's private security force of old soldiers and retired policemen, or in the FBI, and he was well aware that the secret service agents would confine their vigilance to the immediate safety of the president. The protection of Victor Tremont and the Hades Project rested on his shoulders.

His eyes were hooded as they continued to work the crowd. In the cold twilight, the pocks in the tall man's skin seemed deeper in the hollows of his face. He inhaled the pungent odor of wood smoke carried in the cold evening air. The scent reminded him of his nomadic youth around the campfires of northern Iraq. Those were not memories he cared to dwell on. He had come far from those poor beginnings, and the Hades Project would be the culmination of his long escape. No one was going to stop his success.

As he thought that, he saw them.

Smith had disguised himself in bulky hunting pants, a plaid hunting coat, and a ragged black mustache. The CIA woman wore a gray dress, hair darkened with shoe polish, and a straw hat. But they could not hide from him.

He whispered to McGraw and started forward, fighting the crowd. Excitement spread through him.

5:16 P.M.
Lake Magua

His eyes haggard, his back bent, his face so close to the keyboard his sweat dripped onto the keys, Marty battled to overcome the last barrier and assume control of the cable transmission. He had long since ceased to mutter and cry out. He had lapsed into a deep and determined silence as he struggled.

Mercer Haldane stood with the technicians in front of the single camera. It was switched on, focused, and waiting. He continued to mop the sweat that poured down his face under the hot lights. No one made small talk. The room seemed to bristle with tension.

At the studio door, Peter no longer watched the corridor outside or listened to anything but the silence that seemed to stretch endlessly. He did not know what was happening in Long Lake village, but he knew the speeches must have begun at least ten minutes ago, and he hoped that by now Jon and Randi were approaching the platform to shout out their accusations in front of the president, the crowd, the secret service, Tremont, and the worldwide TV audience.

Accusations they would have no chance to prove . . . unless Marty broke into the transmission in the next few seconds.

5:17 P.M.
Long Lake Village

Jon and Randi had reached the second row of packed spectators. Just ahead was the raised stage with its colorful patriotic bunting. The entire throng—all the dignitaries, Victor Tremont, and the president—were staring up at the giant image of the prime minister heaping praise and gratitude on Victor Tremont.

Jon took a breath, nodded to Randi, and they abruptly pushed through the last people and shouted up to the president's turned back.

Smith bellowed: "Tremont is a fraud and a mass murderer!" He waved the printouts of the secret records. "He caused this pandemic himself! For *money*. To extort billions from the world!"

The president turned in shock at Jon's first shout.

Victor Tremont spun to face them, shouting back: "They've got guns! That man is a fugitive from the military, a rogue scientist, and a *killer*. Shoot him!"

The secret service leaped from the platform and ran toward Jon.

Randi took up the cry. "Tremont's still infecting millions of people! He's sending out the virus in his antibiotics. He's shipping infected antibiotics every day. Even *today!*"

Nadal al-Hassan and his men struggled through the crowd toward them. Jack McGraw was bawling orders at his security guards.

Jon battled in the grip of the secret service. He managed to wave his papers. "I have the proof! I have their records. I . . ."

The secret service swarmed him to the ground.

Other secret service and FBI men pounced on Randi. Pain shot through her shoulders. They found her Uzi. "She's armed!"

Nadal al-Hassan had almost reached them, his gun hidden at his side.

5:18 P.M.
Lake Magua

Marty shouted into his microphone, "We're in!"

"Go!" Peter cried.

Mercer Haldane stared into the camera, took a deep breath, and started to talk.

5:18 P.M.
Long Lake Village

On the platform, more secret service grabbed the president to hustle him away.

The giant screen above the milling crowd went dark for a second, and then Mercer Haldane appeared with his white, flowing hair and dignified face. He was standing in the secret laboratory. Behind him the four lab technicians held up giant blowups of the most damning print-outs. Watching from below, the crowd fell into a surprised hush.

"My name is Mercer Haldane." His words boomed. Somehow Marty had managed to increase the volume. "Until last week, I was chairman and CEO of Blanchard Pharmaceuticals. I have news about the virus that all of you must listen to carefully. Your lives depend on it. A great evil has been perpetrated on all of us by Victor Tremont." Shocked by his words, everyone's attention was riveted, including the secret service. "Ten years ago, Victor inaugurated a monstrous secret plan. He called it the Hades Project, and he infected twelve soldiers in the Gulf War, six on each side of the conflict, with a unique and deadly virus he had found in the Peruvian jungle. Then he contaminated Blanchard's antibiotics with the live virus and shipped it across the world. This virus would lie dormant for—"

On the platform, the president had stopped to listen. Still closely surrounded by the watchful agents, he stared up at the mammoth screen, his eyes slowly blinking as he took in Mercer Haldane's story. All the dignitaries had focused on it, too. The great crowd stood in an eerie silence as Mercer Haldane pointed to record entries, to dates, to figures.

The audience began to murmur, softly at first like a distant tornado barely heard, and then louder and louder.

The secret service agents relaxed their holds on Jon and Randi.

On the giant screen, Haldane showed the list of officers and stockholders in the secret VAXHAM Corporation.

As a shudder of understanding and belief seemed to sweep over the throngs, the president barked an order. Secret service and FBI agents went to stand beside Nancy Petrelli, General Caspar, Ben Sloat, an angry General Salonen, and the four officers of VAXHAM.

The president scanned the audience. "Bring those two who were shouting. I want to see the records they were trying to show me."

Randi brushed away the FBI and secret service agents, jumped onto the platform, and handed her printouts to President Castilla. "Sir, you must arrest Victor Tremont at once, or he'll escape and transfer billions of dollars to his offshore accounts."

The president scanned the papers and barked an order. The secret service and FBI agents spread out, looking for Tremont.

The chief of detail ran up to the platform. "He's not here, Mr. President. Victor Tremont is gone!"

Randi searched all around, too. Her voice rose. "So is Jon!"

"Find them!" the president shouted.

5:36 P.M.

The hallways in the storage basement of the main building of Blanchard Pharmaceuticals, Inc., were brightly lighted and filled with boxes, file cabinets, and discarded office furniture and equipment. Beneath that level was the sub-basement where the lights were dimmer. Here spread all the machines to heat, air-condition, supply, and operate the big two-story building. The equipment made a quiet hum.

Under that was yet a third level, unmarked. Seldom visited. It was dark, damp, and rived with narrow corridors. It was not silent. Running footsteps echoes from the walls as Victor Tremont and Nadal al-Hassan rushed along with the speed and certainty of those who knew where they were going. Each carried a weapon. They passed an ordinary steel door on the right. They did not stop but continued on to the wall at the very end. This wall was as smooth and unbroken as all the rest in the dank sub-sub-basement. Simply the end of the corridor, apparently.

Victor Tremont took a small black box from his suit-jacket pocket.

Nadal al-Hassan, his weapon ready, watched warily back along the side corridor.

Tremont pressed a button on the box. The entire wall slid heavily to the left, revealing a hidden vault door made of the strongest steel available when it had been built on Tremont's orders at the time he had Blanchard's operations moved to the Adirondack Wilderness. Tremont was shaking. He spun the combination lock, and the massive door rose a few millimeters up on pneumatic lifts and slowly swung open.

"Clever," Jon said as he stepped from the main corridor, the Beretta held steady in both hands. He aimed it at the two fugitives, who looked up. While Mercer Haldane had been speaking to the stunned crowds, Jon had watched Victor Tremont slip away. Caught in the mass of bodies, Jon had been unable to work his way as swiftly as he had wanted. But in the end, it had not mattered. He had found Tremont.

Nadal al-Hassan never hesitated. A thin smile spread across his narrow face. He swung his Glock and fired before the echo of Jon's voice ceased.

The bullet missed Smith's throat by the thickness of a hair.

Jon did not hesitate or miss. All the horrors of the past two weeks swept over him in an unforgettable second. He pulled the trigger, and al-Hassan fell forward without a sound. He lay spread-eagled, his blood pooling on the gray concrete floor at the side of his head.

Victor Tremont's bullet did not miss either. It stabbed like searing ice through the upper part of Jon's left leg. It hurled him against the wall, which caused Tremont's second and third shots to fly past and ricochet, whining away along the main corridor.

Propped against the wall, Jon fought to stay conscious. He fired again. His bullet hit Tremont's right arm, knocking him back against the half-open door and sending his pistol flying with a metallic clatter to the floor. It bounced and skidded, and the sound reverberated away along the secret corridors like a dying cry.

Dragging his bloody leg, Jon advanced on the mass murderer.

Tremont did not cringe. He lifted his chin, his eyes glowing with the certainty that any man had his price. "I'll give you a million dollars! Five million!"

"You don't have a million dollars. Not anymore. You're dead. They'll electrocute you."

"They won't find me." He jerked his head behind him toward the half opened door. "I destroyed the plans. No one knows an exit is here. I had it built by foreigners. The money's already transferred where no one can find it."

"I thought you'd have some plan."

"I'm not a fool, Smith. They'll never find me."

"Not a fool," Jon agreed. "Just a ghoul. A murderer of millions. But that's statistics. The world will have to deal with you for that. But you killed Sophia, and that's personal. I get to decide what to do. You ended her life with a wave of your hand: Eliminate her. Now it's my turn."

"Half! I'll give you *half!* A billion dollars. More!" Tremont shrank back against the massive steel door, his long body cowering.

Jon limped forward, the Beretta steady in both hands. "I loved her, Tremont. She loved me. Now—"

It was Randi's voice behind him. "No, Jon. Don't. He's not worth it."

"What do you know? I *loved* her, dammit!" His finger tightened on the trigger.

"He's finished, Jon. The FBI is here. The secret service. They've got them all. The serum's on its way to stop the dying, and they've confiscated all the antibiotics. Let them deal with him. Let the world deal with him."

Smith's face was fierce. His eyes glowed like coals. His chin jutted. He took another step closer, the Beretta steady, inches from Tremont's trembling face. The arrogant executive tried to speak again, to say something, but his mouth and lips and tongue were too dry. All that came out was a whimper.

"Jon?" Randi's voice was suddenly soft, close.

He glanced back over his shoulder and saw Sophia. It was her lovely face, her large, intelligent eyes and sweet smile. He blinked. No, it was Randi. *Sophia.* Randi. He shook his head to clear it. He knew what Randi wanted, and what Sophia would have wanted.

He made himself take another deep breath. He glared once more at the shaking Tremont. Then he lowered the gun and stumbled away, his wounded leg dragging. He brushed past Randi and pushed through the ranks of FBI and secret service. Some of the agents reached out to stop him.

"Let him go," Randi said gently. "He'll be all right. Just let him go now."

Jon heard her behind him, but a rush of tears was blinding his eyes. He could not stop the tears. Did not want to. They poured silently down. He turned into the main corridor and hobbled on toward the distant stairs.

Epilogue

Six weeks later, early December
Santa Barbara, California

Santa Barbara. . . . Land of palms and magenta sunsets. Of diving sea-gulls and glossy yachts with white sails afurl on the turquoise channel. Of lovely young women and handsome young men in the briefest of swim-ware. Jon Smith, M.D., formerly of the U.S. Army, tried to occupy his mind with the languid beauty of this soft paradise where effort seemed trivial and appreciation of life, nature, and dreams was all.

It had been a fight to resign his commission. They had not wanted him to go, but he knew there was no other way for him to find a reason to live. He had said good-bye to his friends at USAMRIID, pausing a long time in Sophia's former office. Already an eager young man with a closetful of credentials had scattered his things where her pens, notes, and perfume had lain. Jon had stopped in his own office, which was empty, waiting for its next occupant, with less sadness. Then he had gone to say farewell to the new director. As he had stepped inside the office door, he could almost hear the noisy bombast of General Kielburger, who had turned out to have a strain of decency no one had suspected.

Then he had paid a company to pack up his house and put it on the market. He knew he would never be able to live there again, not without Sophia.

The whole sordid incident of the Hades Project had occupied the news media for weeks as more and more revelations of Victor Tremont's plans were made public and more arrests of once-respected private and public officials were reported. Legal charges against Jon Smith, Randi Russell, Martin Zellerbach, and a mysterious Englishman were quietly dropped. All refused interviews or any official gratitude for their roles. Details were swept under the mantle of national security. He was not pleased when an enterprising newswoman dug up some of his history at USAMRIID, Somalia, West Berlin, and Desert Storm and tried to draw a connection between it and his ability to face down the criminal activities of Victor Tremont and his cohorts. He was consoled by the fact that time would pass, other news would take over the headlines, and if he went far enough away and severed his ties as completely as he had managed . . . interest in him would dwindle. He would not be considered for even a footnote in history.

He had stopped for a day in Council Bluffs, Iowa, to see once again the river town of his birth. He walked through the downtown park with its water fountain and big graceful trees and went out to Bennett Avenue to sit in the parking lot and stare at Abraham Lincoln High School, remembering Bill and Marty and the days of their youth. It all had been so much simpler then. The next day, he had flown on to California to this tranquil resort pueblo with its distinctive red-tiled roofs and easy ambience. He had rented a beachside cottage next to the Remaks' house in Montecito and played poker twice a week there with a group of university professors and writers. He ate at local restaurants, walked the breakfront, and never struck up a conversation with strangers. He had nothing to say.

Today he was sitting on his deck barefoot and wearing shorts as he stared out at the cloud-rimmed islands. The air tasted of sea salt, and although the day was cool, the beaming sun seemed to warm him to the bones.

When the phone rang, he picked it up.

"Hi, soldier." Randi's voice was bright and cheery. In the beginning, she had called nearly every day. There was the business of disposing of Sophia's belongings and condo, which the two of them had worked through as quickly as possible, each choosing important mementoes to hold Sophia's memory close. But then Randi had continued to phone a couple of times a week, and he had realized she was checking on him.

Amazingly, she was worried.

"Hi, spy," he retorted. "Where are you now?"

"D.C. The big city. Remember it? Working away at my lowly, boring job here at the think tank. Oh, for a life of adventure. I don't think I'm going to have a new assignment for a while, but I get the sense they're cooking up something big. Meanwhile, they seem to think I need my rest. Why don't you visit for Christmas? All that sunshine and good weather must be getting on your nerves."

"On the contrary. It suits me just fine. It's going to be just me and Santa. We'll have a jolly old time."

"You'll miss me and Marty. I know you will. I'm having Christmas dinner with him. Of course, there's no way to blast him out of that little bungalow of his, so I have to go there." She chuckled. "He's made Samson part of his fortress routine. You should see them together. Marty's particularly fond of the way Samson can make his fangs drip. At least, Marty claims Samson has control over that particular involuntary bodily function." She paused. "You're a doctor. What do you think?"

"I think they're both crazy. Who's cooking?"

"I am. Unlike them, I'm not crazy. I want something edible. What do you like—traditional turkey? Maybe a standing rib roast? How about a Christmas goose?"

It was his turn to laugh. "You're not going to talk me into going back. At least not yet." He gazed out at the tranquil Pacific, rippling with sunshine. Santa Barbara was where Sophia and Randi had grown up. He had driven past their childhood home the day he arrived. It was a beautiful hacienda perched atop a cliff with panoramic ocean views. Randi had never asked whether he had visited it. There were still areas neither wanted to discuss.

Their conversation continued about five minutes longer before they said good-bye. As they hung up, Jon thought about Peter, who had returned to his California aerie as soon as he had gotten permission to leave Washington. His wounds had been as superficial as Jon's initial diagnosis had suggested, and only the cracked rib had given him continuing pain. Last week, Jon had called to see how he was feeling, but a machine had answered. He had left a message. Within the hour, some officious clerk had phoned to inform him that Mr. Howell was on an extended vacation and could not be reached for a month or more. But don't get discouraged, Dr. Smith. Mr. Howell would be in touch as soon as he was available.

Translation: Peter was off on some operation.

Jon crossed his arms and closed his eyes. A warm offshore wind ruffled his hair and sent the glass chimes at the corner of the deck into a series of tinkling tones. In the distance on the beach, a dog barked. Children laughed. Seagulls called. He propped his bare feet up on the rail and felt himself grow drowsy.

Behind him, a voice asked, "Had enough peace and quiet yet?"

Jon jumped. He had not heard a door open or footsteps tread across the raised-wood floor of the house he had rented. Automatically he reached for his Beretta, but it was locked in a safety-deposit box in Washington.

For just that instant, he was back on the trail of Victor Tremont, wary and alert . . . and alive.

"Who the hell!" He turned.

"Colonel Smith, good afternoon. I'm an admirer of yours. My name is Nathaniel Frederick Klein."

In the open sliding-glass doorway between the house and the deck stood a man of medium height, dressed in a rumpled charcoal suit. He held a calfskin briefcase in his left hand. With his right, he dropped picklocks into his jacket pocket. He had a receding hairline, wire-rimmed glasses pushed up high on his long nose, and pale skin that had not seen the sun for any length of time since summer.

"*Dr.* Smith," Jon corrected him. "Just get in from Washington?"

Klein gave a short smile. "Dr. Smith, then. Yes, came straight here from the airport. Care to keep guessing?"

"I don't think so. You look like a man with a lot to say."

"Do I?" He sat in a deck chair. "Very astute of you. But then, from everything I've learned, that's one of the characteristics that makes you most valuable." He rattled off a short history of Jon's life, from birth through education and the army.

As he talked, Jon felt himself sinking deeper into his deck chair. He closed his eyes again. He sighed.

When Klein finished, Jon opened his eyes. "Got that all in your briefcase, I expect. Memorized it on the flight."

Klein allowed himself a smile. "Actually, no. I've got a month's worth of magazines. I'm behind in my reading. The flight gave me a chance to catch up. *Field and Stream.* That sort of thing." He loosened his tie, and his shoulders slumped with weariness. "Dr. Smith, I'll come right to the point. You're what we call a mobile cipher—"

"A *what?*"

"Mobile cipher," he repeated. "You're at loose ends. You've just had a terrible tragedy that has irrevocably changed your life. But you're still a doctor, and I know that's important to you. You have training in arms, science, and intelligence, and I'm wondering what else is important to you. You have no family, and only a few close friends."

"Yeah," Jon said drily. "And I'm unemployable."

Klein chuckled. "Hardly. Any of the new international private investigative agencies would welcome you. Obviously none of that appeals to you. One look at your résumé is enough to convince anyone with common sense that you're something of a maverick, which means that despite your years in the army, you're really a self-starter. You like to run your own show, but you still have a strong sense of patriotism and a commitment to principle that made the army attractive, and you won't find that in any business."

"I have no plans to start a business."

"Good. You'd probably fail at it. Not that you wouldn't enjoy starting one. You've got an entrepreneurial nature. If you were driven to do it, you'd go through all the hell of setting up a business, make it hugely successful, and then once it was running smooth as hot butter, you'd either sell it or run it into the ground. Entrepreneurs by definition make lousy managers. They get bored too easily."

"You think you've got me figured out. Who the hell *are* you?"

"We'll get to that in a minute. As I said, 'mobile cipher.' I think we've established the 'mobile' part. The 'cipher' refers to how the unfortunate events in October altered you. The external changes are easy to tally—quits job, sells house, goes on a pilgrimage to the past, refuses to see old friends, is living clear across the country. Have I left anything out?"

Jon nodded to himself. "Okay, I'm hooked. Let's get to the internal changes. But if this is a free therapy session, believe me, I'm not interested."

"Touchy, too. That's to be expected. As I was saying, we don't know—indeed, you probably don't know either—how much this has changed you inside. You are, in effect, at this moment a cipher to yourself as well as to everyone else. If I'm right, you feel at odds with the world, as if you've lost your place in it. Also, that you can't seem to find a reason to go on living." Klein paused, and his voice softened. "I lost my wife, too. To cancer. So please know that I have tremendous sympathy for you."

Jon swallowed. He said nothing.

"And that's why I'm here. I've been authorized to offer you employment that should interest you."

"I don't need or want a job."

"This isn't about 'job' or money, although you'll be well paid. This is about helping people, governments, environments, whoever or what-ever is in crisis. You asked who I am, and I can't completely divulge that information unless you're willing to sign a secrecy agreement. I will tell you this: There are interested parties, high up in government, who have taken a personal interest in you. They are forming a very small, very elite group of self-starters like yourself—mavericks who have strong ethics but few encumbrances in the world. It might mean occasional hardship, travel certainly, and danger. Not everyone would be interested. Even fewer would be capable. Do you find this idea at all appealing?"

Jon studied Klein. Sunlight glinted off his glasses, and his expression was solemn. Finally he asked, "What's this group called?"

"At the moment, Covert-One. Officially part of the army, but really independent. Nothing glamorous about it or the work, although the work will be vital."

Jon turned away to gaze at the ocean as if he could see the future. He still carried the pain of Sophia's death, but as the days passed, he was learning to live with it. He could not imagine ever falling in love again, but perhaps someday he would think differently about it. He remembered the brief moment when Klein had surprised him: He had reached for his Beretta. It had been a completely automatic response, and he never would have guessed that he would have done that.

"You've come a long way for an answer," Jon said noncommittally.

"We think it's an important question."

He nodded. "Where do I get in touch with you if I decide that I'm interested?"

Klein stood. He gave off the air of a man who had accomplished what he had set out to do. He reached inside his jacket and pulled out a simple white business card. On it was his name and a Washington phone number. "Don't be put off by whatever business answers. Just tell them your name and that you'd like to speak to me. We'll take it from there."

"I didn't say I was going to do this."

Klein nodded knowingly. He looked across the expansive view. A white seagull flew past, its feet tucked high as it rode the ocean air. "Nice here. Too many palm trees for my taste though." He picked up his briefcase and headed into the house. "Don't bother to get up. I know my way out." And he was gone.

Jon sat there another hour. Then he opened the gate on his porch and walked down onto the sand. It was warm on his feet. Automatically he turned east for his daily walk. The sun was behind him, and ahead the beach seemed to stretch into infinity. As he strolled, he thought about the future. He figured it was time.